TWO WOMEN AND ONE MAN MAKE A DEADLY COMBINATION.

Very few friendships—even the oldest—are strong enough to withstand it. And as devoted as Harriet Townshend and Coralia Suarez were to each other, their relationship became strained when they met Philip Haagersen.

Both fell in love with him.

Harriet was red-headed, flirtatious and vivacious. Coralia, a widow, was quiet and charming.

Each wanted one thing, and each was determined to get it. After all, what's a broken friendship compared to a broken heart?

MISS HARRIET TOWNSHEND

By Kathleen Norris

PAPERBACK LIBRARY

New York

PAPERBACK LIBRARY EDITION

First Printing: April, 1970

Library of Congress Catalog Card Number: 55-5268

TO TEE'S ELLEN, AND THE MEMORY OF MOLLIE BAWN

*The characters and the incidents in this book are entirely the
product of the author's imagination and have no relation to any
person or event in real life.*

This Paperback Library Edition is published by arrangement with
Doubleday & Company, Inc.

Covers Printed in U.S.A.
Body Text Printed in Canada.

Paperback Library is a division of Coronet Communications, Inc.
Its trademark, consisting of the words "Paperback Library"
accompanied by an open book, is registered in the United States
Patent Office. *Coronet Communications, Inc., 315 Park Avenue
South, New York, N.Y. 10010.*

CHAPTER 1

Over the rancho of Our Lady of the Little Columns a California sun shone hazily through a September day. At three o'clock in the afternoon nothing near the hacienda stirred. Chickens and farm hands alike had gathered for the siesta in such shady patches as there were; under the sprawled oaks and peppers back of the low-roofed white-washed adobe barns, in the doorway of the lofty stable, through which there always moved a current of air.

The tile-roofed walls of the house stood on the rise of the foot-hills of the Sierra Madre, and but for the denseness of the surrounding gardens it would have commanded a view of the coast range that shut away the Pacific, fifty miles toward the west. But the successive mistresses of the rain-stained plastered old mansion had come from countries where tree shade is a luxury, a rarity, a treasure to be cultivated, and crowding in among the peppers and oaks of the garden were many planted trees that effectively shut out air and view, eucalyptus, tall and shaggy towers gently moving their fragrant sickles against the pale blue sky, pines and cypress tightly needled together with dusty ropes of cobweb, glossy-leaved magnolias with stained furled blossoms, and for the lower orders, verbena, lilac, pampas grass, and rank overgrown rosebushes.

Through this jungle paths had been maintained, paths edged with thousands of inverted stone bottles that had once brought port from Spain. These paths were impassable in wet weather, and rarely used in dry, for they hummed all summer long with bees, mosquitoes, and a dozen varieties of flies, heavy and languid and metallic-winged, or sharp and active and almost invisible.

The house was pretentious in the grand and simple style

of the nineteenth-century pioneers. Standing four large rooms wide in front, it dwindled to storerooms and sculleries in the rear; it rose to three stories in height, and spread on either side into wings connected to the main building by elegant curved glass passages. Its plaster walls had once been eye-splitting white; the years had mellowed and stained them into creamy-gray softness and beauty. There was no glass at the windows; the deep sills were protected by heavy solid blinds.

Inside, the deep wide main hallway was always cool in hot weather, bitterly cold during the short western winter. Enormous rooms opened one either side, rooms only half furnished, in the true Spanish fashion, with a few rugs, a few chairs, a few holy pictures. A handsome silvermounted saddle was flung upon a table; a jar of trembling grass reflected itself in a dim, gold-framed mirror.

At the back of the hall to the left, however, was a room so doubly, trebly furnished that it at once pronounced itself the social heart of the house. For months the members of the family might not even glance at the other rooms, taking no concern for their rotting window draperies, or the collection of dead flies and wasps on ledges and sills. But the last room, on the northwestern corner, was the room given over to active living.

This room had four tall windows shrouded in fringed dark red rep; windows so close to the dense growth of laurel bushes outside that they reflected like mirrors, and gave the room back its own dark image. There were several real mirrors on the distempered plaster walls, old mirrors like pond water that had the effect of always holding in their depths more than they actually saw; flying draperies, misty faces, strange fuzzy blue lights.

Between the mirrors there were primitive portraits of stony-faced women in bombazines, with black hair dragged back to tortoise-shell combs, lace collars, and fat hands, and matching portraits of plethoric middle-aged men. On the mantelpiece, a stiff narrow mantelpiece in Spanish marble, stood four pink Sèvres vases filled with artificial silk flowers. There were no books in the room, but there were many heavy black volumes of bound songs and piano pieces, and there was a

6

fine square piano, with ruffled green silk panels behind lattices, and a thin cover of scalloped purple flannel. The furniture was principally of overstuffed horsehair, fat chairs and sofas well covered by antimacassars pinned primly in place. Several lamps stood about, in pink china or green glass; there were shelved whatnots in corners, two tables, and a fire screen. Beside these the furnishing was mainly religious in character; the tables bore small statues of saints, rosaries displayed on velvet backgrounds, colored prints of the Madonna, Jordan sand in a glass tube.

There were six women in the room on this warm afternoon. Three, brown-skinned, black-eyed, were alike enough to be, as they were in fact, sisters; prosperous sisters somewhere between forty and fifty. A fourth was a thin nervous woman somewhat younger, and there were two quite old women, one mighty and broad and crowned with heavily oiled silver braids, one small and bent, peering at the world through iron-rimmed spectacles. The other living things in the room were various parrots and dogs, the latter of the fat almost hairless variety, as lethargic as the women, drowsing away the afternoon heat.

The women wore heavy dresses of sateen, lined and boned, placketed and gusseted. Their garments came decently to the floor, but upon movement betrayed voluminous petticoats of fine white eyelet embroidery. On each heavy breast, by jeweled gold loops of ribbon, was pinned a watch; all the round soft brown fingers were heavy with rings.

Through the closed shutters long pencils of sunlight pressed in from the west, dancing with motes and crossed occasionally by flies. They touched the heavily embroidered edges of a cotton table runner there, glinted here upon an oiled black head, sleek as a seal's, showed the dust deep in a tufted bit of buttoned horsehair.

"The girls are lying down," one indifferent voice presently stated.

"Upstairs," another confirmed it.

"My daughter," said the silver-crowned old woman, out of a silence, "about your Coralia. Does she know that this man leaves the rancho today?"

7

"I had Francesca tell her, she would take it better from a girl. But she knew," Coralia's mother said, briefly and unwillingly.

"Take what, Rosa? Knew what?" came squeakily from behind the iron-rimmed glasses and the great woolly shawl in which the shriveled little old woman was disguised.

"The girl is no fool," an aunt said comfortably. "She may like him, why not? He is a handsome boy. But Coralia will marry one of our own. Arturo, perhaps, or Romano."

"Well . . ." another aunt contributed drowsily. There was a plate of small rich egg cakes on the table; she reached a plump brown hand for one.

"She will marry as Pablo wishes; she will obey her father, she is a good girl," the majestic old grandmother pronounced.

"Lola's Maria Dolores will get Romano," a sudden voice spoke out spitefully. It was as if an impalpable veil holding all their tongues had suddenly been split.

"My dear sister-in-law does not get everything she wishes," Señora Ybarra, from the Monterey ranchos, said lightly.

"Lola has always had everything her way!" It was as if the third sister, Señora Dias y Muertas, known here as Tia Ria, spoke against her own will, with a quiet acceptance of a distasteful fact.

"God gave her five sons," cackled the little old lady.

"God gave you none, Mia-mia," said the matriarch unkindly.

"And God gave me nothing but daughters, and you would have been glad enough to have daughters, or sons, or a man," said Coralia's mother, speaking out suddenly against her will. "As to Lola," she added uneasily, "I don't hear that anything is settled about Romano."

"I don't know that two years in a Paris school and kissing the Pope's ring makes a girl ready to settle down with her man and bear her children," Tia Ria said without conviction.

"The satin dress with the beads will not help," said Señora Ybarra, and they all laughed.

"Black satin, and with the train and the ruchings, forty yards," said the silver-crowned old woman. She fanned herself with a dry, rounded palm leaf. "It is hot," she observed.

8

"One reason we all feel that Lola has so much, she is always boasting," Maria Anna Lopez broke out in a brief silence. "For me, I wait for my grandchildren. My boy is only sixteen, my girl will marry. Give Lola time. She will not always be so sure."

"You think it is settled as to Romano Martinez, Tia Ria?" the grandmother, nettled by the possibility, asked in a low tone.

"What of it? She must marry someone," the other woman answered with an air of hardiness.

"But that would be a great catch, with the Morenos and the Bandini ranchos, when poor José dies," Ysobel Ybarra said slowly. "Maria Dolores would be a great lady."

"And have her own four boys! And our Coralia, who will she get?" put in Mia-mia. Except for annoyed glances, nobody paid any attention to this, but it was with a touch of added sharpness that Tia Ria presently said in an oratorical drone:

"Lola was always very beautiful, she has fine sons. Maria Dolores is beautiful too—yes. Yes. And they are very rich, and why would not the one daughter marry well? So our brother Roberto is fortunate in his wife and his children, and how much better," finished Tia Ria, half-hearted in reproof, "than having his house filled with misfortune and his only son die, as Mateo's did. Eh?"

There was a languid murmur at this that might have been taken for agreement, and again silence fell. The sunlight at the blinds had turned red, and burned in the room like rubies.

CHAPTER 2

Coralia Valdez slipped out a side door and went swiftly through little used paths between the stone walls and the heavily massed shrubbery of the garden. She did not risk the

9

drive or the main gate, but stepped over a tangle of ivy and blue-blossomed periwinkle to gain a dirt bridle path that ran for almost a mile under eucalyptus trees to join the highway below. This road was nowhere visible from the house; it was not even used by the ladies of the family when they went riding; it belonged almost exclusively to the cowboys and the rancho hands, and the girl breathed easier when she was safe in its shadows.

She was a well-developed girl, with heavy black braids looped on her neck, enormous soft dark eyes under heavy smoky lashes and brows; smooth creamy brown skin and a face only marred by a slightly too heavy chin, and a wide Spanish mouth crowded with teeth. Her dress was of white embroidery over many white-embroidered petticoats, and she wore over her head and about her shoulders a coquettish white lace mantilla.

She loitered when she reached the safety of the avenue, a pretty figure in the long bars of light and shade. The air here was sweet with eucalyptus balm, and the scent of tarweed and Indian grass. A warm languor lay over the world; the day had been hazy with heat, but as the sun lowered to tip banks of slowly moving clouds with pink, from the western mountains coolness spread and a great blanket of fog moved silently down from the north.

Louis Johnson rode down the lane, and as the girl signaled him, he dismounted and came toward her, the horse's great face looking over his shoulder.

Here was a lover to stir a girl's blood. He stood tall, well over six feet; his clipped mustache and trimmed light beard adorned a face handsome, strong, masterful: his blue eyes, like those of the father who had given him his American name, were always laughing, and when he laughed his white teeth flashed, well set, big, strong, like every inch of him.

"Ah-h-h, you shouldn't!" he reproached her, stooping for a kiss, his arm about her.

"I know it!" she whispered with a conspirator's shred of guilty laughter. "But I had to!"

"But we said good-by at the house," he reminded her with a great bouyant laugh. "Your mother would kill you!"

10

"I know. But when Raff said that all the men were going up to the other ranch, I knew you would be alone. And I had to," she repeated. "Louis, I hate to have you go!"

"And I hate to go, Coralia." He said it. But not as he would have said it a week ago, not as he would have said it then! Everything was different now, stiff and unnatural.

"Because"—she tried for the old dictatorial air of childish pettiness and sauciness that she knew he had once found charming—"because you don't know when you are coming back!" she protested. "Or you say you don't," she added, to give him an opening.

"How can I?" But he was hardly thinking of what he said, and she knew it.

"Louis, you believe what I said to you last night?"

"What was that?"

It was getting harder and harder.

"That—that I am not like girls who—Anna and Inez—not like that——"

"I know that. But I think you are a little hard on poor little Inez," the man reproached her playfully.

"Oh, I don't mean that she—no. But she dances with all the boys, she is always screaming because someone has kissed her. . . . But Louis, you know, you know that when I came up to your room last Tuesday night—you know——"

She stopped, her lashes lowered; her face was close to his shoulder.

"Of course I know."

"But they say a man likes a girl less—respects her less—when she—when she——"

"Who is 'they,' for example?" He was tender enough, but he would not be quite serious.

"My aunts. And Mia-mia."

"They might tell you also that we don't talk of these things in the broad daylight, *chiquita*."

Her face was blazing with sudden anger and despair.

"Oh, I knew, I knew I would be sorry!" she said, breathless.

"Now be sensible, dear. You came to me that night to tell me that Tony wanted to sell me the mustang and that the horse stumbled. You came just for that, and you were an angel to do it and you would not even close the door behind you, remember?"

Watching him, still breathing hard, she did not speak.

"So—I closed the door," Louis said. "And all the next day we hardly dared look at each other, thinking of the night to come, eh? And that is right, Coralia, between a man and a woman. Why, who made us so? It is a thing to be happy about. And I will always love you, and be grateful to Tony." He laughed the laugh of a contented man, unashamed, unafraid.

"But now you are going away," she said piteously.

"Yes. Now I must be on my way. I stop at San Antonio, and go on with Juan tomorrow to San Rafael."

"Then you will see Maria Dolores," the girl said quickly.

"I will see Maria Dolores."

"Is she so beautiful, Louis?"

"Well," he said slowly, his eyes smiling, though his voice was matter-of-fact, "it is not that she is so beautiful. But she walks like a—like a duchess, and the hair, the odd dark gold——" He paused; began again. "She has a funny way of speaking quite seriously, do you see," he said, "and then raising her eyes and smiling. It sounds so foolish, but it is hard to say just how she does it. She came down the stairs in a velvet dress—yes, in a way she is beautiful."

"She speaks French."

"After two years in a convent over there? Oh, yes."

"She played the piano when she was quite a little girl," Coralia recalled. There was another pause.

"And now I must go, and if I write you cold letters so that your mother can read them and suspect nothing, don't be surprised."

"Ah, Louis, but you will write!"

"Whenever anyone comes down this way. Your mother," Louis said as an afterthought, "doesn't suspect anything?"

"It would kill her."

"She need know nothing until we are ready to tell her."

"That we are to be married! Oh, I can't bear to think of that day, I go out of my senses! But Louis, if you write me at all, what will she think?"

12

"We must consider that. I'll manage it, somehow!" He quite obviously hadn't considered it. His face was wrinkled with thought for a second; then he kissed her squarely and hard, on the mouth, and was upon his horse, facing her still, waving his hat, but very much upon his way. The white stallion loped easily down the lane, all in shadow now, and was lost in the dusk that shrouded the highway.

Coralia stood very still until the last echo of the hoofbeats died away, then she turned and went slowly toward the house. Dark was descending swiftly. By this time all the older women would be in their rooms, washing themselves in hot water in chased silver basins, dipping combs in the soapy water to help slap and twist their luxuriant hair into shape. But she dared not chance the side door. She worked her way about to the kitchens instead, stopping to break two stiff artichokes from between their exquisite acanthus-like leaves as she went.

The kitchens were on the basement level, floored by the hard-packed solid earth; they occupied a series of lofty plaster and adobe arches, never wholly closed to wind or weather. Under these arches there was one long range always glowing, its vast iron top occupied by a dozen bubbling pots of all sizes. Stretching all about were tables where women stood, laughing and gossiping as they scraped or chopped meat or vegetables. Kerosene lamps hung over their heads and glinted light on their sleek black hair, the gay bandannas over heads and bosoms, and the brilliant reds and greens of tomatoes and peas, carrots and shining apples.

The columns of the wide arches were fringed with all the implements of the oldest of arts. Hung from a hundred pegs were great spoons, knives, aprons, rags, ladles, pitchers, and casseroles, as well as dried herbs, fat dark sausages, peppers, and long strings of onions. All the utensils were the largest of their type, for the cooks who were sweating and chattering above the stove rarely calculated upon less than fifty diners.

Cauldrons of frijoles or tortillas must go down to the men's bunkhouse at about this time every evening, with long loaves of sour fresh bread, a bubbling pot of stew topped by red beads of fat, or a great blackened ham tied with greasy strings and peeling soaked linen. If the giggling maids whose duty it was to deliver these delicacies to the tired men in the bunkhouse chose to add great wooden bowls of egg-heavy cakes or twists of spiced fried dough, they were warmly rewarded, and returned to the kitchen somewhat disheveled, with their head scarfs dangling in their hands and their laughter less suppressed than ever.

Tonight there were some twenty women in the kitchen, coming and going over the earthen floor through the gaunt high arches; there were, besides, almost as many children, and a vast assortment of dogs and cats. In the mingled dusk and lamplight and the glow of the big range and several smaller furnaces, the figures came and went in a smoky redness suggesting infernal regions. But Coralia was at home here, and made her way familiarly to the enormous figure of the head cook, who stood with her back to her bubbling pots and waved a greasy spoon in a stout greasy brown hand.

"Look you," she said to a group of attentive younger women, each with some detail of dinner preparations arrested in her hand, "Maria Refugia is gone, and I am glad she is gone, and I wish her well. I taught her all she knows, let her remember that."

"You are jealous of her, Señora Nita," said a pretty girl, laughing out of a cloud of dark curls.

"I am not jealous of her. Ha! It would be a funny thing if I was. She looks in a book before she will make so much as a tortilla, and now she is going to work with Chinamen. I wish her well of her Chinamen!" Nita said with great heartiness. "And now get out from under my feet!"

"Nita," said Coralia, presenting herself and offering her artichokes. "Could you cook these for my father's supper?"

The older women in the circle laughed shrilly at this, and Nita, taking the vegetables, said ironically:

"I am to cook them ten minutes I suppose, señorita? Preserve us, our Lady of Guadalupe!"

"Do they cook more than ten minutes?" Coralia asked, hurt and proud. Her cheeks burned scarlet.

"Yes, my dove, my little doveling," said Nita. "And who

is to suppose you know anything of cooking? Your father shall have them tomorrow, with a good sauce made of oil. Now go away, girls. It is nearly six.

"Elena," Coralia said in a low tone, linking her arm in that of a somewhat older girl as they all scattered among the smoke-blackened columns and arches, "will you tell me something?"

"Anything, señorita." The other girl squared about when they were out of hearing.

"It's nothing—only," Coralia said, stammering, "that once someone said—someone said that you were going to marry Francisco—not the big Francisco, the little one, with the flat lip?"

Elena drew up, chilled.

"A man may serve God with a flat lip, señorita."

"Oh, I know that. I don't mean that. I mean—did you love him, Elena?"

"More than my soul. More than my patron saint," said Elena. She looked shrewdly at the other girl. "With you it is the man who came about the calves," she said. "It is Don Louis Johnson, eh?"

"Oh, Elena——" Coralia breathed, glancing about.

"It is he?"

"Oh, yes. But sh-h-h——"

"No one is listening. But I knew it. I watched you, señorita. I saw the way he looked at you."

"Elena, you think he cares? It's true, isn't it? I mean, the way a man cares. They're not like us," Coralia said feverishly, "they're not the same. But they—they care."

"And so you've fallen in love?" Elena asked, pleased and scornful.

"Oh, yes. I guess so. It was so sudden. It was just—that first night at supper and watching him ride away with my father the next morning to see the branding—it was so strange! It was like being made of light and wanting to get away from where he was to think about him. It was every step—everything anyone said."

Coralia's feverish swift rush of half-whispered words stopped; she was looking anxiously into Elena's face. The

15

other girl watched her in silence for half a moment before she spoke.

"That's—of course, the way it is, señorita. We—we girls here don't always have it like that, though, with us it's fun and no harm done! Of course the boys kiss us, and maybe put an arm where it doesn't belong—but Holy Virgin of the Swords, there's no harm in that!"

"But that isn't when you—when you really love a man, Elena. No, don't go—she'll call someone else! Please, I want to ask you. Mustn't you trust him then? If you do—and if he does, too, loves you, I mean——"

Her voice died to silence. The laughter, the hissing of fat and rushes of steam, the chatter of the cooks, went on under the dim smoky arches; smells of frying, of onions and garlic, of cabbage and cooking apples thickened the air.

Elena, her swarthy face serious, studied the face near her own.

"But what are you trying to say, señorita?" she asked, not laughing.

"Well—nothing, except that I'm so unhappy! I'm so afraid. . . . You think he will come back, don't you?"

"I?" asked the other girl, her manner changing to impatience. "I don't know. Did he tell you he loved you? Why worry? You are one of the lucky ones, with Don Pablo rich—believe me, we girls would feel ourselves fortunate if we had such a chance! You can look higher than Louis Johnson!"

"Oh, but I don't want to. I want him, and he knows—he knows all about the ranchos and that my father is rich. And that will help, won't it?"

"Why, señorita, you have everything. You are not afraid he won't want you? We girls have always envied you! Do you remember when they sent you to Marysville to school, packing your trunk with the petticoats and the little red coat? I can tell you Refugia and I cried over that, and because we couldn't start off in the early morning, in the big wagon——"

"Oh, that! That was nothing. I hated it! But Elena, if the priest asks me in Confession——"

"Eh!" ejaculated Elena with another change of manner, with a faint motion as if she withdrew from her companion.

16

"Eh?" she repeated, dragging the syllable out. "But no." And again her sharp eyes studied the shamed face.

"Father Pinzon, and the young father, they come this week."

"But you don't mean, señorita——"

A silence.

"When? With everyone watching," Elena said then.

"But we love each other," Coralia offered thickly, by way of answer.

"But how? Sleeping with Rosa and Rosita and Maria Bella in the room, and your mother with her door always open to the hall——"

"No one waked." A silence. "His room," Coralia muttered.

"He knew you were coming?" Elena was whispering.

"Not the first time, no. It was about Tony and the mustang that stumbled. Late at night, I was trying to go to sleep and it seemed to me he should know—that I must go tell him. And then it was as if a river carried me along."

"Oh, the devil. I knew he was a devil," the older girl said, half to herself. The heart of Coralia Valdez sank like a stone into freezing water. "One of the señoritas!" Elena gasped.

"Elena, what can I do?" Coralia whimpered. "If I don't go to the Sacraments they will all know, and if I tell Father Pinzon he will say my mother must know. Please—please, you don't think it was so bad? Because we are going to be married, he is coming back, he said so. He said so! You don't know all that he said."

"Me, I know all that he said," Elena said quietly, looking with knitted brows into space. "I was a fool once too! This will kill the Señora."

"We are making a great deal out of nothing—or, no, not nothing!" Coralia said, trying for anger and bravado. "It was bad, I know that. But we love each other."

"Do you know where he is?" The question came sharply.

"No. At least, he was to go to San Rafael, to the Alvarados."

"Is Maria Dolores there?"

"Why do you ask that?" Coralia said, swallowing.

"Nothing. Señorita, could you follow him?"

17

Coralia was electrified. Her drooping body, her anxious eyes underwent an instant transformation.

"Follow him!" she whispered.

"You can take the money from your father's desk. He never knows how much is there. You wouldn't be the first," said Elena with a knowing look.

"Oh no, I couldn't follow him. It might make him—make Louis angry," Coralia said, suddenly despairing.

"It would make him angry, yes, but he would marry you. It is a big piece of the rancho, over the hills toward the ocean, that he is trying to buy from Don Antonio. Your father would give it to you. He works with an American man; they bring post offices and houses, like in Yerba Buena, and the Mission Dolores," the girl said. "He will not risk angering your father, not now. He will count on your not telling anyone."

"But if he is doing business with my father, he will surely come back," the younger girl said eagerly. Elena was drawing away. "Ah, please, wait a minute—just a minute——" Coralia pleaded.

"Mind you don't say you told me!" Elena whispered almost fiercely. "I don't want to know—I'll say you didn't tell me—Rita is watching us—I'll say I didn't know anything about it——

"And you should know, señorita—he made love to Ana—and the other Rita—that Gregorio liked—Ana said so!"

"You lie," Coralia said, sick. She breathed hard.

"I hope so!" Elena whispered, frightened. "I have to go, señorita!"

"And you are the meanest girl I ever knew. I'll kill you," Coralia said very low. She was alone in the crowd and confusion; she went slowly toward the open stairs, up and down which continual streams of women and boys were coming and going. She felt cold.

They were piling the table upstairs with heavy white dishes loaded with food. There was no particular order or pattern to the meal; the enormous tureen, flanked by a column of soup plates, was at the upper end of the table; a smoking joint held the other end. Between them other edibles were

18

rapidly accumulating; long loaves of fresh sour bread, bowls
of frijoles, mounds of potatoes, cabbage mixed with heavy
limp cuts of ranch bacon, green beans, boiled eggs, solid
marmalade in cakes from Brazil, yellow corn fritters, chocolate custards, walnuts and honey from the home trees and
hives.

Coralia skirted the moving lines, escaped by a back stairway to an upper floor, hastily did what she could to her
appearance, and was in place at the dinner table before the
last stragglers came down to the meal.

Heart and soul and mind were in a wild confusion; she
could not think, but she could be afraid. She plunged into
the family scene, listening, nodding, eating her dinner, only
conscious that she needed the cover of the herd. The solid
earth had failed beneath her feet.

Her mother sat magnificent at one end of the table; her
father would presently come in to grace the other. In his
absence, her aunt Maria Lopez served the soup. Between the
two women some twenty places were filled, by dark, full-
bosomed girls with black hair still dripping water from hasty
arranging, lean dark pimply boys in white shirts, with nail-
studded leather belts and skimpy light cotton trousers, and
the stout matrons who had shared the siesta hours in the
shrub-shaded living room.

The Señora eyed the full table with satisfaction; serving
food plentifully and indiscriminately was one of the main
interests and occupations of her life. No one who came on the
rancho on any pretext whatsoever—traveler, priest, dealer,
tramp, distinguished guest, or mendicant or perhaps a ragged
adventurer, leading a thin wife and a string of bright-eyed
brown-skinned children, ever went away hungry.

On her majestic trips of inspection of her wide domestic
domain, the Señora liked to find groups of hungry derelicts
down among the arches of the great cellars bending over
bowls of beans or gulping hot coffee. Some of them rose
respectfully as she came by; all tried to look their gratitude.

More than once she had taken a group upstairs for treatment of a swollen breast, or to wash a child's sore little leg.
She would return the child, cleanly bandaged and cleanly

19

clothed, and unostentatiously press a little money into the mother's hand. She did this with genuine humility and piety, and would have done it had she had no audience. But she did have an audience, and the tale of the Señora's holiness spread and strengthened.

The friars who went up and down the Coast on muleback, and came in hot and tired for a few days' blessed rest at the hacienda, knew of it and began to ask prayers of the Señora, and to leave rosaries and medals for her distributing. Her sisters, not without varied emotions, watched her growth in piety. They had known her in very different guise. Maria Ana, Tia Ria, and Ysobel smiled wisely at each other now and then as instances of Rosa's spiritual superiority evinced themselves, and remembered other scenes. Like that one, perhaps, when in a hot, woman-filled bedroom on an insufferably airless night the sixth of her daughters, the little Engracia Concepción had first seen the light. The rage of the then less saintly Rosa, her refusal even to look at the little mottled bundle under the mop of black hair, was fresh in her sisters' memory, although Conchita was now eight years old. "I spit upon her!" Rosa, sweating and breathless, had said.

Also there was the case of the lovely Niña, assistant nurse to fat old Lola, and Rosa's fury as she directed two of the men, laughing on the high seat of the bouncing buckboard, to take the frightened Niña and her carpetbag over to the train at San Jose. The Señora was not so saintly but what she could snatch a knife from the wall when hard pressed. Every woman on the place, from Mia-mia to the smallest, shrillest little kitchen maid, had had her whispered version of what had happened, and knew why the Señor had gone off to San Diego to buy bulls, and why so much murmuring and crying went on among the women in the dim-shuttered upper chambers.

CHAPTER 3

But these events were in the past, with many another scene of Rosa Valdez y Riveras' younger days, the days of dancing, flirting escapades, sunshine, threats, and tempests. Now she was the Señora, serene, devout, matriarchal. Now she was the mother of six lively girls; four of them in Marysville, in school, one little one left to plague her and be spoiled by everyone in the house. And Coralia, the oldest, almost twenty, and a great trial. This girl Coralia, now—this change in her——

The Señora wore her inevitable evening costume of heavy silk; blue, white, and red plaid tonight, made with a basque heavily revered, boned, pleated and fitted with darts, the collar high, the ruffled skirt full. Lifted by her bosom almost to a level position, a heavy gold watch rode on a looped bow of gold. Thrust into her belt was a lace-edged handkerchief. Another handkerchief, for use, was in one of several pockets. She held her head high under its tortoise-shell comb; great gold rings dangled from her ears.

The Señora looked down the table at Coralia. She could not understand the girl. Coralia had all the elements that make for charming girlhood; beauty, a fine figure, a singing voice, clever fingers on the piano, and a willingness to please. But somehow there was no charm. "American," thought the Señora. "Mixed blood is bad blood."

For the Señora had made her own mistakes in youth, too. At seventeen she had eloped with one Carlos Clinton, half Spanish, wholly irresponsible. Coralia had been the baby Rosa, repentant, widowed, had brought back only a year later. Her prosperous marriage had followed; few, even at the rancho, knew that Coralia's story was not that of her sisters. But her mother never forgot the difference.

21

When young men met Coralia they hardly greeted her before turning away. The Señora did not expect them to fall in love with her at first sight; she was not that kind of a girl. But they would not give themselves a chance to know her; and however bitter Coralia's reflections were on this point, and however clearly she sensed it, her mother's reflections and emotions were bitterer still.

"Martin, now if she could be made to marry Martin Salazar," Coralia's mother said in her heart. "Preserve us, Mary, what a thing that would be! He wants her, too. Poor old man—sixty-five to her nineteen. And her father only forty-nine if he lives until Assumption.

"But the Corazón d'Oro rancho, all that cattle, the wealth of him! The pride of my giving a great party here to tell Francisco and Lola, and Paca and all of them! Coralia—he would take her to Barcelona. She would give him sons. Tita's Maria Dolores, so lovely, two years in a French convent, eh? Oh, very good. But she could make no such match as Martin would be. I would like to tell Maria Dolores' mother, 'But Tita, the child is in love with Martin. Her father and I did nothing. She loves him. She calls him her "great bear." Yes, he has given her the emeralds, poor Teresa's emeralds!' Ah how she would hate me!" mused the Señora.

"I would like to get some hold on that girl," she mused on fiercely. "I would like some hold on her, to bring her to my knees. I would like to push her away, sobbing, 'No, no, no, your father and everyone must know this. You have brought disgrace to our family. Your poor sisters will not marry now!' Ah, if I could catch her that way! 'Mama, Mama, Mama, stop!' she would beg me. 'I will marry Martin if you say so, I will be a good wife to him, I will never complain. Only, never tell my father, never let anyone know that I have been so bad!' "

Coralia's eye caught her mother's glance at this point, and she smiled in rather a sickly fashion, wondering uneasily what her mother was thinking up there at the head of the table.

"If he were not quite so short and so black and so greasy," ran the Señora's musings, "and if he would not try to paw the poor child as he does. We could have a quiet, quick wedding

22

because of his bad leg. Señora Salazar y Valdez, eh? It sounds well. And all her poor sisters visiting her.

"Coralia," she said as the girl passed her on her way out of the room, "Concha says that you went down the road to say good-by to this Johnson." She drew Coralia aside, in a bare, plaster-scented hall.

"She saw me, I suppose?" Coralia said with a light scornful laugh. But her throat was thick.

"No, she did not see you, she was ill after lunch and old Lola was fanning her. But she says she knows it; she heard you say 'I'll see you again, I'll say good-by.'"

"Lola stuffs her with sweets," Coralia said reflectively. "Is she sick every day?" Her heart leaped with relief. Concha knew nothing.

"She has a bad stomach. You tell me you did not run after the man like a cheap street girl?"

"Of course not."

"Did he make love to you? And why did no one tell me this until now?"

"It seems to me people have been telling you a good deal, Mother. I wonder you listen. As for Concha, what she needs is what we all used to get, with your whip."

"There are wiser ways than with the whip," the Señora said oratorically. She smiled into far space.

"Mother, you grow more like a saint every day," Coralia said adoringly. It was enough. Her mother turned with a deprecatory shrug, proceeded upon her majestic way to join the other women in the living room and pick up her embroidery.

Coralia stepped out on the veranda, where several of the men stood in the dark with her father; all were breathing rather hard and showing an inclination to stretch their legs after the hearty meal. The girl sat down on the upper step and looked out into the night.

It was full dark now around the hacienda. There was no moon yet, but the warm black sky was speckled with bright stars. The gardens, brooding under tight-packed oaks and peppers and eucalyptus, were without a glimmer of any light, but the far gray hills were outlined against a faint glow

23

still flushing the fog, and nearer, where the cowhands' adobe quarters were, many soft red squares and angles of dull light showed low against the earth at windows and doors, and sometimes Coralia saw figures silhouetted against them.

Louis was gone. But this fact meant nothing now; there was too much else about which she must think. He could not remain away, that was certain; no use wasting time on that. He must either come to her or she must go to him.

Romance must wait, for a while. She must be extremely practical and businesslike. How could she follow him to San Rafael, and if she surprised him there just what approach should she make and just what reception would she get?

She felt old, capable, unafraid. If the business matter between her father and Louis was not yet concluded, then he would come back. Quite simply he would be among the before-dinner group of talking men on the side piazza, and quite simply she would seize her first chance to remind him that they were to be married. Her heart gave a leap of delight——

She reproved her heart; crushed it down. This matter of not daring to make an honest Confession, and so revealing to the world that she could not approach the Sacraments, was serious. The visiting friars would be here in a few days; they would stay for only a few more. If she could not feign illness or could not run away, this must be faced, handled somehow.

"Of course we are to be married, Father," she imagined herself whispering under the seal of the Sacrament. There would be a lot of talk to which she needn't listen, and then the old priest would ask if her mother knew of this deplorable situation.

"And then what do I say?" Coralia asked herself.

She dreamed back over the past ten days. Only ten days. And at the beginning of those days she would have been as horrified as her mother at the thought of any dalliance with the attractive half American who was bargaining with Tony, down at the corrals, about the mustang.

Oh, the soft smoky glory of that autumn morning; the smell of a brush fire; the young horses racing about the field. Coralia had hung on the fence, laughing at the heated Mexican face of Tony, and Louis Johnson had leaned on the fence beside her. Under her feet dry eucalyptus sickles carpeted the ground; high over her head the rough plumes of the trees moved softly in the morning air. Coralia had been conscious of her own radiant youth and vitality, her braids of soft hair on her shoulders, her starched blue morning wrapper with its tassels, her brown pretty hand on the rough fence rail, her brown smooth bosom where the decorous ruffles of the basque dipped down. It had been an hour of singing felicity. For almost from the first moment Louis' hand had gripped hers, and now and then at suffocating ecstatic intervals Louis had given her a quiet, unsmiling side glance.

A strange day had followed that morning. Coralia had floated through it in a dream, not knowing what she was feeling, much less thinking.

Briefly, at luncheon, at supper, she had seen Louis again, and when she did, even though he was not near her, her throat had grown dry and her spine icy, and she had gripped her wet palms together. It was strange, it was even terrifying, but she had not attempted to escape from it.

So night had come, and with it a great blankness. The men had disappeared into a dark leather-smelling, tobacco-scented room where they spent their evenings smoking and drinking, and not infrequently falling asleep.

Subjects supposedly connected with the rancho, the grapes, the sheep, the branding and shearing, the wheat and barley, the bottling and crating of wine, were supposedly under discussion. But the tone of the after-dinner talks seldom reached any intensity. The men were all tired; sometimes only a single monosyllable filled a quarter hour of silence. But it was a time of peace and content, secretly envied by the women of the family, who professed, to a woman, great scorn of the filthy habits of men.

"Lola and I just took some towels up to your room," she had told Louis, passing him in the hall.

"So now you know where I am, señorita," Louis had answered with a quick glance that had confused and excited and pierced her spirit.

And he had gone on to join the men on that momentous

night. Coralia, after drifting about somewhat aimlessly with a pair of girl cousins, had gone to her room.

But not to bed. Once in her fluted muslin wrapper and high-buttoned nightgown, madness had seized upon her and she had walked the floor uneasily, answering the cousin who was already comfortable in the double bed only in absent inconsequencies. Something within her, never felt before, even if sometimes vaguely sensed, had been ablaze. She needed only one thing; to speak to Louis. A dozen words with Louis and she would go contentedly to sleep. She must—but for what reason? She must. She heard his voice again, negligent, audacious:

"So now you know where I am, señorita."

Right upstairs. Across an angle of hall, through a door topped with a glass pane and a curtain; then the near door. She heard the meeting break up; everyone had come up to bed.

"I want to ask Mother——" she had murmured to her cousin. Then she had reached the hall, with one dim candle burning and nothing stirring or making a sound in the wide bare space. "Louis," she was saying to herself, with a dry mouth, "Tony has no right to sell you that mustang. He crosses his forefeet, and he has thrown practically every one of us."

Then she was at his door, her heart plunging, her knock a bare tap.

"I'm leaving the door open, I've only a second," she had whispered.

But his look! His amaze and his deep reverent delight. He had closed the door and put her into a big chair and told her not to be frightened. And he had knelt and laid his head against her knees and locked his arms about her, whispering that he had dreamed of this, he had not dared hope for it.

"I wish I hadn't gone up that night," Coralia thought, writhing. She jerked her mind resolutely back to practicalities. "I did," she said mentally. And once again the gnats of fear and shame that she could drive away only for a few minutes at a time gathered about her. Mother. Father Pinzon. The gap before a letter from Louis with plans in it could be some-how smuggled through. Coralia groaned aloud.

"What did you say, señorita?" a maid, sent out to the porch by the Señora to protect her daughter, asked, rousing from a lower step.

"Nothing." But the hated refrain "If I hadn't—if I hadn't—if I hadn't" began in her brain again. Desired and untouch-able, she would have so much more power over him; she knew that now! Well, what had the nuns and her mother been drilling into her since she was big enough to listen? Men did not respect girls of easy virtue.

"Señorita, for the love of the twelve Apostles," Refugia said, her sleepy head on her knees, "let us go to bed. You are tired, and I was up at four o'clock this morning to keep those wolves in potatoes and pork for their breakfasts!"

"Yes, I'll go." Coralia got up and went indoors, went upstairs and mechanically prepared for bed, washing her face and neck at the silver basin, braiding her heavy hair, kneeling for the prayers, none of whose meaning she could sense tonight.

A new and frightful thought had come to her; had sunk its teeth into her very being, and was tossing and tearing at her.

She got into bed, and the thought came, receded and softened, returned with a savage rush. She twisted, tortured. It would not leave her, and she knew it would not.

It was the thought of Maria Dolores Riveras. Maria Dolores, lovely, seventeen, completely sure of herself, coming down the wide stairway at the rancho up in the Marin hills, candlelight shining on her, her dress perhaps of flattering wine-colored velvet, her burned-gold hair on her shoulders. Maria Dolores on the stairway, and at its foot, waiting, Louis.

Coralia twisted and turned. Her cousin moaned a protest as the jerking of covers disturbed her sleep; managed a drowsy question as Coralia quite suddenly left the bed and went to the door.

"I have to speak to Mother," Coralia whispered.

Yes, that was it. She must tell everything to her mother. Her mother would know how to handle it; what must be told

27

the priest, how the problem of the Sacraments could be met. Her mother would be furious with anger, heartsick with disappointment, but she would show neither of these emotions for the good reason that she could not. Not without exposing herself to the pity and the quiet amusement of all the cousins and aunts.

No, matters were desperate now. The authority of a wise, strong, loyal mother, forgiving and all-powerful, must be called into service. Louis must be quietly informed of the part he must play; the engagement must be announced; the regular and decent procedure followed. What Coralia, her mother, and Louis knew was nobody's business but theirs.

It would be better certainly to have had Louis take the initiative, display the impatience. But he would, of course, as soon as he understood. Why shouldn't he, with one of the heiresses of the house of Valdez y Riveras for his bride? And besides, he loved her; she kept forgetting that. He loved her.

Her panic of a short while earlier appeared foolish now. After the first earthquake shock of her revelation to her mother, there would be nothing to fear. They would go to San Francisco, her mother and she, and stay with cousins, and in no time—this day next week perhaps——

She hesitated outside her mother's door. Her father had not yet come upstairs. Perhaps he was sleeping downstairs this warm night.

How begin? "Mother—there is something I want you to know. I know it will distress you—but wait—it's going to turn out all right." And then in a rush, "It's Louis Johnson, Mother. I know—I know he has no money, only his job, you'll say he isn't one of us—his father's not a Catholic—but we belong to each other——"

The Señora, in the big bare bedroom just beyond the closed door, lying in her bed, was putting her thoughts into phrases too, all unconscious that a tear-wet young face and a trembling young body would in a moment be pressed against her own. She thought of Martin Salazar.

Martin had married a school friend of the Señora's, and even then had been a good twenty-five years older than his

28

sickly little bride. Teresa had lived—lived—there had been
no dying for her. And Martin had gone from forty-five to
sixty—and no child! Now a widower of sixty-five he was
ogreish, dark, bent, frightful in his beaming attention to
women, all women. And of Coralia, the Valdezes' oldest
daughter, he had made a pet for eighteen of her nineteen
years. . . . Yes, he would be almost forty-six years his wife's
senior—oh, what of it! The name, the estate, the great wealth;
Rosa felt she was fretting herself mad at the thought of it.
For Coralia would look bewildered and heavily unresponsive
at any subtle reference to him, and at a direct approach her
mother feared she would incredulously laugh. More than
one of the girls of the finest old families had already rejected
Martin Salazar.

"If I could promise to buy her something—something she
wants. Or if I could manage to get her out of some trouble.
'Do you not see how this marriage gives you an escape, my
daughter? No more playing around with beggars like Johnson!
Do you not see the dignity, the security that this man offers
you? Rather than that your father and I are disappointed and
ashamed and your life ruined, can you not do this simple
thing? All marriages are as one, once you have your child.
Teresa Salazar and I were schoolmates; your father respects
Martin as he does few men. His long marriage to Teresa was
childless, you will give this good man a houseful of children.'

"If she would but steal jewels—money—but from whom?
Then I could say, 'The world will never know. Your mother
will make good the loss, and as a good man's wife you will
be above suspicion.'

"But she would never steal anything!" lamented the Señora
resentfully. "She will never do anything wrong! If she could
but come to me weeping, frightened, shamed, how quickly
all could be arranged! He is dying for her! My promise to
save her, to help her, her promise to me to take Martin, before
we lose him to one of the Guerrero girls, or Maria Dolores
at San Rafael. I promise a pilgrimage to the Shrine of Guadalupe," said the Señora passionately, "if this girl gives me
an opening—any opening, to secure this good Martin, and
make her mistress of the Corazón d'Oro! . . . Come in,

come in!" she said impatiently in answer to a timid tap on her door. Ten o'clock, and here was some imbecile maid with an imbecile problem that could not wait until tomorrow——

"*Coralita, muchachita mia!*" she said, sitting up in bed, arms wide.

CHAPTER 4

On a hot, sunshiny January morning of the year 1872 the bark *Queen Emma,* twenty-three days out from the Sandwich Islands, came to harbor through the Golden Gate.

Across the waterfront she sailed, under quarter canvas, in a languid wind, bringing herself skillfully to her mooring, and immediately dispatching a longboat for the shore.

The blue waters of the bay were as peaceful as rippled satin this morning, the hills of the eastern shores only a shade darker. But San Francisco's heights were sharply etched against the vague pale sky, and patched with shanties and small farms and cabbage fields above the gathered roofs of the city and the long fringe of masts along the piers.

These piers were a seething mass of activity this morning, for other ships were in, and merchandise was displayed on the docks for a constantly shifting crowd of buyers. Chinese dock hands shouted in unison as they hauled on ropes or packed crates to and fro; anxious little freighters from Sacramento and Benicia made their fussy claims; from a sea-scarred old hulk from the Clyde came a long blast to meet the city whistles that were sounding noon, and gulls, as if blown into the air by the sound, fanned up into high space and settled on the long warehouse roofs again.

A woman and a girl came out to the rail of the *Queen Emma* waiting for the tiresome preliminaries of landing to be over before displaying eagerness or impatience. The woman, clad in a decent black silk gown, with a traveler's good black cloak all but concealing it, and a warm heavy Scotch shawl over the coat, wore gray braids wound about a handsome head and a widow's cap with a limp black streamer surmounting the braids. Her face was reddened by the fresh wind that was shaking the sails as they came down, her gray eyes keen and interested; two short silver curls framed her face.

The girl of seventeen who leaned on her arm was of frail, small build, with curly red hair and black-lashed eyes. She also was well bundled in wraps, but with a gallant smile on a very pale face she protested against them.

"Mother love, we can loosen up. That's sunshine. Oh, and that's San Francisco! We're here. It's all like a dream."

"That's a church," said the mother, her eyes mounting the rise of California Street; a street of wooden buildings, with sidewalk stalls where apples and oranges gave bright colors to the picture. Above them were the jumbled flat roofs of Chinatown, and on their southern boundary the solemn tower of the brick cathedral. Above again were empty lots, unpaved dirt streets, and the superb lines of half a score of enormous residences in the building, grand in window glass and brick chimneys, crowning the crest of Nob Hill.

Mrs. John Townshend, born Mary Josephine O'Neill of Cork, Ireland, did not know the names of these streets and hills, but she knew much about them. No steamer in two long years had left San Francisco for the Sandwich Islands without bearing her a letter from her son. Johnny had been with the Wells, Fargo Bank for two years now. He knew San Francisco well; he had written her of the city's wealth and the Flood and Crocker and Hopkins mansions.

Johnny himself was presently waving madly from the dock; Johnny was across the gangplank and on board, Johnny had his sister and his mother in a wild embrace. Tall, changed, but Johnny!

"My God, I've missed you so! It's so good to see you! Hat, you're a beauty!"

"Johnny," said his mother, resetting her bonnet.

"I know, but it wasn't swearing, Mother, it was praying!"

31

Johnny protested with a laugh. But his lean hard face, sporting sideburns and a luxurious mustache, flushed boyishly nevertheless.

"Hattie," he said over and over, bracing his sister with a lean long arm, "you've got so pretty! Are all the boys crazy for her, Ma?"

"They are not, then!" his mother said.

"Oh, Johnny, we had a horrible trip!" Hattie half laughed, half wailed. "I never want to see the ocean again!"

"Well, I was afraid——" His nice homely face at once assumed a worried expression. "It was pretty rough, was it?"

"Hattie was sick every day until evening, and then she was too weak to eat and half frightened to death. I never saw waves like the ones we've been in since we came in toward the coast. Twice we had our rosaries out! Here, boy, boxes right here!" Mrs. Townshend had beckoned two Chinese boys, pigtailed and cotton-clad, to take charge of her luggage. "Where do they take them, Johnny?" she asked briskly.

"Well, you're at a place on Taylor Street. It's quite a bit up the hill; I've a carriage here." Johnny handed his sister down the gangplank, came back for his mother.

"Ugh, that horrible ship, I shall never be hungry again!" groaned Miss Hattie, lifting skirts over her crinolines as she came down. But her color was already beginning to bloom, and more than once as they drove up the hill she laughed with amazement and delight at the scenes about her, and was prettier than ever.

"Johnny, they're Indians, aren't they? Men with long hair, don't they look silly! And the coolies, of course. And everyone richer than Croesus from the mines!"

"I'll talk to you about it later, Ma," said Johnny, squeezed between them and holding a hand of each. "But we ought to put something into these mines. Machinery costs money, and there are always fellows about who are looking for investors."

Mrs. Townshend straightened her fine broad shoulders.

"All I know is keeping boarders, Johnny."

"Well, you're in the land of opportunity now. Someday

I'll show you some of the houses of the big guns, up on Nob Hill here. They all started with nothing!"

"There must be decent people here who want a boarding-house," Mrs. Townshend said absently. She was looking at her strange surroundings with eager interest. Widowed twice at forty-five, and self-supporting for some half dozen years, she had resented the idleness that a month's waiting for the ship had forced upon her in Hawaii, and the long stormy days while the changing Pacific winds had urged the ship inconsequently to and fro in the endless great circle of which it was always the tormented center.

She had mended all the clothes on board, marked linen, learned to cook Chinese dishes on this trip, but at best it was wasted time, and she thirsted for wider activities. This city of San Francisco, with its outlying districts of the Mission Dolores, Tuckertown, Yerba Buena, was her oyster; she felt in her veins that it was a wise step that she had taken. She had done well in Honolulu, she would do better here.

Markets, those were certainly markets, with fish glittering on open tables, and the church comfortingly familiar rising above them, with its tower and its clock. Then came China-town; huddled, teeming with pigtails. But as she knew China itself, this was not particularly interesting; she knew the dark oiled wood in collapsing houses, the rickety balconies hanging over the street, the inevitable banners——

"Here we are," Johnny said, stopping before a gaunt white hillside house back in a garden. The walks were of Portuguese tiling; the long balcony rails wound with bougainvillaea just putting forth leaves. Acacias dropped yellow tassels on the walk.

"Pretty, Hat," said Mrs. Townshend, pausing to look down across the roofs of Chinatown and the piers and the shipping.

"Oh, Ma, it's beautiful! Think of us being in America, everyone speaking English!" Hat exulted. Johnny, grasping boxes, grinned in gratification, and they all went up the wooden steps to the piazza and into the house.

The bare parlors on the right of the wide hall had bay windows draped in Nottingham lace, pale worn carpets, impersonal mismated chairs. A whatnot filled one corner of the

33

room, and a grand piano with the inevitable thin purple flannel covering was in another corner. There was a table holding heavy gift books with gilded covers; Flaxman's illustrations for Schiller's *Bell*, Doré's *Purgatorio*. Several china lamps were on small, marble-topped tables. A pug dog, with a tail as curled as a small doughnut, leaped from a basket and barked as they came into the room.

Mrs. Lomas was a tired, sharp-faced woman who wasted no words on her new boarders. Five minutes after their arrival Johnny had gone and the Townshends—mother and daughter—were established in an immense front bedroom upstairs and were pluming and refreshing themselves in luxury to which they had long been strangers.

"Hot water, Ma!" said Hat, busy with the heavy china pitcher and basin. She had taken off her dress; she soaped her arms thoroughly.

"This is so pretty, Hattie," said her mother, pausing at the window, with her arms full of clothing. "Somehow I never knew it would be such a hilly city!"

"It's so wonderful to be here, and not tumbling around with half your things on the floor," Hattie said, coming to join her. The older woman put a kiss on a fresh, soap-scented young arm, and Hattie embraced her joyously. "I thought we never would! Waiting—and the ship never ready to start," she said. "And then days and days on board—and so hot and no wind! And the weevily beef—and then the storm and every bone in one's body aching!"

"My poor little girl," Mary said lovingly, absently. "Hat, I think we have reached harbor, I think we'll stay here," she added presently. Hattie was dreaming, her head upon her mother's shoulder, the older woman's arm about her.

The new city—it was hardly a city even now, yet it was never to be called or considered a village or a township— lay in incredible disorder and ugliness below them. But its ugliness was that of swift and feverish growth, broken by the unexpected beauty of a church spire here and a straggling line of fresh young eucalyptus there, or a gay lanterned balcony in the Chinese quarter that descended in Oriental color down the steep hill to the piers. Empty lots, tethered goats,

34

shacks and shanties were the setting for pretentious mansions standing isolated on Nob Hill, and comfortable ranch-type homes of two or three stories set in steep gardens. Even in January these gardens showed a flooded glory of geraniums, nasturtiums, roses glowing in the long slanted rays of the setting sun.

"You keep a nicer house than this one, Ma," Hattie whispered.

"Well, I should hope," her mother answered firmly.

"Because—did you see the dead flowers downstairs?"

"Why, your brother said this is one of the finest houses in town," Mrs. Townshend said with an affectation of surprise.

"Now you stop it, Ma!" protested Hat.

"You think I could keep as good a house as this?"

"You stop it. I'll tell Johnny on you!"

"Well, I know I could," the older woman said good-humoredly. She swept a hand down to run her fingers over the rungs of a rocking chair, held it up to display unmistakable smudges of dust. She turned a chair cushion to show white stuffing ready to burst out. And she laughed in quiet triumph.

Her unpacking finished, her toilet completed, she moved the rocker to the balcony and sat back in deep satisfaction, utterly at rest. Hattie brought her her shawl, and she rocked to and fro idly and looked down at the city.

"I saw a good-looking big house with a sign 'to let' on it today," she observed. "I'll find out where the markets are tomorrow."

"Ma, for heaven's sake wait until you get your furniture!" Hat, flitting to and fro, protested.

"I'll get my furniture," Mrs. Townshend said, rocking.

"I'll bet you're off for church in the morning," the girl suggested.

"Indeed, I'm going to walk down to the church tonight," her mother answered. "It gives me a strange feeling, this place, I don't know what it is, here," she went on, after a silence, her hand pressed to her heart. "It's as if I'd died——"

"As if you *what?*" Hat called from the other side of the room.

35

"No matter." She fell silent, saying the Angelus in her heart, the stream of her thoughts serene and irradiated. She had brought her worldly possessions and her daughter safely up from the faraway island that never had been home to her. She was reunited at last with her beloved only son. The years of struggle had left her small visible returns, but even these few hours in this western city had shown her that this was her place, that she could live and work here. The streets, the shops, the hills already seemed to belong to her; the twilight that was scented with acacia blossoms was hers. She had heard church bells tonight for the first time in years; she had heard strangers chattering her own tongue.

The evening was balmy, the bay shining with the last of the sunset that streamed through the Golden Gate, and dotted with the first anchor lights. Over Chinatown a yellowish glow arose; St. Mary's Angelus bells had stopped ringing.

CHAPTER 5

Johnny came up for the plain boardinghouse dinner; clam chowder and venison stew, potatoes and a pale cake with a paler sauce that scented the whole room with vanilla. Hard small prunes were passed, and yellow cheese in cold white bowls.

"So that was what they call cabinet pudden?" said Mrs. Townshend agreeably, as she and her children walked down the hill.

The brother and sister exchanged a mildly indulgent glance and a brief laugh.

"What would you have done to it, Ma?" Hattie asked.

"Well, I'd have put in more than two eggs for seventeen people," her mother answered promptly. But she was too happy, too soothed by the charms and novelties and promise of this new world to be long disturbed by the inferiority of a mere pudding.

They walked upon unpaved streets, upon broken dirt roadways; they walked amidst the high nervous chatter and congestion of Chinatown's dark streets, and came out by the cathedral, before whose plain wooden altar a few dim candles were burning. Mrs. Townshend settled herself to her prayers in the front pew, with a great sigh of complete felicity. Ahh— here they were again, as at home as in Snugborough, "a step to the west of Cork"; here again were the fragrance of Benediction incense, the candles, the altar rail, the sanctuary light!

Her silk dress rustled as it settled about her; her crepe veil flowed back majestically from her strong homely face. Her son and daughter, sitting back in the pew, watched her respectfully. Mother might be all briskness and practicability in daily life, but when she entered a church she escaped them; she became somebody else.

They knew that she was happy; quite suddenly sure of herself and of life; savoring the future and her share of it with strong appetite. But how happy they could not guess.

It was as if she had known that it was to be this way. The days of indecision in Hawaii were over. She had kept her resolution to get away from an atmosphere so strongly Protestant and missionary in its foundations that her Irish faith could not root there; a place in which her conscientious attempts to make converts in return had not made her popular. It was no place for Hattie and the danger of a mixed marriage; and her Johnny might be needing her up on the mainland. Lord knew what the boy was up to by this time!

So she had torn up roots, with no idea of what she would find in fabulous San Francisco; no assurance that she would not regret her venture. Four hundred and twelve American dollars now stood between her and the humiliating moment when she must ask Johnny for help; "God love him," she said now in her heart, pouring out the eager hungry prayers that had been waiting for that altar light, "I'll not have to turn to him, not ever. I've my furniture and my good linen from home, and my health. And there are many in this place who never had a good slice of wheat bread baked in a stone bowl, or slept in linen sheets, for the matter of that."

Her keen eyes missed no building in the uneven medley of

37

structures, large and small, as she and her children walked on into the city. She noted the markets, approved of the street names: Sacramento, Pacific, Mission. There were no street lights, but lamps flickered everywhere on stalls of fruit, behind dull laundry windows, in shanty doorways.

The city, quite decent in its early-morning hours, when Chinese, Mexican, American, and Spanish housewives walked the rough and muddy thoroughfares and bargained at street stalls for rabbits, bears' meat, fresh wet fish, and who sometimes could get white flour and occasionally cinnamon or sherry, reverted to its frontier manners at night. The daytime sidewalk display of hoes and rakes, mining machinery and iron frying pans, had been gathered now into the little hardware shops that were securely padlocked; all the saloons and dance halls, so drab and dull in the daylight, were gushing red temptation across the broken sidewalks.

Sailors locked arms and sang as they zigzagged in trios to and fro; cowboys on nervous horses loped by, letting loose wild screeches; maudlin laughter and song were already ripping into the dark. Harriet walked between her mother and brother, a little frightened. But her mother swept through the hot little danger zone apparently unaware of anything irregular, and soon, to Johnny's relief, they reached Market Street, running at a bold angle against the orderly lines of Kearney and Dupont, and brave in the big padlocked doors of hardware stores, banks, and dimly painted windows marked "Ships Chandlers," "Haberdashery," "Itchi Ban."

Here were the big hotels, the Palace and Grand, and not far from them the Russ House and the What Cheer. Johnny showed them the Wells Fargo Bank, and Sather and Sons Bank, and the famous restaurants Poodle Dog and Jeunesse Dorée. Down at the foot of the street ran the low long sheds of the ferry building, the godowns and the bund; all these places as dark and decorous now as the streets of the "Barbary Coast" were roaring and awake. At the entrances of the hotels high incandescent lights hissed and snickered cold and white, and a few green iron lamps at Market Street corners showed fans of gas in glass hoods.

"I'll have to put forty pounds into groceries," Mrs. Townshend said with relish. "And I'll get my hands on a boy or two to take back the baskets from the market."

"Ma, have you got your egg ring?" Johnny had Hattie on his arm, and Hattie was linked to her mother; they were walking in the old way, a single entity. His laugh showed he was teasing.

"Who else would have it, then?" his mother demanded.

Hattie laughed. "She'll never buy an egg that goes through the ring," she said. "But as for me I'm still on the ship, with the world going up and down like a seesaw. Ma, I'm tired."

"We're on our way home," her mother reassured her.

"You've got your bearings, haven't you, Ma? Knew just what corner to turn," Johnny observed admiringly.

"I've my head on," Mrs. Townshend said dryly.

"By the way, Hat," said Johnny. "Julia Danvers is here."

"In Boston, you mean? She was going to Boston——"

"She didn't go on to Boston. She's here with a Mrs. Garceau. Lin Breyer is here too."

"Oh, you might know *that*," Hattie said after a moment, her mouth filling with salt water. "How'd you know, Johnny?"

"I went to a dance at the Salisburys'—let me tell you the cream of the fancy was out! Julia was there."

"Dance with her, Johnny?"

"No chance."

"I suppose not," Hattie said tonelessly. She did not speak again until they were all inside the house, mounting the stairs by the light of one dim trembling gas flame. "Do they have many dances, Johnny?" she added then.

"One more. I've got you a card."

"My dress'll be horribly mashed. I'll look a fright."

"You—that thought you were going to be drowned in the cold sea this time Sunday night, and now it's dress again!" the older woman said, taking off her long-tailed bonnet and heavy cloak. She hung them, and Hattie's outer garments, on nails in the shallow closet.

Johnny kissed them both good night and left them in their big airy room. Hattie, thinking of Lin Breyer and Julia Danvers, got into bed and was promptly seized by sleep. But her mother, well wrapped in an Oriental dressing gown, her gray

39

hair twisted into strips of white rag, went out to the balcony and sat there in the rocker thinking.

Her thoughts were exhilarating; she had not often known such buoyancy of spirit. She had carried heavy responsibility for many years, eking out a living in the restricted atmosphere of a lonely island far down in the Pacific, maintaining her religious loyalties against the softer and more winning element represented by the well-entrenched missionary families. Teatime in some island home, with the doctor of divinity relaxing in his big chair and the charming wife and children dispensing bread and butter, with the home photographs about and the good talk of hymns and social suppers and Sunday school going round, was a much more warming affair than were the visits of occasional lonely and celibate clergymen who were hardly known to the scattered and minority Catholic groups.

Mary Townshend had taken more than one dangerous sea trip; she feared and hated the sea. With a countrified little maid for companion, she had ventured forth from Ireland at seventeen to rejoin the young husband who had taken his ship out some months earlier. Cold and ocean-tossed and seasick, the two terrified girls had finally seen the brave spur of Diamond Head pushing forth into silky and peaceful water and had found solid earth under them at last. But of the gallant captain and his ship nothing more ever had been heard.

Once again Mary Townshend, her name O'Meara then, had set forth across the deep, this time to Rome, and again to Ireland, and with the nullification of her three-hour marriage at last established, she had found the old world changed and had come the long way back to the new, to unite herself to the dashing, handsome, and irresponsible son of a conservative Boston family, a family that had sent him far, far away and taken good care John should never come home again.

Three years of happiness had followed, happiness whose memories today often made Mary Townshend feel uneasy. But confident in her youth, joy, and love, she had felt no scruples at the time. There had been horses to ride, and rolling green breakers to surmount, beach suppers and native entertainments, and heavenly quiet hours in the lightly built hacienda that she had named "Snugborough" for the old home in Cork. Protestant Johnny had given her the first joy of her life.

Widowed again, she had taken her two children home to Ireland, through the Orient this time, hoping never again to leave the green shores of Erin. Then in answer to warm invitations, she had sailed to New England, to show the children to Johnny's folk. But presently pride and honor took her to a shabby sailing vessel in Boston Harbor, and she faced the roaring Atlantic again. The elder Johnny had left in the Islands a horrifying mountain of debts. She had not suspected it during his lifetime but after his death she had faced it, and over the slow years paid off every penny. And in these years she withdrew in timidity to loneliness again, wondering how she had ever come to plunge into the innocent, church-flavored island gaieties; the psalms and hymns and money-raising suppers.

And then had come Hattie's sudden fancy for a staid young missionary, and her enthusiastic description of his appointment to Sarawak. That had been enough. Mary Townshend had brought down her old boxes, her spacious carpetbags again. It must be America now; it must be the mainland, where her son was, where her children's kinsfolk dwelt. Hattie, not at all displeased to be rescued from a situation in which her good nature rather than her heart was involved, had fallen in with the plan amiably enough, and passage on the *Queen Emma* had been secured.

But this trip had outdistanced all the others in ferocity of weather, perversity of winds, inefficiency of accommodations, endless repetition of delays.

"I'll tell you why we lived through it, Ma," said the high-spirited Hattie. "It was only because we didn't die."

But one gentle little missionary wife had died, and one big sailor had been blown overboard, and Mary, on burning days, had carried just a half cupful, just a quarter cupful of the scant quart that was her daily allowance of drinking water, to the feverish boys in the sick bay, and Hattie had more than once left the table just in time to save herself the disgrace of being violently and publicly ill. Both mother and

41

daughter had ached, shoulders, hips, elbows, from the slips and slides and bumps that were an inevitable part of any moving about, endless day after endless night. They were dirty, sore, frightened, sick, and hungry. The voyage had been one long nightmare, and Mary Townshend had spoken for both when she had said: "God helping me, I'll never think upon it again. Nor I'll never trust the sea again, neither!"

Now she lay back in her rocking chair and sent her grateful heart up to God in a rush of prayer. To kneel in a cathedral again, to have her son on one side of her, her daughter on the other, to feel the miracle of the solid earth beneath her feet, and the goodness and safety of hills and streets, voices and homes all about, this was richness such as she had never known before.

Tomorrow she would rent a house. It would be an unpromising place enough to start with. But with the furniture brought up from the *Queen Emma* and half a dozen beds set up, she could be in business in three or four days. Good sheets, clean tables, good food—there was always need for them in the world. Roughing it a little to start, but with things working more smoothly every day. Mary Townshend visualized barrels of sugar, a sack of potatoes, and flour. These things were all here, with mountains of oranges and cabbages and onions flanking them.

Tall Chinese, with bamboo rods angled across their blue cotton shoulders, swung through these streets with great panniers that tipped and swayed as they went. In their baskets were layered straw trays of fine fruit, lettuce, eggs, lemons, garlic, artichokes. She had seen these fruit merchants, their baskets empty, ready to go home in late afternoon, but they would be back tomorrow, and she would bargain with them, as she had bargained all her life. For cheese and candles and herring and fresh crusty bread in the long market sheds in Cork City, for melons and milk and rice and chickens under the lazy waving palms of her island home, and now for everything—everything, she told herself exultantly.

Oh, she could set a table now! Look at this poor woman's waste of vanilla in the pudding sauce tonight, look at the raisins the children in the street were eating, look at the fish

flapping wet on the counters of the Chinatown shops, with
evening gaslight making the long ropes of cuttlefish shine like
silver! This was a great city, this San Francisco, it had everything she wanted in it. A cathedral, praise to God and all the
saints, empty barns of houses, for hadn't half the men deserted the place a few years ago to run after the gold? There
would be new faces every day, newly come men and women
looking for someplace to eat well, someplace to sleep.

"Ma, stop laughing," moaned Hattie late in the night.

"Was I laughing, dear'r?" She kissed the top of the sleepy
red head that bumped on her shoulder. "I'll ask her to have
dinner with us before the month is out, this Mrs. Lomas, and
she'll eat a cabinet pudden that is a pudden," she said. But
Hattie, worn out, was asleep again.

CHAPTER 6

Then began golden days for Mary Townshend, even as these
were golden days for her adopted city. Sober, energetic, busy,
she studied her new world. Nobody looking at the fresh-faced,
tall, rosy-cheeked woman in the widow's veil, and very shortly
everyone knew her by sight, could by any reasonable process
have deduced that she was one of the happiest women in the
world.

Waking in the cold foggy dark was a delight; her walk
through wet gardens and shanties and empty lots to the red
brick cathedral was a walk through paradise. When she came
out from Mass the whistles would be blowing for seven
o'clock, and the sun pushing back the fog, and Chinatown
agog with scraping feet and laughter and high voices.

Mary Townshend walked over Dupont Street to the markets, and small boys appeared with large baskets, ready to
make the trip to and fro with the day's provisions. Supplies

43

were laid in for the day ahead, and as she strolled up the hill for breakfast, hungry, already a little tired, she would feel a sensation close to bliss.

Then came the stir of the big house. Her eye, her voice, her step, her hand were everywhere. In the long parlors flowers must be fresh, curtains snowy, fire brasses and polished surfaces shining. In the kitchen one general look about was enough, but in the dining room the white tablecloths must be invitingly set with scrupulous care: blue plates and generous coffee cups, smoking rolls and pitchers of thick cream. Apricots, figs, peaches were on every table. Sunshine poured in at the angles of the long windows; two maids in checked calico frocks and enveloping white aprons must be ready for action.

The boarders trickled down, and the mistress of the house laid aside her cloak, flung back her veil, and settled to her own breakfast. But her eyes still glanced everywhere, and her greetings to her guests were interspersed by undertone directions to the waitresses, and to an older woman and a young Chinese, who occasionally came in from the kitchen for orders or advice.

Thus began her day of glory. She walked through her domain, eyes everywhere. She stopped at the doorways of spotless orderly bedrooms for cheerful talk with other women. She looked at piles of new linen being marked and of old linen being mended. She interviewed the newest waitress, conspired with the oldest, and descended to the kitchen to try any suspected egg on the ring.

The ring was old, of black bog oak. Any egg that would go through it was too small an egg for Mrs. Townshend's house, and went back to the market, Samples of macaroni, samples of flour, samples of spice were on her desk; when she sat down to paper work at eleven she examined them, pronounced upon them.

Miss Hattie, in rustles of striped taffeta or trailing, flower-embroidered muslin, would come down for a morning kiss. Miss Hattie had had a marvelous time the night before, while she had danced new slippers to rags, had beaten a small fan into fringes. Miss Hattie had half the eligible young men of the city at her feet and could laugh deep in her heart at the thought that she ever had been envious of Julia Danvers! Lin Breyer had long before this transferred his allegiance.

Girl friends came in, late in the morning, to talk over parties with Hattie, and often a young man or two would join them, on his lunch hour, for a five-minute stay. Great laughter and teasing and discreet morning continuation of evening flirtations went on, and the sunshine, pouring in through opened french windows, lighted as pretty a scene, Mary Townshend used to think, as any in the smiling world.

Hattie discussed all her beaux with her mother, with such pitying laughter and tossing of red curls. The poor things, they were so absurd! Writing her poems and sending her roses —why didn't they save their money, the creatures, or spend it sensibly on some other girl? Why couldn't she and the other girls and all these men just have a good time, dancing at the Presidio and picnicking over in Sausalito, without all this nonsense of getting engaged and married!

Mary listened in fond admiration that was tempered with warnings and advice. She went with Hattie to select the materials for her frocks, and fat old Miss Vilder, on the top floor front, made them up for her. Miss Vilder, born Helga Wilde, but perfectly satisfied with her Americanized name in this land of strange languages and faces and pronunciations, shed actual tears of admiration over Hattie's beauty as Hattie pirouetted in flimsy muslins from Paris and fringed shawls from China. And a gentle widowed woman who adored Hattie, "Gardy Ann," took Hattie to the parties, and sat waiting for Hattie, and wrapped Hattie warmly in shawls for the trip home. Mary never went; she was tired at night. Nine o'clock usually ended her fifteen-hour day and saw her comfortable in bed. Gardy Ann loved to play chaperone.

But Hattie still shared her mother's room, and when Hattie came back from dances and cotillions and dinners her mother got the whole story, the older woman sleepily admiring and exclaiming as the extravagant entertainments of Nob Hill were described, but scanning any possible suitor with a far more critical eye.

"Is he a Catholic, Hat?"

45

"Pierre? Devout."

"Well, that's good. How about this Louis?"

"Luis Morenos? Ma, look at the name! Of course he is."

"And this Jimmy Kane?"

"Well, about him I don't know, Mrs. Townshend, because you'll be surprised to learn that the first thing I do isn't taking out my rosary when I dance with a man."

"You bad saucy girl, you get into bed, and no more talk. Hang your dress in the wardrobe there, your hem's all fringed out again. God bless you, my own girl, good night."

To Hattie, no door in the city was closed. Johnny's life, now that he had his pretty sister to escort, was changed. Her wit, her fresh beauty, her friendliness enchanted him as it did other men. They went into private theatricals, and Johnny was found to be a rare character actor, in *The Lady of Lyons* and *Jim the Penman,* and *Diplomacy.* But when Hattie took her bow there was more furious applause.

The city's hostesses were of varied backgrounds, but they were alike in perfectly appreciating Miss Harriet Townshend. Hattie met their standard. Of fine southern stock themselves, or of sound French origin, or from England's or New England's good families, they had established a genuine aristocracy on the hills of the most western outpost. Manners and customs were carefully observed and regulated; elegancies of table setting and the returning of formal calls were in full bloom. At balls small cards with fringe-tied pencils kept the proper order of the dances, and when Miss Charlotte Billings paid last calls with her mother, just before her marriage, a penciled "p.p.c." on her card meant only that she was making her last call as Miss Charlotte Billings.

Girls were whirling joyously into marriages, many to be followed by honeymoon departure for New York and the opera, or Niagara Falls, or even Europe. And on the night before his marriage, the groom entertained his men friends for the last time. With good-by to his bachelor ways, to gambling, drinking, to affairs with a type of woman of which his angel-pure bride had presumably never even heard, he also said good-by to his old companions, and it was understood that they would make no effort to see him again until they

46

heard directly from his young wife and received an invitation from her.

Into this fine moral atmosphere Hattie was gladly welcomed. Her name was a good one; she was lovely, innocent, cultured, gay. She played and sang Franz Schubert songs, songs bound in big black books with her name in gold on the cover. She spoke French prettily, and so could be placed next to Comte du Mar de la Ferronays at dinner, and keep the gallant old consul happy.

Of course she was a flirt. She gloried in flirtation, and her mother, as innocent along certain lines of knowledge as she was, considered it a harmless girlish amusement, and merely felt sorry for the young men who breathed the faster as they poured their story of young passion into Hattie's little ears, held her small boneless hand in their burning ones as they danced, and went raving home under the moon to try in the terms of Tennyson, Shelley, or Swinburne to write her what they felt.

Hattie was bridesmaid over and over again at the elaborate weddings on Nob Hill and in the elegant parlors of the Palace and Occidental hotels. This entitled her to stand beside the bride when callers, members of the family, and close friends came to call at the new home on the day following the wedding.

The bride, shy and sweet and nervously hospitable in her special "second-day" finery, would receive mother, sisters, grandmother, and bridal party first, and then serve coffee and sherry and biscuits to the circle of aunts and cousins. Much gentle laughter and constrained talk marked these occasions, and the loveliest wedding any woman had ever seen was described with sufficient detail to satisfy even the chief participant. Hattie would be first lady in waiting.

Later, days or even weeks later, when the happy couple left for their honeymoon, Hattie and a few others often accompanied them as far as Sacramento or Benicia, after which privacy was granted them and the world lost sight of the newly wed pair for an entire year.

But even here Miss Hattie Townshend was privileged. She might flutter in to gossip and giggle with the bride any morning she could spare the time. The newly wed Minnie or Mamie or Charlotte would welcome her with joy, perhaps keep her for a tea and oysters lunch and a proud display of lately arrived wedding silver from faraway eastern cousins. The talk would be innocent and restrained; wifely pride on the woman's side, airy boastful complacency on the part of the responsibility-free girl.

No intimate question ever was asked of Minnie, even by her own mother. What went on on the upper floor of Minnie's darling little house was nobody's business but her own. Her only references to her wonderful Willie were laughing apologies because "Men eat so much, Hat!" or a shy "He's just an old home lover, he just doesn't want to go anywhere."

It might happen that when the couple was busy with first dinners given in their own home and in their friends' Hattie would cool toward her beloved Minnie.

"Why don't you run out and see Minnie?" her mother would ask. "Take the Mission Street horsecar and get off at Twelfth."

"Oh, I don't know, Ma." Perhaps Harriet's head would be a globe of foaming suds, the air astringent with the strong scent of Spanish bark. The hard capable hands of Mary Townshend would claw firmly at the white mass that hid the gleaming red tendrils.

"Why, you and Carrie haven't been out there for a long time, dear."

"Well, she was going down to the Winships in San Mateo."

"Wasn't that just for the day?"

"Yes. But—well, her mother's there a lot now."

"Oh, is it that way?" Enlightenment in the older voice, speculation. "I thought, from something her mother said—" A pause. "Well, that's nice."

"Nice!" Harriet would ejaculate, emerging from the last douches of cold water now and rubbing her head with a great crash towel. "I think it's horrid."

"What's horrid about having a beautiful child to love?"

"Oh, everything. I think it's awful. Poor Min, just as they're beginning to have a good time! Staying at home and waiting

48

for Willie to walk around the block with her after dinner—I think it's horrid!"

"What else would Minnie expect, being married, Hat? What more would she want than her own little baby?"

"Ma," Hattie said one day in one such talk.

"What is it, dear'r?" It was pouring rain, at five o'clock on a February afternoon, and the boardinghouse was more than ordinarily warm and cozy. In the drawing room below various ladies sat knitting or sewing, chatting or playing euchre; a bare-armed maid came into the parlors at intervals and put coal on the two stalwart fires that winked behind polished steel bars. At the back of the house, dinner preparations were already hissing and hammers pounding; in the dripping kitchen porch a fish merchant with a wagon full of crabs and prawns, salmon and cod was bargaining with Gardy Ann.

Mrs. Townshend and Hattie were upstairs in the hall bedroom that the older woman used for an office. The flat-topped desk faced the room, and Hattie's mother looked across it at the girl, who, comfortable in a shabby old armchair, was pretending to look at a book of Tennyson's poems and to take only a casual interest in the conversation.

"Ma," she said, "do married people have to have babies?"

"Dear God, what else would they want?" the mother demanded.

"No, but you know what I mean. Do they have to?"

"Well, Harriet, you're twenty-one," Mrs. Townshend said, laying her pen aside with a sigh. "You've seen how it goes. Some have them, and some don't. Look at poor Mrs. Ebbetts. She broke her heart for a baby."

Harriet raised her eyes from a page.

"Yes, but I mean suppose you didn't want them?"

"Then you wouldn't marry."

"No. But there's a lot—that—I don't—understand," Harriet said slowly.

"There's a great deal that you've no need to understand," her mother answered promptly. "Leave all that until you're married. When you fall in love with a man you'll find it all comes naturally and simply, as it ought."

"Ha," Hattie said thoughtfully, and returned to her poetry.

49

After a moment she said, "Nasty little squirmy things, looking as if they'd been boiled."

"You're the one that loves Sonny Howard," her mother reminded her, smiling. "Who went upstairs every night to sponge him off before he went to bed?"

"Oh, my beautiful darling little Sonny," Hattie exclaimed in a rapture, "oh, those little fat hands!"

"Well, you see," Mary Townshend said mildly.

"Yes, and that's all entirely different!" Hattie argued. "Sonny was almost a year old."

"You have to give them a chance to grow up, Hat."

"Yes, but that's not what I mean." Harriet looked up again from her book. "I mean—the wedding and trousseau and the new house and all that are such fun," she said slowly. "And then—well, Minnie's sick every morning, and her clothes feel queer, and she knows she's going to be screaming and yelling for a whole day—with Kate Cozzens it was three days and then the baby died, and—well, it doesn't seem fair."

"Harry Cozzens is as proud and happy as he can be over another baby's coming," Harriet's mother said, disapproving of the trend of the conversation.

"Yes, and it has to be a boy or he'll give it to the ashman," Hattie said noncommittally.

"Well," Mrs. Townshend said indulgently, "they all want boys. Mrs. Keenan said that Harry comes home early, now that it gets dark at five, to take Kate walking."

"Yes, I know. So kind of him," Harriet conceded dryly. Her mother gave her a keen look, but Hattie was reading and did not speak again.

And the happy dancing and flirting months went by, and were years, and every year brought a fresh lot of adorers for Miss Harriet Townshend, with the red hair and the blue, blue eyes, the piano playing, and French chattering. But Hattie did not find the right man, or seem to care that he was so slow in appearing.

CHAPTER 7

To Harriet's mother these years went on, perhaps more golden than Harriet's own. Mary Townshend was in a situation to enjoy every moment of an unusually vigorous life. Her cares as a wife were over; her independence complete. She could revel in the society and the love of a fine son and a lovely daughter. And she was free of the seas, the mainland was firm beneath her.

Her enterprise had moved apace to security and success. In its modest pioneer fashion the Townshend House was famous. Fine people, coming to an unknown city and unpredictable fortunes, knew about her. Other fine people linked her name to that of San Francisco: "Write that down for them, George. Mrs. Townshend's house in Stockton Street," said women in Baltimore and Boston and Portland, Maine.

The property now comprised the adjoining house, a similar wooden structure whose sunny bay windows were brave in looped white curtains, and the staff had grown to quite formidable proportions. Forty-four guests meant more than a hundred meals a day; a spacious basement laundry, with its potbellied stove always adorned with heavy flatirons, was occupied all day long, and Miss Vilder was now permanently employed in the linen room.

The vigilance and energy of Mary Townshend never relaxed for a moment. She was always available, and no detail was too small to engage her attention. The commanding figure, swishing silk in the leisurely afternoons, trailing a widow's bonnet and all-enveloping Paisley shawl in the misty early dawn before Mass, became a familiar sight in the growing city. Her fine homely face framed in four dangling silver curls, her linen cuffs and collars immaculate, her step buoyant as her rich Irish voice, she walked the earth as if the blood of kings was in her veins, as indeed she believed it to be.

Every step in the growth of the mushroom city delighted her.

"Hattie, they're building a blanket works out on Potrero. We'll have our own blankets one of these days," and "Hat, do you know they're making gloves up Napa way, where the wineries are?" she would exult.

"I'll bet they're awful gloves," Hattie might opine.

"They're gloves," her mother would assert simply. Hattie's gloves were of fine French kid and many-buttoned; they fitted her pretty hands and arms so tightly that they had to be stretched by long, scissor-like clippers whenever they were to be worn. Most of her frocks were of imported gauzes and muslins; her tiny satin corsets were Paris-made.

But there were smart shops now on Market Street and Kearney Street, where ravishing materials could be bought, with fans, parasols, lisle stockings inset with medallions of white lace. New merchants arrived every year; black-face minstrels came from the East to put on hilarious shows, and the number of those who remembered applauding little roguish Lotta Crabtree was becoming fewer. Horsecars jingled up Market Street and out to the Mission Dolores, a box at the door of the car ringing a bell as the nickel was inserted, and the driver looking over his shoulder as he drove to be sure the fare was paid.

Mary Townshend went to churches other than the old cathedral, walked up to the big Jesuit school and church on Hayes Street, or took the car out to the Mission Dolores. She went once a week to sew, in a group of devoted women, for the "poor." She had a prominent part in the great Christmas feasts, notably that to which some hundred small children came to get their dolls and their candy, and their handmade small dresses of good durable woolen. San Francisco already had its slums, its rickety wooden buildings that hid other shanties in the rear and sheltered men who lay about muttering in gutters all day long, and shrill-voiced women in wet aprons, whose fingers were swelled pink from washtubs.

Miss Hattie gathered up her frail ruffled skirts as she

tripped after her mother through such scenes, and bent upon the unfortunate women and girls of the alleys and dark stairways and grimy kitchens a glance so heavenly in its sweetness and pity that she was often apostolized as an angel right out of paradise.

She would be serious for a while, and discuss social injustices and the evils of drink while she ate her lunch, but immediately afterward she might flutter away in the prettiest of new dresses for a drive in the park, with a flowered bonnet tied beneath her chin and a distracting miniature parasol with an ivory handle tipped against the sun.

Over to Masonic Avenue, and clip-clip out to the park the phaeton would go, with an ardent young man at the reins and Hattie's lovely little face illumined by the lavender light that fell through the stretched silk of the yellow parasol.

"I don't think you ought to see things like that," George Fitzmaurice said to her one day when they were spinning about the Speedway in glorious autumn sunshine.

"Like what?"

"Oh, those places your mother takes you, places where you see drunks and all that."

"Ma says we have to be charitable," Hattie said primly.

"Well, you don't have to go places like that!"

"I certainly would believe my mother was right before I'd believe you were right, George Fitzmaurice."

"It isn't a question of right or wrong, but you're much too fine and pretty—and well, pretty, to mix up with people like that!"

"Ah, but now look," said Harriet in her most wheedling manner, "let's suppose I was married to you, George, and we had that little white house over there. Wouldn't you want me to do charitable things for the poor? Wouldn't you want your wife—oh, of course we'd dance and go out a lot, I don't mean that——"

"I wish you'd shut up!" was George's reply to this, for they had been over this ground before and Harriet had shown no inclination whatsoever toward taking the steps that would lead to the white cottage and the charitable wife. Her joyous laugh then dismissed all serious talk, and they presently dropped in upon English friends for a cup of tea, Harriet, who had, it seemed, promised this particular hostess that she would find another man for the cotillion, delivering George over to her in person.

There was an increasing number of pleasant tea tables always available now; there were English families who made five-o'clock tea a ritual, and charming southern families who had come West after the tragedy of the Civil War and found a new world by the Golden Gate.

Mrs. Townshend made not even a casual effort to enter the charmed circle that prided itself upon its exclusiveness, and Harriet none at all. But the doors opened nevertheless. The city's most eligible bachelors were apt to live for short or longer periods at Mrs. Townshend's, and for longer or shorter periods were deep in love with Harriet.

She went to parties and cotillions and dinners well escorted, and only anxious to share her retinue with the other girls. And the offers of marriage fluttered about her like moths about a lamp, so that over and over again, as she demurely played the part of maid of honor at some friend's wedding, Hattie knew in her mischievous heart that in the shoes of the complacent bride she might have been standing herself.

In the evenings, when friends came in to the Townshend House, there was music in the back parlor, with the girls and boys in gales of laughter as they gathered about the piano. If there were new boarders in the house, Hattie drew them into the circle, never in any doubt but that they would succumb. Perhaps they had already heard about her, perhaps this was a first glance; it made no difference, they would inevitably be hers, be they a quiet man and wife, a stout cheerful couple whose children she had helped settle down upstairs, a new and exciting bachelor, a gallant captain on his way to the Presidio.

Johnny always had breakfast with his mother, and dined with her four times a week. On other nights he called on Miss Lizzie Carmichael and sat in the Carmichael parlor, with her grandmother knitting or sewing in a rocker just beyond the open parlor doors. He took cigars to her father, and took Lizzie candy and flowers. They were engaged, but with no immediate prospects of marriage. Johnny's name was on the bond with his mother's for the purchase of the annex; Lizzie's mother was dead, and her father and her younger brother and sister were violently agitated at the mere thought of her leaving them.

Lizzie was a placid, pale girl, with a smooth heavy knot of lifeless brown hair on the nape of her neck. Her hands were long and cool. She was in no way Hattie's type, but the two were congenial, teaching catechism in the Jesuits' Sunday school, playing duets with firm counting aloud in all the stiff places, determining to walk regularly, to study poetry regularly, to continue with French. They exchanged Christmas and birthday presents, and thought of themselves as bosom friends.

But Harriet was so constituted that she did not need either to give or take real affection, and Lizzie, who could entertain no emotion easily, was secretly, painfully jealous of Hattie. Hattie fascinated and frightened her, she was so perfect: She was as unconscious of her own beauty as a flower; she chattered in French with the professor, she chattered in Hawaiian to the houseboy; she had traveled around the world, been humored and loved as a child in the Islands, Ireland, England, New England, and she was not spoiled. When she told Lizzie, with a flushed little face and blue eyes as liquid as soft blue fire, that she was terribly sorry to have to say no to Alan, or that nice Baltimore man, or Sally's darling brother, Lizzie felt her heart wrench with pained adoration.

"Why do they all try to get you, Hattie? They know it's no use."

"Well, they have to love someone, I suppose. I don't try to make them, Lizzie. Honest I don't."

"Oh, I know you don't. It's something in you. They don't bother me!" Lizzie might say with a stress on the last word and a forced laugh.

"Well, they would! But Johnny's right there, in the way."

"Oh, long before Johnny! I'm older than Johnny," Lizzie more than once reminded her.

"Lizzie, why don't you and Johnny set the date?" Hattie coaxed one day when she and Lizzie had crashed through the

Second Beethoven Sonata, with the effect of emptying the two long parlors of the boardinghouse of casual sitters.

"Oh, heavens——" Lizzie said faintly.

"Well, but honestly. You've been engaged for two years."

"Not really. Well, yes it is, too. But Johnny wants to buy a house first."

"But look, Lizzie. You love him. You feel the way I did for Monsieur Bonfils, or thought I did. I mean—all excited," Hattie reasoned. "Now, if you and Johnny have been feeling that way for two years I just wonder you aren't burned up."

"Oh, heavens," Lizzie said, suffocating again, "it isn't like that!"

"It must be, Liz. Do you get all weak and your hands wet when he kisses you?"

"Listen, isn't this a silly way to talk, sitting on piano stools!" Lizzie half whispered, with a guilty glance about. "I wouldn't care if we never married!" she added in a rush. "I'd be so frightened—not after a while, of course, like Aunt Dora and Lucie Greene and all the girls who marry, not after a while. But just at first—I mean, undressing, with him right there——"

"I have a nightgown," Hattie said as the other girl paused. "Look—tucks all across here, as fine as hair, and then rose point, and more tucks. It belonged to a lady Miss Vilder worked for, and she died; it's French, she never wore it."

"But of course, after a year or so, it'd be—well, just the way marriage is," Lizzie reasoned, half to herself.

"And then you'd have babies. That'd be the part I hate. Him going off to the office all handsome and shaved and everything," said Hattie, "and you—well, like Fan is now."

"I wish you could skip right into the middle of the next year," Lizzie said with feeling. "It always seems so wrong to me, Hattie, to have a wedding, and veil, and all that just because you are getting married! I don't see how a girl can look people in the face thinking that she's going to their house with him that night——"

"Lots go to hotels," Hattie, who never had given this moment any particular thought, said, a little puzzled.

"I wouldn't," Lizzie said firmly. "And second day," she

went on, her throat almost closed, "with people like Mrs. Welch and Mrs. O'Sullivan bringing you in layer cakes or flowers or peaches or something—I'd throw them at them!"

"Well, we'll take you yellow soap or Pearline," Hattie promised gaily. "But that's what I think would be fun!" she added. "All your lovely presents out, and yourself in your second-day dress! Otherwise, what would you have a second-day dress for? I'll tell you what my second-day dress is going to be; you know that dimity at the City of Paris, blue silk stripes on dark blue, well, with a white embroidered under-dress, not too much crinoline——"

"Whose reputations are you girls cutting to pieces?" said the strong good voice of the mistress of the house as she came in with her skirts pinned back over a blue alpaca petti-coat and old gloves on her hands. "I've been hanging out of the windows trimming the ivy away," she explained in answer to Hattie's "Ma, how is it up the chimneys this morning?" "Your music sounded good," she told them.

The girls jumped up from the piano stools in some slight confusion.

"How's your father, Lizzie?"

"Well, he went down to the store today. Leo was with him."

"And what have you girls been gossiping about?"

"Ma, I've decided on my second-day dress."

"You," said Mary Townshend in loving scorn. "I doubt will you ever wear one! We'll have to settle a lot of things before that. Stay for lunch, Lizzie. Johnnny may come up, it's Saturday."

"Johnny and I were going out to see my little sister in the Children's Hospital this afternoon," Lizzie offered mildly.

"That reminds me," the other woman said, diverted. "Mrs. Salazar and the little boys are here, Hattie."

"Oh, she came?"

"With a nurse for the baby, and a dog. Yes, she has all the rooms upstairs that the Callaghans had."

"Is she pretty, Ma?"

"Well, yes. Not Spanishy, either."

"They're rich as anything. They have that whole Heart of Gold rancho," Harriet explained. "They say it's as big as a

57

county. Her little boy—which one, Ma? She has about ten, hasn't she?"

"She has four," Mrs. Townshend said shortly. "Francisco, the second one, is out in the Children's Hospital with hip disease, the poor little fella. She was crying about it. Maybe you'd just step in and say hello to her, Hattie."

"I will. Is her husband here?"

"Harriet, I told you he had died a year ago."

Harriet retreated on a gale of giggles.

"Then I hope he isn't! Come on upstairs, Lizzie. We'll wash up for lunch."

CHAPTER 8

Señora Coralia Salazar y Valdez was close to thirty years of age, and had been widowed for almost a year when she moved into Mrs. Townshend's house to be near a hospitalized child. When Hattie tapped at the door and came in for a little before-dinner call, she turned from a big black trunk, over which she had been stooping, and straightened up and smiled.

Harriet, who knew of her wealth and her importance among the big ranch holders of the center of the state, had expected to see Latin heaviness, brunette coloring, lavish display of jewelry, and to hear a strong Spanish accent.

Instead, a lean tall woman who looked hardly more than Harriet's own twenty-three years faced her, a woman whose smooth dark skin glowed as if roses were beneath it, whose ink-black braids hung loose on her shoulders, whose mouth widened with a smile as she saw Harriet. She flung a handful of frothy underwear to a maid as she gestured to a chair, and spoke as easily in English as Hattie did.

"Why, you're so nice to come in! Sit down. We're unpacking, Ana Immaculata and I, and I'm tired."

58

"Mother said she'd send us up some tea." Harriet's eyes roved the room, already transformed.

The atmosphere was already that of an elegant woman. There was perfume in the air, a splendid fringed shawl was flung over a chair, and on a taboret a tea service waited, in heavy silver and cheerful frail English china, all ribbons and roses.

Señora Salazar had secured as reception rooms the big front parlors that were now strewn with trunks and boxes, and for herself the large bay-windowed bedroom behind them. An adjoining bedroom was for the nurse and the small boy she had brought with her; and her own maid would sleep in the passage between the rooms.

Harriet, who was not accustomed to such spaciousness and extravagance, was impressed by the arrangement, and all the more impressed by Coralia's simplicity and by her cordial manner. Despite the seven years' difference in age the two were laughing and talking together in terms of easy friendliness and enjoyment before a quarter hour had passed.

Coralia had spent most of her married life on the fabled Heart of Gold rancho; her girlhood years had been divided between her father's rancho and the Notre Dame Convent in Marysville. Harriet had met many of the Notre Dame girls, and there was much to say of marriages and engagements among them.

"And you have four boys?" Harriet had not reached the point of calling her new friend "Coralia" but both women knew it was fast approaching.

"Four. This one, Josito, is the baby. And the little sick one is Francisco. You'll go with me to see him someday?"

"Oh, I would love to! Poor little fellow. But this one," Harriet exulted, catching the small body as it raced by, holding the brown warm sweetness of it, the black curls, the olive skin, the inch-long dusky lashes in a struggling embrace, "this one is a double darling!"

The double darling tore himself free, leaped to a distance, stood eying her like a tousled pony, his hair in his eyes.

"The other boys are at school in Santa Clara," Coralia volunteered. "My husband was ill for so long, and boys are

59

so noisy!" She seated herself at the tea table with a gracious sweep of a crinolined skirt and with a smile thanked the dark-skinned nurse, just returning from the kitchen with hot water. "The Señora will have a fire?" the nurse suggested in Spanish.

Harriet went downstairs half an hour later in a blur of happy and excited feeling. The ecstasy that belongs only to the beginning of friendship enveloped her like a rosy haze. There was magic in the big upstairs room, with the blinds closed against the westering sun, the fragrance of perfume and of tea, the graciousness of this woman who seemed hardly older than herself, the firm, gentle, motherly manner of Coralia with little Josito, her quiet pleasant authority with the maid.

Deeper than that, although she sensed it only confusedly, went her first admiration for marriage, her first vague experience of the jealousy of an unmarried girl for the woman safely established in wedlock.

How independent Coralia was, she reflected. No chaperones for her! No brother or Gardy Ann waiting to wrap her in her cloak and take her home after a party, and perhaps scold her on the way. Quiet mistress of the plain, comfortable old rooms and of the maid and the beautiful little boy, quietly, unobtrusively anxious about Francisco, she was a new type to the younger girl. There was to be a consultation of doctors tomorrow. Harriet was to help Coralia select for the little invalid a dozen toys from Chinatown.

"Could you go down to Chinatown with me, Harriet?" Coralia had asked. "When we were children we loved the little wooden eggs with all the wooden eggs inside, and the paper almonds with surprises in them; do they still have them do you know?"

Harriet had eagerly agreed. Already she knew that whatever Coralia did she would be only too ready, from this night forth, to share.

Immediately they were intimate friends. To both the venture was intoxicating and new. Coralia had never had so close a friend before. The years of her wifehood had been one long strain of illness and pregnancy, quiet days in an old hacienda that seemed to know but two sorts of weather, whispering rain from dark and dripping trees or the burning still heat of summer, when to put her head out of doors was to feel a heavy headache immediately striking through the motionless air that pressed upon her from all sides like the breath of an oven.

The swarming little dark-skinned boys in the nurseries had been her only companions; she had been happiest with them in her arms, all of them: Pablo, Martito, Francisco. And Josito, her baby too; so—so—so—piled up, little naked forms squirming and laughing, soft little faces and wet mouths against hers.

Sometimes her husband would come slowly in, leaning on Indian Wawano, thumping a heavy stick. He would sit watching his wife and his sons and smiling. He was always kind and generous, like a deaf, heavy, amiable grandfather who does not understand but means well by everyone. Coralia, from the raging confusion of emotions in which she had married him, had come rather to like him. She was very much the mistress of his great hacienda, and queen of the vast estate of the Corazón d'Oro. Anything the place could supply, from wild honey to the great salmon that swam in the Pacific, was hers if she wanted it. Hers were dark-skinned women to fan her, dark-skinned men to run her errands. Martin's lovemaking, at first so horrifying that the bride had more than once made an escape, in her nightgown, from his room, was the price of her wealth and luxury, and of her children. She had paid the price stoically, and learned not to think about it.

And then suddenly—dizzyingly—widowhood, and very real and natural tears as she looked at her small, bewildered, black-eyed boys and told them that Papa wasn't coming back any more. Everyone had tried to comfort her, even including Wawano, whose strong arms had caught her on the nights of bridal escape and carried her back like a sack to the amused Martin's arms.

Coralia moved timidly at first, tasting her new freedom cautiously. She went to her old home to her mother for a short stay and talked finances and investments with her father. But very shortly that phase passed. She was more important, richer, more envied, than any of her sisters, or of the older women at the ranch of Our Lady of the Little Columns; she did not have to consult them. Indeed, they were rather awe-struck at her new magnificence and hardly dared make any but the most admiring suggestions.

They saw her pretty, brown, businesslike hand sign papers, heard her young voice delegate authority. They heard her answer when her mother protested that the little boys were too firmly disciplined.

"You know nothing of boys, *Madrecita*," Coralia had said, undisturbed. She had bared the squirming small brown body on her knee and applied a slipper until the little boy had broken free and run sobbing to his silent, agonized nurse. "You had only girls, Mother," Coralia had said kindly, a little breathless. Her mother had left the room.

A great deal of property, money, authority were hers now. But after a while much of it palled. She was lonely and did not know it. She could not fill heart, soul, and mind with the inspection of these acres of grapes and wheat, these hillsides clothed in sprawling oaks. Spring was wet and green and muddy, summer too hot, with the ground sown in squashed apricots and peaches and the air sour from rotting fruit. Autumn meant grape crushing and pig sticking, but not for her. It was the men, the forty or fifty odorous, dark-skinned cowboys, who really lived on the ranch, and the giggling girls of the household, who squealed louder than the pigs.

They feasted and danced, a shadow coming over their liberties and lovemaking only when the Señora came down from the house to look on for a few minutes.

Coralia would hear their shouts of laughter, their fresh bursts of song as she went back to the big dim parlors and halls that always smelled of dust and damp plaster and rotting wood, that always buzzed faintly of flies, that gloomed with old dark curtains and old dark paneling. The boys' nurses, whose numbers comprised all twenty of the women of the household at one time or another, were far more free than the Señora was. They could move about through the back channels of the establishment, the laundries and kitchens, the sheds and paddocks and the stables where the famous race horses idled, magnificent and pampered, in the big box stalls. They could snatch a tortilla there, a great bronzed apricot here, drink cold milk from stone ollas, saunter out to hang on a fence to watch yearlings being broken to the saddle, or the prize bull Re del Mundo snuffing and pawing in the stableyard dust.

If the Señora rode she must ride alone, with one of the men following at a discreet distance. Sometimes she had a small boy or two mounted to ride with her, Tomas and Enrico at the horses' heads. The little brothers, Pablo and Martito, shouted with joy, but to Coralia even their ecstasies meant nothing. She smiled at them abstractedly, wondered what a solitary woman on a lonely big ranch did to make friends, to get away from the stiff occasional visits of aunts, uncles, parents, unmarried sisters.

Her sister Carolina, familiarly "Dodo," had made a foolish love match with the half-Indian foreman of a Mexican *estancia* and had disappeared from view. The other sisters, now well into the twenties, Luisa and Josephina, had married fairly well; Lupe and Engracia were still at home, to their mother's despair. Carolina had protested that she could do little for them; she knew few men, and Paulo had had a long and trying illness. Anyway, the girls infinitely preferred livelier neighborhoods, preferred visiting ranchos near Monterey Presidio or the navy base at Vallejo, where there were men available.

Their unaffected shudders at the mere thought of their brother-in-law had for years offended Coralia. She had visited her mother, a long day's drive distant, at intervals that invariably demanded explanations and apologies. To her sisters she paid, on these occasions, small attention.

When the flurry and panic and shock of little Francisco's bone trouble had come, however, Coralia had sent for her mother. The little boy was to go to the Children's Hospital out on the San Francisco sand hills, and Coralia, distracted, was planning to go to the—the Occidental Hotel, perhaps, or the Palace, she didn't care. Martin had always spoken of the Palace. Her mother had listened, devoured with jealousy.

63

How free this girl was! Widowed so young, and with four boys, and all the Salazar money! She could go to the city, share that life of bright lights and strange faces and fascinating shops.

"The doctor says his bones are like cheese," Coralia had said over and over again. "I will take one of the maids, Rita perhaps, Ana for little Josito. We must leave him in the hospital. I'll go to a hotel."

"You cannot go to a hotel," her mother had decreed calmly. "Quiet yourself. A lady does not go to a hotel. You must go to Aunt Rosa."

"Aunt Rosa! Forty miles away!"

"You can send for the horses." Coralia said nothing to this but her mother had known the set of that firm, handsome mouth. "You can go to Mrs. Townshend's," she had offered suddenly "She is a Catholic, she is very good, she knows all the Jesuits. Inez knows her. Inez sent her boy there when he was in school in Santa Clara and had to go up to see a dentist. You will have quiet, not like those hotels, with the carriages and carts coming and going, and the men, and the spittoons, and the bright lights hissing like cats. Send Arturo in tomorrow to talk to her and take the trunks and make all the arrangements."

Coralia had not given this suggestion her first instinctive veto. Even while her mother talked it had occurred to her that rumor had put more than one attractive man, more than one delightful social event in the Townshend House. Lovely little Miss Townsend was the belle of the city. She had gone to the convent in Marysville to sing and play Schubert songs for Good Mother's diamond jubilee. She had christened a ship with a quart of French champagne. Men fought duels, actual or verbal, over her. She led cotillions.

Coralia summoned her foreman, the aged Arturo, and sent him with Rita and little Josito into the city to investigate the Townshend House. Three days later the unfortunate little Francisco was snug in the Children's Hospital, with a weight upon his left hip and his small spirit diverted by the sight of whimpering or slumbering children in beds about him up and down the long ward.

And so when Harriet put her pretty head into Coralia's room on the afternoon of her arrival, Coralia had given her an eager welcome.

CHAPTER 9

Harriet was a mystery to Coralia, and all the more fascinating for that. The older woman studied the younger one curiously, and with more than a twinge of jealousy. She saw a slim but beautifully made girl with thin wrists and ankles, and square clever little hands as smooth and flawless as dark ivory. She saw a cloud of coquettish red-gold curls about a face wide of brow, narrowed below high cheekbones to come down to a rounded cleft chin and a wide, thin, expressive mouth. Harriet's teeth were big and firm, her smile denied the frivolous fluff of hair and the dancing Irish eyes; hers was a womanly mouth, capable of showing whatever emotion possessed her.

Coralia watched her thoughtfully. What was her secret? Why did every man she met follow her, with his eyes at least, as long as she was in sight? Harriet did not laugh, she was not giddy when men talked to her; she had an intent, uplifted look most of the time, listening, considering. With girls she could be as silly as the silliest; men were a more serious matter and she made them feel it.

Coralia had had small chance to practice flirtation; she had been trained in shyness, awkwardness, diffidence where men were concerned. She had known from the earliest teens that a girl's great objective was marriage, but how to bring men to a declaration of actual intent was unknown to her. She could only redden, stammer nervously, laugh without cause, be suddenly and frowningly silent.

Her marriage had done little to mend this state of affairs. One reason Coralia hated to be with her sisters was that their

65

company made her feel herself once again a stupid, inexperienced girl who was betraying with every word and look her desire to bring any male, any male at all, whoever he might be, to his knees.

Harriet made no such effort; she was as unconscious of these difficulties as an engaging baby of two. Her concern was rather to hold off the declarations that meant the loss of some favorite man friend, at least for a time; to delay making a decision that hurt her feelings almost as much as his own.

The two women had shared more than hours of tea and talk before Coralia felt impelled to tell Harriet some of the details of her marriage.

They had been to church repeatedly, to Benediction, to Confession, to Masses at all hours; they had walked, studied, sung together, and had made almost daily trips out to the hospital. They had sat for decorous hours in Mrs. Townshend's room with Miss Vilder and Gardy Ann, marking new sheets or mending old ones, ripping out tucks, brushing dust from hems.

One October afternoon of blinding rain and wild wind found them in Coralia's lofty room looking down from a bay window at the city streets lashed with gray water and gutters swollen with what Harriet called "café-au-lait." Very few umbrellas were in sight, first evening lights were beginning to show through the gray dusk at five o'clock, and Rita had carried away the tea things.

Harriet flung herself into a favorite deep chair and locked her hands behind her head. Coralia lay on the horsehair sofa, with an afghan over her knees; she had been in the house for a day or two, nursing a cold, and felt a languid reaction after the tiresome aches and coughing.

"Coralia, were you surprised when Mr. Salazar asked you to marry him?"

"Surprised. I cried."

Harriet's delicious laugh rang out.

"Coralia!"

"I know how it sounds. But it wasn't as simple as that." Coralia laughed, colored, and was silent for a moment.

"He was much older," Harriet prompted.

66

"Forty-six years. He had been married for thirty years before that to a friend of my mother. And he was a good deal older even than she was," Coralia said. "No, but I cried because they'd made me feel—I mean my mother and father had—that I was the sort of person no man would want to marry."

"Coralia!" Harriet was eager, girlish, amused. It did sound funny, Coralia not good enough!

"You see, I had liked another man before Martin, a man they disapproved of."

"But, good heavens, I should hope so! Were they mad at a little thing like *that!*"

Coralia considered her answer.

"Some people feel that way," she offered mildly.

"Did you love him—the other one?" Harriet asked, a little breathless.

"Oh, yes."

"But they forbid it?"

"Oo-oo-oo," Coralia said simply.

"And they thought that made you bad?" Harriet asked with relish.

"Yes. So when Martin came along they could—well, balance things. His record against mine. He was old, he wanted a young wife, he wanted children, and he liked me. And on my side, I had fallen in love with a man they wouldn't look at——"

"You let him kiss you!" Harriet breathed in a pause. The other woman looked at her steadily.

"Yes," she said simply.

"Well, Ma doesn't like it," Harriet confessed. "And of course I don't tell them they may!" she added after a moment. "But as for making a fuss like *that*——"

"It was a fuss," Coralia assured her seriously.

"But d'you mean that he didn't want you when he knew that you liked another man!"

"No. I'll tell you. My mother and father forbid me to tell Martin." Coralia paused. "He had asked them for me then."

"Why, if you'd run away with him they couldn't have been any worse!"

67

"No. Could they?" Coralia said mildly. "I wanted to run away, but I couldn't!" she went on. "So one day I thought that perhaps I'd act myself. I thought I'd go to him—Martin, I mean—and tell him that he could make it much easier for me by giving the whole thing up, by saying he'd changed his mind."

"Oh, but meanwhile you wrote to the man you loved, Coralia?"

"Yes, but I never heard from him. He wasn't what I thought," Coralia said, coloring painfully, and a little short of breath, to her own surprise.

"Ah-h-h!" Harriet breathed, disappointed.

"So one terribly hot morning when I was up at my aunt Filomena's house," Coralia said, "I got up at about five and slipped down to the stables and got a horse and rode over to the Corazón d'Oro; Martin was at breakfast. He got up, flustered and astonished of course, and looked around for a duenna. Someone brought me some coffee full of hot milk. I couldn't eat anything solid, I could only wait until we were alone and then tell him everything; I had loved another man, I wanted to marry that other man, my father and mother had forbidden it. I said I could not let him, Martin, believe that I was ever going to love him. I couldn't let my father and mother go on trying to press this match. I said that he had a right to know the truth!

"He listened. He said he would have Juan Rivas—his man who knew everyone—find out this man and bring him back. Harriet, I went home on air, trembling, ready to cry. I don't know what I told my mother—I was beside myself with hope. Hope after such despair. A week later Martin came over to buy two young bulls—my father's wonderful bulls. And as we went out to dinner he said to me, very low, 'Your man has gone with a party to the Nevada mines. He has left no address.'

"That evening they left us alone in the old parlor, Martin and me. He talked to me a long time. He asked me to make my mother and father, and to make him, very happy, and he said that he would make me the happiest woman in the world. He said, 'It is so easy for you to say yes, it saves us all. Come, we'll tell your father and mother now.'

"And after that," Coralia said, "it was all happiness, as he had said. My mother cried, my aunts all envied her, and she loved that. My sisters began to quarrel over brides-maids' dresses, the servants had all the wine they wanted, it was fiesta from morning until night. Then old Father Pinzon was there hearing all our Confessions——"

"You having to tell him, I suppose, that you loved another man?" Hattie put in, half incredulous.

"He knew that before."

"And you never were sorry," the younger woman said, wanting it to be so.

"No. He was always good to me. You see, for years I was very ill, I was lame and sick at my stomach all the time. I was anointed," Coralia said seriously. "And then," she added, smiling, "the time came when I could tell him that I was well again, that someday his son would be born. The whole household then—the rancho——" She left it unfinished, with a smile and a shrug.

"I can imagine!" Harriet commented.

"After that," Coralia said, "I was never downstairs until after Jóse."

Harriet stared.

"You never were—what?"

"No. What with having babies and nursing babies and being ill, I wandered about the upper floors and had trays and waved to the nurses who were playing with my little boys in the garden. But I didn't go downstairs. Four boys—in less than four years. One we lost, and then after four years Josito."

"And did he—Señor Salazar—did he love them?"

"He loved us all, he would cry for joy when he saw them. He never wanted to leave us, even for a few hours. He had what he wanted," Coralia said.

"It still seems to me, even if it all turned out so well, that it was a lot of fuss about nothing," Harriet commented. She took up the pretty work that was to go to the making of a hat, dried peas covered with soft creamy chamois skin and gathered into bunches of tiny grapes. "This green velvet ribbon here," she said, her head on one side as she considered the effect, "and grapes all the way round. All I can say is," Harriet went on, "that if Ma had raised the whole country and engaged me to some old man every time I thought I'd fallen in love, I'd be married ten times over."

Coralia studied her a moment in silence.

"My people were terribly strict," she presently observed mildly. "She—she's like a child," Coralia thought.

"Carrie's doing the leaves," Hattie said, looking up.

CHAPTER 10

The courtship of Johnny Townshend and his Lizzie proceeded decorously. Sometimes on Sundays they walked out together, climbed the rough dirt streets and passed the huddled shanties of Nob Hill, and studied the magnificent homes that were rising on a bare hilltop at the summit. The infant city boasted a brownstone mansion now; every dark block of it had traveled around the Horn to gratify an old millionaire's homesick memory of a New York boyhood. Splendid behind a great fence of brownstone and steel chains, its plate-glass windows shone blandly above the scattered settlement below them, gazed on to the landlocked harbor that was soon to be "the golden gateway to the Orient," and to the heterogeneous confusion from which a great city would be born.

Lizzie and Johnny and their children would be part of the picture; they felt it. They would never want to go anywhere else, never love any other city. This was the full limit of their adventure, a house in Tuckertown, out Sacramento Street way toward the Children's Hospital, or in the sunshiny Mission Dolores. One day they had even looked at a cottage on Howard Street; the last tenant had used it shamefully, broken the kitchen window, smashed whiskey bottles against the wallpaper in the little bay-windowed parlor. But though Lizzie said nothing because she was trembling too hard to speak as they made this daring move—this actual looking at a house for her and Johnny!—she mentally cleaned this house, scrubbed it from doorsill to the bottle-laden narrow kitchen porch, sold all the bottles to the rag-and-bottle man, who went singing with his cart through the morning streets, opened all windows to get rid of the musty smell, and turned it into her fondest, maddest dream of a home.

Walking through its cramped hall over the splintery floor, eying the dingy kitchen and the little stove slightly crooked on three legs, returning again to the Sunday streets and the strolling Sunday families, neither knew what dreams went through the other's mind; they were silent. Lizzie's were dreams of love, of geraniums planted in this strip of flinty garden, and heliotrope and bold bright marigolds, of closing that door with its cheap red paint against night and storm, of dining in that unpromising kitchen, with a little silky head as red as Johnny's resting supremely content against his shoulder, and a bold hurler of all small articles, whose firm-featured face looked like Grandma Townshend's, reigning from a high chair.

Johnny thought perhaps of the hour that would give him Lizzie, this dear, sweet, flesh-and-blood girl walking beside him. Lizzie shy, clean, uncertain in a buttoned white night-gown—in their own little home——

Nothing of this was said. Johnny and Lizzie had passed the cottage on their way from late Mass at Mission Dolores; they tacitly refrained from any mention of their find as they joined Mrs. Townshend's forty guests at the boardinghouse luncheon. The house was hot on the April morning, with an untimely hint of summer.

Doorways stood open; fresh flowers were about. Closed green wooden shutters clicked in the lazy warm wind at the windows. The boarders were hungry and happy at two o'clock, for Sunday's lunch never varied and was the best of its kind. Winter or summer great platters of fried chicken, white and sweet potatoes, boiled onions and mashed turnip, home-canned corn and pickles, soda crackers and yellow

71

cheese, fluffy brown-topped biscuits as white as cotton inside were served from the little dining ingle where the Townshends sat. Second helpings were the generous rule, and the dessert of ice cream and layer cakes was always planned for two big saucers, two big wedges all round.

On other days the menu had variations that already hinted of the city's famous tables in days to come. Mrs. Townshend was a masterhand at curries, she knew about gumbos and guava, the clever use of bamboo shoots and cuttlefish. Her guests said sometimes that they never knew quite what they were eating; Irish potato cakes one day, Javanese *rijsttafel* the next.

"I hope you know what was in that pie," a nervous woman with a nervous laugh tittered one day.

"I'll let you know when we get to the horse meat," Mary Townshend assured her. "Horse meat was all that saved Hattie and me on the *Queen Emma*," she went on thoughtfully. "The captain had a lot on board left from a trip he took to the Arctic. Some of it had green mold on it, but we scraped that off, didn't we, Hattie?"

"Ugh," Hattie said, laying down knife and fork.

Faces grew flushed and warm at the Sunday two-o'clock dinner, and there was a general tendency after it to sit about in rockers and loosen neck gear; elderly guests slept in their rocking chairs. Nothing much went on in the boardinghouse all afternoon, but at half past five pleasant odors of tea and buttered toast began to permeate the halls, and under the guise of a very light meal, for which no one had any appetite, mountains of toast and gallons of tea, with various jams and gingerbreads and pot cheeses once more loaded the board. And after that meal Johnny, who had been sound asleep on some remote sofa, and Lizzie, who had been sitting on Hattie's bed talking shyly, yet with immense gusto, for hours, would go out and sit on the long flight of front steps and stare down at the twilight that was enveloping the city and blotting out the far delicate shadows that were the hills beyond Oakland across the sheen of the bay.

Languor would hold them both, but it was a languor of complete content. When Mrs. Townshend and Hattie came downstairs equipped for the short walk down to Benediction at St. Mary's, Johnny and Lizzie would join them. After which Lizzie must be taken home, to give him only a brief good night in her home parlor, with the interested eyes of brother and father looking on. But Johnny would dance and whistle all the way back to the boardinghouse.

A four-room cottage out in the Mission, eh? Fifteen dollars a month, eh? By golly, Johnny would exult half aloud, things were beginning to move at last! Before he knew it he'd be a family man. He wrote Lizzie a reverent note on the occasion of her acceptance of a diamond chip ring.

"My dearest Lizzie, my own, for I may call you that now," wrote Johnny. "I am still trembling with the ecstasy of your promise. Oh, Lizzie, may God make me worthy of you! A man's life is a harsh, ugly thing, and I the weakest, the least deserving of men. I should aspire to no more than a touch of my lips to the hem of your robe, or a reverent glance following you as you enter the church to pray. Lizzie, when I think of your purity, your faith, the peace and love in your beautiful eyes, I am shaken to the very heart——"

There were four pages to the letter; Johnny wrote a firm large hand, in very black ink, and he was proud of his composition. Lizzie was proud of it too. All the boys wrote girls letters like that before they got married; now she had hers. Hattie read it and said, "Johnny's a saint, you know, he's never so much as kissed a woman. The girls in the Islands all thought he was going to be a priest. Only I wish he wouldn't—at parties, you know," Hattie had added delicately.

"Get drunk. Johnny doesn't get drunk. He's awful quiet when he's drink-taken," Lizzie had promptly countered. "But there's no harm in that."

For already whatever Johnny did was right, and whatever Johnny didn't do was not important.

"Well, he doesn't do it often," Harriet had been obliged to concede.

She and Lizzie looked over the wedding presents so often that they got to know the feel and weight of them all; Irish linen sheets as heavy as boards, blankets from the new blanket factory out on Potrero Street, where the dumps and the slaughterhouses and the Magdalen Asylum were. Six plates from Wangenheim-Sternheim, two small platters, three cups, a chocolate pot, a Dover egg beater and a mixing bowl, and odd spoons, cups, doilies, vases bought at the irregularly stocked city shops or selected from some old friend's treasured collection.

The display of these, in a parlor of the Townshend House was handsomely backed with Mexican serapes, great red Spanish pottery water jars; a *rebozo* with a paper rose pinned on it; a snake rope bristling with horsehair, a stone hollowed for the pounding of corn, and the pestle to go with it, and many smaller articles in wampum, fringed leather, and artificial flowers. And Lizzie's father stood ready to give her the big mahogany bed that had crossed the plains in a prairie wagon, the pots and pans that had held that prairie cooking and were familiar with bear meat and turkey meat and the sweet white meat of mountain trout.

Lizzie and Johnny reviewed their wealth in trembling, smiling unbelief. Johnny's first American job had been as a waiter, and when the proprietor of the Poodle Dog came up to the boardinghouse one night and presented Lizzie with three graded copper casseroles, Lizzie was in tears. But when an uncle in Chicago sent her a draft on the Sather Bank for one hundred dollars she was awe-struck.

"We'd ought to save it, Johnny."

"You're right!" said Mary Townshend. Lizzie flushed with pleasure, for she stood slightly in fear of Johnny's mother and liked to win her approval.

"Us with a bank account!" Johnny grinned.

"You've handled mine for two three years, and you in a bank," his mother reminded him encouragingly.

"Well, sure, but it seems so funny for Lizzie and me."

It was all funny; they were the first man and woman in the world who had ever felt such thrills, such fears, such amaze. It was unbelievable that in a few weeks they would be living out there in the Mission, just living their own lives, with no interference from anyone.

The date was set, far enough ahead to allay the resentments of Lizzie's young brother and sister and her father's reluctance, at least momentarily. Lizzie, too, experienced misgivings, and sent Johnny out to Father Varsi for a full debate as to the advisability of their union. The old Italian prince, however, appeared to be on Johnny's side, for he heartily urged the marriage and sent Lizzie a rosary blessed by Pius IX.

Nothing now seemed to hinder the plan, and the weeks flew. It was full summer; fog enveloped the city in slowly moving veils of white shrouding, until the sun broke through at noon and the trade winds began to blow dust and papers and straw against dingy white-washed fences and store fronts.

Hattie and Lizzie, sometimes with other girls, sometimes with Lizzie's little brother, sometimes alone, went out to the Mission house every day, and exulted over it, and fell in love with it.

Just cleaning the floors and sweeping about the porches and bringing the good scents of ammonia and soap into the place were enough to delight them. But when their daytime meetings were extended to evening hours, and Johnny joined them, and they made coffee on the three-legged stove—now firmly propped with brick and blackened to a mirror shine—then that was living. They unrolled rugs and moved chairs about, and set forth dishes and pans, vases and daguerreotypes; they sank into chairs and with long "Ah-h-hs!" of satisfaction, they burned rubbish in the little grate and put Johnny's heavy set of Dickens and Lizzie's five volumes of Father Faber in the cretonne-covered shelves Johnny had hammered into an empty crate. It was perfect, it was all simply perfect.

Lizzie wouldn't come downstairs at first, on the actual wedding morning, and Hattie, in maid-of-honor taffeta ruffles and pleats, flew down in agony to her mother, and whispered to her, their full silk skirts whispering together, too.

"Ma, she's perfectly quiet and sensible, but she says that it's better to correct a mistake now than regret it later, and that she'll get married in December. It seems her mother did."

"I expected this," said Mary Townshend without alarm. "Did you tell her the priest is waiting this blessed instant at the church?"

"I did, Ma. But she just said, 'Let Johnny go tell him.'"

75

"I'll get her." Mary Townshend headed for the stairs; the horses in Lenhart's best wedding carriage champed at the gate. Layers of fog poured softly over older fog, making ghosts of the garden's eucalyptus and the pampas grass.

Lizzie, red-eyed but composed, came down with Johnny's mother five minutes later, and Harriet kissed her for sheer joy and relief. Johnny and Maurice O'Connor had left the house to walk to church some half hour earlier; the three women got in the carriage together; Harriet held tight to Lizzie's hand.

The church was half filled, an amazing crowd for quiet Lizzie Carmichael's wedding. Her small brother and sister were in a front pew; her old father in the vestibule waiting to give her his arm. Hattie slipped around to the vestry, came in upon the astonished Johnny and his best man.

"Johnny, I know it. . . . I know it. . . . I'm going right back. They're all there, it's all right. . . . No, she looks perfectly beautiful. Johnny, don't look at her and don't speak to her until you're *married*. Do you hear me? Don't say one word——"

"About what?" asked Johnny, bewildered.

"About *anything*. And Johnny, don't kiss her. Not until we get home."

"Oh, for God's sake," said Johnny.

"She asked me to ask you not to. Or at least, she said——"

"All right, all right, all right!" said Johnny, nervous and impatient. Hattie fled away, and the ceremony proceeded along the usual lines, and trailed up the hill to the Townshend House, where it lost its strained and formal character completely and evaporated into feasting, laughter, toasts, kissing, and a surprising amount of crying, too.

"God bless you both. I'll see you tomorrow, Lizzie," said her mother-in-law, with a sound embrace for each of the newlyweds. "Always wanted a sister," said Hattie, crying and laughing, her cheek against Lizzie's.

"I sent old Annie out to be sure your dinner was in the house, and the wood and coal was just being put in," Mrs. Townshend said. "A man was there fixing the pipe, but you've got your pump on the sink in case the water isn't running.

76

Johnny says he thinks there's a mouse out there by the wooden tub on the porch, so stand your food in pans of water until you catch him."

To Johnny, Harriet clung at the last minute as if she could not let him go.

"Johnny dear, we seem sort of young, don't we? For you going off and getting married!"

"Not going far," Johnny mumbled, speaking down into the red tumbled silk of her hair.

"And we never quarreled, did we? Ma said we didn't. Even little kids down home."

"Well, cry about it," he teased her.

"No, I won't. I'm happy." But she disappeared from the group and was not waving with the others when the carriage came back to take the John Francis Townshends to their new home, to take them, awed and nervous, through the gritty windy dusk of the city, and out to the Mission, where the late sun was sending streamers into the western windows of the Howard Street house.

Lizzie's hand, elegant in a glove with twenty-two buttons, was in Johnny's, but she did not know it. Above all other emotions she was swept by jealousy of Hattie, always the fortunate, always the safe, high, laughing one, with no responsibilities, no worries! However on earth was she to get Johnny's breakfast in the morning?

Hattie wasn't riding off with a complete stranger, to spend all her days and all her nights in frightening proximity to him! Hattie was safe in a warm big house with an adoring mother, and had been talking already about the Chamberlain party the next night. Hattie could go to the piano tonight and sing "Du bist die Ruh'" and "'Twas Dying They Thought Her" without a care in the world!

Lizzie cleared her throat.

"Perhaps we ought to stop at Papa's," she said hoarsely.

"What for?" Johnny said, coming out of gloomy dreams.

"To see that the children get to bed." Lizzie's voice died away on a dreary whisper.

"Isn't your aunt there? Beside, the children are still at Ma's."

77

"Oh, yes," gulped Lizzie. She looked at Johnny obliquely. He was frowning. This was frightful—she'd said something wrong already——

Johnny was thinking of Maurice O'Connor, recently officiating as his best man. Maurice's uncle was vice-president of the bank; his father was prosperous in his own lumber and paint and glass business. Sarah Doyle, who was to marry Maurice in January, had already asked Lizzie to be matron of honor.

"They'll have it all over us, he's buying his house," Johnny brooded. "They'll come and have dinner with us and pity Lizzie and me. We ought to drop them right now and never see them again."

"We ought to have something in the house to eat," he said.

"Your mother sent in everything, cream and eggs and everything."

"Oh?" Johnny was comforted. His grip tightened slightly on Lizzie's lifeless hand.

CHAPTER 11

Several weeks after Johnny's marriage Hattie went over to the great Salazar rancho to visit Coralia in her own home.

The occasion was the return of little Francisco from the Children's Hospital, as nearly cured as he could hope to be from the operation for what the doctors called hip disease. Coralia could not come to the city. She sent old Arturo and young Tomas; Arturo to wait with the big surrey in on the Oakland side, Tomas to go over to San Francisco on the ferryboat and pick up Harriet and Francisco with a carriage.

The complicated plan, involving all of Tomas' ingenuity and courage, proceeded successfully from the livery stable to the Townshend House, thence out to the sand hills for Francisco, down the long slant of Market Street to the ferries, and the return trip across the bay.

Tomas could stop sweating then, for there waited old Arturo, with the surrey and the horses, and his responsibilities were over. He could lift little Cisco into the blankets and pillows with which the back seat was lined and place the beautiful gay redheaded young señorita in the middle seat, from whence she could turn about and watch her charge. Then he himself could subside into exhausted silence beside Arturo, his knotted dark hands dropped between his knees, his breath gradually subsiding.

They stayed overnight at a convent in San Jose, Harriet winning the nuns with no more effort than that extended by an irresistible yearling baby, and everyone hovering over the gallant emaciated little invalid. Early the next morning they were gone again, with fresh horses clop-clopping steadily on the dirt roads, switching tails and tossing manes as flies and the day's heat became more and more annoying.

It was nine o'clock at night, and both Cisco and Harriet were shaken from head to toe, deep in dust, half sick with the rocking of the carriage, when they saw light on a wooded rise half a mile ahead and Tomas turned to inform them that they had been driving on the Corazón d'Oro rancho for more than an hour.

A troop of women took possession of Cisco in the dark wide entrance hall. Harriet was conscious of Coralia's kiss, of a glass of hot milk extended by a brown old hand, of an immense upstairs room with a high great bed and high windows swathed alike in white ruffles, of a pillow, fresh sheets, her day clothes mysteriously off and her night clothes mysteriously on, lights lessened, lights out, blessed dark enveloping her as she sank into sleep.

Coralia laughed at her as they idled on the terrace in the autumn afternoon next day. Hattie was fresh and rested; she had slept late, awakening to find a breakfast tray ready for her, and that her clothing had not only been unpacked, but pressed and hung on the pegs of the enormous wardrobe. Wherever she went doors opened for her and dark faces smiled at her. Whichever way she turned the ripened richness of the old hacienda spread itself in such bewilderment of beauty that she could tell Coralia in all truth that she felt herself transported to another world entirely.

Autumn lay gracious upon the place; the hills had long been burned to gold; the mighty oaks threw their strong shadows across them. Cattle stood motionless in the coolest shade; horses were at the paddock fence, their lovely heads and maned necks laced one over the other in a long line. Against the pale blue of the sky the great circle of the mountains was only a faint shadow; over the red-tiled roofs of stables, barns, quarters, sheds, tree shadows lay in patterns and traceries of tendrils and leaves.

The ordered opulent disorder of it enveloped Harriet like a dream. Servants sauntered about, not seeming so much like servants as like players in some magnificent medieval scene. Handsome boys rode horses up to the terrace, Coralia going down the wide shallow ivy-bound steps to lay her hand on a great satiny equine shoulder and give some direction in a low voice. A twisted old Indian came up with an enormous tray on his head and set it down on the broad balcony ledge. Harriet saw that the peaches, the yellow pears, the plums of purple and gold, the black soft figs, and the massed sprawling grapes of a dozen varieties that completed the dish were beaded with frost.

The lame little son was royally installed on the terrace, with someone always within call to anticipate his needs. The two older boys, home for a week end, roamed about scantily clad in shirts and thin old cotton trousers, with red scarfs tied on their dark heads and heavy sombreros topping the scarfs. There were young cousins and friends at the rancho. They all rode horses, climbed the windmills, managed to get themselves soaked in the creek. There was no swimming, but a few miles away up the mountain, there were good trout pools. Coralia laughingly declined; she was no fisherman, but Harriet got up morning after morning to ride up the steep trail and sit dreaming beside the water, in woods that were hushed and dewy, before the sun was up.

She and the boys were back for breakfast, and ravenous; sometimes their catch was big enough to supply a real breakfast dish of fresh fat trout fried in the corn powder made for tortillas. Harriet bloomed like a rose under the stimulus of air and exercise, rest and country food, and the boys' praise of her prowess.

"Madre, she rides better than Zito!"

"How does that happen, Harriet? Boys, you smell fishy," Coralia might say from the top of the breakfast table.

"In the Islands we all rode. I rode alone when I was four."

"You really like it, riding and fishing with little boys?" Coralia sometimes mused.

"Like it! Oh, I've never had such a happy time!" Harriet said joyfully. "I don't know where time goes!"

"No beaux for you," Coralia said.

"Beaux! You should see the way the boys squire me. Our fishing trips are the most delightful things I ever did. But Martin warned me solemnly 'Mass tomorrow,'" Harriet laughed. "He and Pablo tell me they must put on their new suits."

"Then go fishing in the late afternoon, you crazy people."

"Oh, Coralia, we will! Martin," called Harriet, "your mother says we can fish tomorrow after Benediction. That's a beautiful time to fish."

"I think I will have to give you Capitan," Coralia said, her adoring eyes on her friend.

"I wouldn't know where to keep him. No, let Capitan live here, and if I haven't worn my welcome out, I'll come back and ride him again."

"Try to wear your welcome out, Harriet," Coralia said, unsmiling.

"Ma's Chinaman said once, 'Long visit end long friendship,'" Harriet offered. Coralia looked up from her embroidery ring, looked down again.

"There's one bad thing about this visit," she said quietly after a moment. "It's almost enough to spoil it. I mean that you are going away on Tuesday."

"Oh, I have to! I've never been away from Ma for such a long time in my life."

"Yes, I know. Of course." It really made Coralia sad, Harriet thought uncomfortably. No matter how much she loved people she never seemed to mind partings; it would be good to see Ma and Johnny and Lizzie and the Howard Street house again, and then later it would be just as much fun to come back to the magnificent rancho again. No matter how life moved it was gloriously exciting, and she was always right in the center of it, small and redheaded and dancing like a firefly.

After she left the rancho Coralia was in a sort of dream for many days, and when she descended the stairway to join her sons at breakfast in the morning, she crossed to the other corridor and avoided passing the door of Harriet's room.

But Harriet, though she had been in tears at parting, as Coralia was, slept peacefully through the long drive down to the city and chattered her mother almost dizzy as she leafed through a great heap of mail, and of cards that had come with flowers, and retailed every moment of her stay on the ranch of the Heart of Gold. San Francisco was beautiful and balmy in the autumn dusk, and the broad flight of steps that connected the Townshend House with the steep rise of Stockton Street made a grandstand upon which Harriet and her callers seated themselves with a great ruffle of dimity skirt and crinolines, and here their adorers perched in what places were left for a review of past events and a lively discussion of excitements ahead. The Sausalito picnic had waited for Harriet; the dance at the Presidio was imminent; cards for cotillions were already in circulation.

"I've nothing but rags!" said Harriet, as expected. "I've not done one bit of shopping."

But she thought of the café-au-lait gauze with the appliqued flowers in colored felts, and of the love of a lace gown, held up in loops by tiny silver birds, over a delicate petticoat, and she felt no misgivings.

Home, and the bracing autumn sunshine and her bedroom windows above the spread of satiny waters that held Alcatraz and Angel islands, and the shores of Marin, and the silhouette of the Lady of Tamalpais, all seemed magic and new. Her mother, handsome and strong and always busy, was a miracle of efficiency, her new seal coat and tiny seal muff were "just too too," and every hour in the airy big boardinghouse was filled with some interest or amusement for Harriet. She danced through as radiant a youth as any princess was ever destined to know; she was, in fact, a princess in her own right, and the generations of girls who followed her would someday look at the tiny photographs that all the girls exchanged and smile at the pleated hooped skirts of the plaid silk gowns, the frail rose point at neck and wrists, the coquettish curls spread on slender shoulders. Miss Hattie Townshend became something of a legend in the infant society of the infant city; for its first half century prosperous and important men would remember her with a half-amused, half-rueful laugh. "I remember. There was a time when I thought I'd kill myself if Miss Hattie didn't say 'Yes' to me."

Miss Hattie said yes to nobody. She argued with her mother that when one was completely satisfied with life why look around to change things? She pivoted between the rancho and the city now, and only complained that life rushed by too fast.

"There's a time when life can't be all dancing," said Mary Townshend. But her eyes would shine, just the same, at the mere sight of this evanescent, joyous creature, whose world was so different from what her own had been.

It was enough that Hattie had to live in a boardinghouse rather than a lovely home, and was always amiable and sweet in attentions to the boarders. Everything else must be smooth for her; no touch of the sordid or even practical must come her way.

Johnny, now, was different. He was making his own way, and while the boy would never set the bay on fire he was as good and faithful and honest, yes, and good-looking, too, as any mother could want. Didn't he have his own little home and his good wife and his steady job? She had no greater ambitions and no fears at all for Johnny. His high spirits and his nonsense were a delight in the evening parlor. In soberer moods Harriet accompanied him while he sang "Brother's Fainting at the Door," "Bright Things Can Never Die," and other favorites. To hear him in a duet with Harriet on the languorous strains of "Juanita" always brought tears to his mother's eyes.

On a certain November afternoon of drenching rains she

was seated high upstairs in the linen room, pausing often in her knitting to look down across the dark oily balconies and horned roofs of the Chinese quarter, swept with storm, and on to the bay, whipped to whitecaps by the fitful winds. Quite unexpectedly, and out of breath from climbing the stairs, Lizzie came in.

"Lizzie dear, in all this rain," protested the older women. But Lizzie had shed her mackintosh and cap downstairs, and was quite dry. Mrs. Townshend lamented that Harriet was away; she had gone down to Menlo Park with the Floods. Yes, quickly said Lizzie, who seemed pale and nervous beyond even her usual wont, she had known Harriet was away. Her mother-in-law looked at her keenly, returned her eyes to her knitting.

Lizzie talked inconsequentially and aimlessly for some time; she regaled her hostess with the story of Imelda Hannify's vocation, and of her father's quarrel with the City Sewerage Commission. Then suddenly she shifted to a more personal matter and obtained Mary Townshend's sudden and complete attention.

Not that Mary showed it. She went on steadily with her knitting, not raising her eyes.

"That's what you said to Johnny," she presently observed mildly.

"Yes'm. Shouldn't I of?" Lizzie, exquisitely uncomfortable, asked nervously.

"No. It's nothing. Go ahead, dear."

Lizzie went ahead, and was advised, and comforted, and finally given hot tea on the end of the long dining-room table and a motherly kiss at the door. Mrs. Townshend's eyes might have been observed to have an oddly bright yet dazed look during the evening, but no one noticed it, and in the morning she appeared quite herself again.

"She's had no mother since she was eight," she reminded herself more than once. "But you'd think a baby rabbit would know that much! Well—God knows how she'll get out of it, poor innocent that she is!"

But Lizzie had no trouble in getting out of it. Perhaps she was smarter than her husband's mother supposed, or perhaps she was even more childishly simple. It was on that same evening, after dinner, when Johnny had returned from escorting her brother and sister home and was stretched on the parlor sofa with the evening *Post*, that she said quite easily:

"Johnny, you remember what we were talking about last night?"

"I do," said Johnny, absently at first, and then with a sudden dawning of puzzlement and interest.

"Well, here's what I was thinking," said Lizzie, brushing a few crumbs from the cleared dinner and looking down at them in her palm. "I was thinking that in some ways—in some matters, a man has no business to ask his wife anything. He'd ought to tell her. He knows a lot more than she does; you don't know, she might have been convent-raised, and where'd she hear anything there? She'd respect him more did he lay down the law to her—as long as it's God's law, too. And nobody would think any the less of her for being said by him. Your mother said so."

Johnny, staring at her, cleared his throat.

"They'd think the more of her," he said.

"Well, I'll get at my dishes," said Lizzie. She went into the kitchen and closed the door.

CHAPTER 12

When it became evident that little Francisco Salazar was dying, Harriet went up to join Coralia on the ranch of the Heart of Gold. Coralia, agonizing over her child, sent a letter and the big surrey with Tomas to bring Harriet, and when Harriet arrived in the middle of a dark freezing spring night Coralia was awake, padding about the upper floor in noiseless slippers, and ready with a great embrace and a burst of smothered sobbing to greet Harriet at the head of the stairs.

Escorted by red-eyed maids, they reached the apartment that Coralia for some happy months had called "the Señorita's room," and there, white-faced, Harriet heard the whispered news; the child could live only days now. The house was filled with relatives: Coralia's mother, two of her sisters, various aunts and cousins; the uncle who was a Jesuit priest from Santa Clara and the cousin who was a doctor had taken up residence here some days before.

Harriet got into her nightgown, tied her dressing gown about her and crossed the big dim hall to the sickroom. There was a soft light from a single hooded kerosene lamp; Ana Immaculata looked up in alarm, subsided to a weary smile as they tiptoed in. Everything was in spotless order, toys ranged above the fireplace, medicines on a side table, and a special rag dog that Harriet had given Cisco months before lying on the bed, firmly anchored by the languid little brown hand.

The child's head and most of his body were in deep shadow; he did not stir. The two women stood looking down at him until they were convinced of his regular deep breathing; death had marked the sweating little ivory face, but he still lived.

Back in her rooms, Harriet got thankfully into the fresh linen sheets of the big four-poster and sat propped on pillows drinking hot chocolate as she and Coralia talked.

"Don't cry, dear. You know Father told us months ago that little Cisco was going back to God."

"Let me cry!" Coralia leaned back in her chair and held a handkerchief against her streaming eyes. "I've not been able to cry," she managed to say presently. "With my mother and my aunts I've felt frozen—I couldn't speak——"

A silence. Then Coralia said, "If you knew how glad I am that you are here! Just to see you, down there in the dark, getting out of the carriage made me feel right again."

"If I can help——" Harriet said, subdued.

"You've helped me already." Coralia still lay back in her chair as if exhausted, one hand lying on Hattie's hand. "He is leaving me," she said, faltering. Tears slid from her closed eyelids.

Hattie could say nothing. But however inadequate her response to Coralia's need, it was enough, and Coralia clung to her as to a rock of comfort in the days that followed.

At breakfast Hattie met various members of the allied clans; heavy, dark, handsome women, their black eyelashes soaked with tears, slim pimply boys obviously more interested in Cousin Coralia's horses than in Cousin Coralia's sick little boy, the old doctor, the young priest, and two of Coralia's younger sisters, Lupe and Engracia, nervously aware of their unchallenged maiden state.

Hattie's presence provided an element that helped them all; she seemed to belong nowhere in particular, and yet to be everywhere, and her quiet answers, her ready common sense brightened the whole dark house. When the sick child's grandmother, herself almost so crushed that she could not leave her bed, was unable to persuade Coralia to rest or to drink a sustaining cup of coffee, Harriet could manage it quite naturally, and she put her whole heart into it.

Three days after her arrival it was Harriet who touched the kneeling Coralia on the shoulder, and it was in answer to Harriet's low words that Coralia raised her stained face from where it had rested against the child's colorless hand. Instantly sobbing broke out in the room from kneeling forms in the shadows.

"He's gone, dear," Harriet said.

Coralia rose to her feet, her rich hair disordered, her hands pressed against the sides of her head.

"No, no!" she said loudly. "Not Cisco! Not my little Cisco——"

Just how Harriet managed to get her to her room, to get her to lie down quietly, to talk in subdued tones as the older members of the family filed in and out, nobody seemed to know. Coralia was the calmest of them all, and could go into Cisco's strangely changed room late that afternoon and sit there like a statue of grief, with only the beads of her rosary moving through her hand to show that she was alive.

There were two or three dark rainy days of weeping and praying, days scented with heavy crepe and bombazine, and with tuberoses and smilax. Then carriages and mounted horsemen began to arrive, and the drives all about the house were filled with respectable surreys and closed family carriages. There was a Mass, and a solemn procession on foot over wet leaves and muddy ruts to the stone-fenced acre on the hillside where the old Señor lay, and where the small casket of his son was laid beside him.

After that priest and doctor departed, all guests went away, and the older boys returned to school; Coralia's family was the last to go.

"You are a good friend," said Coralia's mother, weeping as Hattie disappeared completely in her soft big farewell embrace. "God bless you," murmured some of the other women. Separate bundles of black, they moved slowly down steps and driveway and went their ways. A great peace, a heavenly silence followed their going. Harriet and Coralia, with the sprawled dogs and the wary kittens, and with the irrepressible Josito, sat on the terrace and watched the light fading from the oaks on the hills and the great shoulders of the Sierra.

Rain had fallen for three days, but it had stopped today, and the sun had shone bravely on the heaped flowers that marked Cisco's grave. Sunshine was lying now in long streaks across the world; everywhere wet leaves twinkled in the light, and the agitated roses and fuchsias threw off little chains of diamonds. The last lily petal had been swept from the wet tiling of the terrace; the great sheaf of white roses that had marked the main doorway was gone.

The two young women sat still, without talking, and let the miracle of quiet take possession of them. Coralia could cry no more; she was apathetic, spent. Harriet spoke now and then to Josito, or the nurse of the moment. Presently she sent them in for supper and bed, and when Carmen approached with some question of an evening meal, she nodded to her in dismissal. The Señora was resting. Rest was what she needed; she mustn't be disturbed.

"How good you are to me," Coralia said out of the dusky silence. "Baby go upstairs?"

"A little while ago. It's getting a little cold."

"Hat, I'm so rich to have three boys left."

"That's what I tell you, darling."

"But he—he was the strongest of the babies," Coralia said, suddenly faltering. "Hat, don't," she added, her hand out, as Harriet made a movement to get up. "Please. I can't bear to go upstairs—and think that there's nothing to worry about any more, that he's not in there, not even going to be there again."

Harriet met this head on.

"I know. I keep thinking I hear his darling little voice calling," she admitted. She held out her hand. "Come on, we'll go up," she said. "And then we'll have supper and go into the chapel for a while."

"Tia Filomena said today that we mustn't pray for him, but to him," Coralia said, slowly mounting the stairs.

"He's safe now. Safe eternally with God." Harriet spoke confidently, firmly. But she herself felt a sickening plunge of her heart as they came to the open door of the room that had been Francisco's. The door was open; one candle was burning in the room. It was in order, there was no sign of its recent occupant. The windows were shuttered; the medicine bottles, the slanted board that was to rest his back, the pillows that were to lift the bad leg away from the bed, the toys and the slate with its red flannel binding, all were gone.

Coralia walked to the bed and laid her hand upon the pillow where Cisco's head had lain; she stood so for a moment, Hattie watching fearfully from the door. Then she walked to the bureau and blew out the candle. Young moonlight struggled through the shutters and lay in lattices on the floor. Coralia quietly closed the door as they left the room, and Harriet went with her to her own room and sat with her for a while. When Joselito came romping in to say good night both women were ready to laugh at his maneuvers before they went down for their dinner.

Three days later they parted, Harriet climbing into the surrey with tears in her bright eyes; Coralia very calm, but without a vestige of color.

"You'll be coming to town, Coralia?"

"In three weeks and three days. . . . Oh, Harriet, I hate to see you go!"

"And I hate to go. This is my other home!"

"If it only were! . . . Harriet, how am I to thank you?"

"By eating and sleeping like a sensible person," Harriet said gently.

"And you will be back, soon?"

"Having danced too much and eaten too much and flirted too much, I'll be back."

"It'll be rainy, you know. And this house can be so dark and big and—and plastery-smelling—you called it that!—in the rain. The eucalyptus creak all day long, and the roads are all mud!"

"I'll love it. We'll practice 'The Poet and Peasant' and 'The Lovely Melusine.'"

"Oh, won't we?" said Coralia, brightening.

"And we'll sew for the poor," Harriet suggested virtuously.

"Harriet, you make that sound absolutely hypocritical!"

Harriet's gay laugh rang out.

"No, but it does always make me feel creepy—oatmealy, when I sew. But we really will sew for the poor. We'll send bundles to Mother Russell."

"I'm sending her all——" Coralia's voice thickened. She fell silent.

"Hate to leave you," Harriet said, holding tight to the other woman's hand.

"Those novices will be here Thursday."

"Not that they'll help," Harriet said ruefully, with a slight stress on the personal pronoun, and she and Coralia laughed together.

Then Coralia went back into the house that had darkened for her for a long time, whatever the weather, and Harriet settled back in the surrey for the long trip home. She would spend the night at the San Jose convent, get an early start in the morning, and be swept back into the world of white-capped bay waters, fog-wreathed, hilly streets, straggling fences and straggling gardens, shanties looking saucily at the mansions whose plate-glass windows stared solemnly and re-provingly back. Again she would flit through the rooms of the Townshend House, carrying a tray of little vases downstairs to dispose of the wilted flowers and refill the jars with the curling stems of gay nasturtiums or bold marigolds, velvety rich-scented heliotrope, fuchsias dangling like delicate tassels in scarlet and purple.

Her mother might come in from a marketing trip, rosy, breathless, sturdy in her great black cañamero cape and her dangling widow's veil, and Harriet would hear the deep voice, "Hattie! You're home, then! Thanks be to God!"

Harriet would get a dozen firm, cold kisses, and a glorious review of the news. Her mother was under the firm impression that the house could not run without Harriet.

"It's like a different place, and the weather seems different," said Mrs. Townshend seriously. "I declare you couldn't see the bay for fog since the day you left!"

"Ma, it was horribly sad, Coralia's Cisco, I mean."

"Of course it was." Harriet went to and fro, unpacking, shaking out her tumbled dresses, and her mother sat watching her with eyes that drank in every beloved detail.

"But oh, I was glad I was there!" Harriet said. "Oh, and Ma, did you go out to Johnny's?"

"I did, then. She'd got up a very nice little dinner; she'd a nice piece of salmon with an egg sauce on it, and a crown roast of lamb. You'd laugh to see Johnny helping her clear and going out for the butter and all. She had a coal fire going, and she'd made ice cream."

"I'll bet Johnny made that. He can't let that freezer alone. He's never so happy as when he's pounding ice out in that shed of theirs, up to his knees in mud, and yelling in to Lizzie to bring out the mashed strawberries."

"Ling Foy puts the ice in a gunny sack here and does it for all four freezers. Has Johnny a sack?"

"A sack of rock salt and a sack for the ice—he has everything. You'd think nobody ever had ice cream before! You'd think nobody ever got married before, the way Johnny shows off how Lizzie makes coffee and how she's got those Lady Washington slips started! I'll go out tomorrow." Harriet went back to the subject of events on the Heart of Gold rancho, and her mother sighed as she listened.

"It's hard to bury them, God knows," she said.

91

"You wonder why they ever lived at all—why should they, Ma? A little boy like Cisco, suffering so much."

"If we could see God's pattern He wouldn't be God," Mrs. Townshend said oracularly.

"Coralia keeps saying 'I had four, and now I've only three,'" Harriet quoted. "As if they were a set."

"So they were, to her. She'll always see that one in the second place. But look at poor Mrs. Monahan, the way she takes it, with two girls going into a decline, one right after the other!"

"Is she just about crazy, Ma?"

"No, she's very quiet, she doesn't talk. Father said she was saintly in her resignation." Mary Townshend's deep bosom rose and fell upon another sigh. "She's only the boy left now, and him wild," she added. "They lost a little feller the year we got here, with croup."

"The Caseys' baby died of croup," Harriet offered. "But that was only a baby. Coralia's Cisco was such a darling, and so loving."

And Harriet and her mother fell silent for a moment as they went down through the big airy halls to breakfast.

But the sight of the dining room, with sunshine checkering the flowers on the long table, a Chinese boy in purple brocades, with his pigtail dangling as he filled the water glasses, a maid in the kitchen doorway ready to start in with the bacon and eggs, and the scent of coffee, and of that same bacon, filling the room, always raised Harriet's spirit again.

She was home, and she loved home. She was with Ma, and she adored Ma. If her mother ever spoke of leaving her by the natural change of death, it was Harriet's custom to break into loud and tearful protests and clamp a hand over her mother's mouth.

No, everything was perfect now, and Ma better not talk of any such gruesome thing! Ma dying—what an idea! Harriet's ringing laugh, the rustle of her silken skirts, her attempts at mealtimes to speak German with the two scared youths from Heidelberg once more enlivened the house; girls came and went, scales rippled on the piano, and everyone was the happier for it. True, she kept a daily journal, which took the form of letters to Coralia and was forwarded whenever occasion served, but they contained no such earnestness of feeling, no such heartsick longing as did Coralia's letters in reply.

These carried but one burden: "Come back, come back, come back." Coralia admitted quite honestly that she could never be happy on the big ranch again without her friend. They had had her people there; she wrote there was a chance that Lupe might marry one of the Escondido boys, Rafael probably. There was a new foreman at the rancho. Rafael was the small homely one, but he was the nicest. She had taken Josito on a visit to her Aunt Filomena's, on the Ybarra rancho; he had played with the grandchildren, two nice little girls with ponies. Coralia was reading *The Talisman;* it was quite exciting. Harriet wrote back that she was reading *Helen's Babies,* and it was a perfect love. Coralia's next letter had a postscript: "Our foreman's name did I tell you is Phil Haagersen, Swedish father—Irish mother." The sentence passed unnoticed through Harriet's giddy head, but her mother noticed it, and observed mildly, when the letter had been somewhat discussed:

"This foreman, now. Did you meet him, dearie?"

"Oh, yes, but it was down at the corral the night we shipped the steers. I couldn't really see him. Big fellow, blond, too."

"Swedish. I'd hope she'd not take him! A Produstunt, likely?" said Mrs. Townshend.

"Take him!" Harriet echoed, shocked. "Why should she?"

"Well. Why shouldn't she?"

"She wouldn't," Harriet said after a moment. Two red spots burned in her cheeks. "They—her mother and everyone, would think she was crazy to marry a—a foreman," she stammered. "Besides, she has the boys. Beside, she has the ranch to run," she added.

"Not if he's already running it." Mrs. Townshend, in the process of fitting up a young friendless Irish lad for his battle to establish himself in a strange city, was darning a gray sock of good heavy Irish wool. She thrust her darning ball into the toe, drew the edges of a goodsized hole together, and began a careful crisscrossing. Miles O'Dea was not of the Cork O'Deas, but it was a good name, and Mary Townshend was glad to give the lad his dinners and keep an eye on his wardrobe until he would be finding a job.

"Oh, Mother——" Harriet protested with distaste.

"Well, she's a dear good woman, and she must be lonely," the older woman argued.

"Yes, I know. But. Well, she won't" said Harriet with frowning pauses between her words.

"She's not been widowed long, Hat."

"She'll not marry him," Harriet insisted.

"If not him, someone else. And I wish you'd marry," Mary Townshend continued in her thoughts. "Foreman or no foremand, you're too pretty to be unwed, sitting up there in bed in your nightgown, with your red hair all in a mop and your cheeks burning that way."

"What you thinking, Ma?" Harriet asked with a joyous laugh. "Don't tell me, I know, I know, I know!" she sang as she swooped upon her mother, settled herself in the capacious lap, and seized hold of the stately gray curls that framed the fine, homely face. "Ma, you're beautiful," said Harriet, putting the end of a curl into each corner of her mother's mouth.

"Get that hair out of my mouth," said her mother indistinctly.

"Ma, you have beauty of soul," said Harriet.

"I'd never doubt it for an instant."

"Did a lot of the boys at home in Cork want you, Ma?"

"They did not. I wasn't wasting my time thinkin' of them."

"What were you doing, Ma? You must have been so cute."

"I was minding my brothers and my sister Meg, and their husbands and wives that all had the runnin' of me," said Mrs. Townshend, her eyes narrowed in reminiscence. "And I was nurse to Tom's and Lily's children that had no mother, and them as big as me, and very saucy to me."

"And then handsome Cousin Captain O'Meara came your way——" Harriet paused in the familiar story. Her mother picked it up.

"Handsome or not handsome I couldn't tell you upon me

94

oath," she said. "For I'd never seen him before the hour I married him, and I never saw him after that very day. He was cousin to the Loughboroughs, and to us, too, but he'd been out on a ship sailing the seas since his father took him aboard at the age of seven. He walked to the church with his father; it was only across the square, and I walked over with all me brothers and Meg, and when we got to the church Meg begun to cry. So Father McNaboe asked was I willing I should be wed, and I said 'Yes, if me brother Joe wanted it, for I'd been said by Joe since me father died,' and with that the priest said would I have a word with Shawn O'Meara, and we stepped aside—I can smell the plaster in the church now, and a wind blowing, and the ivy hitting the windowpane with my mother's name on it. It was a very fresh day—spring it was.

"So he asked me was it all right with me and would I trust him that he'd be good to me, and I said 'Yes.' And then we got married, and Meg gave me my mother's Paisley shawl that I wear to this day, and we went back to the house and they had a big meal ready, and Shawn said, 'Joe, I leave me wife in your care. Mind you ship her off to me in the Islands when the *Oliver Tracy* comes in.' And he said to me, 'You'll follow me, dear?' and I said, 'With Katty Ryan,' and he asked why did she want to go to those faraway places, and I said, 'That she'd pick up a good man, her pushing forty.' And they had a great laugh at me, and I ran upstairs, and when I came down Shawn was gone off to his ship, and Pheeny Rafferty—she was an innocent poor soul—called me by me married name and I gave her a good slap."

Hattie, getting back into bed, gave the expected laugh, and stated rather than asked:

"And that was the last of Shawn O'Meara!"

"That was all annyone seen—saw of him," Mrs. Townshend agreed, dropping the Irish burr with which old memories usually endowed her.

"Though it took you years to get it through the Pope's head that you could get an annulment," Hattie mused.

"You go easy on the Pope," her mother said warningly.

95

"Well, I meant the slowness of ships and mails and all that," Harriet apologized hastily.

"You're a bad girl," said her mother adoringly.

Harriet was silent as her mother prepared for bed, lying staring into space like a bright-eyed kitten. Mrs. Townshend moved about the big bare upper chamber in the comfortable last routine of the long day, opening a window, carrying a jar of roses to the hall, pausing to stare down at the night light of the city she loved, finally kneeling at the bedside for brief night prayers, in which Harriet joined. Then the gas was turned off, and immediately peaceful moonlight flowed into the room and against a sky clear and bright Harriet could see the moving tips of the eucalyptus trees in the garden.

"Ma, what a night!"

"You can see the villages across the bay tonight, Oakland and Berkeley. A steamer was crossing to the Sausalito side, with the moon on her wake." Mrs. Townshend yawned in the darkness, and was immediately asleep. But Harriet lay long awake.

Coralia married. Hattie turned the words over and over again in her heart. Coralia in love, really in love perhaps, this time, and going through all the familiar motions, blushing and shy, confident and proud—Harriet made a face in the dark.

Coralia! She had always seemed set apart from that sort of thing, dignified by her young widowhood, her exquisite attitude toward the small fatherless boys, her wonderful courage and faith when the little Francisco died. Her very wealth in acres of woodland, pasture, mountain range, vineyards, her responsibility for their management made her position unique. A man would spoil it all!

"A husband, well, it would simply be the end for me," Harriet mused. "And a man like that, one of the hands, really, or he was until old Arturo died. Coralia Mrs. Haagersen. It just doesn't sound right."

Her heart began to beat hard. Why, this would change everything! All the happy nonsense she and Coralia talked together, the easiness, the sureness each felt of the other's

96

affection, would be jeopardized. Men were notoriously jealous of their wives' interests; she had seen it more than once among her newly wed friends.

"He would be a lot nearer her than I am," her thoughts ran. "He'd be with her always, and I'd only be there when they decided to ask me. That's funny. That's really funny," Harriet said half aloud. "I never thought of it quite that way before, not when Caroline married, or Lizzie. Coralia and Phil Haagersen. They'd talk about me at breakfast, maybe: 'Hadn't we better ask Harriet again, it's weeks now.'"

She tried to remember the new foreman, tried to remember if anything significant had been said about him when she had last been at the rancho. Had Coralia seemed in any way different? Harriet decided that there had been faint indications of change.

She got out of bed, paced the floor for a few frantic minutes, presently knelt at the window sill and looked out at the moon-washed world. Suddenly she buried her head in her folded arms, overcome by a sudden uprushing of emotion, breathing deep, trying to think.

She remained perfectly still for some time. Mind and soul were in a confusion of emotion; shame and amazement, fear and jealousy fighting in turn for recognition. Harriet had never known jealousy, the very forcing bed of all other miseries of the spirit. She did not know it now that it was sweeping over her in terrifying waves.

After a while she straightened up, as the bells of old St. Mary's rang midnight, and pushed her hands up across her hot face, forcing her hair back from her forehead. She was panting, frightened at the passions that shook her whole being.

Coralia going to be married. Coralia beloved by a man, perhaps already embraced by him, already planning a radiant future on the old rancho beside him. Coralia wondering how she could tell poor little Harriet the glad tidings.

Harriet, a poor despicable fool now in her own estimation, had been satisfied, more than satisfied, with the happy woman friendship; Harriet had felt that their companionship had been perfect! But Coralia—oh, it was impossible to think that

97

Coralia hadn't practiced some deception, hadn't kept this secret only too well! Coralia had known from the beginning that affection between women, all laughter and embroidering and early rides and city afternoons upstairs with the pink teacups and the coal fire, were but a shadowy imitation of the relationhip a man could create without effort, the real, the poignant and thrilling thing!

Had Coralia been giving Harriet her easy, charming friendship even while there burned in her the knowledge of this deeper, more precious feeling, this feeling that would wipe all other loves out of her heart, her husband, her sons, her woman friend?

Harriet moaned, and her mother roused in the wide bed and looked across at the little silhouette in the window.

"Anything the matter, dear'r?"

"Just that it's such a heavenly night," Harriet said a little thickly. But her mother was not in a mood to analyze fine graduations in tone; she merely added to her question the advice not to get cold and relapsed again into sleep. Harriet still knelt at the window.

"We've had such fun," her thought said. "She's liked it as much as I have. But to have a man around all the time—and Coralia nervous all the time, the way the other girls are, for fear she's hurting her husband's feelings, for fear he doesn't like her girl friends! And not to tell me——"

That was the rub. To keep Harriet out of it, perhaps to be smiling at Harriet's blindness, perhaps to feel sorry for her. It was unbearable!

"I know what I'll do, I'll get married, too," Harriet said, as a sudden inspiration sent hope into her soul. "I'll marry somebody. I'll marry Taylor Mowrey or Sid Forester. I will! And when Coralia tells me that she has a secret to tell me, and she couldn't tell me before because only their families know, I'll tell her my secret! Ma's always hinting she'd like me to be married, and I'll be glad, too, and have all this guesswork about men over!"

The lights were all out in the city now, except for faint vague glowing of dull pink or green among the huddled wooden roofs of Chinatown or the dots of yellow that were lanterns swinging on the ships. Tamalpais was a splendid sweep of darkness silhouetted against the pale gray of the moon-washed sky; the night air thrilled with the faint harp strings of spring dark. Harriet, suddenly exhilarated by resolution, by the fire of a new plan, a plan that would answer Coralia—silence her once and for all—got into bed and was immediately and deeply asleep.

CHAPTER 13

In the morning, more temperately, she considered her chances. Taylor Mowrey was for many reasons the best. He was handsome, he was of a socially prominent family; his aunt was the dashing and popular Mrs. Howison Howe, the hospitalities of whose country palace at Belmont were already the most discussed of the time. Taylor drove a smart little trap, often with Harriet Townshend beside him, and loved to scare her by touching up the cob when they reached the Speedway in Golden Gate Park.

But Taylor was dull—heavyheaded dull. He did occasionally have flashes of fun, even sometimes of rather shrewd comment, but he was heavy going most of the time.

Sid Forester was a young lawyer with a brilliant future before him; everyone said so. He wasn't physically prepossessing, being of the square-built, swarthy type, negligent of his appearance, sweaty of brow under the exertion of taking a picnic lunch out to Seal Rocks at the Cliff House or climbing the Sausalito hills. But just his talk, especially if there happened to be another legal mind in the group, indicated that his profession was an all-absorbing thing in his life, and eminence and success were ahead of him. However, Harriet rather disliked the idea of being a lawyer's wife.

The fascinating Jean Bonnefilles with whom she studied

French was another possibility, as was good-natured, curly-headed Tom MacNulty, one of Johnny's closest friends. Any one of these would come running at her summons. Harriet had said "No" to them all, but with such fascinating seriousness and affectionate regret that hope had sprung eternal in their hearts even before they had left her presence.

There was Lord Avery Edward Fox-Spence, too, one of a group of Englishmen of assorted ages and backgrounds who lived in Bakersfield, indulged in light clerical employment of various sorts, if occupied at all, and were regularly helped with delightful draughts in pounds, shillings, and pence, from London banks. Behind these banks were concealed the families of the exiles, who only wanted to know that Cecil or Guy was safe in a faraway land, and not involving his family and friends in any fresh trouble.

Harriet knew little of "Dolly's" resources; she knew that certain members of his circle, very young and callow boys, or quite shrewd and charming and cultured elderly men, were known as being away from home on "tickets of leave." But just what that meant she didn't know, or care. They were, many of them, delightful, their manners and speech were fascinating, and if she knew little of them as potential husbands, why, she knew quite as little of the other men, too.

Upon their qualification as home supporters, as facers of responsibility, as citizens generally, she never meditated. Girls got married, and settled all those questions later.

Girls married drinkers, to "reform them," and succeeded or failed with equal equanimity. Girls married rakes, and patiently followed their fortunes into long struggles for subsistence, for children's needs, for dim hopes of regained solvency and restored self-respect. Girls married the bubble-made pioneer millionaires and went from humble homes to the magnificence of Nob Hill, driving behind their matched grays, among the sand hills and the young green of the Golden Gate Park, wearing their diamonds at entertainments that rivaled the Arabian Nights in extravagant splendor.

But no engaged girl ever thought seriously of the future. They might all have been convinced that the story ended with the familiar promise of living happily ever after. The marriage was the exciting, the desirable goal. After that, well, at least one was married.

Acute jealousy agonized the unengaged girl as her closest friend displayed a ring, went into a rapture of dimples and blushes, and confessed that she and Freddie, or Ray, or Lee, had been keeping the thing secret, "just for the fun," but they did want dear Lily to know! And whatever speculation or suspicion had done to prepare the way, the news left dear Lily with a sense of outrage and shock. A sense of being left out of the big things and fobbed off with the lesser. A sense of icy division between herself and her best friend; she had been babbling of the new man at the Wakefield party, she had been boasting that Winfield Davis had asked her to go to the concert—mere shadows of courtship! Here was her friend, insufferably complacent, with a real proposal and a genuine engagement to announce!

Harriet suffered such emotions as these for many days after the arrival of Coralia's letter. She read the letter several times, trying to extract from that mysterious postscript more than was there. She vacillated between a desire to write Coralia superbly that she had, of course, suspected the engagement, and had been aware all the time of what was going on, and forlorn misgivings, lest by some miracle what she suspected might not be true after all. She hoped at times that she never would see Coralia again.

Meanwhile she pursued her plan of a counterattack, a marriage on her own part, immediately following Coralia's or perhaps preceding it. She went out a good deal, and on evenings at home had at least four swains to swell the musical group in the back parlor.

Various boarders would be sitting about on these occasions. Perhaps a game of whist or euchre would be going on in a corner; some of the women would be knitting, some rocking and chatting in undertones. The gaslight would hiss gently overhead. If a song was popular, or if Harriet's and some tenor voice blended in "Juanita" or "Rosalie, the Prairie Flower" the talk would stop and a little patter of applause reward the laughing performers. Sometimes the younger crowd played Jenkins at the long table. Mrs. Townshend's paying guests really did resemble the happy family she was proud to consider them.

About a week after the first shock of her wretched suspicions of Coralia, Harriet had had an unusually successful home evening, for Avery Fox-Spence had come up from Bakersfield and had made no secret of his intentions, and a sparkling and stunningly handsome new-comer from Boston, who had been in the house but three days, was visibly snared.

It was with a sense of power and satisfaction that Harriet saw the nobleman to the door at eleven o'clock and smilingly dismissed the attractive Nathaniel Babcock. Flirting and singing with men was great fun, after all, especially when one knew that at any chosen moment things could develop into more serious channels.

Harriet turned at the door, went through the empty great double parlors. Two maids had appeared from nowhere and were straightening the rooms, windows were opened to the mild spring night, and white lace curtains stirred uneasily in the breeze that flowed in, sweet from the bay. Harriet went on upstairs. On the upper floor her mother called from the opened door of her bedroom.

"Hattie!"

"Yessum," Hattie answered, weary.

"Coralia's here," said Mrs. Townshend, from her bed.

"Coralia is!" The world rocked.

"Yes. She and Josito got here about ten. They came part way on the train. Josito said he liked it much better than the carriage. She didn't want you bothered."

"Bothered," Harriet repeated, her heart beating hard.

"But she said she'd be awake until midnight anyway, and to come up. And she had that maid of hers—Ana, it is?—she had her light the fire. You might run up. But Hat, it's late now, and do, darlin', do have some sense about getting to bed."

The last words were unheard by Hattie, who had been almost running as she crossed the upper hall and went through a baize-curtained door at the rear, mounted three steps to the hallway of the annex and reached Coralia's door.

But when she got there emotion overcame her, and she

stood shaking and silent for a minute, and for another minute, gathering her courage to face what might be news on the other side of the door. Coralia was in a rocking chair by the fire, and looked up, getting to her feet, arms outstretched, and Harriet was in her embrace before either spoke.

"My dear," Coralia said. "You did come up! I was so afraid your mother had gone to sleep and forgotten to tell you."

Their delight was mutual; they were seated side by side now on the old horsehair sofa, Coralia's right hand gripping Harriet's left. For a heavenly quarter hour they could not talk fast enough, or stop laughing.

Then things quieted down a little and Harriet took her favorite big chair opposite Coralia and Ana brought in two cups of frothy chocolate and some buttered toast. And for Harriet, at least, the hour was one of perfect bliss.

Coralia was just her own old self, only nicer. She reported that things had been deadly dull at the rancho, with the boys gone back to school and the spring rains falling. Harriet listened, rejoicing; the menace of Philip Haagersen faded steadily, the old warm rush of confidence and affection flowed back. "You fool, you hopeless fool," she reproached herself in her heart. "It's been dull, nothing's been happening, they missed you!"

And it was with a radiant face that she fell to planning the happy days of Coralia's visit.

"I feel more and more that I'm—well, I'm more alive, here," Coralia said, putting down her cup and stretching herself on the old sofa. She put up her feet, half closed her eyes as she watched the drowsy fire.

"And I always feel perfectly drunk with excitement when we pass those alders down at the creek and I know we're reaching the rancho," Harriet countered.

Coralia moved lazy dark eyes to her companion's face.

"But you see, I've lived on ranches all my life," she said. "And you've never—well, you've never seen the ranch without you, so you don't know how lonely it can be!" And they both laughed again.

Harriet was staring at the fire, too, her little figure in a child's half-crouched position in the big chair, a tangle of

103

bright hair, like threads of fine copper wire, falling in a cascade of curls on her neck.

"We have it both ways," Harriet said. "Whenever we want to we can go to the beautiful ranch, and I can ride Stella Maris and gather figs and go down to see the prize bull. And then for a change we can come to Ma and put on gloves and hats again."

"Hat, when did you begin to like me?"

The face under the red-gold curls was radiant.

"The minute I saw you. The day you brought dear little Cisco down for his operation."

"Did you really? Did you know then that we were to be such friends?"

"I think I did. I remember that the room was full of your lovely things, and something smelled delicious, and Ma sent us up biscuits and tea. You—I don't know—anyway, that was it."

"Don't I remember it, and feeling at home at once, and feeling that your mother was an angel when she talked about Francisco."

"Ma is an angel," Harriet conceded. She went back to the beginnings; loving to remember every detail. "Remember that I got Cisco some paper walnuts in Chinatown and he ranged all the little animals in a row on his bed?"

"Oh, and remember——"

It was late when Harriet went downstairs to creep in beside her mother with no more noise than the fog was making, the white fog crawling over San Francisco. She lay for a long time without sleeping, her heart so bubbling with joy and relief that it could not at once be quieted.

Coralia had mentioned her foreman, but with such unconscious ease that Harriet had felt more reassured than if she had avoided the name. Haagersen, Coralia said, was going to take his vacation in Mexico to see the bull fights.

"Our Re del Rancho is a fighting bull from the Guerrero. At least he was to be raised among fighting bulls, but Martin bought him when he was only a calf."

"Tell me about him, Coralia."

"Re del Rancho—well, he's just——"

104

Harriet's laughter had broken out like bells.

"No, no, no, you goose! Philip Haagersen."

"You got his name?"

"You put it in your postscript."

"But you asked for it. Don't you remember, the day you left the rancho, you asked me the name of the man who cleared the bulls out of the road for us when we were riding?"

"I'd forgotten. I am an absolute fool!" Harriet added the last phrase only in her thoughts. "You didn't know it then," she reminded the other woman.

"No, asked Ana."

"But you do like him?"

"I didn't at first, I thought he was too good-looking," Coralia confessed with a laugh. "But he really is good with the men, and they like him. He's already suggested a change in the little bunkhouse, and we're going to put a big porch annex on the cookhouse for the hot weather. He's young and he's energetic, I like him. But what with my Spanish baron making a formal call and my mother coming all the way over to assure me that as a baroness I would hold a high position in Barcelona, I've been fully occupied."

"Is he really terrible? The baron from Barcelona."

"Ugh. He's an orangutan. Mr. Nobody from Nowhere!"

"Coralia, you're speaking of a fellow human being!"

"I know it." Their laughter had been easily stirred; it seemed good to both to be laughing together again. "And that reminds me," Coralia said, "I want to go to Confession to someone who doesn't know me. Father Valentini is an old saint, but he knows all about me."

"I'll go too," Harriet said. "We'll pick a strong husky Jesuit." And they were laughing again.

105

They sallied forth in the sweet spring mornings as joyously intent upon adventure as any knights of the Middle Ages. Not a week went by but what some new little shop was opened and fashions in china, neckwear, fans, parasols displayed from shops half the world away. On these visits of inspection Coralia and Harriet found a hundred incidental objects of interest as they walked down the steep hills of Washington or Clay Street, Dupont or Mason. They commented admiringly upon every fresh stretch of wooden sidewalk, every sheet of plate glass laboriously freighted "around the Horn."

Sometimes they took the cars out to the beach and walked in semi-circles of wet sand, with gulls hovering and swaying overhead and seals barking on the Cliff House rocks. The old birdman, who pinched the beaks of his tiny performers if they seemed careless, and the old candy man, with a pitted dark face and a tray of delicious molasses sticks, were warm friends.

Many friends wore pitted faces in these days, when smallpox came in on the ships; the "pest house" out on the sand hills, beyond the Children's Hospital, was always tenanted. Everyone Coralia and Harriet knew had been vaccinated, even the tiny arm of little Josito had worn a bulbous scar for weeks, but there were folk of the humbler orders who liked neither the performance of bloody scratching upon whole skin and forced assimilation of poisoned animal's serum, nor anything else in the whole idea. And these often found themselves hidden in back bedrooms by families less afraid of the disease than of the pest house and willing to take all risks while it ran its course.

Mrs. Townshend usually had a few destitute families for

the younger women to visit, and it was Harriet who always found the right touch in dealing with them, and Coralia who could only stand by tongue-tied and wait to add her silver dollar to the dollar Harriet slipped into some worn old hand. Perhaps Harriet held a damp and odorous baby during the negotiations, a wide toothless grin on the pale little dirty face in answer to her own smile. And more than once, leaving the shabby Stevenson or Annie Street tenement, Harriet would indicate some man lying flushed and semi-conscious in the street and say with a shrug:

"That's her husband," or, "The sick old lady upstairs, that's her son."

And until they left this part of town they might be sobered for a few minutes, passing corner saloons with a haughty glare wondering what men were made of, anyway, to care so little for their families!

But most of the time everything was laughter and delight, from the time Harriet poured coffee for her mother at one end of the long table and Coralia came down to supervise tray breakfasts for the baby and his nurse. After that she would have her own breakfast with Harriet. Often she would wait until late at night, when Harriett, who perhaps had not seen Coralia since some swain had borne her away for dinner, a cotillion, or the theater, would run upstairs in the annex for a last half hour of confidences and reports.

Sometimes, with Josito and his nurse, they went down to the busy piers and walked on the tarred docks that were warm and soft under their feet in the hot spring sunshine. Here there were wonderful smells from crates and barrels that were being unloaded from seagoing ships, and reloaded upon the river steamers, whose side paddles or walking beams went up and down like calipers as the vessels came slowly through the Golden Gate. *Stockton, Martinez, Point Reyes*, were the names painted on the busy little freighters; the larger craft, salt-soaked from the rough last miles of the Pacific, had statelier designations, with cities' names beneath them, *Glasgow, London, Napoli*.

Early in the afternoon, with the rising winds, the fishing fleet came in, its tobacco-brown sails, patched with yellow and blue and tan, filling magnificently against the background of Tamalpais, and the receding hills that flanked the mountain, and the blue western sky. The fishermen, sustained only by flasks of red wine and chunks of sour bread, had been out since the four-o'clock darkness; they were usually happy, getting home for hot food and long sleep, and as they spread their catches on the pier, or negotiated for sales among the backing and filling carts already glittering with old scales, they kept up a shouted conversation in any one of half a dozen Latin argots.

The Chinese were not less noisy; they jabbered as violently on the stimulus of the early-morning meal of rice and tea as did their neighbors. Most of their fish went up to the crowded little oil-dark shacks of Chinatown, but Harriet could bargain for a great pink salmon that still was flapping, or a dozen or more of the crabs that were winding their dark green legs together distractedly in a bucket and waving dangerous claws at any approach.

The air in this open market was salty, fishy, it smelled of Oriental grasses and of the green water, ringed with oil and cluttered with coconut shells, that moved restlessly about Meiggs Wharf. The girls, with the nurse and the fascinated small boy, might saunter on through sheds where sacks of grain, scenting the air deliciously, were stacked, might linger close to a horse trough to watch the great draught horses plunge their velvet noses deep into the water as they drank.

On Bush Street, not far from the Townshend House, was a skating rink, and on Monday nights the fashionable throng gathered there. Johnny, since his marriage, had not attended these meetings, but Coralia and Hattie went regularly, and although Coralia did not skate, she was sufficiently entertained by watching Harriet swim blithely past on the arm of an admirer, the man's tall head bent to catch her lightest remark, Harriet's fur tippet streaming behind her, one hand hidden in a tiny muff. She was an admirable skater, but nevertheless had quite often to be taught rather simple curves and reverses; there were always teachers.

Coralia, known vaguely as the "rich Spanish lady at Mrs. Townshend's," might easily have found an escort to the concerts, minstrel shows, plays and dances, but she felt no special interest in any of them, and liked best to have Harriet go and come back to tell her about them. Harriet saw *Fiske's French Opéra Bouffe*, at Magnin's Opera House, and *The Lady of Lyons* at the Metropolitan, and never missed a show at the new "California."

But when Susan B. Anthony and Elizabeth Cady Stanton lectured on the question of equal suffrage Harriet and Coralia went to hear them, disapproving heartily of their vigor and fanaticism, as did most of the ladies who attended. Ladies were assured by their men and earnestly reassured by each other that they could get anything they wanted from husbands, fathers, brothers, without "stramming" about in bloomers at the dirty polls.

"I like anything at any theater, if it's in the daytime, for instance, like Woodward's Gardens," said Coralia, excusing her indolence. "But I'm all Spanish on the subject of being out at night. Spanish women simply don't go out at night. Home is their place then. That is the reason I suppose that Martin, and my father, too——" She left the sentence unfinished, and Harriet tactfully shifted the subject, gathering that both these devoted husbands were devoted in more than one direction, and to more than one individual.

"But suppose you marry a man who lives the theater, Coralia?"

"Well, then he must learn to love his home, and the women in his home, and talk and music and maybe a little dancing in the evenings. The young people love that."

"But all families don't have other women and young people in them. Look at Johnny and Lizzie. They sit, and Johnny reads the paper, and Lizzie just sits, and after a while she yawns—they get up at six every morning and she gets sleepy, and then Johnny jumps up as if a firecracker hit him and shouts that he'll lock up, it's after nine."

"In the name of God, why does he shout? Lizzie looks as quiet as a mouse."

"She is. But Johnny's like that. He'll go half asleep over his paper and then wake up with a roar."

Coralia laughed.

"I will be very sure of how my husband feels before I pick him," she said.

"You sent the baron away?"

"Us-s-sh!" shuddered Coralia. "And you sent Lord Fox-Spence away," she countered.

"We could have been Your Highness and My Lady," Harriet said, amused.

"Well, what will the other one do when one of us really falls in love?"

"I thought you were."

"Thought I was what?"

"Falling in love."

"With—not with—with who?" Coralia asked, flushing and pleased.

"With Haagersen, on the rancho."

"My foreman? But I've hardly ever looked at him. What on earth put that into your head!"

They were climbing the steep Mason Street hill; they paused on the grass, and sat on two cement barrels that had been flung down on the site of one of tomorrow's Nob Hill castles. Both were breathing fast; their faces were rosy from the climb as they faced each other.

"You told me his name in a postscript!" Harriet laughed.

"And that meant I was mad about him?"

"No-o-o. But it scared me."

"You don't like him?"

"I've never seen him, in daylight."

"Oh, well. And anyway, didn't you ask me the name of the new foreman?"

"I think I did," Harriet admitted slowly, remembering it.

"But you did see him, Harriet, one night down at the corrals."

"Of course I did. But I didn't get a good look at him. Just that he was tall, and blond, and had a nice deep voice—that's all," Harriet said.

"And you thought I might be falling in love with him?"

"No, not exactly. But I was afraid you were."

"That would spoil everything," Coralia said thoughtfully.

"That's what I thought. You know how we fool around at

the ranch, riding, and coming in late to breakfast, and having the dogs come up. I don't know——" She grew vague. "It's all such fun," she finished, her eyes narrowed in recollection. "I seem to breathe differently there. And having a man around all the time would spoil it."

"No danger," Coralia said, getting to her feet.

"No danger here."

Harriet could hardly keep her feet on the ground for happiness as they finished the climb and went panting in for rest, and tea, and baths before dinner.

Twice during this spring visit Coralia was driven in her own rambling surrey, behind the big black horses, to visit her mother on the old home rancho of Our Lady of the Little Columns, or one of her aunts or cousins on neighboring ranchos. Harriet might have accompanied her if she would, but Harriet utilized these occasions to make some duty calls of her own on Lizzie out in the Mission Dolores.

The Mission was connected by the Mission Street horsecar with the main city; wooden houses, sagging on the grassy streets and displaying discouraged marguerites and marigolds in their battered dooryards, had increased in number until they all but connected the two settlements. Sidewalks were of wooden planks, with convenient knotholes here and there for the button games small girls played after school hours.

Lizzie's little house was dark and gloomy on a windy, foggy afternoon. The blinds in the front parlor were closed; glints of wavering light picked up the shine on the horsehair sofa and the pink rose on the china lamp. Lizzie was in the kitchen.

She sat at the end of the small table, her figure drooping, her looped lifeless hair drooping, her hand locked idly in her lap. Every inch of her expressed discouragement and apathy; she moved listless eyes to Harriet as Harriet came in, looked down at the floor.

Harriet sat down opposite her and talked cheerfully. But she smelled a strange stale smell compounded of rotting wood and mice and yellow soap, and she heard the wind whine about the house, and her heart sank. It was to this that poor, adorable Johnny came home.

111

"Lizzie Townshend, did you get out today?"

"I went round to seven at St. Charles's."

"Did you have your coffee?"

"Oh, yes. I guess so. Sure I did."

"Johnny all right?"

"Sure. But he feels terrible bad." Lizzie's eyes, already tear-swollen, watered afresh.

"Oh, heavens, of course he does! But Lizzie dear," said Harriet, leaning across the table and speaking earnestly, laid her hand on Lizzie's hand. "Lizzie dear," she repeated, "you mustn't shut yourself up and cry about it. Ma says it often—often happens with the first baby."

"It was a little boy," Lizzie whispered, in living agony.

"I know." Harriet could add nothing to the two words, and there was a silence.

"I climbed on the apple box, that's what did it."

"Fall?"

"Sort of slipped, and I could feel it wrench through me."

"Oo-oo," Harriet shuddered, absorbed in sympathy.

"So I lay down until Johnny came home, it was only a little while. And he went for the doctor."

"What were you doing?"

"On the apple box. I was reaching for the spider webs up on the ceiling." Lizzie put her scrawny elbows on the table and covered her face with her hands. "Oh, if I hadn't, if I hadn't," she moaned.

"Well, then you'd have been trying to do something else!" Harriet said bracingly. "If an accident can happen as simply as that, it was going to happen, Ma says."

"Oh, Harriet, you do help when you talk that way!"

"Because I think mulling yourself up in the house this way, and crying, is bad for you!" Harriet said, encouraged in her well-doing. "Don't you want to come out and walk? Let's walk over to Mission Dolores. It's only three o'clock."

Lizzie was persuaded to put on her hat and coat, and they walked in the fog and wind. Papers and rubbish were blowing about the wooden sidewalks; the air was heavy and damp. But when they came back Lizzie had some color, and she rose gratefully to Harriet's insistence upon tea. They had

112

stopped for fresh graham bread; they skimmed the cream from a panful of milk that was standing on the table of the narrow rear porch. The hot tea scented the kitchen comfortably. When the gas was lighted the room seemed cozy.

"Now mind you give Johnny a good hot cup of this when he comes in. What have you got for dinner?" demanded Harriet.

"Well, I was going to heat up the stew, and maybe fry him a few potatoes. And we've still got half of your mother's cake."

"And six red apples," Harriet supplemented. She had bought them from the baskets of an old Chinese, wandering with his fresh market-garden wares through the streets. "You feel better, don't you?"

"Oh, I do, Hattie. You're awfully kind!"

"You know God has some reason for all the trials He sends us," Harriet said seriously.

"I try to think of that," Lizzie answered forlornly. "But Johnny and I were so happy," she went on, her lips trembling. "We didn't want for anything; he was laughing from morning until night. And now——" Her voice thickened; she fell silent.

"I know you love Johnny," Hattie said musingly.

"That's the worst of it, breaking his heart," Lizzie said.

"You'd like to see Johnny happy again?" Harriet questioned, after a moment's brown study.

"Oh, God knows I would, Hat!"

"Well, then, you be happy. You tell him tonight that there will be other children, and that crying won't help, and you want him to come home, not to be afraid he'll find you lying on your bed yelling bloody murder," Harriet said simply.

"It's easy talking." Lizzie continued to stare drearily into space. Her eyes filled again.

"I know. Of course it is," Harriet said in quick sympathy. "But, Lizzie, supposing you had a good fire going in the stove tonight and the gas lighted," she went on persuasively, "and supposing you did up your hair and put on the red dress, don't you think Johnny's heart would give a leap of thanks to God?"

113

"I don't know would it," Lizzie said lifelessly.

"You know it would. You could do that for him, no matter how sad you feel," urged Harriet.

"Oh, I don't know will I ever laugh again!" sobbed Lizzie, her head down on the table. Harriet studied her for a while in silence, her face troubled.

"Well, I'm not doing you much good," she said finally, getting to her feet. "And I have to go."

"You were good to come, Hat," Lizzie gulped apologetically.

She went to the door with her guest, and watched Harriet walk away in the harsh wind that was whirling straw and papers high in the air. The street looked gritty and gray; a horse-drawn grocery wagon went by in a cloud of dust. Harriet turned at the corner to wave.

Lizzie went back into the house and stood reflecting for some minutes. Then she went on into the little kitchen and lifted the plates from the iron stove. She shook down the ashes, and put in crumpled newspaper and kindling. Where her bared arms touched the stove they were streaked with black.

When the first crackle sounded she poured in coal and did knowing things to dampers and doors. She filled the kettle, presently subtracting enough hot water to wash her face and hands. She put on the red dress. She went out into the forlorn unfinished street and in various vacant lots found four poppies, six buttercups set in their own delicate spraying foliage, and two stalks of pink mallow. She was arranging these in one of her wedding vases when Johnny came in.

"Hello, Liz——" he began, a little uncertainly.

"Hello, Mister John Townshend," Lizzie said, with a thick throat and a lopsided smile.

Watching her, he put aside his coat, laid the paper on the table. He did not speak.

"I've a steak for you; there's a good fire," faltered Lizzie.

He was across the room, he had her in his big arms, his face was on her shoulder and he was sobbing so violently that he might have frightened her. She had never seen him

114

cry before; not through all the terrible hours of the last month.

But Lizzie was not frightened. She held him tight. She knew that she would never cry any more.

CHAPTER 15

Harriet followed Coralia to the rancho a few months after Coralia took Josito home. She put in certain events of summer gaiety first, visiting Lake Tahoe, going down the peninsula to San Mateo and San Jose. She played tennis, ate picnic lunches in secluded glens and on the Santa Cruz beach, rode half-broken horses on wild gallops to Mountain View and Santa Clara, and danced on the rough wooden floors of country houses, on the green grass of watered lawns, and on the canvased deck of a navy ship that chanced to be in the bay.

She came home to recount triumphs, jokes, comment upon persons and clothing, to her mother. Miss Vilder put all her clothes in order and Gardy Ann escorted her to trains, or to meet her escorts at the Palace or the Occidental. And early in September she was off to the Heart of Gold rancho again.

It was like a home-coming; easy, familiar, flawless. Autumn lay in a haze of gold and soft blue over the rancho. The warm air smelled of grapes. In the dusty leaves of the apple trees near the house the fruit hung red and thick. The corn was all in now, but among the sprawling vine leaves pumpkins were lying; baskets filled with the dark rich comice pears stood about under the pointed shafts of the pear trees.

Everywhere was overflowing plenty. The milk pails that came from the long line of stanchions in the barns were brimming, the foamy top of the milk specked with dirt and cow hairs here and there. Bins were filled with grain; new wine and new cheeses were in the making. In the cellar below the spring house vats of butter glistened with dewy drops.

Coralia and Harriet and Josito wandered about, watching and reveling in all of it. When the farm hands milked they sang, and often the two women were quiet audience at the end of the long barns, listening and amused, watching the switching tails and the munching jaws, smelling the good smell of the cows, and of the sweet new milk and hay and the balmy airs that came in from tarweed and sorrel in the orchard.

When dew brought out the peculiar sweet fragrant pungency of the dust and the dry grass, they would wander up toward the house again. Like most of the old haciendas it stood on the rise, the garden that surrounded it heavily fenced with stunted pines. These old trees were laced with cobwebs through all their lower branches; much dead wood choked their inner growth, only the outer layers of foliage were green.

Tall eucalyptus and peppers and many overgrown shrubs added to the darkening of the rooms of the house, but the brick terrace was always kept clear and the upper stories rose above the treetops. To Coralia and Harriet the depth, shadows, and coolness of the big place were welcome, especially in the hot weather that might come in February or October as well as midsummer. Even in winter they could hurry to bedrooms kept comfortable by coal fires, or to the sturdy coal fires in the grates of the dining room, or sitting room, which burned all day long.

Since her widowhood Coralia had used only a quarter of her big domain, living in half a dozen rooms. But on this visit Harriet discovered a change and was delighted with it. The boys were not to go back to Santa Clara, instead a tutor had been engaged for them, and Martin, Pablo, and Josito were racketing about joyfully, keeping a delightful sense of occupation and activity in the place.

The tutor was one Miles Mulholland, a subdued, studious person whose forty-three years made him seem elderly even to Coralia. He stood thin and straight in shabby garments, and was nervous and anxious in manner, still obviously strange.

But shy though he might be, Miles had made it plain that he would take no position that separated him from daily contact with his church, and he had taken full responsibility for securing the presence of an aged priest, a Spanish missionary of some eighty years, crippled with rheumatism, slightly deaf, but saintly beyond any question, and permitted by his superiors to spend his last years as a house chaplain, considering that there were some fifty persons on the rancho and the administration of spiritual sustenance had before this been uncertain and irregular.

This made a full table, and on the night of Harriet's arrival another guest was included in the long-drawn, bountiful dinner. The new foreman, Philip Haagersen. The smile Harriet gave him as he walked beside her striped black and white taffeta ruffles to the dining room was entirely friendly. Suspicion was dead. He was everything that was nice and tall and—yes, good-looking—and he had a strong hand that practically broke bones in a handshake, but Coralia was entirely out of his zone, with her great hacienda, her chaplain, her sons and their tutor. The absurdity of Harriet's agonies over the situation, only a few months ago, kept her mouth twitching a little, although this was an evening of decorous behavior.

She sat next to old Father Anselmo, who was on Coralia's left. Martin was next to his mother, on the other side, then the tutor, then Pablo. This gave Philip Haagersen the head of the table, and brought him about to Harriet's left. She treated him demurely, saving all her sparkle for the old priest.

"What brings you to California?" she asked Philip.

"The bull," he answered briefly.

"Our new bull?" Harriet often used the possessive when she spoke of the rancho now.

"Bruno."

"You mean——" Her eyes looked like topazes in the candlelight under the copper twinkle of her hair. She stopped, at a loss.

"I was visiting on the Hernandez ranch, at Tia Juana, and old Captain Juan couldn't find anyone else to do it, so I volunteered."

"By railroad?"

"No. They had a flat box truck. Two Mexican boys and I made the trip. It took us fourteen days."

117

"Resting at night—well, where?"

"Resting in the daytime. We had letters. The Hernandez family is well known. We came from rancho to rancho."

"And the poor bull. Did he stay in his box all the time?"

"No, he came out into a corral somewhere, every day, and bellowed at the top of his lungs," Philip said seriously.

"But what fun," Harriet commented, also without a smile.

"Then the Señora here asked me to ask Juan Hernandez, when I went back, to send her a good foreman. And I asked to stay."

"I don't blame you." Harriet was conscious of a struggle to keep the conversation alive. "This is my favorite place in the whole world."

"And how much of the world have you seen, señorita?"

"Well——" She was helping herself to pale pink salmon from a platter of magnificent fish that had been casually placed near her. "The Sandwich Islands and China and Russia —just crossing it," she answered mildly. "And then Ireland, and ten days in England—only London, and a day my brother and I spent at Oxford—then Boston, to my father's people, and Hawaii again, from Boston, and then to San Francisco. Oh, yes, and the ship had to wait in Marseille on the way back from Ireland, for a week, and we went to Rome—my mother wanted to see for herself that St. Peter's was in good shape."

She made the recital carefully, as if it were quite the usual story, looking at him with childlike trust.

"So of course I haven't seen the whole world," she said modestly as she finished. The man cleared his throat.

"No," he agreed briefly, and she knew he knew she was laughing at him. She turned back to her right-hand neighbor and tried on him her student's Spanish with great success.

After dinner there were night prayers in the chapel. The women put on lace veils and knelt absorbed and reverent in the candlelighted place. The abode walls of the chapel were three feet thick, and pierced by high narrow windows of colored glass; the plaster everywhere was discolored and rain-stained, but the altars were rich with mosaics and gold and silver offerings, and the delicate arm of the carved wooden

118

Madonna was covered with jeweled bracelets. Dark heavy paintings of saints were hung along the sides of the long, narrow room; the pews were worn smooth from the hands and knees of generations of the faithful. At the altar rail grooves had been worn in ripples in the wood.

Benediction candles burned brightly on the altar; other candles sent lights and shadows in wavering patterns on the walls. There were but three or four pews. The murmuring, rosary-jingling crowd that came in from the rancho on Sundays could stand or kneel as they chose at the back of the church; a few benches along the walls afforded seats for some of the women and the old men.

Harriet genuinely loved Benediction; her eyes, shining in the delicate shadow of her lace veil, went once seriously to the eyes of Philip Haagersen, and she smiled, completely at ease and happy here in this holy atmosphere. It struck him then, perhaps, that while the Señora always was rigidly grave in church, Harriet was enough at home to smile with no fear of being misunderstood. Coralia was at her loveliest tonight, her beauty set off by her black lace veil.

He was studying her; she fascinated him. He did not return Harriet's smile, and Harriet swept her gaze once more to the ceremony that was proceeding to the last *Laudate*. Incense smoke fumed into the air; the little flames of the candles were made dim and mysterious by it.

The company streamed out of the chapel blinking and smiling at each other; Miles turned with Pablo to the stairs, Martin, who had served as acolyte, joining them as they went. Harriet had promised to go up to tell Josito a story. She was talking to the tutor as they mounted the wide stairway and disappeared. Coralia and Philip lingered to wait for the old priest, and when Harriet and Miles came down they found the others on the dark terrace, under an autumn sky blazing with stars. Harriet seated herself on the top step of the three wide, shallow steps that led down to the garden, and touching the old bricks beside her, invited the shy Miles Mulholland to sit down. And with only an occasional word tossed over her shoulder to Coralia and Philip, seated in the shadows behind her, she devoted herself to her companion, winning from him

119

a luxury of confidence to which he had long been a stranger.

Awkward and low-voiced at first, he warmed to the encouragement of her laughter and the protection of the soft dark night. By the time the moon was splitting the tall plumes of the eucalyptus trees and sending tree shadows against the walls of the hacienda, he was gruffly expansive; Harriet learned of the brother who was studying for the priesthood and the mother who kept a boardinghouse in Cincinnati.

"My mother runs a boardinghouse," Harriet said, pleased.

"Your mother!"

"But does that surprise you, Mr. Mulholland?"

"Well, no. Well, no. But I thought you were"—an awkward outspreading of his big, bony hands—"I sort of figured you for dancing and going about," he said uncertainly.

"Well, you would figure me right! Coralia, this man thinks of me as simply a social butterfly. And let me tell you, Miles Mulholland, that that—is—exactly—what—I—am!" Harriet's laugh rang out joyfully. "No," she said more seriously, dropping to an undertone again, "I'm not, really. But my mother feels that you are only young once, I mean a girl is, and that you ought to have lots of dancing and fun while you can. When I marry," Harriet told him, her eyes gleaming in the moonlight, her small body tucked into a very rose of tarlatan ruffles on the top step, "it'll be housekeeping, and children, lots of children, if I don't want to break Ma's heart—she's named about six of 'em already!—and all that."

"You'll have to marry someone with plenty of money to raise a crowd like that," said Philip Haagersen from the background.

"I'll have you check on his bank account, Mr. Haagersen," Harriet countered.

"I—with many another gallant swain—may have cut my throat by that time."

"Blessed be God," said the broken voice of the old priest as he got to his feet. They all rose, making the response: "And blessed be His holy name."

When he had said his good nights and Miles had escorted him to his first-floor bedroom, the quartette wandered down through the garden to the summer house, a latticed octagonal pagoda smothered in honeysuckle and passion vines, and speckled, inside, with millions of diamonds of moonshine. A cracked round table, flanked with four stout homemade benches pretty well filled the floor space. Comfortably seated about it, they idled for an hour of desultory talk and singing.

Walking back to the house, Harriet and Philip followed the others; they were at the steps when he touched her arm, and jerking his head toward Coralia and the tutor, said casually:

"That's an awfully nice feller. What do you do it for?"

"Do——" Harriet began, astounded. She got no further. In the covering dark she felt the color rush to her face. "I don't do anything," she said proudly, very low. The man did not speak again, and they went into the hall. The big swinging lamp over their heads had been extinguished, and the place was lighted only by four candles burning in a row on the long dark table.

"This is Ana Immaculata's way of saying bedtime," said Coralia ruefully. "And perhaps she's right. Good night."

"Good night!" Harriet was three steps up the stairway.

"Let's ride before Mass, if someone will ask Jose to bring up the horses," Coralia said.

"I'll attend to it, señora," Philip said promptly.

The good nights went briskly back and forth, and then Harriet and Coralia, carrying their candles, went on their way upstairs and could be heard laughing as they went. Harriet was in high spirits, and Ana Immaculata, who slept in a little bedroom adjoining Coralia's, thought they would never be done talking and laughing. The Señorita, of course, had much to report; she came from the city that awed and even a little frightened Ana, and reputedly had a great many desperate lovers, and knew all about the beautiful clothes that came from Paris, and was altogether a most inspiring guest for the widowed Señora.

Harriet in a frail embroidered French nightgown embellished with little roses and a voluminous Chinese wrapper of stiff, plum-colored tribute silk, sat on the edge of Coralia's bed busily brushing her hair.

"It's so good to find so many people here, Coralia! It's always seemed so big and empty."

121

"Oh, it's much nicer this way. It's partly on my sister Lupe's account, you know. One of the Ybarra boys is really in earnest and my mother is all upset, and says she will close the old place now that Tia Filomena and Mia-mia are both dead, and perhaps come here."

"Oh." Harriet wrinkled her expressive little face. "And shall you like that?"

Coralia's smile was dubious in return.

"My mother——" she began and stopped. "Well, first she will be going to Pepita down San Diego way—that's Josephine, whose husband was killed by a stallion last year," she reminded Harriet, beginning again. "And Luisa, too, who is going to have a baby at last. Pepita has a girl, and a boy that is not quite right, and my mother is real use there, and she likes it. She's not happy here. So I brought the boys home, and Miles—did you like Miles?"

"I think he is a dear," Harriet said warmly, flushing out of all proportion.

"Harriet——" Coralia said wonderingly. And then accusingly, "Why, he isn't captivating already!"

"Heavens, no," Harriet assured her, laughing. Her risen color had nothing directly to do with the boys' quiet, bashful tutor. It rose from the sudden memory of the careless words Philip Haagersen had said on the steps. She didn't want to think of those words now, she wanted to be alone when she remembered them.

"But you like him?"

"I honestly think he's nice. And he must be awfully good, too. I mean, he was almost like a priest on the altar tonight."

"I think he would have been a priest if he hadn't had to help at home until just lately."

"Maybe he will yet."

"He thought of it. He told Martin so. Anyway," said Coralia, "I hope he stays in the world until the boys get a good start. They behave like angels for him, little devils that they are." Both women laughed.

"Well, it makes a nice household," Harriet approved. "Darling old Father Anselmo, and the boys, and Josito, of course, and this nice serious tutor. And if your mother comes, so much the better. Tell me, does Mr. Haagersen come up to dinner every night?"

"This is the first time. No, I really need other people about when my mother is here," Coralia confessed. "And another thing, if she comes, I'll want to go down to the city again, and quite often, too, and I can leave all the boys with her and Miles Mulholland."

"He's stunning, and he knows it," Harriet said musingly, after a moment.

Coralia brought her dreaming gaze suddenly to attention. "Who?"

"Don Felipe." Harriet's tone was playful as she used the boys' name for the foreman.

"D'you think so?" Coralia demanded in surprise.

"Well, I should think so. I mean, I should think any man who looks like that must know it."

"He is stunning," Coralia conceded, with a thoughtful emphasis on the verb.

"That yellow hair alone——" Harriet contributed.

"Well, isn't it?" Coralia agreed.

"You know I met him the last time I was here," Harriet reminded her, "but it was down by the corrals, at night, and all I got was an impression of a very tall man shouting out 'Head her off' and 'Shut that gate!' "

"We were shipping the heifers to San Antonio that night, I remember," Coralia said. "I didn't know then that he'd even stay. He's never done this sort of thing before. He really wants to be a doctor."

"He does?"

"Oh, yes. He wants to go to Edinburgh."

"Scotland!"

"You sound surprised." Coralia laughed at Harriet's widened eyes. "Is that so strange?" she asked.

"Well, no. But he didn't seem just that type. Doctors are usually sort of runty and spectacled and elderly." Harriet in turn laughed at her own absurdity.

"But don't they have to be young before they get old?" Coralia demanded reasonably, and this time both women laughed. And Ana Immaculata, writhing restlessly in her bed in the adjoining room, wondered how long they could keep it up, and breathed a mild curse upon the departed Don Martin, who had had these flimsy walls put in to divide the enormous old rooms into bathrooms and linen closets. A few years ago a poor harmless Christian woman trying to get to sleep couldn't have heard giggling through any of the walls of the entire hacienda!

"But seriously," Coralia presently resumed, after a moment she and Harriet had devoted to vague, sudden dreams, "do you remember my writing you what his name was and your worrying for fear I was losing my heart?"

"Perfectly," Harriet answered, with the flames of the same old worry springing up through the cold ashes.

"Which was idiotic, of course," Coralia resumed. "But it did make me notice him, and so when I knew you were coming I thought I would ask him to come up to dinner and let you see for yourself the fate you picked out for me."

"And you like him better than you thought you did." Harriet made it a statement.

"I honestly do." Coralia's manner was deceptively frank and simple. "At first I thought he was too pleased with himself, and proud, holding himself away from the rest of us, you know, and generally horrid."

"I couldn't agree with you more thoroughly," Harriet thought. Aloud she said: "The boys seem to like him."

"They adore him. He's had a funny history; he was adopted by his stepfather when he was a baby, he spent a lot of time in a doctor's house in Boston, with all his vacations down at Tia Juana. Then he was in England, I know. He hasn't much money," Coralia said. "I pay him a hundred and fifty dollars a month, but with that sort of man you never know when he'll be off—for the bull ring, maybe."

"Matador!"

"Well, I don't think so. Not as a life work. But he has killed bulls in the ring."

"But how'd you get all this history if he's not been up to the house before?"

"Oh, riding with the boys, we stop down near the cook-house sometimes in the afternoon, and he's there, lying in

124

the hammock maybe, reading. He comes over and talks."

"Coralia, I have my dark suspicions of you."

"You needn't have." But color had come up under Coralia's rich olive skin. "You'll be the first to get any news of that sort."

"Well, I should hope so," Harriet said.

"There isn't the remotest chance of my ever doing anything so completely silly," Coralia continued, liking the subject.

"You can't call getting married silly if you love the man!" Harriet protested.

"Ah, but that's the rub." Suddenly Coralia dropped her light teasing tone and became businesslike and serious. "This is utter nonsense. I would have to meet someone very different from Philip Haagerson," she said. "Besides, I have the boys to think of, and the rancho. And I'm extremely happy just as I am. Especially," she added, "when Miss Townshend of San Francisco and Hawaii is here."

"It's a wonderful feeling," Harriet said, yawning and stretching as a preliminary to saying good night, "those last miles, after we pass the old lumber mill! Something seems to drop off me, fuzziness and the city headache and the smell of the train, and everything is peace. The air does it, or the trees or something. Anyway"—Harriet got to her feet—"anyway, having the boys here, and dear old Father Anselmo, and our two swains just makes the place perfect. It's too big for just two of us and Josito. And I'm going to sleep deep, deep, deep and get up early to ride."

She stooped to kiss Coralia, plumped her pillows, and went to her own room. Closing the door behind her, she stood perfectly still in the center of the dim, big, candlelighted chamber as if turned to stone.

"No, no, no," she said half aloud. And while still automatically brushing her hair, she stopped more than once, stricken motionless, and whispered again, "No. No. No."

"If she ever does marry him, I did it," Harriet told herself. Coralia to marry, and to marry a man against whom Harriet had felt an instant antagonism. He must have felt it for her too, or he could not have phrased so easily, so carelessly, that stinging reproach as he and she had mounted the terrace steps. Her face burned angrily at the memory. His tone said that he did not care a snap of his finger for anything Miss Harriet Townshend did or did not do, but he rather hated to see a fellow male badly treated.

"Now, what can I do to get even?" Harriet thought as she climbed into the enormous four-poster to lie wide awake in the big shadowy room that was striped with moonshine. "I'll do something. I'll go on paying my entire attention to Miles Mulholland. He's worth ten Philip Haagersens!"

She was instantly asleep.

CHAPTER 16

The boys had the place in an uproar in the morning, but when Harriet put her head in Coralia's door her friend was still deep in sleep, and Harriet ran downstairs to join Martin, Pablo, and their tutor at the carriage door, with its ivy-burdened porte-cochere and its iron poles bearing little horses' heads with rings in their mouths.

Josito and his nurse had come down to wave good-by; everything was fresh, shining with beauty and breathing sweetness in the autumn morning. Yellow leaves had fallen from the poplars and were deep under the horses' dancing feet on the drive; the pepper branches were bowed with coral jewels. The air was champagne; Harriet accepted Miles' hard brown hand for a flying mount to the saddle, and raced her horse for the first mile to get the ginger out of his legs. Her escorts followed at a gallop, slowed to a decorous walk when they reached the meadow road, and turned toward the sierra.

A singing morning. Breezes ruffled the wide shallow pools the rains had left in level places; the gutters ran milky coffee. Each horse had his own temperament to deal with, and the riders patted or pulled at the heads, or loosened the short reins for another spurt. The boys' faces reddened, Harriet's hair flew left and right, and even Miles lost something of his sober quiet.

Riding slowly back to the hacienda an hour later, they saw Philip sitting on a fence watching a field in which a few cows and a few mounted cowboys were riding and running apparently at random. He dropped from the fence and came toward them.

"You're all as fresh as daisies this morning!"

"It's the morning," Harriet offered as the little boys galloped away and she and Miles reined in their horses. "We're now just making Mass without a minute to spare."

"You've time. Your hair," said Philip, "looks to be in anything but a devout mood."

"Oh, my veil will fix that!" She was off, with her back very straight on the side saddle, and her full crinoline ballooning. Miles went after her, with a boyish wave of his hand for Philip that showed Philip how far the thawing-out process had gone. Leaves flew up about them; leaves drifted down in a gust of wind. The high blue sky was paler than the faint line of the Sierras etched against the eastern light.

Philip walked up to the house that afternoon with some samples of leather. The old man down by the mill who was making the boys' saddles wished to know if the Señora would like fringes on the stirrups and pommels. Coralia had just come down from her siesta; she sat on the terrace, where the grass was bare burned brown between the bricks and the ivy had knotted itself into a heavy covering of doorway and walls and balustrade, and seriously considered the fringes. The branches of a tall eucalyptus checkered the old adobe of the house walls with moving shadows.

"That was one of the nicest parties of my life," Philip presently said.

"Last night," Coralia said, assenting. "It's so good to have people in the house," she added. "Harriet was speaking of it at breakfast. Father Anselmo, and the boys, and little Josito coming down in his nightgown. Father is wonderful, isn't he? You're a Catholic, of course?" Coralia asked, her handsome eyes wide.

"Of a sort." Philip laughed briefly.

"Oh? But you come to Mass."

"Sundays."

We'll have to convert you," Coralia said maternally.

"Do you know I think you might," Philip said in an under-tone, as if he spoke to himself.

Coralia felt an odd thrill stir deep within her. She found it deeply pleasant to be sitting here so comfortably on her own terrace, with the autumn afternoon burning itself out in golden lights and shadows, the boys well amused somewhere in Miles' charge, and this most personable young man, with his mop of fair hair and his browned hard lean body seated on the wide upper step, almost at her knee, consulting her about grain and grapes and the hiring and firing of hands for the late crops.

"Harriet was sound asleep when I came down. She may be awake now," she presently said. "But she was up at six to ride with Miles and the boys, and she was falling asleep at the lunch table."

Philip was silent a moment. Then he asked:

"Were you in school together?"

"Oh, no. I've only known her about three years. My little boy who was ill—the little boy I took to San Francisco for treatment—we went to her mother's house. My aunt Maria Lopez had been there, and I was somehow afraid of a hotel. I've never been to a hotel; I came here when I was married, and Martin and I never went anywhere."

"He was an invalid?"

"No, but he never had the slightest interest in anything but the rancho. He was king here," Coralia said smilingly. "No, he was very strong, I was the invalid. What with babies and being sick, I didn't get off the second floor for about six years."

"Good heavens!"

"Happy years, too." Coralia had laid aside some fine needlework to study the leather ribbons. Now she picked it up and began to embroider a realistic fat red strawberry. "Everyone spoiled me, and people, cousins and sisters and aunts, came every day to see the babies and amuse me."

"It's a magnificent place to call your home, isn't it?"

"You think so? I suppose I do too, but I've always lived on ranchos. So the city is the great adventure for me. We do have wonderful times in San Francisco."

"I knew a man who was in love with Harriet Townshend. I knew her name long before last night."

"He wasn't the only man!" Coralia ventured with a laugh.

"I suppose not. She made him very unhappy."

"She can't help it." Coralia's eyes danced with fun.

Philip looked at her thoughtfully.

"No," he agreed finally, in an expressionless voice.

Coralia rambled on into comment on Harriet's charms; Harriet was the finest friend she ever had known. Philip agreed that Miss Townshend was a fascinating girl; he had heard of her conquests in San Francisco. They managed to keep close to the subject of love and marriage, and Coralia felt oddly warmed in heart and spirit when she went upstairs a little later.

She found Harriet awake, but still curled up under the afghan that was made of small gay-colored crocheted squares, and reading.

"Why should you look particularly handsome today, señora?"

"Well, I don't know!" Coralia's laugh was deprecatory. "I like white," she said, glancing down at her white dimity, deeply flounced over her crinoline.

"And white likes you," Harriet said. "What've you been doing?"

"Well, I saw the boys off with Miles, and by the way, I like him better and better. He's wonderful with them. They took Josito."

"Josito! Up the Quito!"

"Simply bursting with pride."

"Ana too?"

"No. No nurses on this trip! But I got hold of little Renzo, Maria Refugia's Renzo. And I told him to go along and hold on to the *muchacho*. You never saw such a happy little face! Then old Anita and I went over the sheets."

"How about some duets?" Harriet put her feet on the floor.

"Love it! We can have a good hour before the children

come back. Oh, yes," Coralia added casually, "Philip Haager-sen came up about the boys' new saddles. This old Indian makes them down at San Jose Mission. Look at the fringes."

She had a bunch of them in her hand; Harriet took them and shook them admiringly.

"Lovely colors! And how was the fascinating Philip?"

"Well, I couldn't say fascinating," Coralia said temperately, over by the mirror now and doing something to the braids and ringlets of her thick dark hair. "But he really is interesting. He has had quite a life. He was at Oxford, you know, when he was about fifteen."

"What on earth was he doing there?"

"His stepfather—he was adopted, you know—was sent there, I don't know why. Studying something for some medical business or something. Anyway, he was there."

"So you got the story of his life?"

"It is a funny life," Coralia conceded. "Swedish grand-father——"

"Did he tell you that? I hope you finally got around to the fringes for the saddles."

Coralia laughed joyously.

"Oh, not today. But the day I met him I had such trouble with his name that he explained that it was Swedish."

"I'll concede you this," Harriet said, tied and buttoned into her own flounces now. She came to the mirror and looked in over Coralia's shoulder. "I'll concede you this, that he doesn't seem exactly the type of foreman for a rancho. Not—well, old Arturo's type."

"Heavens, no!" Coralia agreed heartily. "That's it, I think ——" she added, and stopped.

"That's what?"

"Well, that's what sort of puzzled me. When he came up with the bull from the Tia Juana and they put him down in the cookhouse, I didn't pay much attention. He stayed around a few days, but I didn't happen to see him, and I was sur-prised when he came over to me one day when I was driving my mother and Josito around the place. This was just after Arturo died, and everything was in a mess. We stopped the carriage, and he told me a few things that were all wrong and

130

I liked what he suggested, and asked him—I think I said I supposed that he couldn't stay and get things into better shape. Well, he grinned and said he'd like to try, and I said to come up to the house and we could settle it. But we never did," Coralia laughed. "It was taken for granted from then on."

"Hold on to him," Harriet said.

"Oh, I will! He may not know everything," the other woman went on as if arguing, "but he's modern enough to know where he can learn a lot about ranching that I don't know. And speaking Spanish, and having been on the big Bandini and Hernandez places, he's practical enough to impress the men."

Harriet bent her head, brushed vigorously at her glittering mop, occasionally eying the mirror approvingly.

"Is he really going to be a doctor, Coralia?"

"He says so. He's thirty," Coralia stated inconsequentially. "Harriet, I want to say one thing," she added, with a little effort and very seriously. "I never will marry again."

Harriet was silent for a full minute. She had the mirror to herself now; it was a long mirror, set into a bureau with two blocks of narrow, small, carved drawers on either side. Below mirror and drawers was one long deep drawer, and sides and center were finished with heavy slabs of marble. Gray shadows wavered in the mirror, but did little to mar the picture Harriet presently made in her striped taffeta flounces and delicate batiste fichu. Her eyes met Coralia's gravely in the glass; her heart was sick.

"Why do you say that, dearest?"

"Because I mean it. And you must help me."

"With poison in Philip Haagersen's chocolate."

"No. Seriously. I wasn't thinking of him at all, because Oxford or no Oxford one doesn't marry one's foreman." Coralia had gotten this far when a suffocating recollection of the talk on the terrace smote her, and she had to fold it and put it away for later consideration. "We'll have to convert you," she had said, and Philip had not answered, had said in an undertone, as if to himself, "Do you know I think

131

you might." She mustn't forget a syllable of this. Aloud she said feebly: "So that's that."

"A poet and a peasant are waiting for us downstairs," Harriet said in a somewhat dry voice, after a pause in which she had looked directly at Coralia, and Coralia had looked with great attention at other things; a paper on her desk, her left shoe, her handkerchief box.

"Ready," she said. They went downstairs together, commenting on the soft autumn weather and the earlier setting of the sun.

They ruffled through large black books of bound sheet music; found the *Poet and Peasant* and gave it a brilliant rendering, occasionally counting loudly in difficult corners. Afterward they tried Beethoven's Second Sonata, except the introduction, which demanded too much skill. Both girls were breathless and laughing when they finished, and went out to the darkening terrace to watch for the children's return.

Coralia's mind, against her will, almost against her knowledge, had been obsessed for hours with the need of somehow getting in touch with Philip Haagersen again. There seemed to be no pressure about it, no emergency, but she was obliged to think about it, firstly because it might be a little difficult to arrange it naturally, and secondly because she was unable to think of anything else.

Walking back and forth on the fallen leaves of the terrace, watching the last light die from the day, talking animatedly but abstractedly with Harriet, and afterward with Ana Immaculata, who had come down to inquire about Josito, Coralia argued within herself that she was, after all, the mistress here, that what she chose to do in regard to her employees was no one's business but her own, that the only course to follow was the simple natural one. That it would merely mean turning at dinner to any one of the maids who straggled in and out of the dining room at meals with a request that Don Felipe be asked to come up to see the Señora for a few minutes.

"Not for my sake alone," Coralia thought. "But it certainly makes the evenings a little better balanced for Harriet and

Miles, too. I wonder if he plays euchre? He very probably does."

Old Father Anselmo joined them on the terrace, and Coralia was quick to find an excellent excuse for getting hold of Don Felipe. The old priest was malarial, and pleaded that on certain mornings, now that the mornings and evenings were getting so cold, he would like to feel that a more flexible hour for Mass could be set. He would not often abuse the privilege, but he would like to be lazy sometimes, like any other old sinner, he said. And then, situated as he was, he often found it hard to get hold of a messenger.

"I'll send Pepita or Rosalita," Coralia promised eagerly.

"Wait a minute," Harriet said. "Why not put one of the boys from the adobes in one of those empty rooms next to Father's? Then in any emergency he'd have help there."

Walking slowly, they turned, faced the red sunset that was streaming through the western trees and laying long shadows over the barns and sheds and corrals down toward the farm.

"Miles, of course, is 'way upstairs with the boys. They're too much for Ana now, or even for Rita," Coralia mused aloud.

"Coralia, why not Don Felipe?"

Coralia echoed the name questioningly, with no indication of the sudden plunge of her heart.

"Yes, why not? It's always seemed to me that he didn't belong down there in the bunkhouse."

"Well, that's the—that's the place he picked for himself," Coralia offered hesitatingly. "He has the corner room—that was the kitchen before we built the cookhouse."

"I know."

"You've not seen it?" Coralia spoke with involuntary sharpness. Father Anselmo had taken a chair some moments earlier, and Ana Immaculata had discontentedly disappeared.

"Yes, dear, I've seen it," Harriet answered blandly. "I was there all last night."

"You behave yourself!" said Coralia, and the old priest, as they passed him, wondered why youth always could find laughter.

"We could make one of those rooms comfortable," Harriet

reasoned. "Half of them have beds in them already; we can find a big chair or two. What do you think?"

"Well, I think it would be good." Coralia's spirits were soaring far above any indication in her tone. "If Father feels nervous—— Oh, heavens, what's happened! What is it?"

For a bedraggled cortege was winding its way up the garden, and even at first glance it seemed to bode ill. But the chatter of boys' excited voices and Philip Haagersen's voice ringing above them were reassuring: "All right, don't worry!" and Coralia, at the top of the steps now, could control her anxiety as she called out:

"Josito! He's not badly hurt! He's sopping wet!"

"He's all right, we're all all right," Philip said, repeating his earlier message. "Yes, he fell in the creek, didn't you, Josito? Here, you take him, Ana."

Ana, scorning permission, had already come swooping down like an angry eagle and had taken charge of Josito in a storm of muttered imprecations.

"He'll be all right," Coralia said, breathing again. "How did it happen, my precious? Where was Renzo?"

"Renzo fell off his horse when the horse stepped into a bad board on the bridge," Philip explained. "Yes, take him up-stairs, Ana, and get him dry, and get some hot milk into him. Renzo," he went on, turning to the others, "was pulled off his horse, and as he had Josito's horse by the bridle he came down too."

"Renzo hurt?" This was Harriet.

"Yes, I think he was. I sent Miles for the doctor, and the boys came on with me. Get your horses back to the stable, will you, Martin? And take Josito's. Just by chance I heard them as I was crossing down to see Ramon—I think they're all right, it was only a scare."

"Oh, heavens, I am so glad you were there! You picked Josito up?"

"When Mulholland shouted, Pablo's horse was behaving badly. I was afraid one of them would step on the child. But all he got was a good ducking."

"I'll go up and amuse him while Ana gets him some supper," Harriet volunteered.

"I will too!" Coralia exclaimed.

"I wonder," Philip said, arresting her with a touch on her arm, "if you would come down with me to Maria Refugia's. The boy is there, and the doctor perhaps."

It was hardly a request; it was more like a command. Coralia, aroused to her duty, turned instantly from the doorway.

"Of course, of course," she agreed, giving him a half-confused half-grateful look, conscious only of the satisfaction of feeling a man's authority over the bad moment. As they went down the steps into the deep dusk of the garden Harriet, looking from the doorway before going up to Josito and Ana, saw Coralia gather her light shawl about her and put her arm into Philip's.

"Come back and tell me about it," she had called to them as they left, and an hour later they returned to find Father Anselmo, Miles, and Harriet herself before a good coal fire in the back parlor, with chairs and a welcome awaiting them and their news.

To Coralia the episode, indeed, the whole evening, was sweet and satisfying even though she could not settle her thoughts to analyze what made it so. The touch of Philip's hand on her arm, firm and authoritative, his quiet pointing out the way her duty lay had changed her world.

After that everything was like a dream, or like her part in a play. The hour in Maria Refugia's smoky little adobe hut, Renzo's gratitude, the respectful faces and questioning eyes they all had turned toward her, and the warped, copper-colored old Indian doctor who had waited for her nod before beginning his ministrations, and above all, Philip's presence beside her had bound her in a spell; she was still floating in the dream as she joined the group at the fire. Her role as the Señora, the head of them all, and yet the young and still lovely widow who was someday to be won, was the role she would have chosen, just on this night, out of all the world.

When she had ascertained that Josito was snug in bed, fed and dry, and already asleep, and when the reassuring report on Renzo had been made, they fell into happy idle talk. It was after chapel and evening prayers, and the old priest had gone to bed when Coralia broached the subject of Philip's moving up to the hacienda.

"Father is in that wing we scarcely use at all. It's always been called the priest's room; they gave it to priests long ago, even in the days of Martin's father. But he's getting old now, and someone ought to be always within call."

"I could be down at the cookhouse for breakfast," Philip mused.

"Not if you behaved nicely," Harriet told him, her half-closed eyes on the fire, her small form stretched luxuriously in a deep chair. Philip glanced at her quickly and saw the shadows of the thick black lashes on her cheeks, stained apricot by the fire, and her red slippers emerging from a sea of ruffles.

From her he turned his eyes to Coralia, a picture of opulent youthful matronly beauty in her spreading skirts and dark braids.

"I'd like it immensely," he said.

"I'd feel safer about the boys when I'm in San Francisco," Coralia added, her heart dancing.

"Let's pick out chairs and things tomorrow," Harriet said lazily.

"To get the men started for the day, I'll get out early," Philip said, very especially to Coralia.

"But come up to dinner whenever you feel like it. Don't feel bound," she answered, very much the chatelaine receiving reports from her man of affairs.

There was a long drowsy silence broken by groans of protest as the candles were brought in by yawning Tomas, and the necessity of eventual breaking up was indicated.

"Thank you for picking my small boy out of the Quito," said Coralia at the foot of the stairs.

"Ah, if he never gets into worse trouble than that!" the man said, laughing as he turned to go down through the dark night to his own quarters.

136

For the next few days the women of the household were happily engaged in fitting up a big corner room for Philip
Haagersen. Harriet and Coralia, trailed by the boys, and
helped by Miles Mulholland's willing arms, transformed the
dismal wide dusty place into a man's comfortable chamber,
after Ana and Lupe, Lola and Rita had washed and swept
the rough wood floor, brushed heaps of dead flies from the
sills, cut away the encroaching ivy that darkened the windows,
and brought back the old heavy velvet curtains that had been
banished to the attics years ago, when the drawing rooms had
been refurbished.

Upon a fine old chest stood a pitcher and basin in Portuguese silver, elaborately chased, and on a square heavy table
that was bound in dark, ink-spattered leather and covered
with green felt, was a student's lamp with a green shade, an
iron candlestick, an iron inkwell, an iron pounce box. These
had once been used by the master of the house, but not for
some years before his death, and Coralia, who had rarely
seen them in use, in saying to young Martin, "These will be
yours someday, they were Papa's," felt that she had made the
new arrangement quite understandable.

Philip, coming in sweat-stained and dusty after a full day
on the range, stood in the doorway and surveyed the finished
room with great admiration. It was late afternoon, and at
the drawn curtains sunshine was battling to enter. The floor
was still slightly damp, under a few scattered rugs, and the
air smelled of wet wood and ammonia and late roses. On
the bed a Navajo rug had been spread; the roses were in
one of the many jars that gathered in the vestry, next to the
chapel, for altar decoration; a small coal-oil stove, standing
modestly in a corner, was ready for the first sharp cold.

"I'm on my way to clean up," Philip said. "We've been up on the range since five this morning. I thought you ladies would be lying down. Rita, downstairs, told me you'd been at this all day, and she thought you were resting. . . . Say, this is simply wonderful!" he went on. "This is going to be great!"

"Oh, we hope so," Coralia said, on a tired sigh. Her hands were grimy and her braids disordered, but her face had brightened with Philip's arrival. "It does look nice, doesn't it?"

"And look," said Harriet, from a window recess. "All you do is push the curtains back——"

She caught the draperies in her spread hands, opened them, and turned to face the room. The level light, blazing with rubies, poured in about her. Ivy leaves, framing the window, rustled and twinkled; her red hair caught fire.

"And come here and see your view!" she said. "Right clear over to the mountains."

Philip came obediently, and Coralia, too, and the three stood looking out at the treetops and the tiled farm roofs, the milk cows roaming aimlessly about the pasture; men filing into the tangle of fences and sheds on their tired horses, dogs jumping and barking about them with undiminished vigor.

"It's the loveliest place in the world," Harriet said.

"I think it is," the man said quietly. And then abruptly: "Well, I didn't mean to come in looking like this! I'll go clean up."

"Come back to dinner if you like, and we'll give them their satisfaction at euchre," Coralia said boldly. "Why shouldn't I?" she argued in her heart. "We've had many a man at our table in Martin's day who wasn't as much of a gentleman as this one is!"

"Maybe I'll come back for chapel and the game," Philip said, after a moment's hesitation.

"You had better not. I feel very lucky," Harriet said.

"And move in whenever you like," Coralia told him. "You go to Martinez with Tomas tomorrow?"

"Or beyond, as far as the San Antonio, if we don't find the sheep; down to Santa Maria Mission, perhaps."

"We are buying six young sheep," Coralia explained to Harriet.

"Yes, I know."

"Then move in when you come back." Coralia amended it serenely. They all wandered out into the big upper hall and separated, the small boys mounting still higher to join Miles in their own quarters, the old priest passing them as he went toward the chapel, an old crone hobbling by with an armful of sweet, sun-aired linen, Philip disappearing down the wide stairway, Ana in the usual wrestle with Josito at his nursery door, and Coralia and Harriet into Coralia's rooms.

"Oh, I love this afternoon scramble!" said Harriet.

Coralia was standing perfectly still in the center of the floor with her hands over her face.

"Harriet——" she said in a strangled voice.

"Coralia," Harriet countered, pirouetting before the long mirror and twisting her head over her shoulder to see the effect of her ringlets, freed from the net into which they had been pinned all day.

"Nothing," Coralia said, at the wardrobe now, with her face out of view.

It was not until some days later, the last day of Harriet's stay, that she said the words she had cut short. She had been close to tears all day, life would not be the same at the rancho without Harriet.

"Harriet, when will you be back?"

"Oh, after Ma gets a good look at me and Johnny comes to dinner and after Delia's party and the first cotillion. Coralia, you don't know how I hate to go, much as I want to see them. It's been so perfect here, with Father Anselmo and all of us having such fun—time never has raced as it has this visit!"

"Oh, Harriet, if you only mean that!" Coralia said, her lips trembling.

"But I do. Before you know it I'll be back."

Coralia walked to one of the deep-silled windows. The adobe walls of which the house was built were two feet thick; there was no window glass, but between heavy curtains and heavy wooden shutters winter cold and summer heat could be controlled. Tonight both shutters and curtains were opened to the bland autumn airs; Coralia stood looking out into the darkness for a few minutes; then she said hesitantly:

"Harriet, I want to tell you—you're going early in the morning—day after tomorrow——"

She stopped. Harriet was in the rocking chair that had comforted little Cisco in the last hours of his illness. She was thinking, as she tipped lazily to and fro, of the hot little body limp in her arms, and of the languid little voice. She had been a favorite with Cisco; sometimes he had come to her when Ana and his mother had won only a fretful turning away. "I hope Coralia isn't thinking of him," Harriet thought, watching the fine full figure at the window, the dark rich braids, the voluminous skirts.

"Harriet, I'm afraid I'm in love with him," Coralia said. There was a silence. The rocker stopped creaking.

"Well," Harriet said mildly, catching at one word out of her whirling thoughts.

"But Harriet—I can't. I couldn't," Coralia went on, turning back to the window after one glance over her shoulder.

"Why not?" Harriet asked, after a pause.

"Talk to me!" Coralia came over to Harriet's chair and sank on her knees, her arms linked about the other girl's waist. "Talk to me," she said thickly.

"I'm sorry," Harriet said slowly, eyes on Coralia's face.

"Oh, yes, and so am I!" Coralia said quickly. "But why are you, why are you?" she demanded.

"For the same reasons that you are, I suppose. Because it will change things. Because we don't know much about him—we don't know his people——"

"He stayed with the Hernandezes at Tia Juana," Coralia offered as Harriet hesitated.

"Yes, I know. And we know him, and you can't help liking him," Harriet said. "But Ma—Ma is always worrying for fear they have wives and families in the East somewhere!" she went on with a little shame-faced laugh.

"I know he hasn't," Coralia said jealously.

"Well, I don't believe he has. But it would all be so different —and with the boys—and all—oh, Coralia, I don't want you

140

to get married!" Harriet said on a wail that was half playful, half in earnest.

"I don't think there's much danger," Coralia said on a note of irony.

"Why do you say that?"

"Because I haven't the slightest idea that the man has ever given me one moment's thought, in that way, anyway," Coralia said heroically.

"But wouldn't he have had a good deal of audacity if he had?"

"Audacity?"

"Yes. You're the Señora, everything here is yours, everyone here is your employee. He'd be asking to step into a pretty important position, wouldn't he?"

Harriet drew her thumb slowly over Coralia's thick eyebrows, and Coralia caught the hand and kissed it. She could not help a half-smile that had something of gratification it it.

"Those things don't count."

"Of course they count!"

"I never thought of that side of it," Coralia said slowly.

"I don't suppose you did. But he may have," Harriet said. "I mean—I mean, it might well make him hesitate," she added hastily at Coralia's look.

"He probably isn't in the least in love with me," Coralia said. "And I know there's an awful lot to think of, on my side. Martin's three boys will inherit this place, and the other ranchos, too, and they'll need all the guidance I can give them. It's nonsense—it's nonsense to think of any change. I know that."

"But you love him," Harriet said quietly.

Color burned in Coralia's face.

"I can't help it," she whispered. "I can't think of anything else. I can't get him out of my mind. That day when we fixed his room and he came in all dirty and perspiry, it didn't make any difference. And last night, when he put his hand over mine while we were playing euchre, remember?—it went right through me. When he said, 'Señora, the jack is the

141

left bower,' I thought I would die—really, I felt—oh, every which way!"

"I'll kill him if he doesn't love you!" Harriet sputtered.

"Oh, don't," Coralia said with a broken laugh. "No, truly," she went on, "he has never given me the slightest reason to think that he was interested. He's never said one word of love, or anything like that. This is entirely my own doing. But that doesn't help. You see, it's not like one of the old family friends—one of the distant cousins. It's not like anyone I've known all my life, for whom I might form an affection with a—with something behind it——"

"With a background," Harriet supplied.

"Exactly. I've nothing to go on," Coralia said. "And it isn't anything I can seem to control," she went on, distressed and puzzled. "I'll get over it, I know that. But meanwhile—Hattie, I'm so afraid he'll never care, I'm so afraid he'll go away. And I never have known anyone like him, never. I never have known anyone in the least like him."

"But, Coralia, I can't see how he can do anything else but fall in love with you!" Harriet said generously.

"You like him better than you did?" Coralia asked by way of reply.

"I never disliked him, you know. I felt that he wasn't particularly sympathetic to me, or I to him," Harriet answered, wrinkling her forehead in thought. "He snubbed me the very first time he came up for dinner, the night I got here; that is, he seemed to think I was leading Miles to his destruction, when of course I wasn't."

"He did? You never told me. What did he say?"

"I didn't tell you because it made me mad. Miles can take care of himself. How did he know Miles wasn't flirting with me, I'd like to know!"

"I don't," said Coralia with an irrepressible giggle, "see Miles flirting!"

Harriet laughed too, a little unwillingly.

"Well, maybe not. You know," she pleaded, "I can't help being civil."

"Civil!" Coralia echoed significantly.

"Well, honestly, he isn't unhappy."

"He's too sensible to cry for the moon."

"And look here," said Harriet, suddenly quite sober, and speaking seriously, "if you want Philip, why, there's no question that you can get him. Here you are in the position of the mistress—the chatelaine—he can't do anything without consulting you. You see him every day——"

"Harriet," Coralia interrupted, with a rapt, faraway look, "when I think of what it would mean—if he cared—if he really wanted me!"

"But think a minute. Would you go to Edinburgh if he wanted to study medicine?"

"Oh, yes!"

"Coralia, how long have you felt this way?"

"Oh, a long time. Or, I don't know. I don't know how I feel," Coralia confessed with a puzzled shred of laughter. "It's all so strange! The minute he isn't here I'm planning how to see him. And then when he comes I feel quite cool, and as if it didn't so much matter. But then everything he says I remember, and save up to think about, and it makes me all trembly again."

Harriet tightened her arms for a moment and kissed her companion on the cheek.

"I hope it all comes right," she said, getting to her feet. "And that he's the right person, the right man out of all the world for you. I'm going to pray about it."

"It seems too much happiness to come to me," Coralia said humbly. "I've so much now. My boys, and the rancho, and you. I'd given up the idea that marriage would come my way again.

"After all, what don't you like about him, Harriet?" she presently said as Harriet lingered on her way to the door, turning back more than once to air some undiscussed phase of the fascinating topic.

"I think he's stunning."

"No. But do you mean he's not your type?"

"I'll tell you frankly," Harriet said, coming back into the room, "that he's not a type. He's not like anyone else. A man who has killed bulls and lived at Oxford and will take a job running a rancho is not the usual cotillion partner."

"Indeed he isn't!" Coralia agreed, her eyes shining. "What would your mother think?"

"Oh, disapproval at first. But after that she'd probably fall in love with him too. He certainly would be more interesting than any of my sisters' husbands. But this is all nonsense!"

"And it's not nonsense that you may be engaged any time now, soon," Harriet mused.

"Harriet, I tell you I have nothing to go on!"

"Oh, but that part's all right," Harriet said confidently. "And good heavens, how I'll miss you!"

"But why should you? You don't think this is going to make any difference?"

"It can't help but make some. I've had experiences with new husband and the wives' school friends. But if you're happy I'll be happy," Harriet said, with an April face and in a voice that was not steady. "Good night, dearest." And she was gone.

Coralia sat still, looking at herself in the mirror.

"Life is horrible," she said half aloud, after a while.

The following night was the last of Harriet's visit, and great plans were under way for a farewell party. Both Harriet and Coralia, although neither expressed it, were conscious that the confusion of a party would be a welcome break in the emotional strain of the evening, and arrangements were made to include not only the little boys, but two dark-chinned serious young men from the Santa Clara college, cousins of Coralia.

Benediction in the chapel was as usual, then two fires were lighted in the steel-rodded grates in the parlors, and the old black music books were brought out. First Coralia played, and then Harriet, for endless songs; then Harriet sang "Adelaide" with great feeling. When the boys were sent to bed there came up from the farm a three-piece orchestra consisting of the Silvas, father and son, with two violins, and Jose Riviera, uncle of the senior Silva, to play the piano, and there was dancing.

By this time refreshments of varied sorts had been served;

144

there was a claret punch in Coralia's big cut-glass bowl, and plates of small cakes and sweet breads, chocolates and purple grapes and golden persimmons from the farm were set about everywhere. One of the old cooks, brown of skin and wrinkled like a peach stone, brought up a small bowl of some rich custard that was ice-cold and flavored with rum and orange and cinnamon; the company, warmed by dancing by this time, ate it gratefully from the punch cups and Coralia kissed the beaming cook. It was midnight when the musicians, also fortified with food and drink, went away, and Coralia, Miles, and the two shy cousins sat down for a last game of euchre.

"I'll cut in, I'll cut in!" Harriet assured them. "I couldn't play now, I'm absolutely out of breath!"

"Next game then." Coralia arranged it, looking at her first hand. Harriet stepped across a bare dimly lighted dark hall and through the open door onto the terrace, drawing in great breaths of the cold sweet air and turning her hot face up to the faint night breeze.

A step on the stone flags startled her; a man was coming up from the blackness of the garden. Philip.

"Oh, you scared me!" Harriet half laughed, half gasped.

"I had to see the Silvas down as far as the turn, where they could see lights from the farm. They were all scared to death!" Philip explained, a little out of breath. He glanced toward the oblong of light that was the hall doorway.

"They're playing euchre," Harriet told him. "But Luis and Jose want to go to bed after the first game, so we can take their places."

"And you leave us tomorrow."

"Yes. But fortunately it's a general breaking-up. Ana and Miles and the boys go to their grandmother tomorrow, for Lupe's wedding next Thursday, and Coralia herself goes on Friday. They'll be gone two weeks anyway. So you'll be all alone with Father Anselmo. Yes, isn't it gorgeous?"

They both looked up at the great inverted bowl of the stars and were silent. Harriet felt her hand gripped in his as he stood beside her; other big male hands had held hers under somewhat similar circumstances, but this was different.

145

Her throat thickened and she felt her heart beat faster. She drew her hand away.

"Won't have anything to do with me?" Philip said mildly. Harriet was angry, and did not speak. "What's the trouble, Harriet?" he asked.

They had decided upon the use of each other's given names a day or two earlier, but Harriet had not taken advantage of the decision up to this point, nor had she heard Philip use her name.

"No trouble," she said coldly.

"We just didn't start right. You didn't like me from the moment you were down at the corrals, on that other visit."

"I didn't like being told I was a shallow little heartless fool," Harriet said, betrayed into speech against her will.

"I don't remember using those words, exactly."

"You didn't have to."

Philip said nothing for a moment, but when Harriet made a sudden movement as if to go away, he gripped her hand again.

"I happened to be fond of Stewart Filmer," he said.

"Yes, and so was I!" Harriet exclaimed, her face hot. "So was I! But you can't marry everyone who asks you. I felt very badly, I wrote his mother. He's all right again, he's down with her in San Diego."

"Yes, that's where I met him. I told him no girl was worth that, or half that!"

"I'm sure you were right," Harriet said politely, her voice shaking.

"Ah, no, now," Philip said coaxingly. "Be nice about it. You did let him think he was number one."

"And so he was. And so we were both deceived," Harriet stormed. "And perhaps you will tell me what business it is of yours! The very night I arrived here you interfered with my friendship for Miles, who has no more idea of falling in love with me than that star!"

"I wouldn't be so sure of that."

"Well, I am. He wants to go to Rome, and study, and someday write a book on iconography."

"On what?"

"Halos, he says. Nimbuses. Crowns for different saints."

"Ah!" Philip commented, with a laugh in his voice.

"I like Miles, and I respect him," Harriet said in a hurt and dignified voice.

"You know you don't fool me one little bit," Philip told her, still anchoring her beside him with a firm hold on her fingers.

"I don't attempt to fool you. Your opinion of me is the last thing in the world I care about," Harriet countered.

"You must have a man's complete subjugation, eh? And then be everything that is kind and sisterly as you send him away. But what does it get you? Who's happier?"

"If you'll please let go my hand," Harriet raged, after a sudden futile struggle to be free.

"In a minute. You see, I've known other girls like you, Harriet. Girls whose boast it was that they could get any other girls' beaux away from them. They don't always turn out so well. They've a funny way of marrying suddenly and foolishly."

Harriet stood perfectly still until his voice died away. Then she said mildly: "I wonder if you and I couldn't agree to disagree. I'll be here a good deal. Coralia trusts you; she is delighted you can stay and take over the rancho. Suppose we try just being civil to each other?"

"Suppose you stop talking like a little Puritan who doesn't know what it's all about?" Philip said. Harriet caught one quick breath as he locked his arms about her, and with a big hard hand gripped her chin. His mouth was upon her, and she felt that her ribs would break as he pressed her tightly against him. She made no attempt either to fight or to speak, but when Philip released her she walked back into the house, without a word or look, and came in upon the euchre players, who were just finishing their game.

The round mahogany table at which they were playing was lighted by a heavy lamp, lowered on a chain from the ceiling. The rest of the room was in darkness except for candles burning on the far mantel. If there was anything strange in Harriet's aspect no one noticed it, and as Coralia eagerly begged for one more game, on this last night, and

147

Philip, sauntering nonchalantly in just as the brothers were saying their good nights, seconded the motion, Coralia, Harriet, Philip, and Miles found themselves ending the festive evening with a spirited game of euchre.

"Let's beat these men, Coralia, they're so sure of themselves. We can beat them!"

"Let's draw," Coralia suggested. To Harriet's satisfaction Coralia and Philip were paired by the draw, and she took on Miles, and sparkled away at him so irresistibly that she won from him the reluctant, almost painful laughter in which he so rarely indulged.

Her giddiness finally affected the others so that they were all presently in that state when any word or syllable added to their over-wrought spirits produced fresh outbursts.

"Oh, let's stop this, it's so silly!" Coralia gasped, tears on her cheeks.

"Analyze it once," the serious Miles began shakily. He choked, snatched out his handkerchief, put his elbows on the table and gave way to it, shaking silently, his face in his hands.

"Analyze it," Philip began on a low firm note that rose suddenly to shrillness as he attempted to rush in the words, "and it's simply idiotic!"

Harriet put her head down on the cards and writhed with suppressed hysterics and Coralia in a voice that was like a whinny managed to get out the words "Please stop. Please. I hurt."

After an interval they were all suddenly sober and busy with the game again, and after the game there were brief, weary good nights. The party had been wonderful; now the fires were low and the rooms getting cold. The servants had long gone to bed, and the girls looked jaded and pale. Coralia and Miles went upstairs first; Harriet, to her annoyance, found Philip beside her.

"Mad?" he asked her in a cheerful undertone. Harriet made no answer. "Don't go away mad tomorrow," Philip said. "Aw, be nice, Harriet, we've all had such a good time this week."

148

"See you later, Coralia!" Harriet called as she and her candle vanished at her own door. She did not speak to Philip or look at him again.

CHAPTER 18

Twenty minutes later Harriet, clad in a warm quilted robe securely belted with tasseled cords, with her bright hair loosed in a cloud on her shoulders and her brush in her hand, crossed the dark upper hall to Coralia's door. As she approached it a door that led to the west wing of the house, where the old priest and Philip were quartered, opened and an oblong of weak light illumined the figure of Philip coming toward her.

"Mum's the word!" he said in a low voice. He caught at her hand and jerked his head toward the passage from which he had come. They entered it silently, for Harriet, enraged and half frightened though she might be, instinctively made sure that Coralia should hear no disturbance. To allow her to open her door on this scene would be sheer madness.

Once in the rear hall Philip closed the door behind them and said in a serious quiet tone that reassured her in spite of herself, "I didn't want to disturb Coralia and I was anxious to speak to you. You see you're going away tomorrow, and so I have to talk to you tonight, it's my only chance."

"I honestly don't want to talk at all to you tonight," Harriet said, "tonight or at any other time."

"I see you're still angry. Was that such a terrible thing I did?"

"Is that what you have to say?"

"No. But why was it so terrible? Men have kissed you before this."

Her face blazed.

149

"Whether they have or haven't, what you did was an insult, and you meant it to be," Harriet said very low. "I'm not discussing it. I'm not denying that men I have liked, men with whom I've had good times, have kissed me. But not that way. Now that's all I'm going to say, and if you have anything more to say I wish you'd say it, and from then on let me alone."

"I will certainly do so. What I have to say is that we may not meet again, for I am leaving the rancho."

"For good?" Harriet asked, surprise killing anger.

"Yes. If I'm ever going to do anything I'd better get started."

"You mean for Scotland—to be a doctor?"

"Well, that," he said, and in the dim light she could see a rather twisted smile, "maybe that, someday. But the first thing is bread and butter."

"You haven't anyone to help start you?" Harriet's irrepressible interest in her fellow man had softened her mood now, indeed changed it completely. "This will kill Coralia!" she thought.

"Nobody. I'm a lone wolf. You see I didn't come here just to bring Bruno to the rancho Heart of Gold."

"I thought you brought the bull up from the Hernandez place at Tia Juana?"

"I did. But it wasn't quite like that. It was because old Juan told me that there was a handsome widow here, with fourteen thousand acres in grapes and cattle——"

"Oh no!" Harriet said in distaste. "I don't believe you."

"Well, at least you see that I'm not going through with it."

"You mean to try to marry Coralia for her money—why, what a horrible old man Don Juan Hernandez must be!"

"No. Only European in his ideas. After all, I couldn't get her if she didn't like me," Philip argued. "And I've never given her any reason to suppose that any such plan was in the back of my mind."

"But you do like her?" Harriet demanded, secret hope for Coralia's hopes rising in her heart.

"Of course I do. You have to like her. She's magnificent, with her servants and her horses and her sons. But there are

things that—there are elements that make for—well, romance. And then there aren't. And you might as well expect
to change the weather as to change the way you feel."

"Oh, don't I know that!" Harriet said with a little sigh.

Philip looked at her thoughtfully.

"Yes, I suppose you would," he conceded.

Harriet came to a sudden decision. She spoke eagerly.

"Philip, would it make any difference if I told you that
I believe Coralia would—would like you to stay? I oughtn't
to say this—she wouldn't forgive me—but I think she would
like you to stay."

"No, it wouldn't make any difference. I think I knew that."

Harriet was silent. They looked away from each other.

"That would only make my staying here—my trying to
carry out old Juan's plan—the worse," Philip presently said.
"It was that, I think, that made me see how rotten it was!"

Another silence, which again the man broke with an
abrupt:

"Well, are you going to your room, or in to see her?"

"In to see her. We always do, every night. We talk things
over."

"Good Lord, I should think you would be dead tonight!"

"I am. And we're off at eight in the morning."

They stepped into the wide dark front hall again. Philip
guided Harriet to Coralia's door, and she looked up at him
and whispered good night.

"Good night and good-by, Philip. Come back when you're
a famous doctor."

"Thank you. Good night, Harriet."

He was gone, and she opened Coralia's door and went in.

Coralia was standing by one of the windows; she was still
dressed. As the younger woman came in, Coralia turned her
back upon her. Harriet advanced a few steps, stopped.

"Coralia, what—what—is something the matter?"

"You know what's the matter," Coralia said, half turning
her head. Under Harriet's feet the solid earth plunged. She
could not speak. "You know what you've been doing,"
Coralia said.

"What I've been doing!"

"Yes. Today, and tonight, since I told you——" Coralia choked and stopped short.

"What on earth are you talking about?" Harriet demanded, almost as if speaking in amused impatience to a child.

"Oh, please don't take that tone," Coralia begged, beginning to tremble.

"Then tell me what's the matter?"

"If you don't know, there's no use telling you."

"I haven't the faintest idea!"

"I never would have believed it of you," Coralia said in a low trembling voice. She seated herself at the bureau, facing the mirror, and picked up a brush, studying its bristles intently.

"Believed what?" Harriet was beginning to tremble too. Her knees weakened suddenly, and she sank into a chair without moving her eyes from Coralia's reflection in the mirror. There was a silence, and Coralia began to hum as she brushed her loosened braids.

"You oughtn't to brush your hair in that good dress," Harriet said, almost automatically.

"Dress!" Coralia echoed the word scornfully, but she arose, went to the wardrobe and took out a nightgown and a striped flannel wrapper. Deliberately she took off the gauze and tarlatan ruffles of her dress, stepped out of the frame of the hoops and the embroidered underwear beneath it. Then, robed and slippered, she returned to her seat. Harriet watched her steadily.

"Are you going to tell me what you're talking about?"

"No. Because you perfectly well know."

"I don't perfectly well know. I know we had a beautiful party tonight, and dancing and everything, and I know it's nearly half past one o'clock and I'm dead, and now you start this mysterious talk of something I've done. What have I done, for heaven's sake?"

"As far as Philip goes, you can have him," Coralia said in a bitter voice. "Take him!"

"Philip!" Harriet echoed, bewildered.

"Take him," Coralia repeated, rebraiding her heavy hair.

"You mean that you think I'm trying to get Philip Haagersen!"

"You're trying to get everyone," Coralia said, sorrowful and gentle. "I see it and everyone sees it. Father Anselmo, Miles, my cousins, everyone. But I didn't think—I didn't think——" Her voice thickened and her full bosom rose on a stormy breath that tightened the flanges of her nose and made her bite her full underlip to maintain control.

"I'll tell you what I think," Harriet said, warming to fury, "I think you're crazy!"

"Oh, no, I'm not crazy. I see what I see," Coralia assured her lightly. Still breathing hard, but with her tears dried by anger now, she pinned her hair severely back for the night and put on a lace cap. "Carrying on with him all through dinner to make Miles mad, and then—oh, you'll be so obliging, you'll cut out of the first game——"

"We all cut!" Harriet reminded her hotly.

"Of course we did! And you drew lower than Luis Ybarra did. But you said he and Jose wanted to get to bed early so you made Jose change with you."

"Ah, so I did," Harriet murmured, remembering.

"Oh, now you remember? D'you remember going out on the terrace to meet Philip right afterward?"

"To meet——Coralia, you have no right to talk to me this way!"

"I have a right to talk to you any way I please!"

"Pooh!" Harriet muttered scornfully. "If that's the way you feel——" she began.

"That is the way I feel," Coralia assured her quickly, as Harriet paused. "I feel that the woman I always felt was my best friend has thought it was great fun to show me how easily she could get any man she went after. Oh, don't glare at me, I'm not afraid of your glaring! I'm merely heartsick—yes, heartsick—to think that that was all our friendship meant to you."

"I had no idea Philip would be on the terrace. He was taking the Silvas home. We weren't there two minutes before we came in."

"Will you give me your solemn word he didn't kiss you in those two minutes?"

"What on earth makes you think he did?"

"Will you give me your word?"

"I don't think you ought to ask me that!" Harriet protested.

"Well, I do. Ana saw you."

"Oh, for heaven's sake, is this a convent?"

"No, it's not a convent, it's a place where you could tell a person something in confidence without thinking she would run off and tell everyone else about it!" Coralia stammered with a dry sob.

"If you think for one instant——" Harriet began stiffly.

"Ana saw you," Coralia said simply, in the pause.

"Ana saw nothing of the kind. What she saw had no significance whatever, and anyway nothing meant anything, and she hadn't the faintest idea of what she saw!" Harriet protested somewhat confusedly.

"Tomorrow morning you're going early," said Coralia, giving a deep weary sigh, blowing her nose and wiping her eyes. "I won't see you again. I never thought it would be like this, but since you can't deny that Ana saw what she saw —or at least," Coralia went on, weakening a little, "at least you haven't denied it——"

She paused. Harriet continued her scornful stare.

"And you were in his room tonight," Coralia said.

"How dare you say a thing like that to me!" Harriet's face was white.

"I went to this door half an hour ago and looked into the hall because I thought you might be coming across to say good night, as you always have, as I've always loved you to do," Coralia said, breaking into tears, "and you and Philip were going into the other hall, to his room."

"You mean here—just now?"

"Yes. Before you came in here."

"And you think I went to his room?"

"I saw you!"

"And you're willing to believe that?"

"I believe my own eyes."

"Coralia, never as long as I live will I forgive you for say-

154

ing that! No one ever has spoken to me that way. I stepped into the other hall because Philip wanted to say good-by. I won't see him in the morning. And for you to put such an evil construction on half a dozen perfectly insignificant episodes just shows me that you don't have the slightest confidence in me, you don't believe me, and you're perfectly willing to spoil the finest friendship anyone ever had! No, don't you say a word!" Harriet raged, her Irish blood pitted against the other woman's Spanish anger, and brain and heart in such turmoil that she knew neither what she said nor what she did. "Philip never has paid the slightest attention to me. He came here because he heard how attractive you were, you, you, you! Now good-by, and don't get up in the morning because I never will speak to you again, I never will forgive you, and I never will speak to you again!

"I'm sorry about Josito——" Here tears overcame her, and with an incoherent sound in which jumbled accusations of Coralia's cruelty and of her interpreting perfectly innocent actions in the vilest possible sense, and of Harriet's consternation at discovering that she had had a false opinion of what her love meant to Coralia and that Coralia apparently was incapable of true friendship, Harriet disappeared, closing the door gently behind her. Ana and Josito were in the adjoining room; they mustn't be disturbed at this unearthly hour.

She closed her own door quietly, too, and entered her own cold, big, bare room, so different in the dark silent night from what it was in the heavenly dawn, before Mass, and in the warm daytime hours. While she had been dressing tonight there had been a good coal fire glowing behind the steel rods, and Coralia and Josito and Ana, and now and then one of the other maids, had been cheerfully circulating in and out, all in a gala mood of getting ready for the party.

Now the party was over and the moon had set, the ashes in the grate were cold and the room smelled of plaster and old wood and mice. Harriet put out the candle on her bedside table and sat for a while on the edge of her bed, staring into the dark, thinking.

When she finally got into bed, it was not to sleep. She was too nervous, too physically and emotionally exhausted. The scene in Coralia's room had profoundly shocked her, and she found herself saying half aloud, more than once, "But I don't believe it!"

That Coralia should suspect her of flirtation was nothing. Harriet had aroused such suspicions in almost all her women friends at one time or another. But usually the criticism was expressed with laughter, or with a reproach so affectionate that it caused more fun than hurt.

Coralia hadn't been joking. She had been in dead, furious earnest; she had said terrible things, believed terrible things.

Harriet determined upon a course of action. She would go home in the morning after brief and quiet farewells, avoiding any hint of trouble between Coralia and herself. And then she would never again see the rancho or the boys, Father Anselmo, Ana, the loved chapel, the trails under the redwood trees. She would get no more letters from Coralia and scribble no more long letters in reply. It was all over.

Life looked bleak as she tossed and turned and tried to imagine her days without this friendship. Winter would soon be sharp and clear over San Francisco; Tamalpais cut in gray stone against a gray sky, and the bay ruffled with whitecaps. The pepper trees out at the Presidio would hang with scarlet tassels, and in the gardens of Officers' Row nasturtiums and geraniums and fuchsias would bloom right through to Christmas and bridge the gap until the first acacia came gold and fragrant in January.

Winter would bring the cotillions, and debutante parties and dances, and Miss Harriet Townshend's mirror would be stuffed with engraved invitations. And there was always church, too, and charity calls for Ma, and cheering visits to poor Lizzie in the Mission. There would be blowy days on the bay, on somebody's yacht, and San Mateo visits to some of the big houses with the stone gates. She would keep busy, and in time——

The bitter tears welled up again. They dampened her hot pillow and she sat up, reached about in the dark and lighted her candle, went to the window and let the cool air blow on her face. Suddenly she knew that she must see Coralia—she must do something—this couldn't go on——

There was a crack of light under Coralia's door; Harriet's heart leaped. She was awake, she couldn't sleep either! Harriet crossed the hall, laid her hand on the knob, and stood trembling. It was a long minute before she opened the door and stepped inside. Coralia's candle was lighted; she was lying on her back, with her hands locked behind her head. She had been crying too.

"Oh, Coralia, I'm so sorry! I've been going nearly crazy——"

Harriet got no further. Coralia was out of bed, had crossed the floor, and the two were in each other's arms, laughing and crying hysterically as the agony of the long wakeful hours was washed away.

"Coralia, I didn't mean anything I said! I've been *sick*, I've been lying awake——"

"Oh, Harriet, so have I. I've not been asleep——Oh, what is it, Ana?"

For Ana, in a nightgown of yellow and red, with her heavy black hair tied up into knobs with strips of white rag and her dark face shiny with soap and water, had come tiptoeing in. Being assured that all was well, she did not leave the room, a course that was indicated in her mistress' man- she disappeared, to return presently with two cups of smok- ner, but unobtrusively built up the fire, pouring in a whole scuttleful of coal and clamping on the black tin blower. Then ing chocolate on a tray. Her manner was martyred, virtuous despite ill-treatment.

By this time Coralia and Harriet were seated before the now roaring fire on the old sofa that was heaped with pillows, and with their tired faces radiant and their eyes shining, were deep in the exquisite refreshment of making the peace. Harriet's left hand was held in Coralia's right, their slippers were stretched toward the crackling warmth of good madroña logs and the glowing heat of Coos Bay coal. Both had been crying; tears were still drying on their faces, but they were talking quietly now and the world was all right again.

They welcomed the foamy chocolate gratefully, and Ana could return to her own cold bed in the adjoining room with a satisfied sense that she had taken good care of her young ladies. The talk before the fire went on.

"Let's never think of it again, Coralia."

"Oh, never. I don't know what got into me."

"I was the one."

"Oh, no, you weren't! You never did a mean thing in your life."

"Ask Johnny. I used to torment the life out of him. Ma made him take me off every Saturday morning, when the girls were cleaning the house, and did I pester him and his friends!"

"I wish I'd known you in those days, down in the Islands."

"I was a redheaded devil, I know it. But I learned last night what you and the boys and the rancho mean to me, Coralia, and I'll never risk it again."

"You didn't risk anything," said Coralia's deep rich voice.

"I was sicker than you were! I thought I was going mad."

"D'you suppose married people quarrel that way?" Harriet asked, out of a moment's musing.

"I suppose they do. Martin and I didn't; he was three times my age and I respected him, he was boss here, everyone did what he said, and so did I."

"Coralia, look what's happening at the window!"

"Have mercy, God!" Coralia said in her mother tongue. And then laughing, "Sunrise! Harriet Townshend, we've talked all night!"

They went to the window and looked toward the east. A flaming sunrise had reddened all the sky and was painting streaks of vermilion on the dark trunks of the oaks and eucalyptus. Through the opened shutters the morning air poured in, sweet and cool; it touched their fire-flushed faces as the two women laughed at each other.

"Harriet, your hair! You look like a mop."

"And you look like a lady walking along Dupont Street."

"Listen, if we're going to get any sleep at all, we'd better get to bed. Harriet," Coralia began again, on a different note, "there's one thing I have to say to you. *Mea culpa.*"

The phrase from a familiar prayer brought Harriet's quick look to Coralia's face.

"What mortal sin is on your mind?"

"Not a mortal sin," Coralia smiled. "But just straightening things out. You know that I told you that Ana had said that she saw you and—and Philip on the terrace, while we others were playing euchre?"

Harriet nodded, her face suddenly scarlet.

"Well. I wasn't going to tell you this. But it's only fair to Ana to say that she wasn't snooping—she wasn't spying. She thought it was a romance between you and Philip, and of course"—it was Coralia's turn to redden—"of course she didn't know how I feel about him," she said. "She was delighted to be in on a love affair, and she came whispering and smiling in here while I was undressing and told me she was sure that Don Felipe and the Señorita were in love with each other. It wasn't spying, she had no idea I would be cut to the heart by it. And I didn't let her see it!"

"Well, now I'll tell you something, Coralia," Harriet said, with a little stress on the pronouns, "that I didn't mean to. And I'm not sure now that it's right!

"But anyway, I'm going to. Philip and I were fighting when Ana saw us on the terrace; I was furious. Truly! He said something that made me mad—anyway, I think what he wanted to do was shake me until my teeth fell out. He and I never have gotten along. But here's the thing, Coralia. When Philip came here he was deliberately taking a foreman's position to find out what you were like."

"Harriet!"

"I mean it. Let me tell you. You know old Tio Juan, of the Hernandez rancho? Well, Philip was there, on a sort of holiday, working with the bulls, and someone said that you wanted any bull they sold as not fierce enough for the ring in Mexico City."

"Yes, I know, and he brought the bull up here," Coralia said, staring, puzzled.

"Well. Old Tio Juan had told Philip that you were handsome and lovely and rich and that you needed a man to help raise the boys——"

"He didn't!" Coralia said angrily.

"Yes, he did."

"Then you think," Coralia asked proudly, "that he's simply a fortune hunter?"

"I think exactly the opposite, and I'll tell you why! He came up here, and I suppose that whether he thought you needed a man with the boys or not, he saw that you did need a foreman. So he stayed. And according to what he told me he got more and more disturbed, in his mind, you know, about the idea that you were rich, and he had nothing, and if he did begin to love you and you got fond of him——"

Harriet hesitated, and Coralia, clutching Harriet's arm tightly, but still looking out of the window, said tensely:

"Harriet, do you believe it?"

"I do. Why should he say it if it wasn't true?"

"But then, Harriet——"

"So he's going away. Yes, he actually is, Coralia, you needn't look so surprised. He said good-by to me because he means to be gone before I come back. I don't know what excuse he'll give you, but he said, 'No, she's too fine, she's too nice. She'd find out someday that it was a sort of plot on her uncle's part——' "

"But there was no harm in that plot!" Coralia said, turning a face as radiant as the sunrise to Harriet's. "Oh, Harriet, I'm so happy! I can't help it! You don't know what it means to think that he might care, that he and I might someday be here, running the rancho together. Harriet, this is true, isn't it?"

"Absolutely. And of course I don't know that you can keep him, Coralia. He was in dead earnest. He said that he couldn't bear it if ever you found out that he had known when he came here that you might someday be thinking of another marriage, and that you owned the Salazar rancho, and so on."

"Harriet, do you believe it really is this way?"

"Believe it! Of course I do. And so would you if you'd heard him. He didn't make much of it, he simply said that he had not understood the sort of person you are, and there never had been any chance of his going through with any such plan."

160

"Oh, Harriet, wouldn't it be wonderful if it really came out that way!"

"Wonderful for you," Harriet said dryly. But she smiled, too.

"I believe you'd be jealous!" Coralia exulted. "But not for long. Because we'd both want you, like a sister, in our lives, always, always, always."

"But let me warn you that he's really going away!"

"Now let's see," Coralia said in a businesslike tone that indicated that she was planning a campaign. "First, when is he going?"

"He didn't say. But soon."

"We'll not let him go," Coralia said confidently, speaking half to herself. "Oh, Harriet, don't go. Stay and help me keep him here."

"You don't need me," Harriet said.

"I can't believe," Coralia said, "that he actually was going away because he hasn't the courage——"

"Not exactly that, no. He's going away because he came here with one set of impressions, or motives, or something, and he feels now that they—well, that they aren't what he thought they were, and so he's going away."

"Harriet, doesn't that make you feel that he really is an unusual sort of man?"

"We've always said that."

"I know we have. . . . Remember, I've no business to tell you this."

"Oh," said Coralia fervently, "I'm so glad you did! I won't know how to look him in the face at breakfast, but I'm so glad to know! Oh, Harriet, I hope you are right, I hope you are! It's five o'clock, are you going to bed?" she added as they crossed the room.

Harriet rested her head on Coralia's shoulder, spoke as if out of sleep. Her words were broken by rending yawns.

"I have to. It's hardly worth while, if I'm leaving at eight— but hoo-hoo-hoo—I'm dying of sleep——"

"Tomas never starts on time. Get an hour's sleep anyway, I'm going to," Coralia said. But she knew she would not sleep. She was too happy, too excited for sleep. She needed to be alone, to think over this miracle. When Harriet was gone she went back to the window and kneeled down with her arms crossed on the sill and looked down at the garden, and the orchards beyond, and the line of the mountains again beyond, and fell into a waking dream.

Harriet's thoughts were less satisfying. She felt distinctly uneasy. It had been on a momentary impulse to do and say what would make Coralia happy, what would help wipe out the shock and bitterness of their first quarrel, that she had given Coralia her version of Philip's position. She knew, of course, that Philip was not in love with Coralia; he was not going away because he felt unworthy of her.

Well, Harriet hadn't said that he was in love, she hadn't said that he was going away because his love was hopeless, because his coming to the rancho had been for unworthy motives. She had only meant to give Coralia the exciting fact that she had been talked of as a wife for Philip, she had meant only to indicate that he wouldn't go on under the present circumstances, and let Coralia make what she would of it.

So Coralia was under a false impression—had jumped at conclusions that were only half true.

"That's not my fault," Harriet muttered, abandoning all idea of returning to bed and beginning to pack in a desultory and irresolute fashion. One of the kitchen girls brought her up a pitcher of hot water at about seven, and she joined other members of the family at Mass. After all, she and Tomas and the lumbering big carriage did not get off until long after nine o'clock. Philip did not put in an appearance, but everybody else was on hand to say good-by to the Seño-rita, and even shed a few tears over her departure. Coralia had the last embrace, and Harriet, as they swept down the drive, settled back against the hard cushions consoling herself with the thought that after all, destiny was destiny, nobody could predict the outcome of all these mistakes and misunder-standings; it might as well be good as bad.

She was tired, jaded. Scenes from the crowded last hours kept moving through her mind. She half dozed as the carriage jolted along, and dozed again in the hot train. There was a coal stove in the car; the seats were of heavy red velvet; the air had an acrid taste of smoke. Harriet's head ached.

CHAPTER 19

It was good to get home to her mother. Harriet clung to the big sturdy form like a battered bird to a lighthouse. No, she said, between laughter and tears and kisses, everything was fine, everything had been delightful. But oh, it was so good to get home!

"There's a darling old priest living there, Ma. He's got rheumatism or something and he can't do parish work. He's there because the boys' tutor, Miles Mulholland, who is a perfect dear, but scared to death and sort of half wanting to be a priest—well, Miles said he couldn't come if there wasn't daily Mass, and so Coralia let him bring Father Anselmo. Before that we only had Mass Sundays. And Benediction every night."

"Well, it sounds as if you'd made a Retreat, darling."

"No, Ma," Harriet said virtuously, with her most impish expression, "it was not a Retreat."

She was lying flat on her bed, with her legs crossed at the ankle and her hands locked behind her head. Mrs. Townshend, rocking comfortably to and fro, was hand-hemming diminutive skirts for the Francesca Society. She looked over her steel-rimmed spectacles.

"That means this poor, good, God-fearing tutor," she said resignedly, "got ideas about you into his head, Hattie."

"It doesn't. He—well, he's one of those fellows who really suffer trying to tell you how wonderful you are, as if it was a sin to look at a girl!" Harriet said.

"Harriet Townshend."

163

"Well, I didn't!" Harriet answered the implied rebuke. "Honestly I didn't. I talked—sort of—as if marriage was the last thing in my thoughts, as if you needed me and my duty was here."

She turned upon her mother a look full of sweetness and conscious virtue. Mrs. Townshend's expression lost none of its distrust.

"No. It wasn't Miles. It was Philip Haagersen, Ma. The new foreman. He's really not a cowhand at all; he came up from the Hernandez rancho at Tia Juana, and he's had a good deal of education, he knows books, you know, culture, that sort of thing. He's been in England, and he wants to go back and study medicine in Edinburgh."

"He doesn't sound much like a ranch hand."

"No. He's quite different from what you'd think. What I thought anyway. And what Coralia thought," said Harriet.

"You liked him?"

"Well, as a matter of fact, Ma, I didn't. I like him better than I did. But he and I got a bad start, snapping at each other, smartie talk. I thought he was fresh, and I don't know what he thought I was."

"Well, now, what are you trying to say? Does she like him?"

"Yes, I honestly thinks she does," Harriet admitted, after a moment's hesitation. "I think she's in love, good and hard, too."

"And why on earth wouldn't he like you?"

"Oh, he knows that Filmer boy—remember Stewart Filmer? Remember the carryings-on when he was found on the floor by someone and rushed to the doctor? Well, that prejudiced him!" Harriet said, ending on a laugh.

"Harriet, there was nothing funny about that poor boy's being brought back from the brink of the grave."

"I didn't mean it was funny!" But Harriet's voice was held steady over irrepressible high spirits.

"You'd be sorry," the older woman said thoughtfully.

"If Coralia married? Somehow, I don't believe I would. He's divinely handsome," said Harriet. "And she's bound to marry someone!"

"Don't use that word. Divine is for God Himself."

"If a thing is made by God, I don't see——" Harriet began.

"Harriet."

"Yes, Ma," said Harriet, and was silent a moment.

"You don't suppose that he went there with this marriage in mind?"

"Well, if he did he feels differently now. I mean I think now he's thinking of her not just as a rich widow, but as a mighty attractive woman."

"He certainly would be a useful husband. She might well marry some man who never would be much use on the rancho. Do the little fellers like him?"

"Yes, they do. They're shy boys, you know, rather small and dark. But they do like him."

"Then is it a question of his asking her?"

"He may not. It's rather mixed," Harriet said. "I think it might be exactly what he wants, power over such a big place—independence. And I think—I do believe it's what Coralia wants. I think it's rather a surprise to her to think of it, marriage, I mean. And all the things it would change in her life. But almost anything could upset the whole thing."

"There's something you're not telling me about it, Harriet."

"There's something I don't understand about it, Ma." Harriets face reddened and she sat up, tumbling the coppery tendrils of her hair with both hands. "I mean, how far anyone's feelings go. If all Coralia's people try to convince her that he wants only her money, that might scare her off, for one thing. And if Philip's pride suddenly rose up and he couldn't face everyone thinking it was that——"

"He doesn't fancy anyone else, I suppose?" Mrs. Townshend asked, watching her needle attentively.

"Not me, if that's what you mean, my dear subtle mother," Harriet said, coming over to scramble down on her knees beside her mother's chair, disarranging the sewing and laying her flushed face against her mother's cheek. "There is a sort of antagonism between us. After a while, I suppose I might get in the habit of going up there again. But not for a long while. In fact, never with the same feeling."

"I wish—well, maybe I won't say that, but I'd be glad if

it was you, someday!" her mother began. Harriet sat back on her heels and was all ready for further confidences when a tap at the door announced the arrival of two of her close friends. These fashionably ringleted and beruffled young ladies announced that three hopeful swains were in waiting downstairs and they were all about to go over to Lucie's, where a most interesting announcement was supposedly to be made by Lucie and—who on earth did Harriet think! Yes, Oliver Cartright! Oh, Harriet gasped, getting into a fresh frock, she couldn't believe it! What about Paul Unger? Well, nobody seemed to know the answer to that.

Fifteen minutes later, with a great flurry of skirts and ribbons, feathered hats and parasols, they all departed, and Harriet was back in her old world.

It whirled her joyously through the bright sunshiny winter days; whirled her down to San Mateo and Belmont, where she rode horseback in the rain, whirled her back to cotillions at the Palace, to early Mass and Christmas breakfast with Ma, Johnny, and Lizzie, to a New Year's Ball at which, as Madama Pompadour, she won first prize.

Old Mrs. Fortesque died; a rich uncle of the Duvals died in Holland and left them money; a Father Barchi came out from Rome to be the new Superior at St. Ignatius. And Gardy Ann, the tried and true, the forlorn friend whom Mrs. Townshend had rescued from penury and debt, quietly walked out of the Townshend House and into the establishment of Mrs. Gracie Gracie, a rival establishment a few blocks away.

"She told me she was going South," Mrs. Townshend reported to her daughter. "I took it all for Gospel. But all the far south she went to was four blocks. Now she'll take a lot of my ways over to the Gracie place, as if she was the one thought them up."

"Ma, our house is always full," Harriet reminded her comfortingly. "Someone told me they had fish chowder Friday after Friday!"

"I know it. But her, that hadn't had a full meal for six weeks when she first set foot in this house——" the older woman muttered.

"Want me to go over and see her, Ma, and tell her she's acted like a pretty good old false friend?"

"I do not. What I'd say to her would be a mortal sin."

"That's what she bought the curry bowls for, Ma!" Harriet said, out of dark musing.

"That's what she went down into Chinatown and bought the curry bowls for. Twenty-four bowls at two bits apiece. I asked her what she wanted of them—and this, mind you, two weeks ago," Mrs. Townshend said, remembering, "and she said they were just in from China and she happened to see them—ha."

"Ha," Harriet echoed. Later she herself walked down to Chinatown in brilliant winter sunshine and bought four of the bowls for Lizzie. Chinatown was bustling and chattering; the men were beginning to wear their pigtails coiled about their heads now, but the smells, the laughter, the jostling of straw shoes kept the picture the same. Some of the narrow shops had dark, oily interiors, where the bookkeeper clicked an abacus and carved screens, from floor to ceiling, shut out glimpses of further screens in the depths beyond. Others were food shops, where vegetables in every shape of gourd or pumpkin were buried in feathery mysteries of green and watered conscientiously by the cotton-clad proprietors. On greasy chopping blocks strangled bits of viscera and bone were being shoveled into scraps of newspaper; above the merchants' heads dangled dry strings of oysters and the papery tentacles of cuttlefish.

Harriet loved it all. She was, as always, escorted; it was by a uniformed young man on this particular morning; George Jackman had lived his twenty-seven years in New Jersey, Annapolis, and Brooklyn, and he was fascinated by this glimpse of an Oriental colony. Harriet's nonchalance as she walked the littered, dirty, wet sidewalks that were strewn with rotted straw redolent of Hong Kong, her cheerful greeting to this grinning face or that impressed him. She was such a Dresden goddess to be so at home here! They peered into the doorway of the theater, where two coolies were sweeping out heaped masses of sunflower seeds, and where a high-

167

voiced rehearsal between two actors dressed as girls was going on.

"You go 'way," a slim Chinese boy without a pigtail, who was dressed in American clothes, said impersonally. "You not stay by here. Fine. You go 'way now."

"We like see, John," Harriet told him.

"Too much wastee time," the boy said, discouraged, and turned away. Harriet assured him with a joyous laugh that they would not waste time, and they sat on a hard bench and watched the rehearsal for half an hour. An orchestra seated at one side of the stage banged and whistled on strange flutes and brasses; the actors wore magnificent brocades and headdresses of five-foot-long pheasant feathers, colored chenille balls, and gilt filigree.

Afterward they wandered through the squalid living quarters, looked up dark narrow stairways or down into mysterious basements that had layers of other basements beneath them. The place was honeycombed below foot and overhead, and its inhabitants came and went like rabbits. Aged grandfathers were customarily in charge of infants and carried them along the busy streets with tender care; Harriet took a shaven-headed, fatly quilted, tallow-faced baby into her arms and beamed into the puzzled beady eyes, and the baby laughed.

"Harriet," Captain George Jackman, who had known her for three troubled, ecstatic weeks, said as they walked along Dupont Street, "this may sound silly to you."

Harriet, putting the squashy heart of a lichee nut into her mouth, looked brightly at him. "Stop him," she said in her heart to George's and her guardian angels, "for Pete's sake, stop him! Idiot. I met him at Fannie's Christmas party and here it isn't mid-January yet! Don't say it, don't say it——"

But he was saying it. He knew, he said, that there was no chance for him; he knew that before he ever came up from Monterey Presidio three weeks earlier. Peter Knott told him. But the thing was——

"The thing is," said George, as they paused at the door of St. Mary's, "the thing is, if there was a chance, and I hadn't said anything about it—how I feel, I mean—why, I'd never forgive myself. Are we going in here?"

"Let's. For a minute. Ma always used to make us, and Johnny and I can't ever pass a church. And Captain——"

She laid her small hand, smartly cased in kid and fur, on his arm.

"Captain, it makes me very happy," Harriet said, "to think that you like me so much, of course it does, it would make any girl proud!"

"I'm the one who would be proud," the captain managed to say.

"But I'm not in love with anyone, at least I can assure you of that. I'm not thinking about marriage. So please don't think I'm ungracious," Harriet pleaded, looking down at the little muff which protected her hands, raising the black curled lashes that shaded her blue eyes, and generally making herself as desirable as possible. "And come in," she said, turning to the big swinging door. Captain Jackman followed her in and knelt beside her.

Harriet then took him up to lunch at her mother's table, and afterward they went to the Mechanics' Pavilion, where all Harriet's intimate friends were strolling about, looking at magnificent Kern County potatoes and Santa Clara Valley peaches slumped in tall glass tubes, and pallid pears. There was a horse made of apples, one hoof pawing the air, and there was a dental display of unfortunate extractions that had apparently removed the larger part of certain jaws.

A hundred small booths showed a hundred varied products, from a Japanese plaster figure so accurately done that the story stated that the artist had pulled out his wife's hair, thread by thread, to increase the verisimilitude, to Mexican pottery so tiny that half a dozen little bowls on red and blue strings made attractive tassels.

At many of the exhibits souvenirs were handed out, and the young ladies walked about collecting them; certain gay post cards were soaked with Hoyt's German Cologne, and certain little kegs held pencil-size bottles of Sozodont. Sapolio had booklets of charming rhymes, and Pearline distributed firm paper dolls in sets of three, with their hands linked.

The whole big pavilion smelled of popcorn; molasses taffy was being pulled hour after hour on a revolving frame that caught the rich mass punctually on the instant it was about to drop. A group of tiny bowing and hissing Japanese served tea without sugar or cream for ten cents, and a handful of fortune-telling unleavened cookies with the tea.

Once in the afternoon and once in the evening, at three and at nine o'clock, a sturdy woman in tights, spangled shorts, and a jeweled tight jacket, worked her way up a hundred feet of rope ladder, and to the encouragement of muffled drums and the audible gasp of the crowd, came whirling down from a tiny platform on a rope. She landed on the net stretched below, walked a few plunging light steps on the net, leaped to the group, and disappeared without a glance at her audience, not to be seen again until the hoarse announcement of the feat took place hours later.

Harriet and her captain slipped into the circling group of their friends as easily as a drop of water sinks into a stream, and with her usual generosity she managed to heal the hurt of her answer to his offer, and to make him feel that if she were not marrying him, at least she was not pledged to marry anyone else. She had done this with more than one suitor; it made her feel uncomfortable to say "No," and she tried to blot out the effect of it as speedily as possible.

But things were changing now and she was changing, and was puzzled to find herself, for the first time, estimating the eligible men she knew as possible husbands.

This was a disagreeable thing to think about, and Harriet shrank from it. She had liked a great many men in her day, but as friends. Not as lovers. Not hoarse and agitated, breathing against her neck in some conservatory corner, not eternally bringing the conversation, when the crowd was about, to what "Harriet and I" were going to do someday, "when we give you all a surprise." Not attempting eternally to single her out from the rest, to manage that they should be alone for murmuring avowals of adoration.

Fun and flirting and dancing were all Harriet wanted from men; if her thoughts went on to marriage she thought of the girls who had married, thought of their starry-eyed devotion

170

to their young mates. She had never felt anything like that. She had never felt any jealousy; except in her teens, maybe, of Julia Danvers, and perhaps a little now, and she laughed at the thought, of Coralia. She had truly been jealous when her happy relationship with this adored friend and her happy visits to the Heart of Gold rancho had been jeopardized.

But to marry! To give any man the right to put his arm about her as they sometimes tried to do. To have that mustachy kiss his right, that odor of good shaving soap and woolen clothing and thick pomaded hair close to one's nose, like it or not!

As for further intimacies, as changing from bridal robes for the last time, in one's girlhood bedroom, and going to take possession, for the first time, of a doll house's dainty little new-furnished bedroom! Undressing again, with the husband tactfully taking a stroll or at least pretending that he had to do some unpacking in the kitchen . . . ! Harriet writhed in spirit at the mere thought. One undressed and got into bed; she knew that much. One could keep one's eyes closed when he came in; she could foresee that, too. But what on earth to say, if he said anything, and if he didn't, how long to sustain a silly, uncomfortable silence? A senseless, wretched business to contemplate, Harriet thought, especially when considered in the light of this dancing partner or that. Van, Bill, Taylor, Sid, Avery Fox-Spence. "Oh, horror!" she said aloud.

"What is it, darlin'?" her mother, beside her in bed, asked drowsily.

"I was thinking what if you were my husband, Ma."

A silence.

"That's a nice thought for a girl going off to sleep."

"I was thinking of the different boys I know, and I gave a scream of sheer horror."

"Have you got your rosary there?"

"I have, Mrs. T."

"Well, you say your rosary and go to sleep."

" 'Night!" Harriet murmured obediently.

171

When February came in on a rush of warm weather and bursting green, Harriet had a letter from Coralia. It arrived on a shining morning when all the windows at Mrs. Townshend's were wide open and white curtains streamed out into the fresh, ocean-scented air. In the garden the acacia trees were covered with golden tassels; the eucalyptus buds had burst into sprays of cream and scarlet fringe. Lilacs were showing purple tips on bare branches, and the great cherry tree was a puff ball of white.

Against the sharp rocky rise of Telegraph Hill's eastern front a few chance-planted plum and almond trees were in popcorn bloom, dazzling against the young green. And among the ruts and puddles, the muddy trails and occasional shanties, goats had been tethered; a cow stood at a crazy bit of fencing and bellowed for her calf.

Harriet sat the top of the shallow flight of steps that connected the porch with the garden and read her letter. It contained twenty-seven pages of Coralia's bold, purple-ink writing that always looked as if it were trying to slide off the lower right-hand corner of the paper. The letters were long and looped, punctuation scarce, and exclamation points plentiful.

"The happiest woman in all this world is writing you!" the letter began. "Oh, Harriet, it is true I am to be married again and you know who to—I cannot quite believe it myself but it is really true! He popped the question Friday night, after Father Anselmo went upstairs, while he and I—and of course that magic two-letter word 'he' is going to mean Don Felipe from now on!" Coralia interpolated coquettishly. "We didn't settle it that night we had a long talk. It was raining like mad outside and it seemed as if we two were shut off from all the

172

world, with the fire and in the old library I have come to love so much. But, however, it all began long before that and I must start at the beginning."

This process occupied twelve ecstatic and exhilarated pages, then Coralia was back at the special Friday night of the storm and the fire and the long wonderful talk she had had with Philip. No, he had not said anything definite about marriage at that time, but he had told her all about his affairs; that he had a little more than eleven hundred dollars and that that was enough to take him to Scotland and take care of him for the first months. An old doctor friend had promised him secretarial work to carry him through to his doctor's degree.

Coralia reported herself as listening to all this demurely, thinking of her own fortune and how little money would be needed to insure him freedom to study and work. She had never been so glad to have money. But of course, with three exclamation points, she hadn't said a word of that! Philip had put out lights, and they had walked upstairs in dark midnight with their hands locked, like children, and at her door he had solemnly kissed her on the forehead.

Ana, it seemed, had put her head out of her door at this moment so Ana, presumably, was aware of what was afoot, but who cared, demanded the straggling, long-looped violet letters.

And on the next day, Saturday it has been settled. Coralia and Miles and the children had gone riding after breakfast, and Philip had come across from the corrals to ask her something and had walked beside her horse up to the house. And afterward, on the terrace, he had said very simply that it was for her to say how it would be, and she had said that whatever was ahead of her in her life she wanted it to be beside Philip. As for Tio Juan and his advising Philip to go up to California and meet Martin Salazar's widow, that was pure nonsense. "For we are grown, sensible people," Coralia scribbled. "We know our own minds; just being thrown together isn't going to influence us!"

Well! So Philip was going East, but he would be back in May, and then they would plan. Would it be Scotland for them both, with the boys in a fine school over there? Or would he go and Coralia follow after the long vacation? It would all be bliss, whatever they did.

The letter demanded several postscripts. All this was to be kept secret until Philip came back. But Coralia had said she must tell Harriet, and Philip had agreed, even while saying "But she won't like it!"

"You don't know Harriet! She'll like anything that makes me happy," Coralia had answered.

But this answer required a qualifying postscript too. Harriet was not to think for one instant that Coralia hadn't had had gloriously happy days all through their wonderful friendship. She never had had a friendship like that before. It was perfection; it would always be perfection. This very letter was to order Harriet—mind you, not invite her but order her! —to come back with Tomas as soon as the shipment of machinery on the *Kate Douglas* was unloaded. Philip was going away in a few weeks, and Harriet must join them for all the time she could possibly spare. Harriet rushed with her news to her mother.

"Well, this'll make a change," said Mrs. Townshend. She was in the large, white-painted pantry checking drinking glasses. Her full-skirted calico gown was turned up and pinned behind her; about her head she had a large Mexican handkerchief wrapped and tied snugly. She sat on a high stool writing on a child's slate bound in red flannel; two girls just out from Ireland were up on chairs counting tumblers, wiping shelves, segregating mixed patterns, and otherwise following the strict and mysterious laws of housekeeping that their new employer imposed upon them.

"Won't it though," said Harriet ruefully, with a nod and a smile for Joanna and Annie.

"When's it to be dear'r?"

"No date. He has to go back to Tia Juana, and then East. Next May or June, maybe. Oh, dear," said Harriet, "I don't know whether I'm glad or sorry!"

"You'll like him better than you did as time goes on."

"Oh, I know I will! I mean, when you say 'ranch foreman' you give the wrong impression. She'll never have to be ashamed of him!" Harriet said. "She has so much money that they'll have another foreman, but Philip will always be manager, he'll always be the greatest help in the world with the ranch, and if he gets to be a doctor, so much the better!"

"Would you think, now," Mary Townshend began, as she and her daughter walked back through the big hallways and passages, "that her money had influenced him at all?"

"I don't see how it could help it, Ma," Harriet returned with a troubled look. "In the beginning, anyway. I told you that he had come up here with a sort of half idea that she would be a real catch. Yes, I know I told you! And here"— she ruffled the thick bulk of the letter—"here she says something that—well, it's the only thing in the letter that worries me."

They were in their own room now; Mrs. Townshend already comfortably rocking and knitting; Harriet sprawled face down on the bed, elbows braced, the letter in her hands.

"Here's where she's—this is the place—here's where she tells me about that rainy night. Ma, when they sat by the fire and he told her a lot about himself and she told him a lot about herself, too. I guess. Well, at any rate, here's what she says."

Harriet read the passage aloud.

"It suddenly came to me that all my life might be hanging on that minute," Coralia had written. "We'd had such a wonderful talk, and he was going away soon, he'd told me that, and I wanted him to know—I simply would never have forgiven myself if I hadn't let him know how I felt! For what is money, after all, compared to the companionship of which you have always dreamed? So I—this was when we stood up to go upstairs—I said very briefly that I loved him, that I thought our lives together would be marvelous lives. Was that awful? After all, Queen Victoria did it, and I never heard that Prince Albert thought it was queer! Anyway, he was simply perfect. He held both my hands at my doorway—I told you the rest. The next day he said he would give all his life to making me happy, and he would try to be a good father to the boys."

"What do you think, Ma?"

"Well." There was a silence. "If he honestly cares for her

175

and only her money holds him back, maybe that was the way to do it. There's not anyone else? You wouldn't know," said the older woman, answering herself.

"I'm sure there isn't. But then he may have a wife and family for anything we know," Harriet offered discouragingly.

"They'd get that from someone down there at Tia Juana. The old man wouldn't have told him to come up in the first place."

"Yes, that's so." But still Hattie looked doubtful, and her mother, glancing at her as she reread the letter from beginning to end, knew there was something still unsaid.

"Could it be you think she cares more than he does?"

"Well, I think for her it's all just straight-ahead happiness, Ma," Harriet said slowly, thinking it out. "She likes the money part, too, I mean the feeling that she can do anything for him, show how much she cares by showering him with things.

"But with him it's different," Harriet went on, as her mother made no comment. "He doesn't like the idea of marrying a rich wife and having everyone think—that is, he doesn't like standing before the world as a fortune hunter—at least, that's the way I work it out."

"She says there that she told him she loved him."

"Yes, and I believe she did."

"And do you think he might have gone away and not asked her?"

"Yes, I do."

"Then what's the matter with the boy?" Mary Townshend demanded unsympathetically.

"I think maybe he feels surprised at the whole thing, and that he's let himself into something that perhaps he really doesn't want to go on with—— I may be all wrong," Harriet interrupted herself suddenly. "Probably he's happy to have it settled, and to plan all the things they'll do. Oh, I hope it's that way!"

"After all, you've not been there for more than two months, Hattie. You don't know but what things have changed some."

"No, that's true. That's true." Harriet sounded comforted.

"No man gets this far unless he wants to," the older woman said. "You'll find that they know what they're doing."

"Well, of course! But Ma, I think I ought to go back with Tomas.What do you think? It doesn't mean that I miss Minnie's wedding or Boucicault in *Shawn the Post*. Tomas can't go back until the ship gets here with the things from Spain. That'll be a week or ten days.

"I'll tell you honestly," Harriet presently added, as her mother, always rather a silent woman, looked at her thoughtfully and did not reply, "I know Coralia would be glad. I don't know that he would, and I don't care! But it means a foursome for euchre, and riding, and all that, and it means we all talk together, instead of her feeling self-conscious with Philip—what d'you think?"

"I think you may be right," Mary Townshend said. And it was settled. But Harriet got in not one but two magnificent weddings, and saw the Irish player more than once, and flitted many times to Howard Street to see Lizzie before the *Kate Douglas* entered the bay and Tomas was ready to start.

Tomas gave her but twelve hours' warning, appearing from some congenial neighborhood far down the Peninsula Road, beyond the cemeteries. Here Indians, Mexicans, Portuguese and Spanish laborers, with a sprinkling of Chinese, had a sort of camp or sheds and adobes attached to each other in long strings, their mud doorways shaded by grapevines, and surrounded by littered empty lots, rank growths of mallow and pepper trees, a straggling stream at which goats and donkeys drank, and vegetable plots fenced with rusty wires and unsteady poles. Tomas was quite at home here, but he was glad to be turning homeward, too, and Harriet cheerfully rose in black winter darkness to join him on the high swaying front seat, well muffled and hooded, at five o'clock on a cold February morning.

The heavy ranch team, wild after a week's leisure in a field deep in new grass, took to the dirt road with vigor; the rising sun found them well into the upward slope of the eastern hills, San Jose Mission left behind them. Harriet presently had strong hot coffee and sour bread at a wayside adobe, and consumed them without leaving her buffalo robes or her

177

seat; the first arrows of the sun shot across the world as they went on.

The day turned hot; Harriet loosened her wrappings a little, dozed and waked and dozed again. Spring was flung like an Oriental robe over the hills. Against a background of emerald, orange poppies blazed in masses, buttercups lifted their varnished petals in sheets across the levels of mountain meadows, iris and brown mission bells glowed under the sprawling oaks. In the woods the delicate smoky blue of wild lilac and the pink of currant tassels were sprayed against the darkness of the trees.

Harriet had been dancing until after two o'clock at a wedding so grand that it would presently get full notice even in the eastern papers; she thought dreamily of the perfumed rooms that had been draped in delicate silks, the bride's diamonds, the magnificence of the feast. She thought of Sid Forester, with his nice speech, and his nice titled brother in Ireland, and his modest salary. Johnny had a better salary than Sid. Still Nigel Forester of Forester and Wilkes was Sid's uncle, and would do what he could for him. It would take Sid two years to reach the salary level where marriage was permitted by Forester and Wilkes; he might do better with some American bank, he told Harriet.

Sid had talked of these things in the conservatory last night.

"I'll have to stop going into conservatories," thought Harriet. "They keep making me say things I don't want to say."

She nodded again, this time falling by degrees to rest against Tomas' shoulder. The horses were going more slowly now, with the worst grades behind them and the sun directly overhead.

They stayed that night with the Ortegas: childless, hospitable, always with a houseful of the less fortunate, on the Casa dos Santos, and made an early start again. It was almost two o'clock in the afternoon when they reached the rancho.

Harriet was welcomed only by Coralia and the servants, an arrangement agreeable to her consciousness of fatigue and of being tumbled and mud-splashed.

"Ah, you darling, you darling!" Coralia half laughed, half cried, her arm about Harriet's as they went upstairs. "I was

178

afraid to look to see whether or not you'd come with Tomas!"

It was all too perfect. The great solid hacienda was airy and cool after the spring warmth outdoors. There were flowers in Harriet's room, and a tray with cold chicken and tortillas and sherry. Coralia helped her take off her clothes and get into a thin wrapper, and Harriet sank into the freshness of the wide bed and into deep sleep before there could be anything but a few scattered words of the talk for which they both were starving.

"No, no, no," said Coralia, delighted with her arrangements. "I fixed it so that everybody would be away, and you can rest for three hours if you want to. Then I'll come in and we'll catch up, and afterward dress for dinner and go down. The boys and Miles will be back then, and Father will come and we'll have a big fire."

"Philip hasn't gone already?"

"Heavens, no! He'll be up for dinner."

"Oh, wonderful. And singing, and euchre after the boys go to bed?"

"Everything, everything! Oh, Harriet, isn't it heaven! Now you settle down, and don't say another word or I'll be mad!" And with this childish threat Coralia dismissed a maid, nodded significantly to Ana, and left the room.

Harriet lay still, lapped in rest and fragrance and peace. She heard garden sounds, bird songs and the importunate warning of the sentinel quail, and the cool swishing of water as the plants on the terrace were soaked after the hot day. Afternoon light began to make long angles in the room; Harriet's eyes lazily followed the movements of motes in the slanting beams, the rustle of ivy at her window. Her lashes fell; she was asleep.

When she wakened, refreshed and with her own rosy color restored, Ana was in the room with a great pitcher of hot water, and while Harriet washed at the basin and brushed and dressed her coppery mop, Coralia came in, and at last they were talking, pouring out to each other the little and big events of the separated weeks, with emphasis always upon the engagement and the wedding plans.

"I don't have to ask you if you're happy!"

"I'm only afraid I'll show it and give myself away! We've not told anyone."

"But you'll have to tell people pretty soon."

"Not until Philip gets back."

"Sure you want it that way?" Harriet asked, over a little hesitation she could not define.

"Sure!" She was sure of everything, radiant in new happiness, new dignity, swept away in plans and dreams, all bewildering and new. "You see I'm coming to the city for at least two months," Coralia confided. "I've got to get a trousseau——'

"Oh, fun!' interpolated Hattie frivolously.

"Oh, it will be! And that'll take up most of the time he's away; you know how time flies when we're there. Oh, Harriet, it's all such happiness! It's happines such as I never hoped for, because I never knew there was any such feeling in this life! Oh, and darling, you're glad of it aren't you? You're going to like him too, aren't you?"

"Imagine me trying to do anything else! I'm the sister of this family now, the Tia 'Arriet, as the children call me. I'm the goddess in the machine who pulled the first string."

"Well, you are!" Coralia said, delighted. She put her arms, fragrant and clean from washing and scented with fine English soap, about Harriet and kissed her, and they went on with talk and with their dressing.

CHAPTER 21

The evening was all that Harriet had hoped it would be, and more. She sank into the familiar atmosphere knowing that they all loved her, that the very servants were glad to have the Señorita back. More than one deep bed of coals was glowing in the steel-rodded grates of the downstairs rooms when they went down. Presently they were gathered in one of the vast parlors, whose atmosphere was quite comfortable. The grate here had been replenished by many a hodful of coal; the heavy rep curtains were drawn across the windows. Harriet, rather subdued after the long day, settled her voluminous skirts of pale smoky tarlatan in a deep chair. She was content to listen tonight; these hours belonged to Philip and Coralia.

Miles Mulholland had taken the vociferous boys up to bed; old Father Anselmo was peacefully smoking his pipe by the fire. There was only candelight in the room, and it touched his thin silver hair into an aureole, and twinkled on Harriet's silver slippers. There was a wide sofa at one side of the hearth, and Philip and Coralia were seated on it, their hands not touching, although they were close enough to touch, their smiling faces now turned toward each other, and now to the fire as they smiled and murmured and were silent again.

Philip had joined the group two hours earlier, coming down, brushed and smart, in a dark red house coat and a shirt with fine embroidered frills showing under a flowing collar and tie. It was correct attire, as were the belled full trousers and brocaded vest; Miles wore much the same, but on Philip these garments looked romantic and fitted his handsome fairness, his sideburns, his erect tall figure.

Harriet had met him with simple friendliness and pleasure. If he had ever suspected her disapproval of the marriage, he gave no sign of it now. He sat next to Coralia at dinner, and they had more than one little conference and private joke, and she seemed to absorb his entire attention. Harriet had had her private heartaches already over the consummation of this affair, but she was comfortably tired tonight, too tired to look ahead or look back, glad to sit still, merely sending her eyes lazily about the group. When they rested on Philip it was with an amused recollection of her first resentful estimate of him as a mate for Coralia, her vision of a brawny cowhand stepping in between her and her closest woman friend, of Coralia's self-deception and her later disillusionment; in short, of the general wreckage of relationships everywhere. Philip tonight, relaxed and at home and pleasantly dignified under Coralia's fluttered evidence of happiness, was quite another person.

"You'll get to be a doctor, Philip," thought Harriet "and

181

you'll not want to come back here from Europe and run a ranch. Good enough for Coralia? I wonder if someday you won't begin to think that she doesn't measure up to the life you've planned for yourself. There'll always be the boys' rights to consider, there'll never be any neighborhood contacts to make this place interesting professionally to you; just a baby now and then down at the adobes, or a cut hand, or boils or something among the men. Of course, if you once get to rasing really blooded cattle——"

"Always a pleasure to meet you, Miss Townshend," Philip said with a formal inclination of the head. Harriet's gay laugh broke out.

"I know. I was staring! My thoughts were nine million miles away."

"You're probably half asleep," Coralia smiled.

"No. But I'm completely happy, and just thinking things over."

"You like the present arrangement?" Philip asked, with a hint of significance in the trembling of an eyelid in her direction.

"Immensely." She and Coralia exchanged a mysterious smile, but as the only other person present was Miles Mulholland and he was deep in a book, no one was about to feel any curiosity. Now he looked up to turn his strong, iron-bowed glasses on Harriet.

"Let me tell you this is a good book!" he said, feverishly enthusiastic.

"Ma's crazy about it," said Harriet. "Did you like it, Coralia?"

"I couldn't get into it."

"What is it, Señora?" asked Philip.

"It's French. It's called *A Sister's Story*," Coralia said.

"It's simply terrible," Harriet contributed. "They all get consumption and are exiled out of France when Napoleon comes in, and they live in a damp old castle praying day and night, and nearly everyone gets consumption and dies, and everyone else is resigned."

"It sounds like a book for a rainy afternoon," Philip said simply. The women laughed joyfully; Miles was already deep

182

again in the thick volume. Harriet extricated herself from her chair and went to his side.

"Come on, Miles. Ten minutes of music and then I'm for bed."

He went to the piano with her, lifted a cello from among the various string instruments that had accumulated on the table there, and sounded the strings.

"Want a light?" Coralia called.

"No, no, no, we don't need it! Come in on this when you can, Miles."

She played and sang "The Erl King." Harriet's voice was sweet and pure, her hands were familiar with the music. Miles ventured a few notes, grew bolder, drew the full chords confidently, with the air of loving his instrument that is so particularly that of the cellist. Harriet could look across the top of the old square piano at her audience; fire and candlelight illumined the end of the room with a dull glow that gave her ruffles the effect of wings, and her hair the shine of a nimbus.

She sang "Lesbia Hath a Beaming Eye," and, at Coralia's command, "The Minstrel Boy." Philip brought a candle to the piano and Hattie sang "Sylvia."

The violincello was silent now; the room was silent. Hattie raised her eyes on the last line.

"To her let us garlands bring."

Philip was leaning on the piano and their eyes met. Something about the strong planes of the browned face, the wave of fair hair, the set thin line of the mouth, and the faint frown between the rather deep-set eyes gave Harriet a strange feeling. It was one of almost pure shock; there was no other emotion that she could recognize. "Why, what—what——" she said in her soul, and could go no further.

She smiled at him in the candlelight, went across to Coralia, who was drowsily looking into the fire, and said her good nights.

"Ah, don't go yet!" Coralia protested.

"I'm dying." Harriet went upstairs carrying her candle. Coralia followed her some fifteen minutes later, to find Harriet still fully dressed, seated at her own mirror, her completely absent gaze fixed unseeing on its depths.

"Harriet, are you all right?"

"Fine," Harriet said in a bewildered tone.

"Listen," said Coralia, sitting down. "Don't you think he's wonderful?"

"Coralia, I really do." Harriet knew neither the voice nor what it said.

"I'll tell you, Philip feels things deeply . . ." Coralia was well launched. She had thought things through about Philip. Had Harriet thought him quiet? She felt that he might be even a little confused by his new happiness. He was not demonstrative. He had said he would leave all that to Coralia.

"Leave all that—what?" Harriet asked, turning from the washbasin with her mouth full of the spicy pink suds of Rubifoam.

"Oh, showing affection," Coralia said, laughing. "I reminded him that he was marrying a woman who is half Spanish. You know, to tell you the truth, Harriet, deeply as I respected Martin, and kind as he always was to me, it wasn't the sort of love—I mean, it was a different love from what I feel now. All the years I was married to Martin I was so sick and the babies came so steadily that it was—well, it was quite different from what I had expected. Now——" She hesitated, relishing these revelations and prolonging them.

"Now I know what other girls feel when they get engaged," she went on. "I mean—well, when I'm not with him I'm thinking about him, and when I am with him I keep finding out new wonderful things in his nature. Didn't you ever feel that way about a man, Hattie?"

"Enough to know how you feel," Harriet said. "But what I feel for this particular man," she added in her thoughts, "isn't anything like that. He annoys me—no, it's not that—and he scares me—anyway, he makes me uncomfortable as no human being ever did before! And I am dead-tired and I want to go to sleep."

There was a coal fire in the room, it was comfortably warm, and Ana had put a hot stone bottle into Harriet's bed. She got into bed and stretched upon it, leaning back on her pillows, and concentrated upon trying to keep awake and

184

maintain a brightly eager interest. Coralia was brightly wide awake and full of rapturous revelations.

"I'm going to tell you something. I thought I wouldn't, but now I think I will. This, of course, is secret——"

Harriet dragged out a few words.

"Well, of course!"

"This was only yesterday. Philip and I were out on the terrace before dinner, before Father Anselmo came down. I said I wanted to ask him something and he musn't think I was an absolute fool."

The room faded from Harriet's sight, brightened again. She heard dream voices mingling with Coralia's voice.

"Imagine," she said feebly.

"Well, can you imagine!"

"She really is as strong as a bull," Harriet's drowsy thoughts conceded. "Here it is after midnight, and I got up this morning at four."

"He told me," Coralia was saying, "that he honestly thought he wouldn't have—wouldn't have asked me if I hadn't started it!"

"Well, he would," Harriet commented, stressing the last word.

"I think he would. But that's what he said——" Harriet was off into an agony of sleepiness again. She struggled valiantly, stretching her eyes to their widest, straightening up a little in bed. "He actually said that if I hadn't asked him to marry me—you remember I wrote you?"

Harriet blinked. She found nothing to say.

"You remember I wrote you that, Harriet?"

"Of course I do!"

"Well, he said that if I hadn't, he wouldn't have!"

"You don't think he meant it?" Harriet enunciated heavily.

"I don't know. It seems funny that a man should care for a woman and go away without telling her."

Harriet was suddenly wide awake.

"Mightn't it have been, Coralia, that he meant to get to Scotland somehow and finish up his medical work, and then come back—it'd only be three or four years, with his doctor's degree——"

185

"That might have been it!" Coralia said, struck. "But three or four years—oo!"

"You see, you have everything to offer. And he has nothing."

"He has everything!" Coralia said on a jealous undertone, with a little laugh. "Everything I ever wanted!"

"Well, of course he has, from that point of view. But he'd see it from a man's—the breadwinner and protector, all that sort of thing."

"I suppose so. Aren't they stupid!" Coralia said forgivingly. "But I never did anything in my life I'm so proud of," she went on. "Of course it was terribly hard! I came right out with it. I said: 'Look here, Philip, let's be honest! Why don't you ask me to marry you? You know you want to!'"

"And he immediately asked you."

"No, indeed he didn't! You don't know him, Harriet. The serious side of him, I mean. He looked at me for a minute—it seemed like a month, but I suppose it was only a minute—and said, 'Would you possibly accept me, Coralia?' and I said, 'What do you think?' and he said, 'I don't know what to think!' And then very quietly he said, 'Will you marry me?' and I—I wrote you that?—began to cry. I don't for the life of me know why!"

"Well, I wouldn't marry a man who made my cry when he asked me to marry him!" Harriet said.

"You mean," Coralia said after a moment, in a voice that had a slightly hurt tone, "you mean that in my place you honestly wouldn't marry him?"

"I do truly mean that in any place, mine or yours, I wouldn't marry him," Harriet answered suddenly. She was looking down at her own hands, locked on the counterpane, as she spoke. Now she raised her troubled eyes to Coralia's.

"Harriet!" Coralia said, stupefied.

"I don't know why I said that," Harriet said, burying her face in her hands.

"Well, I should hope not!" Coralia was not angry; she was bewildered.

"But I've wanted to say it—oh, even at my last visit! I mean—what do we know about him?"

"We know everything about him!"

"You mean because they know him down at Tia Juana?"

"I mean that, yes, and everything. You don't think he has a wife and children in the East, I suppose?"

"We don't know that he hasn't!" Harriet stammered, holding her ground.

Coralia came over and sat on the edge of the bed, laying her beautiful smooth brown hand over Harriet's.

"Harriet, what on earth is the matter?"

"Nothing is the matter," Harriet said, gulping back a flood of tears. "Oh, yes, something is. It was tonight—tonight when I was singing and Philip brought over the candles. There was something in his look that was so strange—fixed right on me —it was as if he threatened to kill me—kill us all——"

"Harriet!"

"I know it sounds crazy. But Coralia, don't."

"But, darling, I love him." Coralia spoke as if to a willful small child; she smiled reassuringly, at the mother.

"But if you had seen him——"

"You mean it was devilish, like Mephistopheles in *Faust?*"

"No-o-o." Harriet laughed nervously. "But suddenly I thought, 'Who is he and what is he, and what are we letting Coralia do?' "

"You're not letting me do anything. I've found the man I love out of all the world, and when I think of the happiness of our lives together I—well, I just lie awake dreaming!"

Harriet studied her face for a moment; their hands were locked now. She leaned back against the pillows with a complete change of manner.

"Of course you're right. I don't know what got into me! Except that I don't think anyone in the world is good enough for you!"

"Well, you almost broke my heart!"

"I know. I guess I'm just overtired."

"You ought to be. Now you go to sleep." Coralia tucked in the covers, stooped to put a kiss upon Harriet's flushed little face. You'll see everything different in the morning. Oh, it's so good to have you here!"

"Oh, it's so good to be here!" The candles were out; the

187

door was softly closed; Harriet snuggled deep in the feather bed. Through exhaustion of mind and body her last thought was a soothing one. She had warned Coralia; she had at last expressed the misgivings that had troubled her from the very beginning of her knowledge of Philip's new position. As foreman of the ranch he was all very well; as master here he would be too powerful—he was already too powerful to leave room for Coralia's happiness.

He would take her to Scotland; Coralia had already talked to Harriet of winters spent there, of the house she would find in Edinburgh, of Ana's accompanying her to look out for Josito, of their return to the rancho, of course, for the long summer holidays.

Coralia, whose whole life had been spent in the sunshiny valleys of San Joachim and Santa Clara, freezing in some stony house in a stony street under the stony skies of Scotland! Coralia, who had had great bowls of grapes and figs and bronzed ripe apricots within reach of her soft, idle hand half the year around marketing in a town whose commodities Harriet dimly visualized as consisting of large plain white fish and whiskey.

Harriet had never seen Scotland, but she remembered the conditions of her Irish uncles' dairy farm outside of the city of Cork with singular vividness. She remembered putting her feet into her mother's muff as a protection against the bitter solid cold of heavy linen sheets, and her disgust at the strong lean bacon and the dark oatmeal porridge. She, like Coralia, had come into the dour soft cloudiness of Ireland from warmer skies, from balmy southern isles. She had been homesick there, for gently clicking palms and sun-drenched beaches, and the great cluster of ripening bananas that never was missing from the veranda wall.

"Well, anyway, I told her!" she reflected drowsily. "She knows now how I feel. If he's a murderer and he kills her, I've done all I could!"

She reached for her rosary, got no further than the first "Holy Mary, Mother of God——"

188

Coralia was proved right. In the morning everything looked bright, everything promised nothing but happiness. The household was in the chapel for early Mass, but Philip came in at the last moment, bent his head to Coralia's for some murmured confidences, and left before the ceremony was over. Harriet saw him no more that morning. Her one glimpse of him had set her to wondering what all the fuss had been about the night before. Here was merely a handsome, loosely built big man with a slick-brushed mop of fair hair, pale blue eyes, brown big hands, a man healthily set upon a good marriage, a man who was going to make Coralia, Harriet's best friend, a proud and loving wife. Nothing in all this to cause a hysterical uproar! Harriet's nerves quieted down, and she began to stretch her luxury-loving soul in the leisurely, familiar round that was the daily life at the rancho.

Breakfast was hilarious, for today was a holiday and the boys and Miles were alike exhilarated. Coralia and Harriet sauntered out after breakfast to inspect the various rambling outhouses, paddocks, sheds and corrals where the special pets of the family were installed. Some forty dogs, twice as many cats, and several hundred chickens had the full range of the rancho, and almost as many owners, but the Señora's animals were differently housed; the horses Harriet and Coralia rode had their box stalls; the dogs were individually tended. There were always puppies, kittens, baby colts to watch. Morning hours fled while the two women, accompanied by the boys and stray children from the adobe settlement, with a sympathetic following of maids from the hacienda, wandered idly about ready for any interest that presented itself.

This morning was soft, and scented with brush fires. The sweet pungent smell of burning eucalyptus drifted through the world of fences and sheds and whitewashed adobe walls, where tree shadows crossed the narrow lanes in even bars. Fog was high on the western hills, but only odd drifts of it clung here and there in the long slopes of the canyons. The visiting party peered into little pens where small bull calves butted against buckets, gates, walls; they lifted up the velvety puppies that were established in a deserted manger. Cats peered down at them from high beams on which the soft powder of bran and oats had settled inch-deep; one or two old dogs solemnly accompanied them.

Harriet was happy. Not only had she a deep sense of relief, in that she had said all she wanted to say, and more, to Coralia in dispraise of Philip, but Coralia apparently wasn't going to take it seriously. Harriet's conscience was clear, and matters were already returned to their old comfortable footing. She thought the late winter day, with the sun piercing the soft mists and vapors, was the loveliest of the year, and that the mellowed old roofs and sheds had never been so picturesque.

They sauntered back to lunch, after which everyone took a siesta. Philip did not appear for lunch; he was usually too busy on the ranch to keep household hours. It was only when everyone was riding, in the mellow soft light of late afternoon, that they saw him again.

Then, as the horses turned into a lane between tall, bare-limbed poplars, he turned from the doorway of the forge, where he was standing with two or three of the hands, and came over to the horses. His nod was for them all, the boys, Miles, Coralia, and Harriet. He stopped and put a hand on Harriet's saddle, not looking at her.

"Who cinched this? I told Tomas the ladies weren't to use this saddle."

"It's all right," Harriet said. "I looked at it. Tomas said the Indian put a new strap in there."

She had felt a little flutter of last night's vague apprehension as she saw him, but it vanished under his matter-of-fact, indeed annoyed, tone.

"Guess that's all right then." He went across to Coralia, spoke to her briefly, nodded to all of them, and went back to the forge. The riding party went on, up past barns and cabins of whitewashed adobe, up through a long lane of tall planted trees, through a hillside vineyard of stripped vines, and so on, higher and higher, under mighty solemn redwoods where there was no underbrush and the ground was sown deep in needles and was as cleared as the nave of a mighty cathedral.

All so peaceful and quiet at one minute, with the faint jingle and clink of the harness rings the only sound, and then suddenly—what—what——

Coralia was on the ground, tumbled in an odd boneless lump against the bole of a great oak; her horse was tugging, kicking, was free, and trotted a few feet away.

How Harriet left her horse, how she ran the dreadful fifty feet over the redwood spines to kneel where Coralia lay, she had no consciousness whatever. She was there, she had Coralia's head against her arm. Coralia gave no sign of life.

"Miles—she's hurt! Go as fast as you can for Philip. You're all right, Coralia darling, you're just shaken up! Open your eyes. Be as quick as you can, Miles—no, I wouldn't move her, it seems to hurt her if we move her. Oh, God, let her open her eyes!"

Miles was already riding away at a full easy lope along the rough forest trail; the small boys dismounted and came to stand close beside their mother. The sight of their horrified little dark faces brought quick reassurance from Harriet; they mustn't worry, Mother would be all right, Philip was coming straight back, they'd get her home.

A low dead stick of a redwood bough had driven its way up through Coralia's breast and protruded again above her shoulder. How deep it went Harriet could form no idea; Coralia was breathing heavily, and now and then she moaned. Once she said "Martin" indistinctly in a quiet conversational tone, and as she spoke a bubble of blood formed at her mouth.

Harriet crouched at the base of the redwood, attempting to take some of the weight of Coralia's body off the shaft. She was afraid that at any moment the breathing might cease.

Too terrified to think, she could pray automatically, "Oh, God, help us! Don't let her be badly hurt! Help us!"

The scene would be forever burned into her memory. Everything as far as human life was concerned was deathly still in the wood, where the red level last bars of sunlight were painting the redwood shafts scarlet and sifting like gold dust through the oaks. The little boys had seated themselves on the bole of a fallen tree and were watching, apprehensive and silent; the horses grazed idly in a grassy space near by.

But of animal life there was the usual afternoon stirring and cheeping, flashing of blue jays' wings and watching from the beady bright eyes of chipmunks. Flies spun in a cloud in a clear bar of sunlight; the sentinel quail called stridently from the meadow, where new families of baby quail, no larger than walnuts, were stirring in grass and leaves. All so beautiful, all nature at her peaceful loveliest, and to Harriet full only of brassy terror and menace.

After endless ages voices were heard below, in the forest, and the jingle of harness, and immediately help was at hand. Philip and Miles were mounted; Ana beside Mateo on the seat of the long-bodied farm wagon. Two young ranch hands leaped down, holding a strip of canvas, stretcher fashion, as they fearfully approached Coralia's silent form.

"Look at the stick—into her——" Harriet whispered to Philip, bending beside her. Ana waved an apron, and the flies that had been walking on Coralia's white face scattered. "I'm holding her up as well as I can."

"My God——" Philip said, under his breath. "It goes through, does it? Has she spoken?"

"Yes, she said 'Martin' twice. She moans, too. We're taking you home, darling, we'll have you fixed in no time!" The last phrase Harriet crooned to Coralia as if she were a baby. Philip touched the murderous sharp spear that pinioned her by the shoulder.

"It went right through her habit."

"Yes. Oh, Philip, dare you try to take it out?"

"We'll have to. Unless we could break it close to the tree. And that might hurt her terribly. Rico, Gregorio, here!" Philip's face was a mask of pain and apprehension as he cautiously freed Harriet's arms, substituting the strong brown arms of one of the younger men, and moved between Coralia and the tree, placing his hands on her shoulders to lift them.

"Should we saw off the branch?" Miles whispered.

Philip hesitated.

"If we had brought a saw," he said. "But we mustn't wait, now." And catching Coralia strongly about the shoulders, he drew her toward him, and the branch slowly drew away. A gush of warm red blood flowed onto Coralia's blue habit and a deep cry broke from her. Harriet walked away, her face ashen. Ana's muttered prayers were suddenly audible. The next moment Coralia slumped into real unconsciousness again, and was laid on mattresses in the body of the wagon. Mateo led Harriet's horse; Harriet crouched beside Coralia, holding one of the limp, scratched hands.

The sorrowful cavalcade wound through the now darkening woods, only a few monosyllables being exchanged, as when Philip rode close and turned his anxious face to Harriet's.

"How does she seem?"

"Still breathing."

She was still breathing when they carried her up to bed, and when Ana and Harriet had cut away her habit and exposed the wounded area. Careful sponging revealed that the branch had only pierced the flesh, and although Philip immediately diagnosed a broken arm, he gave Harriet the first reassurance she had had on that dreadful afternoon when he said that the injuries seemed superficial and that the blood-stiffened mouth need mean nothing, lips were easily cut.

It was dark night when Coralia awakened in a candlelighted room and found the doctor from San Jose Mission beside her. Philip handled the shoulder; Harriet hovered near. Ana had gathered most of the older women of the rancho in the chapel for very special prayers.

A broken arm, a dislocated shoulder, an ugly wound, and a painful assortment of bruises and cuts were the full story; there was no concussion, there was no internal injury that could be discovered. Harriet made hospitable arrangements for keeping the doctor overnight for a next-day report.

"Yes, that was a close call," said Peter Wormsley, the doctor from San Jose Mission. "An inch nearer the ribs——"

"God is good!" Harriet whispered. She still wore the challis riding habit in which she had left the hacienda so many dreadful hours earlier; her crisp coppery hair was carelessly dampened and brushed back; she had had a late supper at the end of a long empty table only a few hours earlier; the household was disorganized tonight, and nothing was going according to rule. Philip and Peter Wormsley took turns in visiting the sickroom; Coralia knew where she was now, and that she hurt in several places, but laudanum had done its merciful work; and she was drowsy. Ana had moved in strange dark bedding, blankets and pillows, as a bed for her own occupancy, and Harriet had determined to take the big chair with pillows for most of the night.

They sat about the fire in the "old Señor's" room, subdued and thankful, and talked in low tones, even though Coralia could not have heard them had they shouted.

"Miss Townshend," said Peter, "this is all very different from what I expected. I've heard of the Corazón d'Oro rancho ever since I came to California, but somehow I thought of there being only Spanish people here."

"No, we're all mixed," Harriet told him. "Mr. Mulholland here is Irish, I'm Irish and New England. Even Mrs. Salazar is half American and as for Mr. Haagersen——"

"Mother Irish," Philip supplied, "father Swedish."

The words echoed in Harriet's head; for some reason they made her tremble. She had not looked fairly at Philip all through these evening hours. Now she looked at him and saw that he was looking at her. Not quite with the strange expression that had so troubled her last night, but oddly enough to send the eyes behind her upcurled black lashes down to the ground, to the fire that showed dying red bars of coals between the steel rods.

The doctor made a final visit to Coralia's room, took his candle, and went to bed. Father Anselmo, who had said the rosary prayers in the chapel for all of them an hour or two earlier, had already gone to his room. Harriet roused herself from a half drowse and found herself alone in the big softly lit room with Philip.

He was half asleep too, in the chair opposite her own; both were tired, by emotion as well as by the strain of Coralia's accident. Minutes went by, and still neither moved, or looked at anything but the fire.

"You're staying in her room tonight?"

"Well, most of the time. Ana'll be there too, and this nice doctor—Wormsley, isn't it?—said not to hesitate to call him."

"She'll sleep right through."

"I hope so. The doctor's nice, isn't he?"

"And he thought you were," Philip said dryly.

"Oh, did he? That's nice, too," Harriet said composedly.

"And was it nice to let Miles walk on red-hot coals, too?"

There was a silence. Then Harriet said clearly and coolly:

"It would interest me very much to know exactly what you think a girl's conduct ought to be, with young men. I presume if I shaved off my hair like a nun and put a patch on my left eye, you would feel I was treating your remarkable sex fairly."

At this point the picture she painted amused her in spite of herself, and she broke into a laugh.

"I never thought I'd laugh again," she said, faintly apologetic, with a jerk of her head in the general direction of Coralia's room.

"She got out of that accident today by a miracle," Philip agreed mildly.

"I was surprised at how much medicine you knew," Harriet said, sealing the peace.

"I ought to know more. Well, I will someday."

"You mean you'll really go on with your medicine?"

Philip raised surprised eyebrows.

"How d'you mean 'really'?"

"Well——" Harriet also glanced up, looked back at the fire.

"What made you think I wasn't in earnest?" the man demanded.

"I didn't think that. I just asked."

Silence. Then Harriet said suddenly:

195

"You'll change your plan now about going so soon?"

"Yes. I'll wait now until she's really on her feet again."

"Shall you go to Scotland before coming back?"

"I don't know. I said something to Coralia about looking the whole scene over, the Edinburgh scene, seeing about rents and conditions generally."

"Or Coralia said that to you," Harriet amended it. "She's determined not to stand in your way!"

"I could see myself living there in a house full of Spanish servants and small boys," Philip began again, after a silence in which he had glanced sharply at the slight figure curled in the big chair.

"She'd be perfectly happy having things go along as they are, living here as you are."

"Yes. I suppose so. Unfortunately——" Philip did not finish his sentence, and Harriet also was silent for a space.

"What I was going to ask you," the girl began again, ending it, "was something else. It was this. If it hadn't been for the accident, would you have gone away and never come back to the ranch?"

"What on earth gave you that idea?" Philip asked with a shred of rather mirthless laughter.

"I don't know. Or rather I think I do," Harriet answered hesitatingly. "I've felt it for—oh, I don't know. Lately."

"No, I was not coming back," Philip said steadily. He had dropped his linked hands between his knees; he did not turn his head as he bent over, looking into the fire.

"Philip!" Harriet breathed in a shocked whisper.

"No. I couldn't."

"Philip, you'll break her heart."

"One way or another, yes. That seems to be my destiny."

"Oh, but why—why? Is it just the money? Is it that you feel you have to get started in your profession first? What is it?"

"It seems the wiser way," Philip said slowly. "She'll have you—you're worth ten of me where Coralia's concerned. She has sons and wealth and youth—she's not thirty-two yet."

"She's half Spanish. They're proud and they're—tenacious," Harriet said, reaching for the word.

"That's it. She is proud. Well, better to end this thing now, when even her mother doesn't suspect it, than to wait until everyone knows."

"But—but you asked her!" Harriet accused him.

"Yes," Philip said, glancing over his shoulder at her distressed face, "and I am running away."

"You'll write her that it's all ended?"

"Immediately. And you'll be here, I hope, for her to talk to. That's the one thing that can help."

"But Philip, what's changed everything? She loves you so! Surely, considering everything, this would be a wonderful place to—to marry into?" Harriet finished whimsically.

The man laughed briefly.

"Too wonderful. I wouldn't feel I was even worth my hundred and fifty a month."

"Oh, heavens, I don't know what to do about this!" Harriet said half aloud, in a distracted tone. "I can't imagine how she's ever going to be told, or how she'll take it, or why you're doing it!"

"I had an idea you could," Philip said.

"Could what?"

"Could perhaps imagine what was the reason."

"Reason for—for jilting Coralia?" Harriet demanded, almost indignant, whispering the hard words.

"Well, if you put it that way."

"What reason could I possibly know?"

"The one invincible one," Philip said slowly, not looking at her.

Silence spread like rising water in the room; solidified like a wall, deepened. Harriet's lips were closed; her nostrils fluttered with her long-drawn breath. Looking at her briefly, Philip saw that her eyes were narrowed on space in an expression almost stern.

"No," she protested, swallowing with an effort.

"Yes," Philip said simply. "I thought you must know."

"It couldn't—it mustn't——" Harriet began. She stopped, and again there was absolute silence in the big, clumsily furnished room that still held Martins bed and table. The walls were crowded with old pictures, and with the stuffed heads of deer and foxes. The empty bed was formally covered with a magnificent pink spread of handmade thread lace and brocade, and on the bedside table stood Martin's favorite picture of Coralia, with her first baby in her arms.

"I've known since the night you came back," Philip said. "You remember, at the piano? I was afraid I had told you then."

"No, please——" Harriet whispered. She locked both hands on the arms of her chair and tried to get to her feet, but reeled backward and was seated again. Philip crossed to her and held out a hard, thin brown hand.

"Yes, you're tired, you want to go to bed," he said. "Come on. Try to get some sleep. I'll be up early and see how she is." He lowered his voice in the hall. "Good night!"

CHAPTER 23

Harriet slipped inside the bedroom door, closed the door noiselessly, went to sit in a chair by Coralia's bed. One candle was burning quietly, Coralia's face was in deep shade, she was asleep. The flickering light fell upon her bandaged hand and on the coil of her dark loosened hair. Harriet sat still for a long time watching her. She was not thinking at all; she was stunned.

It could not have happened. It had happened.

"I had an idea you might have known," Philip had said. He had made no protestations. He had not explained. He had thought that she must know. And she did know, in every fiber of her being. The volcano had erupted at her very feet, everything in her life was blown sky-high. Now the dust and the cinders had fallen, the world was settling into its old contours. And still her mind seemed to hold no thought steady.

"You remember that night at the piano? I was afraid I had

told you then." Philip had said that, too. But to remember it suffocated her. "I was afraid I had told you."

No, no, he hadn't told her. Not that night. She had believed everything else; she had never come near the truth. She had thought for months that she disliked him, then that she liked him well enough but that he shouldn't marry Coralia, then that she was entirely resigned to Philip Haagersen's presence on the ranch no matter whether he was good or bad, or whether he ever liked her or not. And on the night when he had brought the candles over to the piano, and she had sung "Who Is Sylvia?" she had been puzzled and annoyed and even frightened by his manner. But with no suspicion of this.

This was not like anything she ever had felt, anticipated as the experience of loving. No joy in it. No satisfaction. Far from it, there was only a heavy sense of something huge and shadowy over her, close to her, and something light and fearless—something that had always been a part of Harriet Townshend—forever lost. This was going to be with her always, and no joy in it, no satisfaction, no peace, just the frightened darkness that held no speck of light.

"Now what, now what, now what?" she said with a dry mouth. After a while she lay down on the bed Ana had fixed on the floor; Coralia slept on deeply; Ana had disappeared. Nobody had the faintest idea what time it was; everyone was asleep, drugged like Coralia, or worn out like Ana. What did time matter, anyway?

Harriet leaped up from her robes and comforters and went to the southern window. Across the east a level streak of orange light burned like a flame. Morning was near. She went to Coralia's bed and looked down at her; Coralia slept on, breathing deeply. Once or twice she sighed, almost with a moan, otherwise she lay still. She had not changed her position all night long.

Harriet went to her own room, washed her face with cold water, and brushed her hair with a wet brush, tying the ringlets back severely, buttoning herself into a warm woolen dress, for the dark morning hour had been cold and she was shaking. She went into the chapel; the red sanctuary light burned waveringly in the shadowy place. Harriet lighted candles before the Blessed Virgin's altar, and knelt down in her accustomed place. Prayer would not come, but she was glad to be there alone. Her familiar black lace veil gave her a sense of being sheltered, and the enveloping silence and the sweetness of winter roses on the main altar sent lines of scent through the air. Silence and solitude were as refreshing, as the quiet minutes went by, as spring water on a burning day; Harriet's whole being drank them in. She could hear the waking songs of birds now, out in the garden; the eastern windows began to show diamonds of red and gold and blue on the robes of mighty St. Paul, and mild little Agnes with her palm, and the very Virgin herself, in the shell oval of Guadalupe.

Harriet was half asleep when old Father Anselmo came quietly out to kneel at one side of the altar and fall into prayer; a few minutes later Miles, serious, bearded, and eye-glassed, was lighting the Mass candles and setting up the book and the framed prayers; all the windows were pouring in light now; the day had come at last.

The chapel was well filled this morning as Mass began. Women who had been praying together until the early-morning hours had gone for a few hours' rest to their various cabins, or to remote rooms in the hacienda, and were now returned to whisper and weep and click rosary beads again. Harriet could hear them scuffing straw slippers and breathing prayers behind her. She wondered if Philip had come in, and the doctor from San Jose Mission, was he here?

She did not turn her head; she waited until everyone was gone and then went to Coralia's room, afraid that she might find Philip there, but knowing it must be faced sooner or later.

Coralia, just waking, was alone except for Ana; she was slightly feverish, she smiled at Harriet, but complained that whichever way she turned some part of her hurt. Her mouth felt thick and dry and her head ached.

"That's the laudanum," Harriet said. "It'll take you a little while to wake up, but believe me, Señora Salazar y Valdez, you are lucky! Only your arm broken, and it might have been your neck, and just bumps and scratches and the cut

200

shoulder. Ana, get some hot water will you, dear? I'm going to wash the Señora's face and fix her pillows, and we'll give her some hot coffee and be all ready for the doctor!"

"What doctor?" Coralia asked, brightening.

"From San Jose Mission. Enrico went after him and had him here by nine o'clock. You remember? He bandaged your shoulder."

"I thought I dreamed him," Coralia said dazedly.

"Too hot, darling?"

"No, lovely. And Pears' soap, it smells so good! What's the horrible smell that makes me feel that I'm going to throw up?"

"Carbolic, maybe. Carbolic and chloroform, he gave you chloroform when he fixed your shoulder. Father Anselmo said he must scrape the last of the bark out——"

"Bark?" Coralia was interested, and the warm soapy treatment had opened her eyes and freshened face and hands.

"Bark! You had a tree through your shoulder. It stuck out six inches and jabbed right into your chin!"

"Oh, Harriet! Were the boys frightened?"

"They behaved beautifully if they were. They just whispered now and then. I sat and held your shoulder up. You were saying 'Martin' now and then, so we knew you weren't dead. Miles rode like mad for—for help."

"What happened to Chito?"

"Your horse? Oh, Muchachito put his foot in to a hole. It seems there was a sort of culvert there, where the water used to form a pool, long, long ago and old Arturo said it was washing out the trail, so he put a drain of tiles in, with saplings on top. And it gave way."

"Chito wasn't hurt!"

"Not at all. But in the funniest way—— Ah, here's your coffee! In the funniest way that horse did seem troubled, Coralia. He came wandering over——"

Harriet chattered away as she went about the room opening shutters to the golden soft morning sunshine and folding the assorted bedding upon which she and Ana had tried to get some rest in the night. She was reassured by the natural sound of her own voice. No signs of last night's earthquake remaining. She was tired, of course, and she saw her face reflected rather wan and pale in Coralia's mirrors, but there was nothing to rouse suspicion or give her secret away. The accident and the Señora's condition were all the household could discuss this morning.

"We took all your flowers into the chapel last night. Some of the girls prayed all night; Inez and that wild-headed granddaughter of hers were there when I went in. As for this worthless Ana here, she didn't go to bed at all!"

"Señorita?" asked Ana, hearing her name.

"I say to the Señora that thy prayers went to God all the night."

"God is everlastingly good," Ana observed simply.

"Pablo told me yesterday that if you once take flowers into the chapel you mustn't take them away because the Blessed Virgin has already given them to some poor sick person somewhere."

"Oh, Harriet, you're magic, I think! I feel so much better."

"Head better?"

"Oh, much. Harriet, does it hurt if I move this thing?" Coralia glanced at the bandaged arm and shoulder.

"No, he said not. But here he is. Good morning, Doctor. Your patient hasn't the slightest recollection of you, so there's one for your vanity."

"Oh, I'm vain, am I?" Peter Wormsley sat down beside the bed, his fingers on Coralia's wrist. "How do we feel?"

"I did feel awful. But Harriet here, and Ana, have been doing all sorts of things for me, and I really feel—— Ouch! Except when I move, I feel fine."

"That's wonderful. I've been wondering if we ought to get you up to the San Francis hospital, but it may be—if everything goes well——" The stethoscope was at Coralia's chest now, and she could even giggle a little as it moved back and forth. "You've had your breakfast?" Peter asked Coralia, shaking down the thermometer. "Half a degree, that's not important. It's very surprising that it didn't go up," he said to his patient.

"You have had your breakfast, Harriet?"

"Not yet. No hurry." She turned to Coralia. "I'll go down

202

now if Dr. Wormsley hasn't any directions. I'll do your hair afterward."

"I wish all my invalids had a Harriet," said Peter.

"You'd lose them all," Coralia said hoarsely, with a little smile.

"I certainly would. I shall prescribe Harriet from now on. I shall say 'Half an hour of Harriet twice a week,' and charge a small commission.

"Unfortunately, other people have the same idea," said Philip's voice quietly. He was standing near Harriet, but his eyes were all for Coralia. "How goes it, dear?" he said, and Harriet saw the doctor's look move quickly from one face to the other.

Coralia smiled up with all her heart in her look, and Philip sat down, holding her free hand.

"Did you look in for a moment early this morning, Philip?"

"I did. And the look I got from Ana sent me reeling back against the wall."

"Oo-oo, I slept!" Coralia said. "And when I waked up I ached all over. I never felt so awful! Was I pretty bad? Harriet came in and told me that lots of the girls were in the chapel—— Where'd Harriet go?"

"She went down for some breakfast, probably," said Peter. "We were speaking of it. My God, that's a beautiful girl!"

"Harriet," Coralia said proudly.

"That's one of the loveliest girls I ever saw in my life," the doctor said.

"And she's as lovely as she looks, isn't she, Philip?"

"She certainly is."

"But tell me about her. Live here?"

"As much as I can make her," Coralia told him. "She lives in San Francisco, where her mother has a private sort of family hotel."

"Harriet Townley, huh?"

"Townshend," Philip said briefly.

"But how do you mean private?"

"Well, you have to know somebody, you have to recommended."

"Let me think who can recommend me," said Dr. Wormsley, and Coralia laughted.

"Here," said her physician immediately, brought to his senses. "You must be quiet, and you ought to get some sleep."

"Harriet said she'd do my hair."

"Well, then, after that, rest. I'm going down now to see if I can make an impression. I suppose there isn't a chance, but I've got to follow this up."

"There isn't a chance."

"Why d'you say that?" He stopped on his way to the door.

"Because she's had every chance. Men have asked her, and gone away, and come back to ask her again. She could be an English 'my lady' and an Italian baroness. She just doesn't want to marry."

"All girls want to marry," stated the doctor. "Well, I'll be back tomorrow night, and then see you again Thursday, and if you go on this way all you'll need is quiet, and not jerking the arm about."

"Philip, this changes things," Coralia said, holding to his hand when they were alone. And she could not help adding mischievously: "Were you scared?"

"Scared! I've never been so scared in my life. You were the crumpledest-looking thing, banged up against that redwood ——"

"I don't remember Chito stumbling, even."

"Those things happen like a flash."

"Harriet said her hand was stuck to mine with blood." Coralia gave a shiver of enjoyment.

"Yes."

"And she was so cramped, Miles said, that she couldn't stand when she tried to get up."

"He caught her. Yes."

"This changes things, doesn't it?"

"In what way, dear?"

"I love to have you call me dear."

"Then I'll remember to call you that."

"I mean, I want things to change," Coralia began again.

"Tell me how. And then I've got to get back to the barns. Johnson, my new assistant, if you please, is good. He's got a head on his shoulders. But we're shipping tonight, and I want the steers cut out."

"Where do these fellows go?"

"Moffit. Up Mission Dolores way."

"This is the change," said Coralia seriously, rubbing her thumb back and forth on the big hand that held hers. "I want you—us—I want to be married before you go away."

Philip, watching her attentively, found nothing to say.

"I'll tell you why, Philip. I think you'd feel—and I know I would—much more settled, that way. Of course not for a week or two, not until I'm around again, but then—let's be married quietly, with just my mother here, perhaps, and then when you go you're my husband, and when you come back we start our life here.

"You see there's something I want to do while you're away," she went on, as Philip did not change his position or his expression. "I'm telling Harriet that what I want to do in San Francisco is get my trousseau, all that. But what I really want to do, when I go back with Harriet, is see old José Gonzales. That's Martin's cousin, and he and young José look after all my affairs, and the boys' affairs, too. And I want an arrangement made by which half of all the money that comes in is yours. After the boys' ranchos are taken care of and the crops sold—the grapes and the beef and the wheat, you know—whatever money comes in is half yours. It comes to—well, you know what we put into the bank every little while."

"Coralia, you are very generous," Philip said slowly.

"It's not generosity. I've so much more than I need. And if you had that, Philip, why should you go away at all? Why not just stay here, managing things? We could take holidays, we could go abroad when Josito is old enough for school. We could do anything!"

"But for a penniless man to marry a very rich woman . . .?"

"Oh, nonsense, Philip! When it's our happiness, when we love each other!" Coralia's look was all love and sweetness. The doctor had given her something that took away her pain

205

and made her feel drowsy and happy. It was deep, utter content to lie here in peace, with Philip's hand over hers.

"I'll have to say to you what you say to the boys," he said soberly. " 'We'll see.' "

"We will see!" she smiled, turning her head toward the door as it opened. It was Harriet, coming in with her hands full of flowers.

"I thought Philip had gone," Harriet said composedly, going toward the washstand, immediately busy with vases, her back to the room.

"Acacia. I love it!" Coralia said.

"And wild lilac. Tomas brought these in. And cherry." Harriet fussed with her arrangements, and Philip kissed Coralia's beautiful limp hand and got to his feet.

"I'm late. Johnson will have been cooling his heels half an hour!"

"Back for lunch?" Coralia asked.

"Not today. It's ten o'clock now. You get some sleep."

"I had ten solid hours of sleep!"

Harriet came toward the bed with a small white and pink vase full of golden buttercups. She put it on the bedside table and said mildly:

"A shock like yesterday stays with you some time, Coralia. Johnny was thrown from a big black horse we had, down in the Islands, and he was queer for three days."

"I'll be in to see how you are sometime this afternoon," Philip said from the door.

"Well, I should hope so!" Coralia said with a weak little laugh from her pillows.

He was gone. Harriet went to find brushes, came back to loosen Coralia's heavy braids and replait them in firm ropes that hung on her shoulders.

"Pain now, darling?"

"Only when I—ouch—move it!"

"Does it get cramped?"

"It did in the night. It was awful when I waked up. Harriet," Coralia said, with a change of tone on the name, "Philip and I have been having a wonderful talk. He seemed so gentle, and so—I don't know—considerate. Did he seem quiet to you?"

"I wish you'd try being quiet. You're not to get tired!"

"I know." Coralia was still for a moment, her eyes shining. "We had the most wonderful talk, we never have quite talked this way," she presently said. "About plans, and finances, everything. It's so comfortable to feel the way we do, no excitement, you know. Just comfortable."

"Did I jerk your hair then?"

"No-o-o. Harriet, I've a good mind to tell you something."

"Go ahead. There, that's that. Now lie back. You look lovely."

"It's this. We may be married before Philip goes away. What are you looking for in the wardrobe?"

Before she answered Harriet established herself in the rocker, with a big basket of boys' socks beside her. She looked up from threading a needle.

"No trousseau," she said mildly. She had no idea what she said; she was concerned only with the fear that Coralia would notice something strange in her manner. Or was there anything strange in her manner; did it just seem, as she herself felt, dead?

"Oh, that——" Coralia said. "That doesn't matter. But I think he would like it. He would feel sure of me, for one thing. And then I want to make some legal arrangements—"

"We'll be making funeral arrangements, *querida*, if you don't lie still!"

Coralia lay still for a moment, and Harriet hoped she had fallen asleep. But Coralia's eyes opened suddenly as she said:

"Harriet, don't you think it's a wise idea?"

"Think . . .?"

"I mean, don't you think it's sensible, our getting married now, before he goes away?"

"But then he'd leave immediately after your marriage, Coralia. That's not much fun."

"He might not leave at all," Coralia said, with a mischievous look.

"But you don't want to be married with your arm in a sling?"

"As if that mattered!"

Harriet appeared to be thinking this over, her head tipped, her needle touching her cheek. She was, however, incapable of any consideration except the confused one that included Philip's words of last night, "I thought you must know. You remember, at the piano? I was afraid I had told you then."

"You see I want to make some adjustments," Coralia said. "I talked to him about it, only this morning, and he agreed. That is, he didn't disagree. My name will be changed; I'll have to fix that at the bank. And then arranging for him to have a rightful share. I don't see what more a man could want. I mean, loving the ranch as he does, and talking about riding down to Mexico someday to see bullfights——"

"You think he really doesn't care about being a doctor?"

"Oh, he does. He does. He wants to stand on his own feet," Coralia said loyally. "But what I feel is, there's no hurry."

"I wonder if he is thinking the way I am—if I am thinking at all," Harriet was musing, deep in her being. "I wonder how long this feeling lasts. I wonder how much of its shows. Then you may not be coming up to the city at all?" she said aloud.

"Oh, yes, all of us, for clothes, after we're married, when he goes away," Coralia said happily, too deeply absorbed in her own dreams to notice anything odd in Harriet's manner. "My arm won't make any real difference. Isn't it funny," she went on dreamily, "that the accident seems to have sort of cleared the sky? It seems to me that I am the most fortunate woman in the world, Harriet. It's all so different from the time I married Martin. I don't mean we didn't love each other; we did. He was always kind to me, he wanted me to have everything in the world. But it was different!

"This," her happy drowsy voice went on, after a moment of silence, "this is such a new feeling for me. That Philip and I are both young enough to travel, and to entertain—you see, Martin never wanted people here, not in my day, anyway. I imagine that when he was married to Pia Lopez he was gay enough; they used to have tremendous parties here. I don't think she ever liked them. But I was always sick, I lived up on this floor most of the time.

"It'll seem so funny going places with my husband, and such a husband! Harriet, are you asleep?"

"Not quite."

"You poor thing, you were awake practically all night, while I slept along here like a log. Why don't you go lie down? Ana's upstairs again, she'll come in."

"I believe I will." Harriet smiled sleepily, put the big basket aside, and carrying a double handful of mended stockings, went from the room.

In the hall she saw Philip standing against the opposite wall waiting for her. He touched his lip with his finger, and Harriet silently followed him about an angle of the hall to the deep embrasure of a window. They stood looking out at the garden, and the orchards, and the dull tiled roofs of the long row of adobe cabins down the hill. The sun had gone behind a bank of fog, the sky was low, and all light and color seemed drained from the world.

"I had to see you. I am going away," Philip said hurriedly.

"Now?"

"Tonight, I think."

"What will you tell Coralia?" Harriet was speaking in a lifeless, weary tone; she did not look at him.

"Nothing."

"You can't do that."

"I have—to do something."

"That's what I think I wanted to ask you."

"What do you want to know?"

There were pauses between phrases, and both continued to look out of the window.

"What—why—why I feel so—sometimes so frightfully happy about what you said, Philip, and sometimes——" Harriet's voice lowered, broke. Tears bit at her eyes.

"Do you really want to know?" Philip asked, also in a low voice.

"I think I do."

"I think it's called falling in love," Philip said.

"No," Harriet said, turning to him for the first time her shadow-ringed blue eyes. "I've been in love before. It's nothing like that. This is more like sickness—weakness—I don't know what it is like."

"You and I have fallen in love. It's too bad. It's the last thing either of us would want to do. But that's it."

She looked at him, looked away again in silence.

"I can't sleep," Harriet said presently. "I lie awake and I begin to tremble, and then I think of Coralia and I wish I were dead."

"Yes, I know. I'm doing that, across the hall, all night long."

"Philip, don't tell me that."

The man was silent, and after a while Harriet said timidly:

"Would you be unhappy—would you be disappointed—if you did marry Coralia, now, before you go away, and then went away and thought it all over and came back perhaps feeling differently?"

"No. It can't be that way. Not now," Philip said definitely.

"But what can we do? What can we do?"

"Harriet, I don't know."

"If I went home to my mother," Harriet said, "and stayed there, and you stayed here, would it—would it make any difference?"

"I don't think so."

"But how," she asked desperately, "can we go on? And what else can we do? What do people do?"

"I thought my leaving—without good-bys——" Philip began, and stopped.

"No. No, that would kill her," Harriet said.

"It's too bad," the man offered, after a pause.

"Oh, yes, it's too bad," she said hurriedly. "I see now, I never did before, that it—that loving—can't be helped. If you stay here and I go away—I'll say I'm coming back, to stay for a longer time, when you go——

"But no, that won't do. Because Coralia wants to be married right away, and come down to Ma's for a long visit. Could you—could you—set the date, maybe, for six weeks from now——"

"That's what I'll have to do. It's not right, but it's the safest way."

"Then I'll go home, promising to be back for the wedding, that will give us time, anyway."

"You see now that I couldn't go through with it."

It was not a question. She said seriously:

"Oh, yes. Now."

"And you didn't know—the night I brought the candles over to the piano, Harriet?"

"No. But I felt strange—that there was something strange." Harriet widened her eyes as she turned to him. "And I feel strange now," she added simply.

A smile twitched at Philip's lips, but he spoke without smiling.

"It is all strange. As strange to me as to you. It is not like anything I ever felt before. It is destiny, maybe. I looked at you that night, while you were singing, and the only thought I had was 'This is she. This is the woman for whom I would have to search the world over, for whom I would have to wait all my years, if I lost her now. This is the face that will be opposite mine, at our own breakfast table, in the good times and in the bad times. She is part of me, I am part of her.' "

"But if it can never be that way?" she asked pitifully, again turned toward the window.

"Then we have this," he said.

"Yes, we have this."

She was gone, with the words, and he was alone.

CHAPTER 24

Coralia's convalescence was to her a time of rapture. She was not expected to make any effort; she must protect the injured shoulder, and give up riding, walking, dancing, for a while.

This was no hardship for her, under the present thrilling circumstances. Coralia had had long illnesses in this dark big hacienda before, but those had been painful; boring slow preludes to that day—or possibly those dreadful two or three days—when she had strained and struggled and burned in the fever of giving birth.

She remembered her bedroom of those days. It was airier now, with frail curtains and a pink moquette rug; it had been a dark and heavy chamber then. It had been curtained voluminously in green rep that was tied with tassels; there had been China matting on the floor. The dark, hot place had smelled of oils and flannels, warm milk and flax-seed, and the coal fire; a great many women had come and gone as the endless flaming hours had dragged from dawn to sunset, sunset through to dawn again.

Everyone else had been comfortable, sympathetic, and uninvolved. Maria Pia, the midwife, aged and experienced, was fertile in expedience. Maria Pia was a soft bag of an old woman, adroit in handling the mottled, worried-looking, undersized boys that Coralia produced. She did not like long labors, they made her nervous, but even Coralia's eventually ended, and the exhausted girl, lying back in the pillows, usually could manage a weak smile when she first saw the black mop and crinkled saffron body of the newborn son. But for days afterward Coralia lay brooding in a world that was still darkened by the memory of roaring and blazing pain. She had no pleasant memories or recollections of those illnesses that seemed to have been merged together, so fast they followed.

Now rich, independent, and in glorious health and spirits, everything was different. The magnificent acres of redwood canyons, vineyards, grain fields, and foothill ranges were all hers, the adobe village where her people lived, under lines of eucalyptus and oak and pepper trees, the infinitely ramified lines of corrals and barns, fences and paddocks, and the grand old hacienda—all hers. And to lend the last touch of pride and romantic pleasure to the picture, here was a lover ready-made, tall, intelligent, masterful, Coralia's very ideal from the rich waves of his fair hair to the soles of his feet.

Coralia dreamed of a long heavenly future, spent for the most part on the rancho Corazón d'Oro, with Philip.

212

They would travel, of course, someday. But there wouldn't be much likelihood of Philip's following up the medical school idea, in Scotland or anywhere. He would be too happy right here, on his own wide lands. She would make him independent of her own purse; a sure way to save his pride and secure his loyalty to her.

They would go to San Francisco, stay perhaps at the Palace Hotel, which was the city's boast. Harriet would be married, too, one of these days, and the four of them would visit every restaurant and theater in town. Then they would all come back to the rancho, to spend delicious days in the atmosphere that was making this time so radiant, so unbelievably sweet. Harriet's children and hers would have their ponies, their playgrounds and playrooms; their dancing feet would explore every foot of the old house.

And at dusk in the winter, or in the long shadows of sunset in the summer, the men would come up from the barns, tired and dirty, glad to find their women fresh and cool on the north veranda. They would disappear into the upper regions, presently to come down shaven and shining. Philip's white garments, his crisp sideburns and shining crest, his long, fine-featured brown face and his lean, sensitive hands, the very tones of his voice reflecting the satisfaction of the tired ranchero, when his flocks and herds, his vines and orchards, his wife and his children are all in order and his soul at peace.

Then would follow the heavenly evening hours, with Tia Hattie at the piano, a fire blazing in the steel-rodded grate, lamps lighted, children coming and going with lingering good nights, and Father Anselmo, or some other old chaplain, dreaming in his big chair. Miles, still and always to be the boys' tutor and companion, would take his favorite seat under the lamp, and Coralia and Philip, their hands linked, would exchange quiet smiles, with now and then a phrase or two, while they basked in an utter content that needed no words.

"What more could we have, Philip?" she asker him, talking of these halcyon days ahead.

"I don't like it!" he said suddenly one afternoon when, for the first time, Coralia had been tenderly escorted downstairs

213

and was luxuriously established in robes and pillows on the old sofa by the fire.

"Philip!" Coralia gasped, half laughing, half shocked. Harriet, crocheting busily in the shadows beyond the lamp, looked up.

"No, you too generous person," Philip said. He was in a low chair, looking at the fire, his linked hands hanging between his knees. "Don't you see that all these lovely plans mean that you're giving everything and I nothing? I've got to balance the scales a little better than that."

"Not by waiting. Not by separation," Coralia said confidently.

"Years from now, how do I know you wouldn't think me pretty weak to have taken so much, my dear? I'd be here, enjoying a king's privileges, not having contributed a penny. Suppose you someday said to me. 'You were just a cowhand when you came here——' "

"Please, Philip, don't tease." Coralia's tone was hurt.

"I'm not teasing. I want to be someone of whom you—of whom my wife will be proud. I've never fooled you about that, Coralia!"

"Harriet, he goes on this way all the time! What are we going to do with him? Harriet, can you see what you're doing over there?"

"Yes, this is fine."

"Tell Philip that it would be wicked—it would be too stupid not to take the happiness that is right here at hand and go wandering off across the ocean."

"Oh——" Harriet started up with a faint guilty laugh. "I promised Father that I'd fix the chapel for Benediction—I wonder if someone brought up the candles——" She was murmuring to herself as she hurriedly left the room.

The whole outer world was a rush and drip of rain on the March afternoon, and the big halls of the hacienda were dim and cool and smelled of adobe. Harriet reached the chapel door and stood there, leaning against the wall, writhing, writhing.

"Oh, what are we going to do?" she whispered. "What can we do! My best friend—and she trusts us both! And she's so happy! This spoils it all—my coming here. I can never come again, after all we've had together! And there's no way out!"

She went into the chapel, knelt down, still féeling her body twist with emotions she could not master. There was no light in the long narrow room, except the red winking eye of the sanctuary light, the dim glow of yellow on a saint's robes, and the glint of the Madonna's crown in the high western windows. Harriet bowed her head and tried to pour out her heart in supplication, but not only did words fail her, but feeling, too. She could only breathe hard against the hands she pressed against her face and struggle for calm.

There was no calm. After a while she went across the altar, feeling as if she limped because of the weight of her heart. She automatically folded the Bible stand and carried books and Mass cards away. She came out from the vestry with the six-branched candlesticks, the vestments, the censer, and put them carefully into their places. Then she knelt down again, and all the world was a desert and there was no refuge anywhere for her thoughts. Rain rapped on the tiles of the high roof.

This was the end of her visit. Tomorrow afternoon, with Tomas or Enrico, and perhaps a bawling calf or two occupying the old wagon, she would be going down the hill, away from the adobe cabins and the overhanging oaks and eucalyptus, the sheds and fences, the old garden that surrounded the hacienda, and the hacienda itself. She would be going away from what was the essential lifeblood of her being. She would not see Philip again for a long time; perhaps never again.

Other women had lived through this; she must live through it. The way to live through it was not to think about it; hard—hard—hard when there was nothing else about which she could think.

She was the daughter of a boardinghouse keeper; Philip had nothing. She might more than once have decided upon an advantageous marriage. Philip might marry wealth and power, right here at his feet.

Too late to think of that now, or of Coralia's wrecked happiness, or of the vagueness, the remorse, the regrets of any

215

future that could possibly present itself. Everything was lost now, until this burning fever in her veins quieted, until she was far away from all this, alone with her own soul.

The Benediction group was gathering; Harriet went to take her place at the organ in the choir. The first chords of *O Salutaris* sounded in the dim space; the first threads of incense crept through the air. The windows were dark now; a black-headed small boy had lighted the requisite twelve candles. Two or three teen-age girls, half Mexican, half Indian, heavy of long black braids and immaculate as to white cotton blouses, suppressing their eternal tendency to giggle, came up to lead the singing. A languid boy pumped the organ; Harriet heard the voice that thrilled through her whole being admonishing him. Then Philip's lips were close to her ear.

"Riding—tomorrow—six too early . . .?"

"Oh, no, Philip!" she breathed back, life flowing into her veins and heaven opening.

"By the bull pen," he said. That was all, he was gone. Through the evening he sat near Coralia and talked to her, and Miles and Harriet tried different odds and ends of music at the piano.

Harriet excused herself before nine o'clock. She said she was tired, but she was moving on wings. Six o'clock was not too near, but the interval would hardly give her time to think what it might mean to be riding before sunrise with Philip beside her. She stayed awake dreaming, with her eyes wide open, until it was time to go in and kiss Coralia good night. Coralia was in a state of quiet transport as ecstatic as Harriet's own.

"I think his lordship and I have come to an understanding," Coralia reported with satisfaction.

"You mean about getting married before he goes? . . . Be careful there, Ana, put the pillow under the Señora's shoulder." Harriet was busy, lifting the covers over Coralia, smoothing them flat.

"I mean that he may not go!" Coralia laughed. "I don't think that young man is quite as anxious to get away from the rancho as he sounds."

"Well, your accident of course made a difference. You

yourself agreed that it wouldn't be much fun to go on a one-armed honeymoon," Harriet said, holding a pill on one palm, a glass of water in the other hand.

"I know, and it's only a few weeks. It's almost two already, and the doctor said six should do it." Coralia gulped down the pill obediently, settled back against pillows, looked at Harriet with a radiant color suffusing her face. "It is such fun to plan with Phil," she said. "Except that he's so horribly serious!"

"Serious?" Harriet echoed the words somewhat indistinctly as she straightened the prayer book, the *Imitation*, and *The Heir of Redclyffe* on Coralia's bedside table.

"Oh, yes. Never laughs at all. I have to remind him that this isn't a funeral we're talking about," Coralia said gaily. "He keeps putting in things about 'if all goes well,' and 'if nothing prevents our carrying out these plans,' and 'if you really think it wiser to be married before I go away, dear.'"

"Ha." Harriet was over by the door now, close to Ana; she had a few words of low-toned direction for the maid. "Don't let Josito come tearing in here too early," Coralia heard.

"How you all spoil me!" Coralia said luxuriously.

"You don't spoil. Now, what else?" Harriet asked, returning to the bedside.

"Nothing else, except sit here on the bed a minute and talk. Harriet, wasn't Philip wonderful tonight?" Coralia mused, her dark eyes dreamy. "That sounds silly, of course. But I mean that just these last few days he has seemed so much more serious, more responsible, as if taking on a wife, three sons, and fourteen thousand acres was a rather big job after all! He's just determined to show me that he isn't an idler, drifting about from one place to another, but that he can stand on his own feet. When he first came here," she went on, as Harriet, leafing through a copy of the *Ave Maria* did not speak nor look up, "he seemed just a sort of adventurer. He talked of all sorts of places and all sorts of jobs, and he told me that of all the things in the world the last thing he wanted was to settle down.

"Well, he's changed that tune now!" she exulted. "Now he's hardly willing to stay here, he wants to prove how much in earnest he is—managing a rancho isn't big enough. That's not the word—I mean it isn't——"

"Significant," Harriet supplied, looking up.

"Well, yes. Too much like being still my foreman. Which of course is pure nonsense. But, Harriet, I would want him to feel that way."

"What way?" asked Harriet, laying aside the magazine and clearing her throat.

"Well, wanting to be something himself, not just marrying a rich woman. But believe me, he'll get over that. Don't you think so?"

"I should think so."

"In the first place, we need him here. He says this new man, Johnson, knows twice what he does about ranching, but I say Philip's the best we've ever had. And in the second, third, fourth, and fifth places," laughed Coralia, "I love him. And I told him so! Oh, Harriet, I hope someday you feel about someone the way I feel about Philip. Only you mustn't feel it about Philip. He's mine!"

"I'm half asleep." Harriet was at the door; her back turned toward the room. She leaned her head against the wall.

"Of course you are! Oh, listen. I forgot. Philip may be off very early, and he said if he didn't come back to breakfast to say good-by and not forget that you're coming back in two weeks."

"If Ma doesn't break my leg to keep me home," Harriet said, turning to flash a good-night smile toward Coralia before she closed the door.

CHAPTER 25

Her heart beating so hard that she imagined she could hear it, she dressed in the black darkness of five o'clock, stole downstairs, and stepped out into the chill of approaching morning. She was ready for Ana, or any of the other servants should she encounter them, with the explanation of headache, restless night, need of fresh air.

But she met nobody. The doors of the house were always unbarred; there were no locks at the hacienda. Harriet crept down one of the winding garden paths holding the heavy skirts of her habit away from brushing against shrubs heavy with dew. The night was just breaking; outlines of trees, gate, fences began to show darker gray against the gray. The sky to the southwest was a troubled confusion of woolly clouds against a long streak of cold silver.

At the corral corner Philip was standing, the reins of the two horses looped on his arm. Harriet and he did not speak as she rose into the saddle with her own practiced lightness. Her narrow bronzed shoe, buttoned high in scallops, hardly touched his hand; then she was settling her skirts about her, and took the reins with the hold that started her mount off at a flying pace. Philip was close behind her; they took the trail that led away from the rancho straight up into the heavily wooded foothills, and were presently riding abreast under oak and madroña and scattered clumps of mighty redwoods.

The corduroy road was packed deep in damp leaves, the air was rich with aromatic scent. Fallen trees had been sawed and built into sturdy woodpiles, over which chipmunks in trim little striped coats flashed busily, but the birds were not yet awake.

There was a mountain meadow some miles above the rancho, and here Harriet checked her horse on the brink of the hill and sat facing the east and the rising sun. A blazing red never seen at any other hour on land or sea flushed the sky; the tumbled little clouds were tipped with gold. Suddenly the sun showed, and Harriet turned her dazzled eyes toward Philip and spoke for the first time.

"Have you thought what we can do?" she asked, like a child.

He was on his feet, and now she dismounted too, and with her skirt bundled on her arm she came to stand beside him, watching the red light catch on the dark tips of the redwoods

219

and pierce with spears of gold through the layers of their foliage.

"I've thought—something," Philip said. "I've thought what we can do first. It's not much."

"There's no happy way out for us, is there?" Harriet started bravely, but her throat thickened and she had to lower her voice to finish.

"Not that I can see. Not for a long time."

"No," she said slowly.

"But someday there might be."

"Yes, I know," she said. They looked at the sunrise.

"What are we to do?" Harriet presently asked.

"Our engagement, Coralia's and mine, of course," Philip said, "is the trouble. You find it hard to understand how that came about, I suppose?"

"I know how it came about."

"I don't think you do."

"Yes. She told me."

She saw his face flush under the sunburn.

"That she asked you," Harriet said simply. Nothing seemed to matter much, now. At another time she might have shielded Coralia, out of sheer loyalty. But all such considerations were meaningless this morning.

"She is generosity itself," the man said. "She has so much to give!"

"I don't know why," Harriet said with a little effort, "it had to be this way. It would have gone so—so right for you both if I hadn't come into it."

"I don't know. It might not have been so right."

Long pauses. The horses grazed on the new fresh grass, dragging their reins.

"Well, this is what I've been thinking, and you see what you think. You go home today—that ends one phase of it."

"So much ends, forever!" Harriet said with trembling lips. "Our morning rides—our singing at night—all our talk——"

"All ended. You go home today, but you're expected back here in two weeks."

"Do I come back?" Harriet asked with tired docility.

"Yes, unless Coralia decides to go into town to stay at

220

your mother's. The boys will be in school, she may bring Josito and Ana, and settle down for a month or two of shopping. I'll write her there. I'll make the break quick and final. And you'll have to help her through it, Harriet."

"She told me only yesterday that in case you really decided to go, you would be married first. When she's in the city she wants to do tremendous things for you, she wants to make you rich."

"I know it. I know how generous she is."

"But that doesn't count?"

"No. As far as a hurried marriage goes, several things are against it. One is that her arm is in a sling. Another is that Father Anselmo will be gone. He goes on Retreat in ten days, and she wants him, of course, to marry us.

"The day after he goes," Philip said, as Harriet, watching him with tragic confident eyes, did not speak, "I will get a letter from my brother telling of my mother's illness. I will leave that hour, and with her blessing, too."

"But how will you get that letter?"

"I have it, here in my pocket. There is a traveler going through the rancho almost every day, north or south. I will say he brought it."

"And then, Philip?"

"Then time, Harriet. Time. That's our only hope. I am going to ship on the first boat I can get out of San Francisco, to Scotland, I hope."

"There's usually one from the Clyde in harbor," Harriet, born to the watching for ships, said, with an anxious little wrinkle between her brows. "Unless you want a special one. Is that—is it expensive?"

"Not if you ship as extra hand or second mate or any other of a half dozen jobs. And when I get to Scotland then I find another job, as hard as I can make it. And when I come back, a doctor, it will be different, maybe. It will be years. Unless something happens."

"I'll wait," Harriet said briefly.

"Harriet——" he began, and stopped abruptly. He walked away from her, turning his back, and stood looking off across the mountain ranges. When he came back it was to speak briskly, although his voice was hoarse. "There are hours in your life that are too hard," he said. "This hour is too hard for me. And because of you it is hard for me."

"Years are not too long," Harriet said bravely. "If we are to be together after that—always——"

"Harriet, you are not to promise, that wouldn't be fair! But I want to promise."

"You needn't." The girl spoke simply; her eyes were wide with dreams. "If there is anything true in the world," she said, "you will come for me. And meanwhile I'll be busy. I'll do what Gardy Ann did for Ma. I'll take care of Lizzie's babies."

"And you know—you do believe—that no matter how long it is, I'll come back."

"Yes. I've often thought what it would be like to wait for your life to—to come true that way. Other women have done it. Now I'll know."

"We can write," the man said.

"Oh, don't you think better not, Philip? I don't want to know where you are. That'll be the first thing she'll ask me. Have I heard?"

"Not for a while, then. Yes, you're right. So then there's just one thing more, Harriet. I love you. I'll never change. No woman ever meant to me what you mean, or ever will. You changed my life, you made me want to get into a world of hard-working men, men who support homes with wives and children in them—the only life for us humans. I want the hard days, laboratory days, and to come home to you, and books, and a fire, and nothing else."

"Tea. And thin brown bread and butter," she said shakily. "And a nice little girl with a mop of red hair to lean against your shoulder and tell you the news of the day."

"You," he said.

"I? Listen to him! I'll be boiling the kettle and buttering the bread. No, that'll be your oldest girl—let me see, Teresa. Ma's name is Mary Teresa, so that fits. Do you know what Teresa means?" His arm was about her; her raised eyes were below his own.

"No, my darling."

"It means 'carrying ears of corn.'" And in her musical Irish voice, always with a hint of tears close behind the laughter in it, she quoted the beautiful passage:

"'Going they went and wept, casting their seeds. But coming, they shall come with joyfulness, carrying their sheaves.'"

Her face was wet with tears as she disengaged herself from his arm and walked toward her horse. Without speaking Philip followed her and gave her a hand to mount. And still in silence they rode down through the awakening forest, that rang now with bird songs and flashed with the movement of wings.

Half an hour later she quietly peeked into Coralia's room.

"You got up for Mass?" Coralia questioned.

"I did indeed. And I went out and walked. It's delicious out. What sort of a night, dear, and does that bandage still feel loose?'"

Harriet was still in a state of bewilderment, daze, and fatigue of spirit, but Coralia saw nothing amiss. Ana was brushing and braiding her heavy hair; candles had been lighted in the room, but now the first red rays of the sun were streaming in at the southeastern windows and over the wide sills poured the racket of a thousand birds in the garden.

The small boys came in to greet their mother. Miles had promised to take them on a long ride to see miners panning gold up in the hills. Two stout girls in bursting white cotton blouses came in with the Señora's breakfast. The hacienda was awake and stirring, and Harriet's secret emotions were lost in the general confusion.

Philip came in; he had had his breakfast. Harriet went down for hers, which was shared by Miles, the three boys, and the old priest. When Philip came in to say a brief kindly good-by to her it was with these witnesses. But her heart was singing wildly of that half hour high up in the hills, and the glory of it stayed with her during the long slow trip home.

CHAPTER 26

Harriet went to the door and looked up and down Howard Street. No sign of a doctor's buggy racketing over the rough dirt road. She went into Lizzie's little kitchen and poured the untouched cup of chicken broth back into the main soup pot. Lizzie hadn't wanted it, poor girl. It was nine o'clock in the morning, but all clocks since yesterday at two had apparently slowed down. Their hands barely moved.

After she had washed the cup and spoon Harriet straightened the kitchen, threw out the coffee grounds, set the oatmeal pot to soak. She brushed the floor and fed two scavenger cats who rose from the porch railing at her approach and stood curved and bristling, ready for instant flight. They finished Liz's bowl of cold cereal in three gulps.

Two old women were in Lizzie's room; one her previously engaged midwife, the other a friend, also a midwife, who had been called in to exert supposedly superior powers. But they could not seem to help Lizzie, and Lizzie was tired, and the general, but unexpressed, fear was that the baby would be getting tired too. Now Johnny, impatient and apprehensive, had gone for Dr. Swann. He would run to Mission Street, take the horsecar downtown, and catch the doctor at his club. And when the doctor was ready they would come clop-clopping back in the doctor's phaeton. It was this clop-clop for which Harriet listened; it was this muddy buggy for which she watched.

She and her mother and brother had had an early breakfast. Now the older woman had gone home; she had been on duty all the long night. She needed a wash and a change and early Mass to restore equilibrium, and she would come back, the promised, in time to kiss "your big boy." Lizzie had been unable to smile at this parting; she had entirely forgotten that a baby's birth was involved in this hideous chain of events. She had lost track of time, she had almost lost all sense of her own identity.

One of her nurses had tied a roped sheet to the base of the bed, and occasionally and enthusiastically suggested that she "pull good" on it. But Lizzie couldn't do that any more, and Harriet, herself desperate with anxiety, suspected that Lizzie's attendants were as relieved as herself that the doctor was coming to explain this apparent deadlock.

In Lizzie's small bedroom the curtains were drawn tight, it was dark; her bed was tumbled. She writhed and twisted in it, sometimes her dark rumpled hair all that was visible as she dug her face into the pillow; sometimes she sat up, wringing her hands. Harriet would watch for a space, her face working as Lizzie's worked, then rush away, if possible out of the sound of the immortal battle. She was at the corner of the street when Johnny and the doctor came into view, and went in to tell the good news to Lizzie. One of the nurses was asleep on the parlor sofa, the other stepped back from the bed, breathing hard, and announced in a whisper that was perfectly audible to Lizzie that the baby was probably dead. Harriet's heart stood still.

However, Dr. Benjamin Swann, born in Vermont and laconic and unemotional as became a Vermonter, was of a different opinion. He came in with a breath of fresh air, and asked his patient cheerfully if she didn't want that baby. If she did, she'd have to go ahead and have it. He was real fond of Lizzie, but he couldn't have the baby for her.

"That there's a smart baby," said the doctor, busy with unwashed hands that smelled of leather. "He told me he wa'n't goin' to show the tip of his head—stand back, Miss Harriet, this ain't for you, I'm goin' to make her mad!—he wa'n't going to show up until I got here. I've known many a baby to die cause there warn't no phy-sician. All right, you give one more yell like that and we'll——Well, here we are, here we are! Someone's comin' to town. Hot water, Mrs. Howden. That's it, you yell, and you tell old Dr. Ben that he ain't no gentleman——"

Lizzie's hoarse shrieks, torn from the innermost fiber of

225

her outraged being, died away suddenly. She said faintly, "Shouldn't it cry?" and sank back, as a dark lump in the doctor's hands, a lump spotted and shapeless, and topped with a black mop, gave forth a shrill "Oo-wah."

"You've got as pretty a little girl as I ever see," said the doctor.

"Oh, let me, let me!" Harriet, as wan as Lizzie was, sprang from her knees and came to peer eagerly. A moment later she had the baby in a blanket, and doctor and nurse were busy with the exhausted but radiant Lizzie. "Oh, you darling, you cross little disgruntled darling!" Harriet, in the rocker by the fire, breathed ecstatically.

"Where's Johnny, Harriet?"

"He was running full speed across the lots," the nurse volunteered.

"Get him back. She's asking for him."

Somebody got Johnny back; and Margaret Mary Townshend was put down in a washbasket that was ruffled with pink dotted swiss, and as Lizzie sank off to sleep, everyone else gathered in the kitchen for a cup of coffee. Mrs. Townshend, returning cold and fresh, was in time for the weary first of the rejoicing; Johnny, before reporting at the bank, lay down on Lizzie' bed and slept. Harriet went home for a bath and change, and the day settled itself into a regular day.

"Ma, is it always a hooligan's picnic like that? Yesterday at two until nine this morning?" Harriet asked, later in the day.

"Well, the first one——" Mrs. Townshend conceded. "But she's got her beautiful gir'rl now——"

"Mother."

"Well, it is a beautiful child, as fat as a muffin, with good lungs on her, and eyes set like yours."

"Mother—I ask you——"

"You'll see. She's going to be a beauty. Margaret Mary, my mother's name, and Lizzie's mother, too. My mother gave all her children the name of Mary, boys and girls alike; Johnny is John Martin Mary. Well, it's over," Mrs. Townshend said, with a deep, contented sigh, "and another little native-born San Franciscan in the world. God bless her."

"Will Lizzie just get over this as if it was nothing, Ma?"

"Well, no, dear. But she'll not resent it. It's all part of her growing up. They say women forget the birth pains—that is, men say it. But they don't, they're not fools. It's only that they've learned not to cry before they're hurt, and they don't talk about it."

"At eight o'clock last night I thought she couldn't stand any more of it, and then to have it go on all night, and that old ghoul of a Howden telling her the baby was dead——"

"That's the way it is, lovey. I wonder what Hattie Townshend is thinking about now," mused Harriet's mother. "She's got that funny faraway look in her eyes. She's not been the same since she came back this time from the rancho. She wouldn't have fallen in love with that very devout young Miles somebody that teaches the boys? Or is it she's breaking her heart that Coralia is going to get married? Well, she'll tell me someday."

It was two days later that Johnny hired a carriage and brought his mother, sister, and daughter to church. Lizzie, upon their return, was lovely in a flowered pink wrapper as she gathered her "little Christian" to her heart. Margaret Mary had not bleached out sufficiently to make anything but a dark little pulpy contrast to her filmy long white robes. She had, however, cried just the right amount as she was christened, and was the object of much flattery and congratulation.

Lizzie seized an opportunity during this long happy spring Sunday to have a word aside with her husband's mother.

"Mrs. Townshend," said Lizzie, slow to use a more familiar term. Margaret Mary was having a midafternoon snack, and the two women were enjoying complete privacy in Lizzie's room. "Would you do something for me?"

"Well, of course, dear'r. Is it bills?"

"Oh, no. My father helped with them. He gave Johnny fifty dollars."

"Johnny told me."

"It's this. I want Johnny to know that—that there won't be any more children." As Lizzie spoke her eyes filled.

"I see," said Johnny's mother with a wise nod.

227

"You see, I nearly died, and if I had, and had left her——" Lizzie said, weeping.

"I know, dear. I know how you feel."

"Mrs. Howden said she never saw anyone suffer as I did. She said she thought the baby was dead. Ess, her did, ess, her did," Lizzie crooned, gathering the baby suddenly to her heart.

"I better take that dress off her, dear, and put her down. She's dropped off the nipple."

"She does that, and then she comes back and tugs like a little ferryboat. Will you do that for me?"

"I'll tell Johnny that for the time being——"

"No, not that! For all time," Lizzie said jealously.

"I'll have a talk with Johnny," Mrs. Townshend said, scrupulously avoiding any exact promise as to its tenor.

"Mrs. Howden says that if the men had to have every other one, there'd be hers, then his, then hers again, and that'd be the end," Lizzie offered, trying to laugh naturally, but not quite sure of the effect of this speech.

"Oh, yes, I've heard that one, many's the day."

"And another thing——Oh, look out for her head! She said always to—yes, that way. Another thing, Johnny himself said that he never could love another one the way he does Margaret Mary, and he don't think it would be fair to the next one."

"That's the father for you," Mrs. Townshend said indulgently.

"And will you speak to him? Because I honestly couldn't go through that again."

"I'll speak to him indeed. Johnny," said Mrs. Townshend to her son a few days later, in response to a confidence from him, "she said something like that to me, too. But give her another month or two and then you'll be the one that won't hear of having any more."

"Ma?" questioned Johnny, surprised.

"Yes, you be the one that don't want any more, that says you can't afford them, and that you wouldn't have her go through that again for twenty children, and that one's enough."

"Aha," Johnny said thoughtfully. "Ma, you're smart. She says now that we're going to be brother and sister for the rest of our lives."

"She'll be all right. Give her her head," his mother advised. "Once married you're always praying they'll come or praying they won't, and it's when they don't come that it breaks your hearts. Johnny," she said, changing the subject, "have you noticed anything about Harriet?"

"You bet your life I have."

"Is it Coralia's marriage, dear'r?"

"Nope. It's my guess she's in love."

"Johnny! She acts that way. Who with?"

"Ma, I don't know. It could be anybody. She was down at Belmont before she went over to the rancho, maybe it was Taylor Mowrey—his aunt's Mrs. Howe. Or it could be that ass from Bakersfield——"

"No, she said no to him only a few days ago."

"Could it be that tutor over at the rancho?"

"He wants to be a priest. She'd let him alone." But Harriet's mother looked worried. "That's it," she said. "She acts just like a girl in love. Harriet!

"She getting letters?'

"No. No extra letters."

"Any special feller coming here?"

"No one special. The unmarried O'Connor boy, but he's always here. And that Renault man—the Frenchman, and Sid Forester."

"I thought he was after Meg Reinhart."

"Well, he is, but they live in Alameda, and he drifts in here a good deal. Johnny, could it be that it's Coralia's getting married, and her feeling lonely, and that things won't be the same at the rancho and she'll just take the nearest man?"

"She'd be an awful fool if she did."

"She's not eating," said the mother. "Oh, she eats enough. But she sort of fools with her food. And she isn't going off on Van Montgomery's tallyho party."

"She could have him," her brother said thoughtfully.

"I'd be glad to have her marry, Johnny."

"Yep. So would I. And whoever it is, she's crazy about

somebody now, betcha any money, Ma. Let's hope she gets him."

"She'll get him," her mother predicted halfheartedly. "And I'll wish she was back home with me again!"

CHAPTER 27

Coralia Salazar y Valdez sat in the afternoon sun on the terrace and basked in a sense of peace and well-being. About her the rancho glowed in the full hot beauty of an April afternoon. Acacia blossoms were gently waving their yellow pompoms everywhere; the old woody lilacs were tipped with plumes of lavender; even the eucalyptus wore tassels of vermillion and cream.

Ringing the rancho, the far mountains were a misty blue against a scarcely darker sky. At the hacienda everything slept in afternoon stillness; birds were still, and from the farm down the slope of the hill, only the pulsating deep murmur of doves sounded, accenting the silence rather than breaking it. Coralia could hear them, although they were out of sight, and imagine them coming and going at the tiny doorways of their whitewashed cote, wings fanning the red roof, all bustle and concern, and singing their deep, full-throated music.

Coralia's sling was gone; the arm was supported now only by a gay handkerchief. Within a week that would be gone, too, and then her darling plan would take shape and begin to be realized. She feasted her mind upon the approaching train of events.

They would be married, she and Philip, on the day Father Anselmo returned from his Retreat. With the boys, Ana, Miles, and a couple of farm hands, men to manage the carriage, and run city errands, they would go to San Francisco. The entire upper floor of the annex at Mrs. Townshend's would be turned over to them, and Harriet's amazement and her joyous help in getting them settled would be part of the fun.

Harriet's shout of "No! Not married! Tuesday? Well, Mrs. Haagersen, what a cheat you turned out to be!" and Harriet's smothering embrace, and Philip's kiss for Harriet, and the first happy jumble of explanations and plans would start the visit off on a note of laughter and jubilee that would last right through the two or three weeks before Philip went away.

For he was going away; that is, he said he was. That was his condition as a part of the contract that included an immediate marriage. When Father Anselmo came back, when Coralia's arm was free, then they would be married and go to the city at once to settle the details that would make Philip independent of his wife's fortune and free to complete his medical studies. Coralia worked out these plans with excited satisfaction; everything was coming right after all.

And when he knew how generous she had been, and when he experienced the delights of the city visit, with thoughts of the rancho, partly his rancho now, to which they might in triumph return, mightn't he weaken? Coralia was sure he would.

She was dreaming over her embroidery frame when a shadow fell across her work, and she looked up to see a man standing only a few feet away from her.

He had approached noiselessly, but it was not that that gave her heart a sudden plunge of fright and her lips the taste of brass. It was a certain reminiscent familiarity in his look, a sort of confidence in his half-smile that somehow sickened her more than it surprised her. She laid her work aside and looked at him apprehensively.

"Why, you're—you're——But what brings you here?"

"Yes. I'm Louis Johnson," he said. "May I sit down?"

He sat down without invitation. Coralia's spirit was in a daze; she was incapable of thought. She knew this was not pleasant; she told her disturbed heart that there was nothing of which to be afraid. But she was uneasy. She was sorry to see him again.

"Were you riding? How did you happen——" she began,

231

and paused. She mustn't be rude or inhospitable; he mustn't sense at once that his appearance was not welcome to her.

"I've been on the ranch five weeks," he told her. "I'm the new foreman. I'll be running things when Don Felipe goes away."

"You've been here!" She was stupified.

"Yes. Since February. I didn't know whose place it was until I'd been here a week. Then you came down with the Señorita to talk to Phil Haagersen and I saw you."

"I didn't see you," Coralia said, swallowing.

"No, you wouldn't notice me. But I got a good look at you. And then I began to question some of the fellers a little, and I found out how it had all come about."

Coralia merely looked at him. This was no ordinary conversation; there was no need to keep it going. The golden globe of the spring afternoon had broken with a crash, there were black spots in the sunny air, thunder rumbled far, far away. She felt cold.

"You've been working on ranchos ever since?" she asked, after a pause in which he expertly rolled and lighted a cigarette.

"Exactly," he said. "But further down. San Diego way. Mazatlán."

"I heard the name Johnson, of course. I didn't identify it."

"Naturally not. Common name."

He was settled back comfortably, blowing rings into space. Coralia spoke against her will; she did not want to lead.

"Did you want to ask me something? We surely have not anything to say to each other now."

"No, nothing special," he said vaguely. "Just perhaps that after you're married it's understood that I stay on here as foreman. At Haagersen's salary, eh?"

"If I marry," Coralia said sharply, "that would be entirely for Mr. Haagersen—for Don Felipe to decide."

"Oh, I don't think so," Johnson said mildly. "I'd want it understood with you. That's really what I came up to say. Haagersen marries into all this money, cattle, horses, vineyard, ranges, everything. All right. That's his luck. He'll never have to do another day's work in his life—he'll have it soft.

Well, maybe I want it easy too. He's never going to fire me. You take care of that."

"I want to tell you something," Coralia said, trembling, and fired with sudden fury, "I don't want you on the ranch. I'm sorry, but I don't. There's no use our trying to come to any understanding—there's no meeting ground between us. I don't know why you came up to see me today; there's nothing to be said. You treated me very badly ten years ago. I'm not blaming you, I'm not discussing it at all. I simply ask you to go away, that's all. I won't mention this to Don Felipe. Go on here as things are, if you like, until you find another place, and then go."

"I'd never find another place like this. He trusts me and he likes me. I know my job."

"That isn't my affair." Coralia felt how weak the words were as she said them.

"Come now, it is, if it's anyone's affair! You promise me that nobody ever will upset my authority here; I'm to have the say of everything, run things when you're away visiting or traveling. Is that understood? Good. I'll go back now and see what the boys down at the farm are doing, and everything will go on as if it was yesterday."

"Don't you realize what a preposterous suggestion you're making?" Coralia demanded warmly. "It would be—it would be monstrous to have you here. You must be crazy to think of it. Will you please—I am going indoors directly——"

"Wait a minute," he said. "Don't be in a rush. I'm not hurrying you. This isn't any threat. I'm simply saying that because of our old friendship I have certain rights——"

"You have no rights!"

"Well, I'm just using that word. You'll admit I have an argument."

Coralia, seething within, said nothing. But her look was carefully calculated to express boredom and contempt.

"Now don't get huffy about it," Johnson said, himself apparently unconcerned. "I'm not threatening anything, I'm merely saying that I like it here, I'd like to be the person to run this place. You and Haagersen won't be here much of the time. I'm merely——" He shrugged.

"You're merely blackmailing!"

"I've not said anything that isn't so."

"And what do you think you could do? Is anyone going to believe you? Do you propose to gather my people together and make them a speech just because—because of what—because of what happened——" Coralia floundered, and hated herself for it. "They would tar and feather you," she finished scornfully.

"No, no, no, nothing like that. I would go to Philip and tell him that before you ever promised to marry him you promised to marry me."

"You promised!" she corrected, stressing the pronoun.

"And if it were not for Philip, I could win you yet," the man said seriously.

To this Coralia made no answer.

"That's the life I'd like," Johnson said. "I'd like what he's got. The rancho, the hacienda, a ready-made family of three sons—and the Señora!"

"You would have no way of proving anything you said to Philip," Coralia said suddenly, out of thought.

"You mean your word would mean more than mine?"

"I certainly mean that. He would know you for what you are, a blackmailer, and you would have to leave the rancho. And that would be the end of that!" Coralia said, trembling.

"I have two letters."

She paled a little; spoke boldly.

"Not from me!"

"One is from you, speaking of that promise of marriage, holding me to it. Your phrase was—I remember it, for I've read it often, 'I will die of shame—I will tear myself to pieces, unless you come back and tell me you were in earnest.' And you said that you were praying."

She remembered those prayers, remembered that tearful and despairing time.

"Oh, if this was only over! He can't do anything—he won't do anything. But I wish this was over!" thought Coralia. "If I were only upstairs watching Josito make trains of the chairs, listening to Ana. Oh, if only Philip doesn't come up while he's here, the low, contemptible—beast! How can anyone

234

be so low! He goes right on talking, and what can I do? You said my mother!" she exclaimed aloud, catching at the word.

"Yes. She wrote me too," the man said simply.

"How could my mother write you!"

"She wrote me care of Wells Fargo Bank, in San Francisco."

"My mother did!"

"I have that letter, too. All I would do is ask Philip if he thought that old promise should hold. If he did not think I had a claim."

"Well, I can't see any good in going on with this," Coralia said, rising and catching up the thin Indian blanket under which she had been resting. "I don't see that any purpose is being accomplished by this sort of talk."

She walked slowly to the door that led to the hallway, her step leisurely and head high. But she was frightened. Angry, too, but anger wasn't important. With anger she could deal. But with this fierce cloud of stinging, deadly flies buzzing about her, she could not think.

"I shall do nothing," Johnson said.

"Do anything you please," she said wearily in the doorway.

"I will do nothing, of course, until we talk again. But I want to feel secure. I've proved I'm useful here. When Philip moves out I'll be more useful. If Philip hadn't been here at all," Johnson went on, as Coralia, halted in the doorway, did not speak, "I would certainly have reminded you that you and I have good reason to be friends. That's all."

"What do you expect me to do?" Coralia asked over her shoulder.

"Nothing. Except to agree that it's a case of least said soonest mended. Philip will always be boss, and he'll never know from me that you and I have anything—well, let's not say anything to hide. Let's say a secret between us. This is merely to clear up what might complicate matters later. If you had a big dinner up here someday for a bunch of cattlemen, you wouldn't want Philip to ask me to come up and see me then for the first time?"

Coralia was walking away, she did not turn her head or speak again. After long minutes, safe in her room upstairs, she looked from the window and saw him slowly walking down the terrace steps. He was gone.

And gone, too, was peace of mind. Gone was pride; gone were dreams. Coralia felt exhausted; she walked to the hearth and sat back in the big chair, rested her head against it, and shut her eyes. Her injured arm began to ache; she clamped her free hand upon it and held it tight to hold down the pain.

There was nothing to do, nothing to plan, nothing even to think about. The hideous situation had burst upon her full-blown; it was indelibly there.

If he had come in a stranger from the outside world, he might have taken her bank draft for—well, what? Ten thousand—twenty thousand dollars? She had no idea how one treated a blackmailer, the mere thought of dealing with one at all was enough to frighten her.

Whatever arrangements she made, or promises she extracted, she was quite smart enough to know that the relief would be only temporary; he would come back and back, even if she succeeded in immediately driving him away. She had small hope that such shreds of honor as he possessed would prompt him to play fair with her. Why should he, having opened his campaign in this dishonorable way? And worst and most hopeless feature of all, he was here, entrenched at the rancho, liked, useful, accustomed. To attempt to dismiss him against his will might mean that he would appeal to Philip. Coralia shuddered and tried not to think about it. She would do something, she would contrive something.

He might take the money she gave him and go to sea and get drowned. He might take it and disappear, never to trouble her again. Coralia moved through the remainder of the day in a somber dream. The house was quiet and lonely. Harriet was gone, Father Anselmo was gone; just before dinner Philip came downstairs with his own quota of bad news. Coralia received it apathetically.

Philip reported that he had received a letter from his stepfather; his mother was ill. He was needed at home, and had already made arrangements to start on the long road to New Jersey.

"Old Don José sent this up to me by the Brandini boys. They've come up to Santa Clara for a reunion, and they sent a couple of their men over here with it. So—that breaks up our plan——"

"Of course," Coralia said. She felt as if she had known from the first that this happy marriage, this handsome husband, might never be hers. She was widowed again; she was destined to live on here alone, filling her heart with memories of Martin and care of her boys. "I wish Father Anselmo were here, I wish we had not waited," she said half aloud. "But you will be back soon!"

"I don't know how I'll find things there," Philip managed to say, as if too abstracted by anxious thoughts to answer.

Coralia, gracious, lovely, broken as he had never seen her broken, laid her hand on his arm.

"You will come back, Philip? You won't just disappear into space? I love you so much, dear. I need you so!"

"Why, my dear——" He was really touched, the more so as he had at once noticed a change in her manner and had wondered if she had a premonition that he did not expect to see the rancho again after tonight. "My dear, you look— you've overdone and you're tired!" he said.

"No. It's right for you to go. And you'll write me, and maybe I'll go to Harriet for a while." In her heart she said, "I must be patient. Perhaps God's hand is in this. I may be able to do something, I may be able to get rid of Johnson, it may all come right. And if it doesn't, I must write Philip that I have changed my mind——"

Miles and the little boys joined them; Philip thought he had never seen her look so handsome as when she stood between her young sons, turning toward him her pale face and shadowed eyes. They all went to dinner together.

"We are losing our Don Felipe." she told the newcomers. The boys showed only polite surprise; Miles began with an impulse "But I thought——" And fell silent.

"Everything must be postponed," Coralia said. She took her place at the head of the table and listened absent-mindedly to Philip's carefully calculated explanations. He hadn't seen his mother for more than a year, he said, and while it seemed a long trip to make just to cheer her up, there was a lot more to it than that.

"My sister's there, the one who was widowed at Sarawak, and she has her little girls with her—I've never seen any but the oldest. And with our plans uncertain here—I mean whether we go or stay—it seems a good idea to get things at home straightened out."

"Any plan that suits you doesn't have to be uncertain," Coralia reminded him gently.

"You're an angel. I'm not worrying about anything like that. You are magnificent tonight, Coralia," Philip said in an undertone as Miles drew the small boys' attention to the subject of melting chunks of sweet butter the size of hens' eggs that they had put on their frijoles.

"I'll not feel magnificent until you come back. I don't even want Harriet to come, to remind me of the happy times we've had! Philip, will you find some way to let me know when you are coming?"

He had to say that indeed he would; he had no choice, with the beautiful dark eyes fixed upon him with their new wistful look, their new appeal.

"I'll keep your California family in order," she said whimsically, with a sad little smile. And with the phrase came the hateful reminder of Louis Johnson's words only a few hours earlier. "A ready-made family of three sons—and the Señora!"

"My mother's always been rather delicate," Philip was saying, all the concerned son. "But it seems she had a fall a few weeks ago—Don, that's my stepfather, says no immediate danger, but she's been talking about me a lot. Which," he added half seriously, "I don't deserve."

"Our numbers are thinning," observed Miles. "But Father will be back next week, and maybe we can lure Miss Harriet back."

"Not until I somehow get rid of Johnson," Coralia thought. "She would suspect something in a moment."

"I'm leaving everything to Johnson," Philip was saying. He had known that Coralia was not listening to him; now he

238

saw that the mention of his departure had riveted her attention suddenly.

"When—when do you go?"

"Tonight. Johnson's driving me down to the railroad, and will stay in the village and bring those tools up in the morning. I want to talk things over with him, anyway. That's a great feller, Coralia. He knows men and he knows cattle. He's a rough diamond, but he's no fool, and they all know it down at the adobes. I'll see Hardisty in San Francisco——"

Her face brightened.

"Oh, you'll see Harriet?"

"I guess so. I'll see Hardisty at the bank, and explain about Johnson. He'll get the men's pay in San Jose and take care of all that. Leave things to him. By the way, did he come up here today? Ana said something about it."

"He was looking for you, I think."

"Leave any message?"

"No."

"Well, I'll be seeing him anyway. You know he's moved into the old house that your husband's father lived in when they first came here to California."

"It's full of deers' horns and buffalo heads and stuff," young Martin contributed.

"He showed us," Pablo said with his mouth full.

"Yes, I think he regards himself as a fixture, and I hope he does," Philip said. "I'm pretty well packed, and we can get started. I know there's a washout by the old bridge, but how far we have to go round it I don't know."

"The boys got through with your stepfather's letter," Coralia reminded him.

"They were on horseback. But we'll make it all right!"

"We'll miss you!" Coralia followed him to the hall when he came downstairs with a roped box and took both his hands in hers. "Oh, Philip, it's going to be so long!" she whispered, on a half sob. "You won't forget how I need you, how I love you! I'm so afraid—seeing new people—going new places ——"

"I'll not forget!" he said, very low, as she paused.

"I think I've always been afraid of happiness, Philip, afraid

239

it wasn't meant for me. Not this kind, the happiest of all, in being married to the man you love and admire and—and need——"

"My dear," the man said, with genuine feeling, "there are many happy years ahead for you!"

"Oh, I know it!" She raised her face for a quick good-by kiss, and as he ran down the terrace steps turned back to the hall, a small son on each side of her. "All gone, Miles," she said unemotionally. "No Harriet, no Philip, no Father Anselmo."

"But all coming back, Señora."

"Please God."

"Mass and Benediction again on Sunday!" Miles rejoiced.

"Oh, yes. It'll all come back."

But she did not feel sure of it as she went alone into the big, sparsely furnished bedroom and walked to an open window and looked out upon the lonely night. The talk on the terrace with Johnson this afternoon had shaken her to the depths of her being; she was trembling from it still. "Contemptible!" she said half aloud. "To hold my letter and Mother's letter all these years. Perhaps he hasn't got them, perhaps he was lying. But even if he is, he could make Philip feel that I was holding back something he should have known that put him in Louis Johnson's power. And then he'd never feel the same toward me, he'd feel Louis was sneering at him. He'd never forget it. No man would if it was his wife! And meanwhile that snake coiled right in the middle of the ranch, making himself liked, making himself more and more valuable——"

The sky was crowded with stars; there was no moon, but the earth sang until there was a clear faint note filling the air.

"If there were just one person I could talk to!" she thought. "If I could be sure what to do. I can't ask Harriet to come up, I don't want her, with Johnson apt to come in at any minute and destroy that friendship, too!"

Something must happen there before Harriet could come back. Somehow the Johnson matter must be settled, buried, before there was any danger of Philip turning to her with bewildered, unbelieving eyes. Coralia felt in this moment of despair that she was unequal to the challenge that life had so suddenly flung at her. They had all failed her; each and every one of them had had his part in laying her life in ruins about her. Father Anselmo had gone away at the crucial moment that might have been the moment of Coralia's marriage, Harriet, seeming curiously abstracted and remote, had gone, Philip had gone; the old happy days of games and talk and evening music and ruffled taffetas and crinolines were gone like the substance of a dream. And Johnson might make it impossible for them ever to be recovered.

Now she must settle down to the old ways, her children, her books, her embroideries, gossip with her servants. Even if Johnson, by some miracle disappeared, even if Philip need never know, even if Harriet brought all her enthusiasm and gaiety to the wedding that was duly to take place, nothing would ever be the same for Coralia. She had been proud, purified by the maturing years, and by her dedication to her husband and home and children. She was no longer the undeveloped, restless oldest daughter of the ranch of the Little Columns; with beauty and wealth and position and her own spiritual growth toward goodness and dignity she had learned to hold her head high.

Now all that was dragged in the dirt under the insolent assault of an enemy who had lain silent for years only to spring at her at this, her happiest moment, and bring her head low.

It was a tired, a bewildered head that she leaned against the window opening, and the eyes that looked out at the dark and the stars could find no relief in tears.

CHAPTER 28

Harriet had not been a fortnight at home before her mother had had the truth out of her. Mrs. Townshend instantly noted the change in her, the new quietness, the unwonted gentleness and adaptability that were not at all characteristic of Harriet. While Harriet's mirror was as well filled as ever with charming little notes of invitation, notes written in shaded chirography and flowing violet ink, and decorated with scallops, borders, or hand-painted violets, her mother saw that she paid small attention to them, and spent her evenings at Johnny's or entertaining the boarders in the long double parlors.

Sometimes there was singing, sometimes Harriet played euchre with three other ladies, or cribbage with old Captain Lucas. She had learned cribbage on her first sea voyage as a small girl, from other captains, and could give the old man a hard fight, with her exultant "fifteen ten" and "one for his nibs."

Hopeful swains came in as of yore, and watched the games, or drew her into games of their own, and she went to Dion Boucicault's opening nights in *Shawn the Post* and *Arrah Na Pogue*. But her mother saw with how indifferent a heart.

Harriet kept the books now, took many responsibilities from her mother's shoulders, wrote menus, and introduced new dishes. She was always beside her mother at early Mass, and afterward shared the exciting hour in the long sheds of the markets, walking over fish scales and crushed lettuce leaves, buying pearly little new potatoes, ripe black cherries, salmon that only an hour or two earlier had been drawn from the tumbling waters of the Golden Gate. This time grew to be one of the delights of the older woman's life, the girl then was so full of her old fun, spirit, friendliness; with the exquisite hour in the old cathedral behind them, and a good hot breakfast in the sunshiny dining room ahead, Mary Townshend felt life almost too felicitous, too full of triumph and delight.

After breakfast Harriet bustled about the two big houses, talking to maids, to tradespeople, negotiating with the Chinese basket men at the doors. It was then that her courage began to flag.

And after lunch there was a lull, a hard time of discouragement. Harriet no longer flitted away for a drive, a walk, a luncheon, her flowered shell hat tied beneath her chin, her parasol tipped at its most bewitching angle. She pleaded fatigue, and sometimes lay for hours on the sofa in the big bay-windowed room she shared with her mother, staring at the climbing green vines and pink roses of the wallpaper, hungering with every fiber of body and soul for just one word—just one of those words from Philip that she once had scorned so lightly, just the sound of that voice that had said to her, "I thought I had told you that night." Sometimes it seemed to her that she would go mad if she could not hear it.

"Harriet, it isn't that tutor—that Miles What's-this-now that you're thinking about?" Mrs. Townshend demanded abruptly one warm spring afternoon when from her rocking chair and her mending she had been watching Harriet for some time.

"How d'you know I'm thinking about a man, Ma?"

"I've known it since the day you got back."

"You're smart, Mrs. T. No, darling, it's not poor Miles, he's destined for Holy Orders if ever a lad was. His uncle is a priest in Baltimore——"

"Who is it then?" the older woman asked, sharply cutting short these irrelevant details. "You're thinning down, you wake up with tears in your eyes, you don't want to run around to the balls and dinners any more, and there's no special one that comes here that I can see. So who is it?"

The weakness of a sudden longing to make a clean breast of it shook Harriet to her very vitals. She had made up her mind that no hint of the truth should reach her mother, but no resolution could hold against the rush of yearning for sympathy, for understanding from this nearest and dearest confidante.

"If there is a man," she began a little thickly, "he isn't one I could ever marry—I mean, he isn't free——"

"Married?" The single word came like a bullet, with a sharp glance over Mrs. Townshend's glasses.

"No-o-o. But engaged. And engaged in a way—in a sort of way that makes it impossible. I mean, I couldn't——"

There was a long moment of silence. Foghorns from the Golden Gate droned through the soft afternoon, and a sharper horn sounded from a fish cart idling up the steep street.

"We've plenty, I got crabs and cod," Harriet said of the fish.

"Then the man doesn't like you, darlin'?"

"The—the man. Oh, yes. Oh, yes he does, Ma."

"But, Hattie, no man would stay engaged to one girl if he liked another. What's the matter with him! Let him be off with the old love before he's on with the new!"

"Well," said Hattie, wishing she were somewhere else, "it isn't exactly like that."

"He told you he was in love with you while he was engaged to this other girl?"

"Yes. But not—not right out. He—Ma, he feels as badly as I do!" Harriet said in a burst.

Her mother was studying her face curiously. Now she said slowly: "Harriet, who is this man?"

Harriet, who had been sitting on the edge of the sofa, crossed the floor slowly and pushed a hassock into place at her mother's knee. She sat down, and laid her crossed arms on her mother's lap, and dropped her face on her arms.

"It's Philip, Ma," she said in a whisper.

"Philip?" Mrs. Townshend repeated the name bewilderedly. "But that's—Harriet, not the foreman at the rancho?" she asked.

Harriet glanced briefly up, hid her face again.

"But, dearie—not the one that's engaged to Coralia?" Mrs. Townshend's voice was pleading. Harriet nodded her head violently without looking up.

"Harriet, you wouldn't do that."

"Ma, I didn't *do* anything. It just happened."

"Your best friend," said Mrs. Townshend slowly.

"I know." There was a silence.

"Hat, I can't believe this of you. What happiness can you possibly get from stealing another girl's man? With all your flirting, you've always given the other girls a chance. And Coralia—of all of them—and she's angry at you, of course——"

"She doesn't know, Ma. We—he didn't tell her."

Harriet looked up to meet her mother's round-eyed stare.

"He certainly isn't going on with his marriage!"

"No. No," Harriet said, hesitating.

"Then what is he proposing to do?"

"I don't know, Ma. He's going away. He's going East, and then he's going to write her and say it was all a mistake."

"And that he loves you?"

"No. I'm afraid that would just about kill her, Ma. And I want to be there when she gets his letter. She'll need me."

"Harriet, you can't do that! And he can't do that! What's the matter with the man that he doesn't know his own mind!"

"Ma—please——" Harriet said, choking.

Mrs. Townshend studied her daughter's flushed and distressed face perplexedly.

"I love him—so terribly," Harriet whispered.

"And this had been going on right under Coralia's nose?"

"Nothing went on. Coralia didn't see anything. There wasn't anything to see. It was just that—that we found out we cared for each other, and we—well, we had to think what to do."

"Oh. And what *are* you going to do?"

"He's going away. He's going to Scotland."

"And you going with him, Mary help us!"

"No. I couldn't do that to her. I don't know what I'm going to do. Maybe, after a while, something'll happen. Something could happen that would—well, maybe change things."

"He's going to be a doctor?"

"In five years."

"And who's paying for all that?"

"Nobody. He hasn't any money. Coralia wanted to be married, right away and give him enough money to do anything—she was coming down here next week to see lawyers and bankers and things. And then he suddenly had to go East—at least that was what he said when I came home——"

"She thinking he'd go to Europe as her husband?"

"That's what she said. She's been terribly happy about it," Harriet said with a sudden tremble of her lips and brimming eyes.

"Poor girl. And now he's to go away and write her that it's all over? And all the while she planning to be married before he went?"

245

"Yes. But Father Anselmo had gone away on Retreat, her letter said, and before he gets back, Philip was going."

"And did he go—this Philip?"

"In her last letter she said he had heard of his mother being sick, and was going that night."

"You've heard from him?"

"No. I said that if Coralia asked me I wanted to be able to say I didn't know."

"Well, this is too bad, dear," Mrs. Townshend said, after a long silence, in the quietest and most sympathetic tone she had yet used.

"It—it just ends my life, Ma."

"You love him, Hat? Not just that he's in love with you?"

"It doesn't feel like being in love—like anything that I ever thought it would be like. It's a feeling that makes me get cold, and shaky, and just want to hear his voice all the time, and think about him," Harriet said simply. "I want to be with him, always. Always."

"How long have you known this, dear?"

"Since just before I came home. Since one night when I was playing and singing, up at the rancho, and he came—Philip came over to the piano with the candles—Miles was there with his cello, and Coralia called out from the fire and said please to sing 'Sylvia' and Philip leaned on the piano and looked at me. I thought it was the candlelight because he looked so strange—sort of savage, and something took hold of me like—like claws—like teeth——"

The rush of words stopped. Harriet looked up at her mother.

"And after that, Harriet?"

"Then we only talked three times—or twice, I think it was. He said that was what it was, our loving each other, and one morning very early we rode to the top of the hill and talked, and I was back in time for Mass, and Coralia never knew."

"You're very sure she doesn't know?"

"Oh, I'm sure! She talks all the time of what she is going to do when they are married, about business, you know, so that Philip will be free to go away if he wants to. But she

246

doesn't believe he'll want to! She's so terribly happy, Ma. She's really in love. And this spoils it all!"

"You've no plans, Harriet? You and Philip Haagersen?"

"How can we have? Just," Harriet said, in a tired tone, "that he's going away, and I'm going back to stay with Coralia for a little while—I don't know—then I'll come back and do something—maybe I'll take painting lessons from old Mrs. Vandercook. Oh, Ma," she went on, putting her head down again, and with a break in her voice, "tell me if you think it could ever come right? It wouldn't matter if it was years —years— but could it ever come right?"

"What makes you think you won't change, Hattie? Girls do."

"Because it isn't me any more. It's—someone else."

Mrs. Townshend considered this.

"You've prayed about it?"

"Ma, I've done nothing else! But how can you pray against a stone wall? I can't pray that Coralia dies."

"And do you think you can go back to the rancho, and listen to her when she reads his letter, and watch her heart breaking, and not tell her?"

"I think I can. It's—it's bad for me whatever I do!"

"Time will help you, Hattie. You'll be going down to Santa Cruz and Del Monte in the summer——"

"I guess so," Harriet agreed lifelessly, in a silence. She got to her feet. "I'm going out to Johnny's, Ma. Liz gets tired this time of day and she likes to have someone come in and help with Margaret."

"Well, now, wait a moment!" Mrs. Townshend said briskly, getting to her feet. Here was a problem more in her line. "Run down to the kitchen and send Juanito for a cab. There's usually one of Lenhart's down at the corner of Mason."

"Listen, Ma, I have no more need of a cab than the cat! It's a heavenly afternoon——"

"Yes, but I'm sending Lizzie the brown clock for Johnny. That was your father's clock and Johnny wanted it fixed. I had the foot put on. And there's the baby shirts Mrs. Cunningham got Margaret. And see what you find in the pantry —a cake maybe, or a pan of beans. I'll tell you, Harriet.

247

Get Aggie to wrap up one of the cut hams from Sunday. Pick one with a good deal on it. Oh, and those plants old Dr. Rogers has been nursing along for Lizzie——"

"You win, I'll take a cab," Harriet agreed. "I'll be home early, Ma. Johnny'll walk me to the car, she said, departing.

"There's nowhere I'd rather have you than in your brother's house," her mother said.

"And there's nowhere I'd rather be!" Harriet called back.

She meant it. Because Lizzie so openly adored and needed her she loved Lizzie, and she and Johnny had never been so near. He had sensed what was wrong from almost the day of her return, without knowing any of the particulars, and had treated her with special tenderness, and Harriet clung to him.

As for Margaret, the little bundle of fat knees, dark curls, blue eyes with black lashes like Aunt Harriets, and petal hands that had already learned to stretch themselves to those she loved, her mother and father had but one fear, that Margaret was altogether too complete, too good to live. Enchantingly responsive to affection, she was like a live doll that could be picked up and admired, bathed, smiling until soapsuds stood up in a drake's-tail on her small head, put down for naps, picked up again for exhibition purposes, formally arrayed in starched embroideries and zephyr wool, or equally delicious in a bedraggled double gown and sodden little bedsocks.

Mrs. Townshend and Lizzie's family and Harriet and Johnny gloried in Margaret. But Lizzie regarded the baby reverently, as a miracle, and never recovered from awe in the fact that this scrap of girlhood, once so dark and angry-looking, once the fruit of so much agony, could turn into the rosy warm treasure in her arms.

To have Harriet with them doubled the rapture of the young Townshends in their baby. Life was going well with them. In the newborn city men of Johnny's caliber were needed; Johnny was no longer a mere teller in a bank, although that was still his title. He was manager, on the side, for some of the investments of the bank trustees, quite a few of whom had once been his mother's boarders. And he

248

had quite recently acquired, in conjunction with his mother, the ownership of three small houses on Capp Street.

Lizzie knew of these ventures without taking much interest in them or in the least degree understanding them.

"What's Johnny want to take all that trouble for?" Lizzie demanded of Harriet.

"Oh, everyone's talking about how fast you can make money here, investing and building, doing things like that," said Harriet.

"All I'm afraid of," said Margaret Townshend, gesturing with her round little arms, and speaking through the voice of her aunt Harriet, "is that sometime my da will be so rich I'll have to have a nurse!"

"No, he'll never be that," said Johnny himself, coming in at the kitchen door in time to get this performance.

The happy warm intimate hour went on, the kitchen was scented by the good smells of fried onions and baked potatoes and steak. Margaret went to bed without a murmur; Johnny installed the new clock. Lizzie washed dishes expertly as Harriet expertly wiped them, and plans for the almost whole ham were made to include Lizzie's brother, sister, and father, who would come in for lunch after "the eleven o'clock" on Sunday.

"Who you in love with, Hat?" asked Johnny then. Harriet, pale up to this moment, flushed to the copper tendrils of hair on her forehead and laughed uncomfortably.

But Johnny was too sure of his shot; Lizzie too keenly interested and sympathetic, and Harriet's heart too full for long resistance. Johnny built a fire in the parlor and Lizzie got out a pink cashmere baby coat only partly finished, and Harriet scrambled herself on the floor, with an arm on the seat of her usual chair, and her eyes on the fire, and told them the whole story.

Johnny took his pipe from his mouth to laugh delightedly.

"Well, so you got it yourself at last. Miss Hattie Townshend! And got it hard. Now you know how it feels!"

"Oh, Johnny, don't laugh!" Lizzie protested.

Harriet turned her head to look at her brother over her shoulder.

"I don't like the way it feels!" she said, tears in her eyes.

"It'll all come right, Hat. A man doesn't let a girl go like that!"

"But if he's engaged to Coralia?" Lizzie asked anxiously.

"He never was in love with Coralia!" Johnny said confidently. "She's the one that's been dreaming this whole thing up!"

"But she does love him," Harriet put in, her heart warming to Johnny on a rush of adoration. Johnny caught her look and knew that he was right. "She's the Señora, it's all hers, she's a widow and so she's independent," he pursued. "He'd naturally feel like a fortune hunter. I'd bet something that she did most of the talking."

"Oh, Johnny, she did!" Harriet squared herself about now, and dragged herself up backward into the chair. "She says so. She is sort of proud of it. She told me long ago that she was the one who finally said 'Why don't we get married?' and over and over again she's told me that Philip wanted to get his doctor's degree before he got married, but that she wanted to be married first. She says so!"

"It's hit you hard, hasn't it, Hat?" he asked affectionately.

"Oh, yes, Johnny!" she said thickly, her eyes wet.

"D'you expect to see him again, Tatsie?"

It was his old little-boy name for her; Harriet had not heard it for a long time.

"Not for years. Not ever, maybe."

"He'll write you," Lizzie said, rapt with sympathy.

"I asked him not to. Not until—something changes."

"Well, no man's going to give up the woman he loves just because he's engaged to another woman," Johnny said confidently. "He'll write Coralia and clear it with her, and then— I'll tell you, Hat. If Ma goes over to Ireland for Uncle What's-his-name's golden wedding in July to show off her fur coat——"

"Johnny!" Lizzie reproached him.

"Well, she said she was going to take it, July or no July. She says the climate of Cork is very damp entirely, and she'll need it. And didn't she walk into the steamship company's office and find out which was the quietest month on the water, and he said July, and July it's to be. She says Uncle Joe was a father to her—there were thirteen of them, and she's the youngest—and she was always spoken by him.

"Anyway, you go with her, Hat, and get married over there."

"Oh, Johnny, if it could only come out that way!"

"But Harriet said she'd never go on the ocean again," Lizzie offered.

"I'd take a rickety boat if it was burning plowshares!" Harriet said fervently, and they all laughed.

"You've got it bad, Hat," her brother said.

"Yes, and I never knew what it was like to be in love before," she answered honestly. "I've seen men—you know the men who've liked me, Johnny?"

"I do," Johnny admitted with feeling.

"Well, you know the things they say, and the way they act, but it never occurred to me that it was like this."

"You just feel he's the one," Lizzie suggested, enthralled.

"Yes, no matter what he's doing, or what he says, or what we talk about, or whether we talk at all," Harriet said.

"It's a nice mix-up," Johnny presently observed. "Her being in love with him, and you being her best friend."

"What can happen, Johnny?" Lizzie asked anxiously.

"Nothing," Harriet answered heroically. "There won't be any August wedding in Cork! So that Harriet Townshend becomes San Francisco's romantic old maid, with a disappointment in love. Oh, it's happened to other girls," she said, "and it happens in books! But somehow you think it never will happen to you! And Johnny, if you'll walk me to the nine-o'clock car, I'll be on my way."

"Harriet, I'm sorry," Lizzie said, as they walked out to the wooden sidewalk and looked up at the starry sky.

"Well, I'll not die," Harriet said. "And go on praying for me!"

"Gosh, she looked little and alone," Johnny said, going back to Lizzie and Margaret half an hour later. "There wasn't anyone else in the car, and she did look so darned little!"

The days that followed were the dullest her life ever had known. If she kept her place in the round of Easter gaieties it was an absent-minded and indifferent place. Harriet did her best to fill the great vacuum that her world had become.

Everything that reminded her of Philip was agony, and the memory of the days when she could see him every few hours, could hear his voice, and watch his going and coming were so poignant that she resolutely put them aside. For that reason, she shrank half-consciously from the thought of going back to the rancho; it would be hard to be in the familiar environment, to love Coralia and all the people and things of the rancho as she did and have to play so hard a part.

The dark-skinned servants coming and going, the window blinds that were opened across the wide sills to admit morning freshness and sweetness, the horses, bridles over the fence post as they sidled and shifted, restless, awaiting their riders, the damp roads deep in leaves, the winter sunshine that shook itself over the discolored old row of discolored adobe cabins, duets at the square piano, Benediction in the pale candlelight of the chapel, joyous meals with all of them ravenous and talkative—small boys, sober, spectacled Miles, old Father Anselmo, gracious and lovely Coralia at the head of the table, Philip always with some report that started them all talking, and herself, Harriet, at the foot, the unacknowledged queen of them all. They were not the same when she was away, they admitted it, they told her that she brought laughter and activity to the rancho, and she knew it was true. She was the pin that held the whole structure together, hers were the voice and the laughter that spurred Coralia, and Miles, and even Father Anselmo, into his or her most spirited mood. As for Philip, she knew now what he contributed, she knew that it was Philip who put the priceless ingredient into her every mood, and she knew that he never would be back at the rancho in the old way again. And so for her it would never be the same.

It hurt her to suspect, from Coralia's rare letters, that Coralia was not urgent in pressing an invitation to the ranch, and yet it was a relief, too.

Coralia's letters were no longer pourings forth of her loneliness and unhappiness. A certain restraint was noticeable in them; she reported that she had had one short note and one

252

dispatch from Philip and asked if Harriet had had any news. Harriet could quite truthfully answer that she had not; for her, Philip had disappeared into a great void. At any minute she expected from Coralia the letter saying that her life and her happiness had been shattered by the stunning, incredible news that he was breaking their engagement, but it did not come.

"Write me everything, dearest," said Coralia's letters. Harriet sensed the subtle restriction. Don't come, write. For some reason Coralia was apparently as reluctant to stir up the past as Harriet herself was. She wrote Coralia, but found her own end of the correspondence dry and unsatisfactory. Some spring was broken. Even the simplest of sentences sounded strained and false because of those other sentences that she could not write. Had Coralia had the dreadful letter, and was this her way of taking it? Harriet wondered. Or had Coralia read between the lines of the letter, and did she suspect that Harriet was the cause of it?

The days went by and were weeks, and there was still no word from Philip, and no news from the rancho. Harriet was quieter than she ever had been; she grew thinner, she spent much time with Lizzie and the baby. Otherwise her mother had her constant companionship, and these were wonderful days for the older woman. She and Harriet began the day together at early Mass, went through its busy morning hours together, consulted, planned, talked or were silent, in a harmony of perfect understanding. "The ones that marry aren't always the lucky ones," Mrs. Townshend reflected. "She's happier than she knows."

CHAPTER 29

It was some time after her first talk with Johnson, and after Philip's departure, that Coralia saw Louis Johnson again.

He came up to the hacienda one afternoon to find her with

the boys and Miles in the room used most often for family gatherings; the boys were playing jackstraws beside the fire; Miles was reading, Coralia was at the piano trying over various songs and humming them as she played them. Several dogs lay by the hearth and Coralia's big white cat was posed watchfully on the high back of a chair.

"Interrupting you?" Louis said from the doorway.

Her look was cold, and her voice colder. She felt sick.

"No. What is it?"

He came to lean on the square piano.

"Well, it seems that there's a wedding going on on Thursday at the Ortegas'. About twenty of your people want to go, take both wagons, and get back Saturday. I didn't know how you'd feel."

Coralia, taken unaware, hesitated for a second, glanced at Miles, glanced at the children.

"Well, I—what did Philip say?"

"I don't know that he knew of it."

"How many want to go?" Coralia rose from the fringed revolving piano stool and walked to her usual chair at the hearth. Miles, with a murmur of cleaning the boys for dinner, took them away, and Johnson sat down in Philip's chair, opposite his hostess.

"May I smoke?"

"Certainly." Her glance and voice were contemptuous.

He took out a leather sack of tobacco, shook some into a strip of dark brown paper. Leisurely in his movements and apparently quite at his ease, he stooped to light a spill at the red coals of the fire.

"Well——" This was exactly the attitude she did not want to take, but her words seemed to come with no volition on her part. "What do you think?" And as he continued to look at the fire, she added, "Louis. What do you think?"

He grinned suddenly, glanced up and glanced away again.

"I think they'd go anyway. They're roasting whole pigs and they've killed a steer over there, and I hear the band's come up from San Benito. The girl who's getting married is your Ana's goddaughter, it seems."

"Oh, well, then. D'you mean little Ria?" Coralia said, in-

254

terested. And immediately she frowned at the fire. "We can manage without Ana," she added in a level voice.

"Ria it is. One other thing. Have you any objection," Louis said, "to my putting a pretty strong fence across that cattle crossing they're tramping out for themselves—you know where I mean—by the corral where we had the Soares bull?"

"Oh? Oh. But why shouldn't they?"

"You'll have 'em streaming over the road where the men come down from the range," Johnson explained. "I wish you'd come down there and watch it some night. Around four o'clock, when they're making for the milking sheds. You never saw anything like it. The boys put their broncos straight at the cows and the cows rise up in the air bellowing and ramping about——"

She was trying not to smile.

"What should they do?" she asked steadily, not looking at her companion.

"Why, they ought to come down the old way, back of the cabins, through the corral where we had the two sick calves."

"I do think they ought to be stopped crossing the road."

"I'll see to it."

"If everyone goes away, can we manage?" There she was talking in cozy, companionable fashion again, the last thing she wanted to do!

"Oh, yes, only about half our crowd is going. And I'll keep an eye on them and send home anyone who gets too gay."

"Oh, you're going with them?"

"Would you like me to?"

What could she say but "You're needed here, aren't you? What do you think?"

"I'd rather not go with them, I'd rather be here. But I'll ride over every day and get a report from old Suez and Enrico or one of the other older ones." He took a notebook from his pocket and looked at it. "An old woman—I think she's Arturo's widow——" he said, hesitating.

"Oh, yes. Nitka. She's part Eskimo."

"Well, I asked one of the girls—Rosa Pilar, I think it was—to round up someone who would come up here and take Ana's place for those few days and she sent Nitka over. She looks clean, she looks a decent old thing. She's not going to the wedding because she's a widow and she doesn't like fiesta anyway."

"That'll do nicely. You are acting," said Coralia, on a sudden rush of resentful feeling, "exactly as if you had not come up here to threaten everything that makes—that makes my life worth while, with blackmail—that's what it was, blackmail. Have you forgotten that?"

Johnson laughed huskily in embarrassment.

"No. I kinder wish I could," he admitted after a moment. "I mean—you kinder took that wrong. I'd been talking to Philip, and he was so sure of himself, so sure he'd be boss here before long——"

"Jealous," Coralia said contemptuously.

"Weren't you ever jealous?"

She thought of Harriet, and of the time when she had accused Harriet of trying to attract Philip, and of the tears and vigils of that dreadful night.

"I have been, I suppose." Another thought came sharply: the thought of beautiful Maria Dolores Riveras years ago, beautiful and seventeen and traveled. Johnson was in this memory too.

"Well, I was burned with it."

There was a pause. Since this stage in the conversation had been reached—a stage quite different from anything expected before its commencement—Coralia felt she could hardly ask in the Señora's dismissing voice if there was anything more. She was relieved to hear the boys' voices in the hall, and to have them come in freshly brushed and with well-scrubbed if still grimy hands. Johnson got to his feet, flung his consumed cigarette into the fire.

"I am riding to the bank at San Jose Mission tomorrow to get them all some money," he said. "I'll be back early in the afternoon. If anything comes up—but maybe you don't like to be bothered with all these small matters?"

"But I do like it, very much," Coralia said authoritatively. "You see, my husband never wanted me to know about the rancho, and so I was left without any experience at all. And

I want to know everything. I feel very much to blame for not knowing."

"I should think you'd want to know, for these fellers' interests if not for your own," Johnson said, with a jerk of his head toward the little boys. "This is a darned valuable property."

He went away, and Coralia went down to dinner with her children feeling oddly comforted. Johnson had come to his senses and changed his manner. Philip would not be gone forever, and meanwhile there were many ranch responsibilities that she must not shirk. Deciding on the cattle run, and that her people might be away for four days, and that old Nitka had been delegated to look out for her in Ana's absence, all this was important. Money was to be drawn from the bank, too, to pay wages; she must enter that in her account book right after breakfast tomorrow. These were her responsibilities. Harriet, who had a perfectly uncanny cleverness at double entry, had straightened out Coralia's books, and from now on they would be scrupulously kept.

Her fear of Johnson mitigated, Coralia's heart was relieved. She and Ana said five decades of the Rosary aloud in the chapel after dinner, and Coralia slept more soundly than she had slept for a long time.

After that she saw Johnson almost daily. There was always something to be seen down by the barns and corrals, some point to be settled. The sheepshearers came, and were detected in killing a fat lamb for a later barbecue, and were reprimanded by the Señora herself. The pruners came, and Coralia walked for the first time in hot April sunshine in her own wide vineyards, and saw the sturdy sprawling tentacles of the vines trimmed back to their clumsy, lumpy bases. There had been another wedding and another fiesta, just before the Señora's accident, this time at the Corazón d'Oro rancho, and the Señora went a long way in providing wine and good cheer. Laughter and young voices and dance music sounded among the whitewashed adobe cabins, and in the orchards and up through the forest all day long and well into the night.

New foliage scattered tender and trembling shadows on the white walls, and across the terrace of the hacienda itself,

257

where Louis Johnson sat talking to his employer. Spring was pouring like a river in spate over the rancho, bloom and fragrance and color were everywhere, the lengthening days were warm, and the birds were going mad with joy.

Coralia's arm had long ago dispensed with the sling; she wore a gown of some thin flowered stuff that showed dim flowers in pinks and blues against a soft gray ground. Her usually pale face wore an unusual color, and sprays of her dark hair lay in rings on her damp forehead.

"It was wise to buy right then, I think," said Louis, "because, according to the old man from San Antonio who was here last week, there isn't a lamb left anywhere. We got in before the price went up."

"The boys and I saw them yesterday," Coralia said. "They're little beauties. Josito shrieked because he couldn't bring one up to play with him."

"He could have one, fooling around on the grass here," Louis assured her. Coralia's face brightened. Louis was always nice to her boys.

"Louis, he would love it! The things you think up to amuse those boys! That fishing stuff you brought down from the city —well, I haven't heard anything else for days except did I eat my fish at breakfast, and can they go further up the Azulita, and so on. And Miles is as crazy as they are."

"Well, you see," Louis said, getting to his feet as an indication that this mornings conference was closed, "I've not made any secret of it; I should guess that you know."

"Know what?" Her throat closed and her heart gave a quick beat as she asked it. Oh, she was going to have to snub him!

"That I'm not beaten until I'm beaten," the man said without embarrassment. "That until Philip comes back and you're married, I'm in the race. Oh, I know how it sounds, it sounds nervy. All right, I'll risk being nervy not to miss what you mean to me. You are the straightest, simplest woman I ever knew; I get along with you, you get along with me. Let's assume that Philip writes you, he comes back, you're married —all right, if that's the way it's going to be. . . . No, don't say anything, I know how you feel. I know you didn't expect

258

this, neither did I. But so far, there's no reason on God's earth why I shouldn't put in my bid. I talked rough to you once, right here on this terrace—I've apologized. You saw me throw two letters into the fire last night; the past is all over. I'll stay here until Philip gets back, then I'll try my luck, and get out. You'll not be bothered this way again. That's all of that. You'll be down to see that horse of yours when it's a little cooler?"

"I want to see him," Coralia said faintly, rallying her forces.

"I think he's going to get over it. The Lord knows what he ate. Anyway, he tried to get to his feet this morning, Juan said, and drank a lot of water. I was there until around two o'clock, when he went to sleep. I'll tell Juan you're coming."

He went down the terrace steps, a burly, bearded figure in his loose blue shirt and fringed cowhide breeches. Coralia sat quite still for long minutes, then she went in and mounted the stairs to the bedroom floor. Everything was quiet; Josito was asleep. To the other boys Miles was probably reading, upstairs, in their own third-floor quarters.

Ana had turned down the quilts and counterpane of the big bed and drawn the shutters against the hot afternoon sun. Coralia took off the flowered dimity, pinned her heavy braids more snugly, and slipped on a thin sasque. She lay down, staring at the high discolored ceiling, whose pattern of age and rain had taken so many forms in the days of sick fancies a few years earlier.

A fly made a zinging noise about one of the windows; from the garden came the buzzing of bees deep in plum tree blossoms and the faraway barking of a dog. Motes danced in the swords of sunshine that pierced the closed blinds. Coralia closed her eyes, but she could not sleep. Mind and body were at peace, but her heart was in a strange maze, where one path ran into another continuously and confusingly. She hungered for Philip, for his first letters—so slow in coming, so brief— and for his return! And suddenly it would be Louis who was in his place; tomorrow she was to take the boys and Miles on a fishing trip and picnic far up beyond the dam, and Louis was making all the preparations; she could not fit Philip into that, she would be afraid all day long that he was being bored. Now she was explaining to Louis that she had no reason to trust him, every reason to dislike him; now she was telling Philip that it was impossible to resent Louis' easy assumption of responsibility for her safety and comfort.

"Philip," said her racing thoughts, in apology, "of course it has never been anything like friendship; with Louis, it's not anything except gratitude, really. You were the one who broke up everything here, and it's just luck that you left us in such good hands." And then a distressed, "I'm sorry, Louis, but it just isn't right to make plans for our coming down to the adobes for the Mardi Gras party or going over to buy the pony for Josito, because Philip may come back at any time now—well, he doesn't understand——"

Philip was everything: her future, her happiness, her ideal. But Philip was gone, and Louis was where she could see him every day, where indeed she must see him every day, to decide and solve the farm problems that were hers, although neither her old husband nor Philip had ever asked her to share the responsibility.

She enjoyed her very real obligations; Louis was not just amusing her with a shadowy authority. She was indeed the chatelaine, the Señora, and whenever there was a contract to consider, or a change to be made, hers was the deciding vote.

Louis brought up papers for her to read, greasy invoices from the sheep ranches, fancy letterheads from the wineries, with colored pictures of lovely bare-shouldered girls pouring wines. They were walking up the lane together one afternoon, he and she, when he put to her the problem of Lolita, old Nitka's granddaughter, about whom some unpleasant rumors were afoot.

"Any truth in it, do you think, Louis?"

"Yes, unfortunately there is—or was. She's always been straight as a string before this. He's left the place, it's over. But she admitted it to Nitka."

"What does Nitka want?"

"To have her stay here, and behave herself, and let the thing die down. But the mother, that little sharp-faced Lotta, wants her sent away."

"Could she live with Nitka?" asked the Señora, pacing slowly and speaking after a moment's thought.

"That's what Nitka wants. I believe if you approved of that, it would do a good deal to straighten the thing out."

"Then let it be that way. I have reason," Coralia said, with a significant quick glance and rising color, "to be lenient with such a girl." And as he was about to speak she diverted the conversation abruptly. "Send Lotta up to speak with me. I'll have Father Anselmo give her a word too. Lotta seems to have a very poor memory. Since her widowhood—well, send her up, anyway. It'll make her feel important. God has been very good to me," Coralia finished in a low tone, "and I have to do what I can!'"

"You are the best woman I ever knew," Johnson said.

Coralia was already mounting the shallow steps, well smothered with ivy, that ascended from the garden to the terrace. She turned at the top to nod him a good-by and went into the house.

Quietly stitching at her embroidery frame in the late morning hours, with Josito playing about on the floor with clean redwood blocks from the mill for trains and Ana darning sheets in the sunshine of the south window, Coralia began to mull over the problem again, putting Philip in the place of Louis, building Louis to Philip's stature. What would Harriet think of the situation?

Everything in her attitude to Philip was unchanged. She was quite keen enough to know that he felt no rush of passion in the contemplation of their marriage. Once married, she felt she could win him by rendering him independent, by gifts, by her own loving adjustment to his will. But his marriage would mean sacrifices for Philip, and already she had experienced some uncomfortable moments as she tried to reconcile his ideas to the rhythm of ranch life.

Louis, she reflected, was in no way comparable to Philip. Louis wasn't to be considered in that or any other connection. Not as a friend, companion, not in the picture at all. He was rough, blunt, easy-going, he took nothing seriously, immensely and noisily loved his present job, stirred everything and everyone with whom he came in contact into excitement and animation.

And Louis was easy. Just easy to handle and direct and be with. He wanted to share everything, whether it was the discovery of a quail's nest in the flat, hot, forty-acre meadow, or an eclipse of the moon. Coralia told herself that she must never let herself like him, never be anything but relieved if and when he left the rancho. But she thought of him, in one way or another, almost constantly.

She had given no hint of this in the letters to Harriet that had become so strangely hard to write. Coralia was aware that Harriet wrote less often and less freely, too; Coralia had never before, in their friendship, felt herself so much out of touch. Did Harriet suspect she was holding something back?

But how could she write Harriet the truth about a situation whose values she herself was completely unable to analyze? How could she say to Harriet, "You were surprised at my acceptance of Philip when he was my foreman, as a prospective husband, even though he was—and is—a man traveled and educated, and a man of good family. What would you say now if I told you that I have come to depend very much upon the assistant foreman, Louis Johnson——

"There is no reason why Philip shouldn't depend on Louis as I do and let him go on planning for the children and keeping me informed on all the farm business," Coralia might reason on in her mind. "We'll always have to have a foreman here, especially if we travel, and we certainly couldn't get a more interested one——"

But she interrupted her own thoughts. Louis wouldn't stay long after Philip was installed as master supreme, and she wouldn't want him to! Philip's word would be final on every point; Philip's place at the head of the Señora's table; Philip stepfather and guardian of the Salazar heirs. And, once married, Coralia would be in honor bound in every case to defer to Philip. There could be no siding against her husband, especially in favor of the burly giant who had so openly wanted to take his place.

For Philip she had come to feel a great respect, almost a nervous respect. She did not understand him. He did not want to depend financially upon his wife, he did not want to marry a rich woman and settle down as her estate manager. He wanted his own career; he wanted to be a surgeon in his own right, and to practice—where? Certainly not here on the rancho. He must live in some city or town, or settlement at least, to gain the position that would satisfy him.

That would mean no position at all for Coralia and the boys; she was quite sharp enough to see that. Eventually the boys would be in religious schools, in summer camps, uniformed and absorbed in their own affairs, far away from their mother. And eventually she would turn all the ranches over to Martin and Pablo, and be simply the rich wife of Dr. Haagersen, who had property somewhere in California.

On the other hand, if Philip had proved to be surprisingly acceptable socially, surprisingly polished, Louis was correspondingly crude in many ways. He was tremendously forceful, he could say nothing vaguely, do nothing halfheartedly. His first statement to her of his hopes to win her right over Philip's head had not only lacked hesitation or timidity, it had indicated confidence. He had told her since, sometimes in words, sometimes in small actions more impressive than words, that her feelings for him would yield to his for her, that the past was swept away, that they were man and woman facing a new clean world.

"Look at it, Coralia," he said to her one day when they had been riding with the boys and Miles and had stopped their horses at the top of the foothills. And he had flung out one of his big arms to indicate the spread of canyons, lined with solemn marching redwoods, of vineyards, orchards, and ranges where the young cattle had already been turned out on the new grass. The sun shone down on the rancho's adobe roofs of red tiling, huddled together under the shafts of eucalyptus, and on the tangle of white sheds and fences, and the long sprawling lines of the hacienda fringed with close-packed trees and shrubs.

Even from here they could see young horses galloping in a paddock, see the tiny dots of red and pink that showed where women were moving between the cabins, and now and then catch on the wind the outraged bellow of the famous bull.

Amigo Real had been to all the western states for blue ribbons; Mateo Olivera, who had charge of him, did nothing but groom and tend the monster, polishing his small aristocratic hoofs to amber, shining the milky terrible horns with their blue ink streaks at the tip. Amigo had his own shed, his own corral and water trough; Mateo slept on a sort of shelf above his stall.

"All yours," Louis said, looking down.

"It is beautiful," she conceded.

"It makes a man wonder what on earth anyone wants that isn't here."

"Men love cities, Louis, and clubs, and meeting other men."

"Cities and clubs," he repeated, musing. "And other men! My God, who is fool enough to think he meets other men in a city! You have to see them in a place like this, Señora, fighting and drinking and loving, women furious over lovers, women crying because there's going to be another child, people playing cards and cheating, men praying all night because a horse stepped on a child, men breaking their hearts over a dog's death—that's real, isn't it?"

"A little too real, perhaps," she said with a laugh and a shudder.

"You've not found it so. I took you down to Sepulveda's cabin the other night. You didn't seem to have any trouble with the baby."

"Oh, well. It was bites, you know. Ana got something for them, they're all gone. In his crib was a dirty blanket simply hopping with fleas! And all the women had decided that the child had smallpox."

"Smallpox! They ought to know better than that. Some of 'em are all scarred with it. You've never seen it?"

"No. But Harriet knows all about it, and leprosy, too. From the Islands, you know."

"Harriet? That's the girl the men call the 'little Señorita'? Why doesn't she get married?"

"She actually doesn't want to. I think she wants perfection. Or else too many men have wanted her. She's never been really in love."

"She'll get it," he said with an indifferent laugh.

"And I suppose she'll get it hard," Coralia added, ashamed because she was pleased at his indifference.

"There goes old Amigo again," the man said, as in a moment of silence the strong call of the bull came on the breeze.

"What's the matter with the poor brute?" Coralia asked thoughtlessly.

"We'll take care of him," Louis said easily, and once again she was impressed by that knowledge that is power; the comfortable confidence in his own experience and judgment that made him sure of himself, and made her feel sure of him.

The truth came to her slowly. Philip had never belonged here at the rancho Corazón d'Oro. Louis supremely belonged here. With Philip life would be one long apology and compromise. One long adjustment of his desire to go away and her longing to be right here, where she was mistress and owner and important. He would grow more and more restless, less and less interested——

And suddenly her mind was at peace. It was Louis, of course, not Philip. Philip's name evoked infinite complications, evoked the mental worries Coralia so hated. The thought of Louis—yes, with all the past and all the future considered—was peace. She could never be nervous and self-conscious with Louis, she understood him too well. He was a type familiar enough on all the ranchos, part American, part Spanish, an adventurer, but an adventurer whose whole dream of experiment and daring would be contained right here on the spacious and famous acres of the rancho.

He would grow bigger and broader and browner here, including the boys in his pursuits, training and disciplining them, deepening the respect and affection they were already showing him. And if other children were presently racketing about the hacienda, why, that would only be new joy, with a hundred warm hearts and a hundred good farm sounds to welcome more boys and girls.

The moment the thought came to Coralia she knew it was the answer. Like all true answers, it solved everything. The mountain that telling Philip of this awkward situation might have been was a mere molehill. What did she care if Philip protested and grew angry? She was safe. Writing the truth to

Harriet? Why, that also was no longer formidable, because it was so secure and obvious. It was just supremely comfortable, and Coralia had not been comfortable in her life or her spirits for some time.

The Señora's husband would be Don Luis, the big man running the ranch as few other ranches were managed. Not caring much about dress, or appearances, but loving to have the place filled with guests and children, and to have his visitors exclaim over the dairy cream and the fat turkeys and the rich wild blackberry jam.

There would always be fine horses to ride, fine streams to whip for trout, fine cattle to show at the fairs. And no strain, no explaining, no great changes, no trips or upheavals, no taking of second place. Harriet would be a regular visitor, of course, with whatever husband she chose, and they would always be bosom friends, but not in the old way, because a woman and her husband had a very intimate and unique relationship, and when their bedroom door was closed none could intrude, even in thought. Harriet would understand.

"With Philip, I would have had to depend on Harriet," Coralia reflected. "She amused him, she always knew what to say. But with Louis—well, we two are always going to be happiest when we are alone here, with the children. It's true, so why not say it? I'll always love Harriet, and what she has meant to me and to mine, but I'm going to be much busier now, and just as Louis says he gets so tired that he falls asleep the moment he gets into bed, I'm getting far more exercise than I ever did before, and I'll be tired too. And if Harriet wants to sit up she'll have to talk to Miles or Father Anselmo."

She thought of herself as already promised to Louis, and felt an inward glow in the situation; she merely had to wait her opportunity to clinch the matter. Louis came up to the hacienda every morning for a report, and Coralia found herself looking forward to that hour, when she dawdled over the end of her breakfast and he sat at her table taking a second cup of coffee. His own breakfast was served in the cookhouse with the men's breakfast at seven.

When her mind had thoroughly cleared the tangle of conflicting desires and commitments in which she was caught, she found Louis' presence increasingly enjoyable. He had shaved away the bushy beard and wore a flowing, well-trimmed mustache and imperial, slicking both in cowboy fashion to points as sharp as those of Amigo's horns.

Coralia found the change immensely improving; Louis was a younger man, a more handsome man, with his well-trimmed head. She spoke to him of having a bathroom put into the adobe cabin when modern plumbing was introduced at the hacienda. But Louis was quite satisfied with his own arrangement.

"There's always a sheet of water blowing off the windmill," he told her. "I keep a towel and a bar of soap there and get a good wash every morning."

Looking at him, Coralia would think that he was as wholesome as the air that blew down from the redwoods, as native here as the creamy fog that crept in over the western hills on summer mornings. Not for any other environment, not for cities or dinner parties or streetcars or offices. But for the dusty roads, where the tarweed and yarrow grew along the ditches, and the corrals, where the young horses galloped, and the high mountain meadows blotted here and there with the shadows of great spreading oaks, and noisy with the bawling of newly branded calves. She knew her own heart now; she knew this was her mate, and that complete fulfillment as a woman, so long denied her, was just ahead.

But how to manage the transition, how let Louis know that he was the man, and how tell Philip that his day was over, she did not know. Coralia was tenderhearted; her attitude toward all men had something of the mother in it. She thought of writing Philip, shrank away from the hard words. She was not sure where a letter would find him, for one thing. She, of course, was not entirely certain of Louis' attitude and intentions, for another. She dreaded the moment when Philip might be expected to return to the rancho. She told herself she must write him that her feelings had changed, and yet the full and happy days drifted by and she made no move.

CHAPTER 30

On the great occasion of her viewing the Pacific Ocean for the first time, the father, mother, and aunt of Margaret Mary Townshend assumed joint guardianship of her person and carried her by turns.

Margaret duly saw the great Pacific and the long miles of beaches that bounded the city on its western frontier, and she saw the seals and the little performing canary birds and she rode on a horsecar, a cable car, and a smoky, noisy little train. After all this she was as fresh as a daisy, but Johnny, Lizzie, and Harriet were exhausted.

They came home to Howard Street house and sank into chairs, Lizzie too tired to do more than untie Margaret's bonnet and unbutton her pink coat before handing her over to Harriet, who took off the baby's tasseled pink kid shoes and cupped her warm little feet in her own hands.

"Liz, if this kills us, what'll we do when Montmorency comes along?"

"I don't know how women do it."

"Gosh, I do think it's remarkable," Johnny said. "A kid that age going through a day like this! That climb up from the beach, an hour and five minutes wait on a windy corner for the train, no seats in the cable car, and then bump, bump, bump up Mission Street. I tell you she's as tough as a horse!"

"Light a lamp, will you, Johnny, and I'll nurse her and put her off to bed."

"She was up in your arms the whole day, Johnny, she didn't climb the hill."

"I know. But she was bundled about, and nursed in a summer house and sat down on sand—she's a trooper, aren't you. Meg?"

"Hungry, Hat?"

"I am—starving. But I couldn't move to get supper if you offered me Seal Rocks!"

"I'll take you all down to the Poodle Dog," Johnny said.

"Johnny, this child doesn't go anywhere tonight!"

"That's right, I forgot Margaret." Johnny stretched himself on the couch and instantly snored.

"What's in the house, Lizzie?"

"Oh, dear knows—not much."

"Any more corned beef?"

"Not a scrap. I put it all into the sandwiches."

They hung over the baby, who was following her father's example by falling heavily asleep.

"Here you, wake up," said Lizzie. Margaret opened gluey blue eyes, swooned off with her small pink mouth still half open and bluish milk still clinging to her lips.

"Is she divine," Harriet stated rather than asked.

"Oh, well——" said Lizzie.

"We could send Johnnie for some eggs."

"We've some of your mother's Irish bacon," said Lizzie, rousing from a sort of swoon on her own account and forcefully shaking herself to attention. "And there's a grand loaf of new bread Mrs. O'Sullivan brought me yesterday. We've butter and some cream from yesterday's milk. And there's jam."

"What's that?" Johnny sat up as if roused by a pistol shot, and all three looked at the doorway that led to the parlor.

There was a small metal bell screwed to the front door of the cottage, and it was this bell that had trilled violently, like a small fire engine. Johnny disappeared into the dark parlor, and they heard him striking a match and speaking to somebody.

When he came back a man was with him, a tall man with fair hair, wearing sideburns, a familiar blue cotton shirt piped with turkey red, a brown suit, and a loose old brown overcoat. In his hand he carried a broad-brimmed straw hat such as farmers wore in summer.

"Philip," Harriet said, both her hands in his.

"Harriet," he said, in a voice that was slightly hoarse.

They stood looking at each other. Johnny and Lizzie

269

moved noiselessly into the bedroom; there was a long silence.

They sat down on the horsehair sofa, still holding hands. But they found nothing to say.

"Coralia isn't with you?" Harriet finally whispered.

"No. No, I've not been to the rancho."

"You wrote her?"

"No, I've not done that, either. Have you had news?"

"Not much. I imagine she's been lonely—I imagine she's been having a bad sort of time."

"I was delayed at home," Philip said. "My stepfather died, as a matter of fact, and I could help settle things for my mother and my sister; I was glad to be there."

"I'm so—glad to see you," Harriet said inadequately.

"Yes, I know."

"We are like children lost in a wood," the girl said after another pause. It was broken when Johnny and Lizzie emerged from the bedroom, and Harriet performed the introductions.

Philip shook hands, smiling his wide smile.

"Sit down," said Johnny. Lizzie liked him at once, and wondered if she might not wake Margaret and show her off. "Harriet here has just been telling us that you're bound for Scotland."

"I'm supposed to enter classes there in June."

"Not until June?"

"Well, my reason for going there as soon as I can," Philip explained, as Harriet sat with her hand in his, taking in every word, every turn of his brown wrist, every change of expression in his face, "is that old Dr. Kerr, who was down in Mexico when I was, is on a hospital board there and he can give me a lot of help before I start."

"And what brings you to San Francisco?" Johnny asked. Philip gave Harriet a quick glance.

"I wanted to see Harriet again," he said simply.

"You've been here before?"

"Never before."

"And what do you think of us?" Johnny asked as he clanked the blower into place over the suddenly roaring coals,

270

He looked over his shoulder with the Californian's confident smile.

"Terrific. I've not seen much. I came up on the *Costa Blanca* and she only docked an hour ago. I went up to your mother's house, but they were all at dinner. I wouldn't have her disturbed. One of the girls told me where Harriet was and how to get here."

"You've had dinner?" Lizzie asked, with a motion of getting up from her seat.

"We had pork and beans at three o'clock because we were supposed to dock at four. But we got our lines fouled with a tug that was fussing round the wharf and a barge with a crane on it, and we all got out into the middle of the bay again!"

They all laughed; Lizzie disappeared into the kitchen, Johnny built up the fire, but Harriet sat on in a dream.

"You've not been to the rancho for weeks then?"

"No. I felt——" Harriet hesitated. "I felt almost as if she didn't want me. I know she's been lonely, but she never made it very definite about my going. And I felt so badly ——" Harriet's throat thickened and her eyes filled.

"I know. But we'll get all this cleared up. That's what I came back to do."

"Coralia's sister was there, with two babies, but she's gone. Father Anselmo is there, and Coralia's letters were all about the Will of God and how things change and our lives go into other channels. Do you think she suspects, Philip?" Harriet asked anxiously.

"No. I'm sure she doesn't. There was a letter for me here at the bank. That's only two weeks old. She does write differently, but not the way she would if she knew."

"I'll see what Lizzie's up to," said Johnny. He went into the kitchen.

"Is it the same with you, Harriet?" Philip asked.

"Just the same. It was that way when I was born, Philip. It's not just loving you and needing you because you're a wonderful person. It's—because we're one. I'm half of you, you're half of me. Nothing else matters. Whether we're having soup for supper in an Edinburgh hospital or we're on

271

a ship going to Africa or we're out here—building a house on the hills in Sausalito—it doesn't matter. If you're there, I'm complete. Well or sick, or rich or poor."

Philip said nothing. Johnny came in with a tray, followed by Lizzie. The delicious aroma of tea accompanied them.

"Johnny, get some spoons and napkins," Lizzie said, panting. "The kettle was boiling to break its heart," she added, in an aside to Harriet, "so all I needed was to bust into the new package of tea. It's got the good Chiney smell."

The fresh brown bread was sliced; Harriet set at once to toasting by the fire. The tea scented the air. They were all young; they fell upon the collation as if they had fasted for days. To Harriet the homely little room sparkled like Aladdin's palace. She was floating in aerial dizziness and light. She was conscious of her physical being as something miraculously perfect, complete; her hands, her feet, the straight strong lines of her body, the vigor of her small hands, set off by cuffs of Irish lace, the sparkle of blue eyes behind black lashes and the metallic glitter of her hair. She was a unit, made of a hundred units, and every one of them was alive now, thrilling now. She would not have been anyone else but Harriet Townshend at this hour to become the proudest and richest woman in the land.

"Harriet will have told you that we feel badly about this," Philip said, looking at Johnny.

"Harriet didn't have to," Johnny answered with a rueful smile.

"And it's come to me," Philip pursued, "that I'll have to go back to the rancho, just for a few hours, and have a talk with Coralia. This isn't the sort of thing you can write."

He looked from one to the other, and Harriet saw that his face was haggard and there were shadows under his eyes. Johnny nodded, his own face serious.

"I mean—just to thank her," Philip said, finding words with some difficulty. "Just to say that it was a mistake, and that as far as appreciation—and affection——What do you think, Harriet?" he asked, in a pause.

"I think yes," Harriet said. "I know her. That's what she'd want."

272

"I'll go tomorrow or next day," Philip said. "I'll go from the rancho to Sacramento afterward and so on East. Are you going back to your mother's tonight?" he asked Harriet.

"Yes. Now." Johnny brought her her coat and hat and she kissed Lizzie good-by. She asked Lizzie if Philip couldn't have a look at the baby, and Lizzie gladly went to bring Margaret into the parlor. Margaret was beautiful and bright-eyed and happy over this unexpected innovation, and didn't intend to go to sleep for a long, long time.

But it didn't matter, she looked dewy and rosy and blue-eyed in her father's arms. And Philip said that he thought she was the prettiest baby he ever saw.

When Harriet and Philip had gone the Townshends looked at each other.

"Well, they have got it," Lizzie said in an awed voice, with emphasis on the last two words.

"I never saw anything like that in my life," Johnny said, gently biting the fuzz on his daughter's hair as she languished on his shoulder.

"They hardly said anything to each other, Johnny. But did you see them hold hands? Only not laughing—not kissing."

"Nope. It goes too deep for that."

"Did you see Harriet's face!"

"From the minute he came in. She looked as if she was looking into heaven. And him—he's a nice-looking feller, Lizzie."

"Oh, he's stunning!"

"Perfectly businesslike, you'd think he was talking about insurance or real estate. It was just as if he said, 'We got into this jam. Now we've got to get out. That's got to come first.' "

"My goodness, it *is* a jam, Johnny."

"You bet your life it is!"

"What can they do?"

"Well—with Coralia her best friend and the way she loves the kids and the rancho—whatever she does she loses."

"But she couldn't marry him now. He hasn't even a job. And if he'd married Coralia think what he'd have!"

"Yes, but since this thing hit them, that doesn't matter any

273

more. Poor old Tatsie, she wasn't ever going to care for any man!"

"And she's so sure of it, Johnny, and you can see that it's made her terribly unhappy!"

"Well, I'll be darned——You're going back into your basket, young lady, and not a peep out of you! I'll be darned how I can see it coming out right," said Johnny.

"It simply can't. How could she go up there to visit, feeling the way she does! How can she stay with Coralia, week in and week out, and not give it away!" Lizzie paused in the kitchen doorway with the tray.

"Worse if he married Coralia, Liz."

"Oh, heavens, yes! I don't know what we'd do with Hattie then. Put her down, Johnny, and hang the bath towel on the back of the chair when you light the lamp. Goodness knows when she'll get off again, but didn't she look sweet when I brought her out?"

"I never thought I'd see Hattie this way," Johnny mused. "Didn't she look pretty when she took his arm, in that fur outfit——"

"Her seal that your mother gave her for Christmas," Lizzie said thoughtfully. "I've been jealous of Harriet——" she said.

"You have not!"

"Oh, indeed I have. I thought she had everything. But I felt awfully sorry for her tonight." Lizzie went with her tray to the kitchen, returned to put the blower up against the fire, straighten chairs, carry the empty scuttle to the kitchen, lock the parlor door that was also the street door. She went into the bedroom to find Johnny still playing with the baby.

"She yelps like a seal every time I put her down."

"Here now, none of that nonsense," said Lizzie, reaching for Margaret. She felt a wave of sheer content and pride. Here she was a married woman, having gone through the ordeals of wifehood and motherhood, and left those frightening days and nights behind her, and here she was possessing the amazing and ambitious Johnny and exquisite Margaret, and here was poor Harriet not even engaged, not likely

274

to be engaged, facing years of separation from the man she loved, forced into deceptions and concealments——

"I'll nurse her, maybe she'll sleep through the ten o'clock," she said, sitting down in the rocker and reaching for the baby. "Oh, Johnny," said Lizzie, unbuttoning a flap in the breast of her long-sleeved, ribbed undershirt, "aren't we lucky to have such a head start! Our home and our baby and each other, and all the beginning parts over!"

CHAPTER 31

Harriet and Philip walked along together through the dark streets to Mission Street. On Mission Street shops were still open; carboys in the drugstore windows sent long streaks of color to quiver on the sidewalk; the candy store was busy; giggling girls and boys were buying brown, pink, and white taffy, broken from great lumps by a little silver hammer, and baby cream, and rock candy. Both saloons were open, the little hinged panels that formed their doors were swinging constantly to emit gushes of dull red light, sounds of deep laughter, and smells of beer and whiskey.

The little one-horse car, jang-janging through the night, passed Harriet and Philip, but they did not see it; they walked slowly, Philip's big hand cupping her furred elbow. Block after block, down Mission to Market, and across on Sixth to Mason. Neither was conscious of exterior circumstances at all, and Harriet was mildly dazed when she found herself mounting the steps through the terraced hillside garden to her mother's door.

The wide hallway was hospitably alight. Various persons were scattered about the long parlors; a game of whist was in progress. Standing at the foot of the stairs, imposing in striped taffeta silk made full in skirt and sleeves, fringed and beaded, and with delicate undersleeves of fine embroidery, stood Mary Townshend. She was talking with the old family doctor, who was spending the winter months in her house. Her face, with its strong homely lines and its frame of silver curls, was absorbed, intent. But she glanced sideways as the front door opened and saw Harriet come in and went toward her.

"Ma, this is Philip Haagersen," Harriet said, glowing and a little breathless. She laid a hand on her mother's arm.

Mrs. Townshend measured the tall man with an appraising glance.

"Well, I am glad to see you," she said, unsmiling. "Will you come in—the little bookroom, Harriet, between the two halls. Let's step in there. And get my knitting from the back parlor."

Harriet lighted the gas in the little bookroom, and revealed it to be a small square apartment obviously cut out of some other room, and made comfortable with rugs, a table, and two great chairs. Except for one narrow tall window, the walls were lined with books; Scott, Dickens, George Eliot, Father Faber.

Philip took one chair and his hostess the other. Harriet perched on the arm of her mother's chair.

"Now," said the older woman simply, her eyes on her knitting, "tell me what brings you here. I know, of course, how things are between you and Harriet. Did you know he was coming, Harriet?"

"No, Ma," Harriet said dreamily.

"I didn't know it myself," Philip said. Harriet was silent; her mother interposed only an occasional shrewd question, and Philip talked. Harriet was content to watch him. She watched the lines of the keen, long-featured face, the characteristic jerk backward of the heavy fair hair, the bending forward of his long lean body in the low chair so that his linked hands hung between his knees. And she heard his voice again.

"No, no," said Mrs. Townshend once, almost sharply. "There's never been any sin in it, an engagement isn't a marriage, man! There's many an engagement better for being broken. It's only that the circumstances here make it hard to settle without hurting someone."

276

She subsided again, and again was a listener. When Philip had finished his story she rose from her chair.

"Well, these things must be left for time and the Lord's will to decide," she said. "But I am glad you came here tonight. The only way to treat this is honestly. You'll go your way to Scotland, and Harriet'll show herself to be the good friend she's always been to Coralia, and we'll see what another year brings about. I'm going out to make sure Delia fed the kittens and set the cracked wheat to soak, Hattie," she added, "and you might light the fire here. I'll be awake when you come upstairs so don't be too late. Good night, Philip," Mary Townshend concluded, holding out her firm, friendly hand.

"I've got so little to offer her, and she's so wonderful!" Philip stammered, holding fast to the hand.

"As to that," said Harriet's mother, with a glance at her, "she's a good dear daughter to me, and she's as good-looking as most of them. But what you offer her is the best any man can offer any woman, his love and his protection and the chance to stand beside him as he takes his place in the world. I would ask no better than that for her."

Philip looked after her as she closed the door behind her.

"Whew!" he said in a tone of awe. "What a person!"

"Ma?" asked Harriet, her eyes glistening.

"Ma," he said. He sat down beside Harriet on the old sofa, and she slipped her hand into his, and they sat without speaking for a long time.

The seal coat and cap went to early Mass the next morning; Harriet had made no appointment with Philip, but she knew it when he came into the pew behind her and her mother. Afterward they walked through the markets, and bargained for cherries and asparagus, and climbed the two steep blocks to the boardinghouse again for breakfast.

And over these hours hung an enchantment that Harriet had never known before, a sense of happiness and security that was new to Philip as well. The steep streets of the sun-washed city, the liquid glisten of the serene blue bay, the far soft lines of the eastern hills beyond the water, all took on a magic brightness that was enhanced by the romantic smells and sights of chattering Chinatown, always awake two hours earlier than the rest of the city, and the dim sweetness of the cathedral, with its wavering candles and the glow of the red altar light.

Sunshine flickered in the dining room, where Harriet and Philip lingered over breakfast; then she came with him to the door, and watched him go down the steps to Stockton Street. He did not kiss her good-by, too many interested eyes in hallway and parlors were trying not to betray curiosity. They did not promise to write. He went away, and Harriet went upstairs to try to quiet the tumult of joy and pain that rocked her. To her mother, when they were busy with month-end bills an hour later, she put only one question. Harriet had been crying, and she was pale, but she was quite composed now.

"Ma, you liked him?"

"You could trust him," Mrs. Townshend said briefly. She made some errand for herself elsewhere in the house and for the time being nothing else was said. The clear morning had clouded over; a dark sky hung close above the city; a willful wind blew papers and chaff about the streets. Foghorns sounded far out at the Gate.

All afternoon Harriet moved in a dream. Now she was in Johnny's warm little parlor again, again hearing the knock at the door. Now with her arm snugly drawn through Philip's she was walking over the uneven streets in the warm soft starlight. Now it was Philip's voice in her ears, then the high laughing voices of Chinatown, and the warm Italian dialect of the markets. Sometimes she tried to visualize Philip's arrival at the rancho, Coralia's eager welcome, his restraining smile, his "Coralia, I've come to say something. This isn't easy, my dear, and you'll have to forgive me——"

Yes, and then suppose, Harriet mused, that Coralia became all motherly and understanding and amused; he mustn't take it so seriously! Money wasn't really a consideration. What if she had a lot and he hadn't, so long as they loved each other?

It would make it hard; it would make it almost impossible to say no, no, no, over and over, to insist that there must be no engagement, no understanding even, she must understand that this must be good-by.

And then, after that, was he to settle down to have dinner with her and the boys, Father Anselmo, and Miles? Or would he and Enrico ride down the long dark miles to the village and the railway, and would he sit in the sun-peeled little station drowsing and waking, shifting about uncomfortably as he waited for the train?

In a few days she herself would be expected at the rancho. Dared she go knowing what she knew now? Dared she risk Coralia's suspecting the truth? Could she really keep up the surface sympathy, the tender understanding of Coralia's crushed love and outraged pride as they wandered through the wet garden on spring mornings, knelt together in the chapel, dreamed through long quiet afternoons on the terrace?

Coralia would go over and over the story, not blaming Philip so much as grieving at his blindness. Just his pride, she would tell Harriet, had cut him away from the woman who loved him, the wide acres of the rancho Corazón d'Oro, the authority of ruling over this glorious golden corner of the golden state and the security of having his own personal fortune.

"Of course I know I'm not as smart as Philip," Coralia would say humbly, "but people don't have to be smart to love each other, and I was ready to give him all I have." And she might add, as Harriet foresaw with dread, that perhaps he did not know his own mind and heart even now, perhaps one of these days he would come back.

"He'll remember, as we do, or at least as I do, all the happy times," Coralia would say, "those evenings when we all played games, remember? Wasn't it fun, when my cousins were here, and we all sang, and went to Benediction, and Father Anselmo told us about Mexico and the miracle at Guadalupe?"

Harriet would listen and agree, her own heart heavy with its secret, and Coralia would lean on her and tell her that she could not have borne these days of shock and loneliness without her.

279

"I used to love the rancho, Ma," said Harriet. "Now I dread it! I hate the thought of going there!"

"You'll not have to stay long, lovey. The first chance I get I'll send you a letter to come home."

"And when I leave her, I leave Coralia with nothing. I mean nothing that counts."

"Her children and her home."

"I know, Ma dear, and her rosary and her good health and her eyes—think of the people without eyes." Harriet said with an impatient laugh.

"Well, you bad girl, if we had the love of God in our hearts all we need do is the duty that lies nearest—and do it with a good will——You're not listening!" said Mary Townshend reproachfully.

"I really am, Ma. And I love you," Harriet said repentantly. And she continued to stare at the weather-stained ceiling of the lofty bedroom, and the flies that walked about upon it, and the slits of light that rose toward it as the sun went down on the hot spring garden below the windows, and the wilted city, and the turquoise sheen of the bay.

CHAPTER 32

Only three days later Harriet came in after a well-spent day, at about five o'clock. Rain was very near, and in the parlors of her mother's house, and in the hall, gaslights were burning brightly.

The day was Wednesday, and Harriet had seated herself beside her mother all morning, in the sodality room of the Jesuit college out on Hayes Street, sewing diligently for the children of the poor. There was a Pauper Alley in San Francisco, lying like muddy dregs below the rising hills and the fabulous mansions of Nob Hill, and to this place every week went clothing for babies and tiny children, little wrappers, double gowns, blankets.

Harriet's mother never missed a meeting of the Francesca Society and of late Harriet had been earning golden opinions as a dependable member. She disliked sewing, but as she stitched on tiny garments she thought of the fortunate Margaret, always so dainty, so fragrant, so safe, and love as well as care went into her work. And on this morning surreptitious tears and secret prayers made it a comfort that kept her hands busy.

After this effort, she had gone with her mother to make two hospital calls, returning home for a late lunch, and at three had sallied forth again to attend the cake sale at the cathedral hall, taking three cakes with her and buying three others to bring home to the boarders.

Then a walk up the hill in the somber afternoon light and a long weary sigh as she carried her cakes to the kitchen, hung her raincoat in the back hall closet, fluffed up her deep curly bang with an indifferent hand, and in the front hall again met Alma. Alma said there was a gentleman to see her.

"Don't keep him long, dear," said her mother, joining her at this moment on her way back from some kitchen errand of her own. "Whoever he is, send him packing, and get some rest before dinner. Were there many at the sales?"

"Packed! The whole place smelled of raincoats. Mrs. Welch took all our cakes. . . . Philip," whispered Harriet to the man who stepped from the back parlor door and encountered them.

Philip's familiar old coat was rain-spattered and his bare head was damp. He looked pale and excited as he caught at Mrs. Townshend's hand and said breathlessly, "No, don't go. I want to speak to you—to you both! Can we go in where we talked Saturday night?"

Bewildered, Harriet and her mother turned toward the little bookroom and Harriet turned the lighted bead of gas up to full power.

"Coralia——" she stammered. "Is anything wrong?"

"No, not wrong," he said. "But I had to see you!"

"You told her. Philip, she didn't—she didn't——"

"No, it's all right! It's not what you think!" They were still standing, Philip holding a hand of each of the other two. "You see, I didn't have to tell her! . . . No, don't look like that, Harriet, she's happy. I never saw her so happy! And after we talked she was still happier. She's married, Harriet. She was married in the chapel last Sunday, with Ana and young Martin and Miles for witnesses."

"She——" Harriet reeled and sat down. Her mother sat down heavily. Both looked at him blankly.

"Let me tell you," Philip said. "I'll begin at the beginning. I got there Monday afternoon—late, because nobody from the ranch was down in the village. The men always have an extra horse in the stable down there, but it took me so long to get it out of someone's field and get started that it was dark when I got to the rancho—just before dinner. One of the maids, that cross-eyed girl who married José—the fiddler——"

"Refugia," Harriet supplied automatically, out of stupor.

"Refugia. Well, she was crossing the hall, and I asked her to tell the Señora I was there. She looked as if she had seen a ghost, and said, 'Señor, you must not harm her!' Of course I had no idea what she was talking about. I stayed in the hall, wishing it was all over, and Coralia came down and put both her hands out to me and said: 'You will forgive me, won't you, Philip?' and just then Louis Johnson came running downstairs, and it struck me as queer, his being in the house at all. He came over and joined us."

"Louis Johnson! That's the assistant foreman, Ma. Oh, Philip, I can't believe you! I can't believe you!"

"The foreman? You never spoke of him," Mrs. Townshend said, bewildered. "How on earth could she bring herself—but go on!"

"Well, this is what she told me. A few days after you and I both left the rancho, he showed up on the terrace, and reminded her that they had known each other years ago."

"They'd known each other years ago?"

"That's what she said. So of course they renewed old times, or I suppose they did, and he got to explaining things on the rancho to her, and getting her interested——"

"And you weren't there."

"No, and you weren't there, Harriet. And after all, he was

an old friend. So after a few weeks of this, it seems, he told her that he was going away, that he couldn't stand to have me come back and run things while he was just an employee on the place—something like that. Anyway, she realized that he had remembered her all this time——"

"Oh, I remember, she told me one night about him! He came to her father's place and they fell in love," Harriet said with an awakening face. "And that's why she married old Martin Salazar."

"What did that have to do with it?" Philip demanded, surprised and diverted.

"Well, her mother was so mad at her for falling in love in that secret sort of way with a man who wasn't a member of the old Spanish crowd that she told her father and they talked her into marrying old Don Martin——Oh, yes," Harriet said, remembering, "and she told me that she went to him first and told him that she had been in love with another man. It seemed a lot of fuss about nothing to me, but that's the way Spanish parents are! . . . Oh, but go on, Philip!"

If Philip and her mother exchanged a mild yet enlightened and significant glance over her head, Harriet never saw it. She was eagerly listening as Philip went on.

"He's a marvelous foreman, as a matter of fact his whole heart is in the land, and gradually—well, I don't know whether gradually or not, but somehow—Coralia told me, she got used to the idea that that was the more sensible marriage for her, that they were the right people to marry. Only she wanted to see me first; she said it didn't seem right to have him talk about it until she saw me, and Johnson, it seems, ruffled up and said no, he couldn't wait for that, he wasn't going to stand around and let her look us over and take her choice. Father Anselmo was right there and Coralia decided suddenly that their marrying was the right thing to do."

"But Philip, does she love him?"

"She's completely happy, Harriet, and she looks wonderful! I mean she's gracious and easy and simple—I've never seen Coralia just like that. If you saw her, and when you do see her, you'll know what I mean. No more uncertainty or self-consciousness—she's laughing all the time——"

He spread his hands, stopping short and smiling from one face to the other.

"The Lord's ways are not our ways, nor His thoughts our thoughts," Mrs. Townshend said, drawing a deep breath. Harriet slid from her chair to her knees beside her mother.

"Ma, that means that you—that means that we—Ma, is it all right?" she stammered.

"What do you say, Philip?" said Mary Townshend, looking up, with her hands on Harriet's shoulders.

"Mrs. Townshend, I am asking you for the hand of your daughter Harriet," he said, tears suddenly in his eyes.

"God bless you both," Harriet's mother said in a voice that wavered into faintness. They were all standing now, and Harriet linked them with her arms.

"I've not much to offer her now," Philip said, his voice fairly singing.

"That doesn't matter," Harriet said. "Coralia married! Mrs. Johnson. And I thought the Lord himself couldn't get us out of this! What shall we do first—what shall we do? Ma, may Philip and I go down to church for a minute?"

"I wish you would," said her mother. "And don't go stravaging through Chinatown all night long. You've got tomorrow."

"We've got all the tomorrows," Philip said as Harriet ran upstairs for her coat.

They walked down the steep blocks to St. Mary's, and knelt together in the dim, candlelit place; they walked through nighttime Chinatown, missing nothing of its gaudy colors, its high, laughing voices, its mingled odors of the Orient and the ocean, the straw-packed crates that stood on its wet wooden sidewalks, the twisted pigtails and the rustle and scrape of bamboo soles in the street. They went into the old market and sat at a dark oily counter eating shrimps and hot sour french bread and drinking coffee.

And for a few ecstatic days the tomorrows were theirs. It was heaven to Harriet to awaken in the dark and to bundle herself into her good coat of London cloth bought by her mother in Ireland many years earlier and to patter down the hill to church. Philip would be kneeling there, and their cold

284

hands linked themselves together for the half hour of prayer.

Then to the markets, with fish still flapping in the carts, and dark green crabs scrambling and sidling in great baskets of seaweed. Breakfast counters were already busy, crab shells and shrimp shells piling up, coffee scenting the air. Gulls flew over the open sheds of the market, breaking into the mild faraway drone of foghorns with their shrill cries.

There were few women downtown so early, but men from the little markets far out in Tuckertown and the Mission Dolores were bargaining and buying, and errand boys dashed among the older folk with big baskets. Mrs. Townshend had her own favorite boys in line and sent them back and forth briskly. Harriet's gay laugh rang out as Philip asked seriously whether the boarders would eat this vegetable or that.

Afterward, climbing the hill for breakfast, they would see the strengthening sunlight pointing its long shadows over the city and silhouetting the line of the eastern hills. The outline of Tamalpais shouldered against the sky; little side-wheelers paddled across the serene blue bay, leaving fans of snowy lace in their wake.

Harriet and Philip crossed the bay on the little ferryboats, picnicked in the Sausalito hills, lunched at the Palace Hotel, in whose famous court carriages were clattering, in and out. Harriet saw trunks plastered with strange Oriental labels, and she and Philip thought that they would come back to San Francisco someday with trunks of their own. They went to the Mercantile Library, and were impressed with the proud statement pasted on every book; seven thousand volumes, that was a library indeed! They rode on a jangling little train to the Cliff House, and watched the seals, sleeping on the rocks, barking and quarreling for place, plunging into the rough water. And the hours were not long enough for all they must feel and must say.

And so came the morning of parting, and Harriet and Philip and her mother sat on the top of the steps above the garden and looked down at the city and made last plans.

"We'll be in Cork in August for my brother's golden wedding," said Mrs. Townshend. "Harriet has enough cousins there to set up a dozen weddings, though indeed most of them are older than my children. I was the youngest of thirteen, and Joe—that's the one that's going to have the golden wedding—is the oldest. It was him married me off to my first husband that I'd never seen before that very day. And a good man he was, by all I've heard, though I never saw him from that hour to this."

"I told you," Harriet said to Philip, "Ma followed him out to the Sandwich Islands, and he never appeared. And Lloyd's listed him and his ship as lost."

"But didn't I have to write to the Pope before I'd get permission to marry on anything Lloyd's said!" said Mrs. Townshend.

"Then you will write me?" Philip asked. "About coming to Cork."

"From Edinburgh. It's no great trip. And you come down, and Hattie'll be married in the church where I was, and my mother, too, and hers before that! They'll make a great to-do over it."

"Mother, if your first husband turned up now, would he be my stepfather or would I be his stepmother, or what?" Hattie put her tumble of copper waves down on her knees to thoroughly enjoy the laugh.

"You'd be a bold-faced girl, that's what you'd be," her mother said discouragingly. "Meanwhile," she said to Philip, "you'll look about to see what you can do——"

"I'll do more than that, Mrs. Townshend. I'll get hospital work, if it's only cleaning instruments. Dr. Kerr has written me twice that he needs me, and has room for me, and for my wife, too, if she'll come. There's another old doctor with him, but it's a big place."

"That's when he thought you were going to marry Coralia?"

"Yes. Then I have two hundred pounds in London, Mrs. Townshend, and while it's not much, it will help. If Harriet and I have rent-free quarters, and I can make myself useful, we needn't be afraid."

Mrs. Townshend smiled dreamily down at the city descending steeply from the Mason Street hill, and the spiked line of masts framing the waterfront, and the panorama beyond.

"You'll not be afraid," she said.

"We'll live on haggis and cockaleekie," said Harriet.

"They've got an old cook there, at this doctor's house. She'll know how to make them. And we'll walk all over the town, and up to the castle, Harriet, and when we come back —who knows?—I can take my last years of medicine here."

"And grow with San Francisco," said Mary Townshend, with something like reverence in her voice. "It'll belong to you, and your children—the hills and the bay and the waterfront with the old ships coming through the Gate. And the eucalyptus trees out by the park and the ocean front, and the fogs crawling over the sand hills. In the end it'll be at St. Mary's that your children learn their catechism."

Harriet laughed a little thickly, and leaned her head against her mother, tears in her smiling eyes. Philip laid his big hand over Mary Townshend's capable and work-worn one. And he and Harriet said "Amen."

Also By Kathleen Norris

THE CALLAHANS AND THE MURPHYS
ELLEN MURPHY WAS PROUD.

Everyone knew Clem loved her. It seemed that she cared for him, too. But life had turned bitter for the Murphys, and Clem could no longer reach Ellen, who had become a bitter, cold-voiced stranger. She didn't want his help, and she certainly didn't want to be known as "poor little Ellen . . ."

This pride, and ironically, both success and catastrophe, held them apart. Ellen almost lost Clem forever.

Then one day she realized there was more to life than pride. But was it too late for Ellen and Clem to rediscover their love?

(65-292, 95¢)

==